A PHILOSOPHER'S QUEST
FOR A LOST CHILD

*Pebble Bnch,
CA
93953*

Sun Valley, Moon Mountains

AJAX MINOR

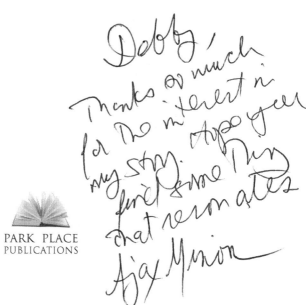

*Debby,
Thanks so much
for the interest in
my story. Appo you
find some thing
that resonates
Ajax Minor*

PARK PLACE
PUBLICATIONS

Sun Valley, Moon Mountains
Ajax Minor

PRINT ISBN 978-1-943887-09-5
E-BOOK ISBN 978-1-943887-17-0

First Edition April 2016

Park Place Publications
Pacific Grove, California
parkplacepublications.com

Cover design Gene Harris
Interior design Patricia Hamilton

For Linda Leckie Sinsar, wife and mother,
and Katherine Leckie Sinsar, our daughter,
Feb. 12, 1992-Sept. 9, 1992

FOREWORD

———

Who is Ajax Minor? If you've read About the Author, you were directed here. Let me explain.

One January afternoon, a few months after our daughter Katherine had died, my wife Linda and I were stretched out in our bedroom for an afternoon snooze. It was a brilliant and frigid day in January in Colorado. Our bedroom had a western exposure and tremendous solar gain, so the atmosphere warmed us like a blanket. Within minutes Linda was breathing deeply, but I just lay there soaking up the warmth and soaking in the silence. Suddenly, a thought tickled my brain and I had an idea for a story. I was filled with nervous energy and couldn't lie still. I decided to get up and start the project.

I didn't have any writing paper but didn't want to drive to the market for a composition book and break the spell. I remembered that I'd tried my hand at some essays and written some doggerel in a notebook that I'd shoved into an old suitcase of mine from college days, stuffed in a closet downstairs.

To my surprise, when I opened the grips I found not one but a half dozen composition books. Opening the first of the unfamiliar ones, I plopped on the floor and began to read. A story, remarkably like the one I had contemplated a few minutes before, unfolded. It was about a couple who had lost a child to a birth accident, as we had, and fled to the Rocky Mountain West. The protagonist had been a bond trader, as well.

At once, I recalled a bit of quantum mechanics and the idea that histories unfolded through time along various paths called 'worldlines'. While conventional theory was concerned with subatomic particles, a physicist by the name of Hugh Everett had written a dissertation that asserted that macroscopic objects also obeyed quantum laws and evolved along multiple timelines, which branched at critical decision points into a variety of 'multiverses'. It was also true that Everett's theory was completely consistent, mathematically, with quantum theory.

It occurred to me instantly that perhaps my own worldline had crossed with that of a doppelganger, whose history had branched from mine at some point in the past and who had suffered the same tragedy we had. Ultimately, I wove his tale into my own and eventually finished *Sun Valley Moon Mountains*, along with two other manuscripts for subsequent books.

I felt it only right to give attribution, but I didn't know my double's name. His main character was called Jaq and he had studied Classics, so the author must have loved Classics, as I did. Ajax quickly came to mind. And if my doppelganger had my own stature, as he surely must have, he wouldn't have appreciated Major, so I made his surname that of the Lesser Ajax in the Iliad.

Worldlines and alternate histories form the basis of the 'Ur Legend' series. Perhaps it is fitting that such histories are not simply conjecture but have a basis in fact, as I found out.

Paul Sinsar

N.B. Two passages from literature are quoted in the text and given attribution at the end of the main body of the novel. They are marked by an asterisk (*).

List of Characters

JAQ: Husband of Kate and father of Ur, bond trader, amateur philosopher and classicist

KATE: Wife of Jaq and mother of Ur, Wall St. banker, realist

UR: Kate and Jaq's daughter; ghost or goddess?

NICHOLAS MARDUK BEELE: Jesuit priest in Sun Valley (Ketchum), ID

TIAMAT: ancient Sumerian goddess, one of the 'old gods', both primordial Chaos and the Creatrix

BILDAD PROUD: Fundagelical preacher in Sun Valley

INDIAN JOE: proprietor of a Native American crafts store in Sun Valley and more

LEVINE: office manager at Coogan & Co. in Sun Valley

JOHN FADDLE: bomabastic stockbroker at Coogan & Co.'s Sun Valley office and its biggest producer

TIA: stockbroker at Coogan & Co. in Sun Valley and misanthropist

VINNIE: office assistant to Levine, math prodigy

CLARA: recent Stanford graduate and trading room assistant at Coogan & Co.

SARAH: Levine's wife

DANIEL AND DAVID: the Levines' sons

DANA: Ur's nurse in Sun Valley and a deaf mute

FRANKIE HOWARD: owner of a local flower store

HARAS: gracile Lunan and doppelganger of Sarah Levine

ENIVEL: gracile Lunan and doppelganger of Levine

BOTTA BOOM AND BOTTA BING: doppelgangers of David and Danny Levine on Luna

ELDAF: doppelganger of John Faddle on Luna

ANAD: doppelganger of Dana on Luna

KAK ZHAL: robust, differently abled native of Luna and
     companion and guide to Jaq and Kate

Historical Characters

HECTOR: greatest of the Trojan heroes in the Iliad

ACHILLES: greatest of the Greek heroes in the Iliad

ODYSSEUS: cleverest of the Greek heroes and architect of
     the Trojan Horse

SENECA: first century C.E. Stoic philosopher

MOZART: himself

THE ILIAD: Homer's epic poem and the story of
     the Trojan war and the events of its ninth year,
     culminating in the slaying of Hector by Achilles

DESCARTES: 17th century Rationalist philosopher
     famous for the phrase: 'Cogito ergo sum', 'I think
     therefore I am.'

BISHOP GEORGE BERKELEY: 18th century radical
     Rationalist, postulating that all which exists is in the
     mind

DAVID HUME: 18th century Empiricist who believed
     that a world exists outside of ourselves and is as we
     perceive it

IMMANUEL KANT: 18th century philosopher who
     synthesized Rationalism and Empiricism, postulating
     that the mind 'categorized' external phenomena and
     that the 'real' nature of things, the Noumenal world,
     lay beyond the grasp of the mind

HUGH EVERETT: 20th century American physicist who
     extended quantum theory to the realm of macroscopic
     objects and whose ideas led to a 'many-worlds'
     interpretation of the unfolding of spacetime

Suggestions for Further Reading

The Iliad by Homer, translation by Richmond Lattimore

The Ancient Near East, edited by James B. Pritchard, The Creation Epic

A Treatise concerning the Principles of Human Knowledge, George Berkeley

An Enquiry Concerning Human Understanding, David Hume

Prolegomena to any Future Metaphysics, Immanuel Kant

The Hidden Reality, Brian Greene, see Hugh Everett III

God: A Biography, Jack Miles, see Genesis and Job

SUN VALLEY, MOON MOUNTAINS

CHAPTER 1

Jaq pushed himself off the bed and stumbled badly. His feet missed his slippers, but he ignored that and lurched toward a sound, wet and windy, and punctuated at irregular intervals by deep, soft huffing. Pausing to gain his balance, he tried to pry his eyes open, but they remained glued shut by sleep. Sleep and *gin*, he thought, as the taste of juniper washed over his tongue. An insistent groaning focused him and he followed it.

His eyelids unfastened and low yellow light, seeping through shutters inset into the wall, bathed his eyes, the soft glow a balm, the shutters muting sobs that thrummed off of the louvers.

Gently, he turned the door latch and stepped inside the master bath to find Kate sitting on a small brass stool, her face in her hands, her breathing deep and moist and irregular. Jaq planted a delicate kiss on her cheek. He ran his tongue over his lips. They were wet and tasted of salt. Kate sniffled and Jaq heard a gurgling sound. He ran the back of his hand across her chin. "You've been crying."

"Brilliant!" Kate drew the sleeve of her robe across her face. "Yes, I suppose I have."

Jaq's arms hung limply from his shoulders. "What's wrong?"

"What's wrong?" Kate snapped.

Jaq sat on the floor and took Kate's hands in his. "Ur?" Kate sniffled again. "I'm sorry, I—"

"No." Kate slipped her hands through Jaq's fingers and laid them across her lap. "What's wrong is I've been making a habit of it."

"I didn't know."

"Of course not. For you ... ." Kate tossed her head back, "How did you put it? 'Sleep is a refuge.'"

"Sleep and gin," Jaq said sourly.

Kate's face softened. "So you have a martini—"

"Or two."

"Not often. And it helps you—"

"Deny. Which is precisely what you're doing now."

"No!" Kate's words ricocheted off the hard green tile. "I need this time alone."

"Look," Jaq said softly, "I'm not an alcoholic, but drinking myself into a coma every night isn't going to solve anything. I think it's time for me to stop." Jaq smiled. "My mom and dad escaped with liquor. From what I still do not know. But I hated it. The boozy breath, the eyes like wet newspaper, as if whatever was written there wasn't for me to read." Jaq smacked his lips and tasted juniper again. "So *I* escaped to my grandparents. But you know all that." Kate nodded. "I felt safe with them. Both of my grannies, especially. Do you feel safe with me?"

"Yes. Do you feel safe with me?"

"I never really thought of it that way. But I trust you. I guess that's about the same thing." Jaq reached out and held Kate's hands again. "Do you always do it in here?"

Kate inhaled a couple of sharp, staccato breaths. "Always. Right on this stool where I used to feed her when she'd fuss."

"I have never heard a sound," Jaq said, as if speaking to himself.

"Good. They're *my* feelings and I don't want them to interfere. I wouldn't let them interfere with my being a mom when she was alive and—"

Jaq laid his fingers on her hand. "And you were a great mom."

"Well, I sure as hell am not going to let feelings interfere now; with our lives and with us."

Jack smiled. "Still the Stoic, huh?"

"Yeah. How else could I have functioned? How else could we have functioned?" Kate wiped her face again with the sleeve of her robe and smiled. It was not a brave smile, but a genuine smile, and that made Jaq feel a little better. "Although, I've become one by choice, while you," she said, poking him in the chest, "are one by inclination."

"Now don't start on me_____" Jaq paused, thoughtfully. "You know, both your parents and mine drank. Too much. And I guess that has a tendency to harden you off, to force you to compartmentalize. To deal objectively with the good as well as the bad. But..."

"But what?

"But I think, temperamentally, that I may be more predisposed to a gloomier view of the world."

"Like your hero, Hector?"

Jaq shrugged and grinned. "Maybe. Maybe just that I'm a fuzzy minded philosopher. While you're a realist."

"Jaq, I know that the way to your heart is through your brain. And I do love you for it. Or in spite of it."

"Stop!" Jaq grinned and ran his fingers across Kate's upper lip. He rubbed them in his palm. They were smeared with snot. "So how bad is this habit becoming?" Kate smiled weakly. "That bad, huh?

"Look, Kate, we agreed that each of us might deal with this thing differently. I'm not asking you to change. I can't do that. *You* can't do that. I know we can't help thinking about all that Ur lost. But try, just a little, to think of yourself."

Kate averted her gaze and picked at a finger.

"Kate," Jaq said, slapping his palms against his thighs, "let's have a party. We haven't been particularly social since we moved here." Jaq pulled her down beside him onto the dark green tile.

"A party? Now what are you saying? I'm a recluse? A shut-in?"

"Of course not. But I get out more. It's easier with a job."

"I still advise my old banking clients in Mexico," Kate said defensively. "Besides, Jaq, you don't have a job."

"Well, okay. Not really. But it looks like a real job. I have an office and a desk and I lose money once and awhile and ...."

Kate breathed deeply and ran her fingers through her hair. "Oh, I don't know."

"I've got an idea! We celebrate the Winter Solstice, don't we?"

"Sure, but I don't see—"

"The Solstice is the day after tomorrow. It's the shortest day of the year. That's a *fact*. We'll bang drums and blow bone whistles. The celebration is rooted in reality, in good old-fashioned facts. In that sense, it's very Stoic. It's *our* holiday."

"But, Jaq, I won't have time to get ready for it, not unless we bag our fishing trip today, and I was really looking forward to it. That's being a little bit selfish, isn't it?"

"It'll be small. I promise. I'll ask a few people at the office, and you ask Frankie and Dana. And I'll help. I'll go in this morning and clean up a few things. You swing by around nine thirty. Water temp won't be up 'til almost noon anyway. Then, tomorrow, I'll take the day off to do errands. Presto! Party."

"Oh, all right," Kate said. "I suppose we really haven't been very social— fun social, that is—since we moved to Ketchum." Kate rose, then took his hand and helped him up.

"Anyway, you're right, you know. I suppose we really ought to connect more." She put her arms around Jaq's shoulders and gave him a light kiss, grabbed his hand and led him back into the bedroom. "So let's connect."

Jaq kissed Kate back. She pushed him gently down onto the mattress, took off her robe and slipped her nightgown over her head. Then she lowered herself slowly down onto him and kissed him deeply, while her hair, thick, soft and golden in the low light, caressed his face.

Within minutes, Jaq could hear her breathing heavily. His consciousness drifted. Where *was* Ur now? Then the room went deathly still and Jaq fell into a deep, dreamless sleep.

◙ ◉ ◙

CHAPTER 2

Jaq dropped the old pickup into second gear, prompting a loud whine, and pulled into a parking space in front of Coogan & Co.'s offices, housed in a modest, cabin-like structure.

He trotted up the front steps and, fumbling for his key, dropped some loose change onto the porch. "Damn," he swore softly, stooping over. In the fistful of coins, he noticed a penny, minted in 1992, the year Ur had been born. "Dumb penny," he mumbled, and stuffed the coins back into his pocket.

The trading room was dusky at that hour. Objects stood in their proper places, in silence. While the grayish-white dawn light did not deny existence, it seemed to question substance, as if the true forms of things manifested themselves, no longer imprisoned by detail. On the dozen or so desks in the office stood CRTs, with bright green ticker symbols and price quotes branded on their screens. They glowed like small stoves.

"*God*dammit!" he said. Jaq reached into his pocket and picked out the penny. He felt a niggling twinge in his side and went back out onto the porch.

"Gotta let go. Just a little," he said as he tossed the penny into a pile of snow across the street. After all, that *is* what he had told Kate a few hours ago.

Jaq swallowed hard and turned to go back inside, but the door was gone. Coogan & Co. was gone. He gazed out onto a vast expanse of thick green grass covering low rolling hills. Filmy, gray dawn had been replaced by burnished twilight.

Jaq could not move and he could not breathe. He felt trapped in a present so immediate that function and flow had no meaning. Yellow-orange light enveloped him in amber.

Jaq gasped. Time started again. He wheeled about quickly to face an unknown that cinched his stomach into a thick knot. The prairie unfolded in front of him, broken only by a solitary structure, bordered on one side by a row of lush shade trees. The dwelling struck him as familiar, though unremembered.

The house was wood clapboard and of Victorian design, yet simple. Two stories high and boxy, it had been painted light gray and trimmed in bone white. A soft wind stirred. Curtains billowed gently outward through the open windows.

As if some unseen hand had slipped its fingers beneath his ribs, Jaq was drawn to the porch of the house with movements that felt fluid and graceful. His muscles functioned without the slightest stress, and his joints slid across one another, as if the most delicate of lubricants had been applied.

While he was barely aware of his body, the porch had a solid feel that served as a point of reference. It circled the house and created the illusion of a sturdy rampart, though the balusters and rail were slender and the deck only a few feet above the immense, grassy expanse.

Twilight caressed the landscape. Thick, orange light that slipped in at the horizon, shooting over the tops of the low deciduous trees that bordered the grassy field, illuminating the vault of the sky, whose albedo decreased with increasing distance from the treetops. Long leaves of simple rye reflected the day's dying fire and pulsed in time with the fickle breeze.

Jaq sensed that he was no longer alone and felt compelled to enter the house. He glided inside and up the stairs to the second floor. Methodically, yet swiftly and with an increasing sense of urgency, he searched the bedrooms until at last he reached the master.

Furnishings were spare. A rug, a bed, a side table; and an oil lamp fashioned from two, frosted crystal spheres, one balanced above the other, with the lightest scalloping encircling the vent. Jaq thought the room exquisite in its emptiness and order.

White curtains billowed about double hung windows, tangling from time to time with a simple, straight-back chair set slightly askew to the windowsill. Beyond, the grass of the field fairly glowed from the reflected light spilling in at the horizon's edge. Vibrant green grass, each blade reflecting the yellow-orange light. Each blade reflecting the other.

Jaq turned back toward the narrow hallway, but found he faced instead a set of double metal doors inset with opaque glass. "Jesus-H-Fucking Christ! No!" he screamed inside his skull. Jaq was in the scrub room at the hospital where Ur had been born. On the wall hung a bright green surgical gown and beneath it was a pair of green slippers. He understood that he must enter the O.R.

Mechanically, he stuffed his shoes into the booties. As he reached for the gown, he saw shadows moving hurriedly behind the glass. One of them carried a tiny figure whose head was slumped on its chest. *No!* "Ur"! Jaq shouted, as he burst through the doors, only to find himself in the still, dark hallway of the house.

A sound reached him from the murk at the end of the hall. An unpleasant scratching, like stiff bristles being drawn across a hard, horny surface, sounded purposive as it drew closer. Down the stairs he flew, out of the house and into the field. Nothing seemed substantial beneath his feet.

The house receded, framed by grass and sky. Jaq was leaving something he craved, something ordered, familiar and solitary. A place filled with sense and thought. A safe place. The house was like a tunnel that connected his inner and outer worlds. Fear gripped him as the house receded further, like a lighthouse when a boat sets to sea. Yet like a lighthouse, it would somehow lead him back.

Jaq lowered his head and ran. Without wasting time to turn and confirm his fears, he knew that the presence he had recognized in the house was following him, and at great speed. It made a scratchy, skittering sound as it moved through the tough grass. Yet his pursuer also possessed mass. Its bulk declared itself in the vibrations broadcast through the thick sod. He headed for the border of dense trees and found it to be just that. A border. Two-dimensional. There. Not there. And then he found himself on a frozen dirt road that led in only one direction. It wound downward, precipitously, and he took it. Or, more precisely, it took him.

Slippery and rutted, the road slowed his progress considerably, and he sensed that the predator was gaining on him, when suddenly the way smoothed and a vacant plain lay before him. Vacant but for a low, cabin-like structure not far off the path. Jaq sprinted for it. Burnished twilight had turned a soupy, elastic gray, and the cabin would have seemed a desperate refuge, except for a tiny, yellow light that lit a single, small window. Snow had started falling and it stung his eyelids as he hurried on. He reached the hut and dove through the open doorway.

The ceiling was low and protective. Support beams were exposed in a single room. On a rough, wood table stood the lamp, glowing softly. Jaq relaxed, but only for a moment.

Through the window, it thrust a single spiny member, black and shiny and bristling with short, stiff hairs. Shooting straight up and off the skin, the hairs on Jaq's own forearms began to quiver violently. He twisted the fingers of his right hand into a fist. Slowly and deliberately, the creature lifted a leg segment and advanced it toward him. In a futile maneuver, Jaq twisted his head to the side to check for an avenue of escape that he knew did not exist.

When he turned back to face the creature, two flat black eyes, absent any emotion, stared back at him. It had entered the room. *But how....* It meant to touch him, to lay its horny hide on his soft flesh. It had committed him, and without his consent. As if She needed it. *She.* Jaq could smell its sex. He clenched his teeth and ground them, as if he had received a jolt of electric current. Then, She thrust a glistening wet palp in his face. A kiss? A small space inside Jaq's abdomen went warm and runny.

He drove his back flat up against the wall. As if there was anywhere to retreat. As if the small distance he put between himself and his predator mattered. Slowly, the quivering palp advanced once again. Jaq tried to dig his fingers into the rough wood wall. Frantically, he pressed his palms against the planks and pushed up. He stood on his toes, trying desperately to climb. Light flickered faintly in the two black beads that stared at him. The palp, soft and seductive, stretched to touch his lips.

"Jaq!" a remembered voice called. Everything in the trading room came into focus. Tia, a broker at Coogan, faced him. She was gripping his shoulders with her big, muscular hands and shaking him. Her hair erupted from her head in an angry black mass. Each strand had a purpose and direction all its own. She had an angular face, large, full lips and gleaming white teeth. Sweat flew off her forehead and splashed Jaq's face as she continued to shake him. "Jaq, what in hell is wrong with you?" Tia's eyes tossed about like bottomless, black water.

"I, um, left my key in the door and something startled me," he answered weakly.

Tia let go of his arms and wiped the perspiration off of her forehead. "Bullshit."

Jaq looked behind him at the entrance to the office and sensed the experience he'd had outside that door receding, quickly, like the house he'd fled.

"Where'd you get those?" Tia asked abruptly, pointing to his feet.

Jaq stared at the green surgical slippers. He'd dropped those slippers, the *real* slippers, into a burn bag, or whatever they called it, when he'd left the O.R. where Ur had been born. At least he thought he had. What *had* happened out there, outside the front entrance to Coogan? Had anything at all actually *happened*?

Jaq ran his hands through his hair. "Oh, it's kind of sloppy out there this morning and I didn't want to get the floor wet." Tia just stared through his explanation. "You've seen workmen, plumbers, you know, put on these kinds of, um, booties …."

"I thought you and Kate were going fishing."

"We are. I'm going to tidy up a few things and then she's picking me up. What about you? Did you run over here?" Jaq asked, focusing now on how much Tia was perspiring and straining to grab a fistful of reality.

"No. I got a workout at the gym and *I* came in early to clean a few things up, too. Then you blow in here in a freaking panic. Whatever Kate sees in you ..." Tia stepped toward Jaq and he moved to the middle of the room, edging away from an unseen web. "Miserable male," she said, with a peculiar rasping sound.

At that very moment Tia's skin began to gleam, though dully, like brushed metal. The hair on her head bristled and her facial features melted into an empty, wet maw. Jaq's limbs began to tremble and he backed up instinctively, nearly tripping over a chair.

The door rattled open. Jaq turned quickly toward the sound. "Hey, Clara," Jaq said in a high, soft voice. Tia retreated into the half-light.

"Hey, Jaq," said Clara. "Hey, Tia?" she called, but received no response.

"Um, still cold out?" Jaq asked, his words wobbly.

"No, it's eighty and sunny. Hell, yes, it's cold out." Clara pulled off her hat. "Sounds like your teeth are chattering."

"Guess I got chilled in the old truck." Jaq sat down in his chair, his hands still shaking. "Boy, would I love to see this kind of weather hit Florida through the New Year," he said, trying very hard to anchor himself.

"In case you hadn't noticed, it has. What do you think all those poor guys are doing down there, running around in mittens and overcoats, lighting smudge pots? We're the ones who should've been growing oranges up *here* the past month," Clara said.

"You know, every once in a while that poor pea brain of yours has an idea. Maybe I'll plant some groves next year and pull a long squeeze," Jaq said.

"Pea brain? If you had any brains at all you'd sell your Juice. Today. If you don't, the only thing you'll ever pull is Herman."

Clara, fresh out of college, had worked at Coogan for nine months. Jaq had taught her as much about the practical and technical aspects of securities and securities trading as he could. And he had tried to toughen her for the rigors of the trading room. Although he couldn't duplicate the pace, he could give her an impression of the culture, which was puerile, offensive and relentless. Jaq knew that if he didn't, when she arrived in New York she would conclude that all traders were assholes (which they were) and quit. Clara was just too damned good at markets not to give them a shot.

"Hey!" Jaq shouted, looking very angry. "You ought to show more respect for a bigshot client like me." Then he smiled broadly.

Clara chuckled. "Bigshot? If you were such a bigshot you'd be able to afford a pair of boots. What are those things anyway?"

"Hang up your stuff and get your butt over here," he said gruffly. Then, hurriedly he stuffed the booties into his jacket pocket.

Clara returned in a flash. Grabbing his chart book off of his Bloomberg machine, Jaq threw it in front of her. "So, you think I should sell today, huh? Why?"

Clara bit her lower lip and then, breathlessly, launched into a three-minute monologue about trend lines, symmetrical triangles, RSI's, volume and open interest.

"Finished?" he said to her at last. She nodded. "I know all of that."

"Then why aren't you selling? Have you met your price objective?"

"Yes."

"Have any variables changed? 'Cause if they haven't, you've got to sell. If you've met your price objective and nothing fundamental has changed, you're *supposed* to sell. That's *your* rule, Jaq."

"And it's a good rule. But the market just *feels* to me as if it's going higher."

"At tops, markets *always* feel as if they're going higher."

Jaq's eyes flashed. *This kid really got it.* "Okay, so how does it feel to *you*? What's your gut tell you?"

Looking at him with a mixture of profound seriousness and repressed excitement, she said, "It tells me to sell."

Pausing, Jaq looked down at the chart and back up into Clara's young, eager face. "Then sell it. Trade me out of it as best you can."

Clara appeared shocked. And scared. Jaq understood the feeling. This was *it*. She was going to trade her own position. No more intellectualizing, no more 'paper trading'. This was real money.

"You'd trust me to trade your money?"

"Yup," he said.

"But, Jaq, I'm not even registered. I mean, if I screwed up and you got mad and told Levine, I'd never be able to work in this business again. Ever!"

"I'm trusting you. Do you trust me?" Jaq asked firmly.

"Of course, I do," she said, lowering her eyes.

"Then get me out of this Juice and don't screw up."

"I won't."

He thrust the chart book into her hands. "Now, get going. The market opens in a half hour."

As Clara hurried off to her desk, Jaq followed her with his eyes. Of medium height and a trim but athletic build, she sported a short crop of straight, sandy hair. Light green eyes swam above a sea of freckles, and pale, full lips sat invitingly atop a strong, square jaw. Hunched over charts and staring wide-eyed at her Bloomberg, Jaq could not help but think about Ur and his throat thickened. "Damn," he swore softly.

The front door slammed shut, rattling the jamb. The sound sent an electric shock through Jaq's body. "Jesus Christ, Vinnie!" he cried.

"Ay, yo, Mister q. I'm really sorry, but it's fucking cold out there." Vinnie was Levine's, the office manager's, assistant. He had followed Levine loyally since his first job clerking at Coogan's office in Brooklyn Heights. Levine had brought Vinnie out of the mailroom, and for that Vinnie would be eternally grateful. But Jaq knew that Vinnie had talent, and soon Levine would have to do him a second favor and send him back to New York to make a career for himself—if Levine survived that long.

"It's always cold in the Rockies in the morning, Vinnie. Even with this heat wave. So watch your language. You're not in a trading room, yet."

"What?" said Vinnie in a flat monotone.

"Fucking, Vinnie. Fucking," Jaq said.

"Oh, yeah, right. But Mister q, it's like, you know, a function of years of conditioned response. You know, like that guy Skinner and his boxes of rats. Or maybe it goes deeper. Like all dumb guineas from Brooklyn have the adjective 'fucking' hard-wired into their brains at birth."

"Vinnie, you're not dumb. But I'll accept your premise that 'fucking' is hard-wired in all Brooklyn Italian male brains. So hook it up to a little switch," Jaq continued, in a calm voice and with a pleasant smile on his face, "and turn the goddamned thing off when you come in here!"

"Okay, okay, Mister q. I'll remember. I'm sorry, okay?" Vinnie said, looking down at the floor.

Jaq suddenly realized that Vinnie looked more than chagrined. His face was bright red and his pompadour of black hair was covered by a sheet of ice.

"Vinnie, what did you do? Drive in with your head stuck out the window?" Jaq asked.

Vinnie raised his arm and gently touched his hair. "Wow." Clara giggled. She had been watching the whole scene. Vinnie crimsoned deeply. "No, well, you see, I sold my car."

"What, did you walk here?" Jaq asked.

"No. See, I bought a bike."

"As in cycle?" Jaq ventured incredulously. Vinnie worked out daily in the weight room, but, like most self-respecting Brooklyn boys, wouldn't be caught dead doing anything aerobic.

"Nah. Come on." Vinnie laughed. "As in motor! And it's gorgeous."

Clara giggled again.

"Ay, what are you laughing at anyway, huh?"

"A gorgeous motorcycle?"

"Yeah. Real gorgeous, okay? It's a lot better looking than you."

Clara seemed stung.

"All right, you two, knock it off." Jaq knew that Vinnie's reply was puerile and he knew that Vinnie had a crush on Clara. But it surprised him that she looked hurt.

"Okay, Vinnie, you traded your car in for a bike. In Idaho? In mid-December?"

"Yeah, right," Vinnie said matter-of-factly.

"Great, Vinnie. Good move."

"Thanks, Mister q," said Vinnie sincerely.

"What about getting a helmet, Vinnie? Bikes are dangerous."

"What are you, my mother?" Vinnie said.

"Don't get smart."

Vinnie looked down at the floor. "Sorry, Mister q, but a helmet would mess up my hair."

"The helmet would mess up your hair." Jaq nodded thoughtfully. "So will the pavement when your skull hits it at sixty."

Jaq could see that Vinnie was chewing that one over. "Good point," he said at last.

"Thank you. Now you'd better go dry off. You're starting to melt."

The sheet of ice covering Vinnie's hair was beginning to stream down over his ears and neck. Vinnie wiped a dollop of ice water off of his motorcycle jacket. "Geez. Right." He started to sprint towards the bathroom.

"Hey, Vinnie?" Clara's voice stopped him in his tracks. "Where'd you learn that stuff about Skinner?"

"College, where else?"

"Where'd you go?" Though Vinnie and Clara had worked together for several months, she'd never bothered to ask him. In fact, she'd never bothered to ask him much of anything.

"Baruch."

She looked puzzled.

"Bernard Baruch."

"Oh, right," she said, now *sounding* puzzled.

"Where'd you go?"

"Stanford."

"Four year school?"

Clara's face froze, flat and expressionless. "Yes," was all she could manage.

Vinnie turned and strode into the bathroom. As he shut the door behind him, his face exploded into a huge grin.

Clara sat in stunned silence, slightly flushed, body squirming, her mouth agape.

"Catching flies?" Jaq shouted in her general direction.

"What?"

"I said, Juice opens soon. You all right?"

"Sure. Yes, of course."

At that moment, Vinnie emerged from the bathroom and Clara jumped visibly at the sound of the door opening. Then she plunged her head into her charts, as if Vinnie, like some male Medusa, might turn her to stone. Jaq smiled and turned back to his Bloomberg.

But the smile faded as Jaq now sat alone, facing an array of bright green symbols. For a moment he began to shake again, like a mutt during a thunderstorm, as he remembered running, running. Maybe he should just go home and hide in a corner.

No! It hadn't been real. At least it had not been of this world. Did that count as an hallucination? Jaq breathed deeply. He had work to do. He needed to clean a few things up. He'd said so. And he had Clara, a protégé, to protect. And *he* had proposed the party to Kate, so he had the responsibility of offering invitations. Yes, he had responsibilties to Clara and to Kate.

And, besides, he and Kate were going fishing. Goddamit, they were going fishing. Jaq grabbed his charts.

◙ ◎ ◙

The office had begun to fill up. Whooping and harumphing and stamping, people blew in through the door, banging it shut behind them to keep out the cold, except Levine, the office manager. He would always open the door just wide enough to squeeze through and then would shut it softly behind him, tapping his feet lightly against the jamb.

Atop his head sat a black hat of curly lamb's wool, matching his moustache in color and texture. He had been stuffed into a beige corduroy car coat, and his feet swam in rubber boots secured by light, metal fasteners of a kind believed to be long extinct. Jaq knew, as everyone else did, that his wife, Sarah, had dressed him.

Crossing quietly to his office from the coatroom, Levine slowed as he passed Jaq's desk. "May I speak with you for a moment?"

"Sure, Levine. What's on your mind?"

Determination replaced consternation on Levine's face, a kind of biological board in a game of semiotic Scrabble. "In my office, if you don't mind."

Jaq, intrigued, cocked his head. "Of course."

Levine closed the door very quietly behind him. He did not turn on the fluorescents, leaving the office submerged in a murky, half-light. With a sweep of his hand, Levine motioned toward an ersatz- mahogany chair, upholstered with institutional gray tweed, as he moved behind his desk. He flicked on a small table lamp, placed the tips of all ten fingers on the black blotter in front of him, eyes cast downward, and lowered himself into his chair. Levine cleared his throat, then bit his lip and glanced about the room distractedly.

"What is it?" Jaq asked gently, as if he were coaxing a suicide off of a ledge.

Levine rubbed his forehead and sighed deeply. "I want to be professional about this. But, Jesus, Jaq, I'm scared." His eyes flitted about the room, seeking any perch but Jaq's gaze.

"I can't help you if you won't tell me what's going on. Is it Sarah? Is it you and Sarah?"

"Oh, no! Of course not."

Of course Jaq knew "… of course not."

"Then what?" Jaq said slowly and emphatically.

Levine was shaking, his face ashen. Clearly, he hadn't slept well. His eyes looked like two piss holes in the snow.

"It's a problem here at the office," Levine said.

"Okay," Jaq said very slowly. "Is the problem my being here, in the office? Am I a distraction? I used to be a partner at Coogan. And I know that Tia—"

"No, it's not that at all."

"Is it Clara? Maybe I've …."

"No, no. Of course not!" At last Levine seemed to gather his resolve. "Well, you know what happened in St. Louis?"

"Sure. And Chicago and Dayton and Brooklyn." At the recitation of his peripatetic career, Levine made a face that looked as if he had swallowed a bolus of bile.

"Oh, shit, no, Levine. Not again. Levine, you're my friend. I like you. I really do. But Coogan doesn't have an office in Barrow, Alaska."

"And even if they did, I'm not sure I'd get the job."

"But who …." There was no 'who' question in Ketchum. There was only Faddle. "Oh, no, Levine. Piss off the Pope for Christ's sake, but not John Faddle."

Levine's palms smacked the blotter that lay on his desk. He was shaking. "John Faddle is not above the rules. No one is above the rules."

"You're right. Of course, you're right," said Jaq calmly. "Tell me what's going on."

"Dammit, it looks as if he's churning accounts, Jaq. You know, there's been excessive trading in his customer accounts."

"I know what churning is," said Jaq.

"I, I'm sorry. I'm not trying to be condescending."

"Forget it. I know that. But tell me, have any of his customers *lost* money?"

"No."

"Have commissions been a large multiple of profits?"

"No. In fact, quite the opposite."

"So what's the problem?"

"Dammit, Jaq, the problem is you don't turn little old Mrs. McGillicuddy's account ten times a year. Strictly interpreted, the rules would say his conduct is not that of a prudent man. Overtrading catches up with you."

"Maybe. But in Faddle's case he might die first. He's been doing this for almost twenty years and has never, ever burned his book. Hell, he's never lost a single account because of performance. Maybe he's lost a few because he pissed them off. But the guy's financial record is impeccable and you know it."

"The higher they climb, the farther—"

"Stop it. Faddle isn't gonna crash and you know it. 'The higher they climb,'" Jaq said in a sing-song voice.

Levine winced.

"Look, I'm sorry—"

With a wave of his hand, Levine stopped him. "No, no. You're right. I'm a little twit."

Levine cast his eyes downward, picked up a pencil and rotated it slowly on the blotter's surface. Jaq sat patiently. At last, Levine let the pencil fall. It hit the blotter with a crisp smack.

"Levine," Jaq said deliberately, "rules can't cover every contingency. The exercise of judgment's part of your job."

"And my judgment is that today, in the current climate, rules ought to be strictly interpreted. At the very least, I have to show that we've looked at the matter. Look at what happened to Drexel. Then Pru. And it's in John's interest as well."

"Come on, Levine. Faddle's no Milken. Besides you could lose your job," Jaq said. "You can't afford that. You can't do that to Sarah and the kids again."

"You're right, Jaq. So could you talk to him?"

Jaq heard the catch click, and then a shock wave rolled through the room as the door slammed shut. "I don't churn!" the big broker shouted, all seventy-seven inches and three hundred pounds of him, though not so loudly as to be heard on the trading floor. Faddle was no fool.

Jaq cleared his throat. "Good morning, John," he said.

"Oh, hi, Jaq," Faddle replied, barely acknowledging his presence.

"Levine, I don't fucking churn," Faddle repeated, this time in a tone of controlled anger that was even more threatening.

"John, who's saying—" Levine began.

"New York's telling me that *you're* saying. Telling me for a fact."

"I'm just doing my job, John. Reviewing records. And the rules, strictly construed—"

Faddle took a step toward Levine's desk, his huge fists clenched.

Levine pressed his back into his chair and held up a hand. "I was just telling, Jaq—"

"Tell *me*," Faddle growled.

"I'm doing it in the firm's best interest. And yours."

Faddle blinked beneath his big, black bushy eyebrows. "Let me worry about my own best interests," he said menacingly. "Let me worry about that." Faddle opened the door and gazed out across the trading floor with an angelic smile. The place began to whir once again and he closed the door gently behind him.

Silence descended on Levine's office with a thump, like the padded paw of a large predator. Levine appeared to lose corporeality, held together only by the faint light that tumbled like smoke, thick and yellowish, from the tiny table lamp tucked in the corner of his desk.

His hands shaking slightly, Levine lifted a small picture of Sarah and the kids, framed in rich red leather and stamped with fine gold filigree. "Did you know that after my first promotion to manager of the Montague Street office of Coogan in Brooklyn, I purchased this in a small art gallery on the corner of Clinton? I didn't buy it on a whim. I'd coveted it for a long time. It seemed tangible evidence of the beginning of what I hoped would be a steady climb up through the ranks of management. I imagined I might even run the whole damned retail organization one day. Then I'd buy myself an antique bowl." Levine spread his palms as if he were lowering the bowl gently onto his desk. "I was going to fill it with fresh fruit every day."

Levine's eyes were glassy, as if he had a high fever. His lips were moist and red, and he was furiously rubbing his thumb against the opposed index and middle fingers. "I don't give a damn about this frame. I love my family. But my work is my center. Don't you see? You must. And it's the doing of the thing that matters. That's where the morality lies. Even the outcome doesn't count, really."

At that moment, the low-slanting rays of the rising sun struck the windshield of a car parked across the street. Smacking Levine in the face, they blinded him temporarily. He winced, appearing lost and alone. The sun climbed quickly. Now its light bathed only the top of Levine's head, casting the shadow of a few wisps of hair against blobs of golden yellow that splattered the wall behind him.

"Faddle likes you a lot," Levine said. "He'd listen to you. I'm sure he would. I just need his cooperation."

"Faddle doesn't listen to anybody, Levine," said Jaq, getting up from his chair.

"But he likes you, Jaq. And, and he respects you. I think you're the only person he does respect. Around here at least."

Jaq shrugged. "I suppose he does, but somehow I don't think that'll matter when it comes to business." Jaq paused, holding the doorknob in his hand. "All right, but I'll have to do it on Wednesday. Kate's picking me up in a few minutes. Can it wait?"

Levine nodded.

"And Levine?"

"Yes, what?"

"Do me a favor and lighten up on him. It's dangerous. I don't think Faddle would hurt you. But there are other people in an organization like this who won't tolerate somebody screwing with a big shot like John. They don't want to jeopardize their cut. But of course you know that, or we wouldn't have had this talk, would we?"

Levine's eyes glazed over.

"Levine?"

"Oh, yes. Sure. I'll, um, do as you say."

"Good," Jaq said. "Oh, and Levine, would you and Sarah like to come to a little party Kate and I are having Wednesday? We're going to celebrate the Winter Solstice and—"

"Yes, of course, it sounds lovely and, um …."

"You'll mention it to Sarah?"

"Yes, of course."

"I'll have Kate give her a call."

Levine did not reply. He sat at his desk staring blankly at the pencil that lay on the blotter in front of him.

As Jaq shut the door behind him, he thought he heard a soft groan. For a moment, he stood outside Levine's office, his hand resting reflectively on the door's brass knob. He rubbed his hand over its smooth surface.

Jaq grabbed his coat and on his way out, stopped at Clara's desk. "I'm leaving. And I'll be out tomorrow. Good luck—"

"But I—"

"We'll talk on Wednesday."

Clara nodded.

◙ ◉ ◙

CHAPTER 3

———

Kate was puzzled by the tiny traffic jam. Then she spotted the Reverend Bildad Proud moving down the line of cars, smiling, extending his arm toward the church parking lot in a gesture of invitation. *Son of a bitching, moralizing bastard. 'God is good,* all *the time.' That's what he'd had to say about Ur's death.*

When Proud had finished chatting with the people in a car directly in front of Kate, he straightened himself up, which appeared to involve some great effort though very little range of movement, and, spreading his fingers across his ample stomach, rocked back on his heels and grinned broadly. His eyes caught Kate's.

At once, Kate's features, hardened and supported by anger, dropped. Her stomach felt as if it had tilted off its axis. Proud yawed toward her car. Instinctively, Kate pressed her back into the seat.

Well-fed flesh stretched the seams of Proud's trousers and there was a roll of fat where his genitals should have been. Gray Hush Puppies collapsed over their own soles. A bloated pink face, inset with watery blue, porcine eyes, poked above a dirty down parka.

Proud tapped lightly on the window, leaving two small smudges. Kate's nose wrinkled, and she smiled weakly. Proud tapped again. Kate checked quickly in the rearview mirror, then ahead of her. Traffic remained jammed. Proud had certainly reeled them in. "Not this one," Kate muttered. She felt heat rise in her face and rolled the window down.

"And how is the lovely Kate this morning?"

"In a hurry, thank you."

"A hurry, yes. So are we all these days. But to what purpose?"

"In our case, fishing. Jaq and I are going fishing. He's waiting for me and I really must—"

"I'm fishing, too, as you can see." Proud's eyes, Kate thought, flickered downward for a moment. She pulled her own down vest closed over her shirt with her fist. Proud kept talking. "Come in, just for a moment. We're having Monday morning Bible class. Don't be in too much of a hurry. All eternity lies ahead of you." A large gold ring on Proud's hand flashed its zircon message, TRYGOD, as it caught and reflected the sun's rays. "The Lord's word—"

"Is not to our taste."

"Oooh. Not to your taste. My, my. But grace is not a matter of choice, my dear Kate. It is bestowed on you, or not. No matter what Father Beele and his misguided brethren may say about, um, good works. Ha! Works are neither good nor bad. They are amoral."

Kate flashed a phony smile. "Well, then, I suppose Jaq and I are damned."

"There you may be wrong. That is what salvation is all about." Proud's pale blue eyes lost what little color they possessed. Kate found herself staring at two hard-boiled eggs. The preacher peered into the cab and down at the space between Kate's legs. "Let me save you, Kate. If talking of faith embarrasses you, come to me alone, anytime." He made a move to reach into the car, but Kate must have anticipated him and was rolling up the window.

Proud's fingers left two streaks on the glass. Kate stared straight ahead and saw an opening in the traffic. She sped off. Glancing in the mirror, Kate saw Proud where she had left him, grinning broadly, rocking slowly on his heels.

◙ ◉ ◙

"How did your morning go?" Kate asked edgily, as she unbuckled her seatbelt and popped open the door of the truck.

"How did *yours* go?" Quickly, Kate explained what had happened with Proud."

"Well, fuck *him.* Let's—"

"No," Kate said sternly. "Fuck him. Today's about us." She took a deep breath. "Let's start over. So, how did your morning go?"

Jaq nodded. "Okay. Well …." Then his face fell. "Well, I don't know, really. Kind of mixed."

"Want to talk about it?"

"No," he said emphatically, "today *is* about us. Not Tia or Levine or anyone else."

"Oh, Jaq, you didn't fight with Tia, did you?"

"Nope."

"Good. Did you ask everyone to the party?"

"Well, not exactly."

"Oh, Jaq!"

"Look," Jaq said, "would you mind calling Tia tomorrow? It'd be easier. Oh, and I mentioned it to Levine but he was a little distracted this morning, so would you mind calling Sarah to confirm? I'll get in touch with Faddle. And Beele." Jaq took a quick peek at Kate. "Deal?"

Kate smiled. "All right, all right."

"Great. That's settled. Today is about us. It's about being selfish. We're going fishing."

Kate reached over and tousled Jaq's hair. "Yes, we damned well are going fishing, aren't we."

"Chinese fire drill?" Jaq shouted. Kate laughed and unbuckled.

As they gained elevation, the sun danced brightly along the ridges of the hills that flanked Trail Creek Road and its eponymous little creek. And as the morning shadows slid down the slopes, Jaq's hands relaxed their grip on the wheel. Kate blurted a small cry of surprise as the Jeep lurched off the pavement and onto the dirt road that wound its way up to the pass.

"You've been somewhere else?" Jaq asked.

"Yes. But you've been kind of quiet yourself. Are you mad at me for wanting to ask Tia tomorrow night?"

"No. You know, I might actually get to like her if she wouldn't take everything and everybody so seriously. She's got potential to be a real character. No, I was thinking about Ur. I guess you were too?"

"Yes."

"Sad?"

"No. Not really. I mean, not especially." Kate tossed her head back. "Ur was beautiful, wasn't she? She looked perfect. Her eyes were such a clear, deep cobalt blue. Bluer than that sky. But they couldn't see. Her brain was too full of holes. Guess that's what lack of oxygen will do." Kate picked at one of her fingers. "Did we do the right thing, Jaq? Did we? Letting her die, I mean."

Jaq was silent.

"I know. We've been through this a thousand times. It's only when I start feeling selfish that I even let myself ask the question. I guess there's a piece of me that's always a little sad when I think of her. Even when a memory comes to mind that makes me laugh."

"I know," Jaq said. "I call it 'the hole in my soul.' I'm always aware of it, and I'm also aware that it'll never completely close. But that's okay. Part of me never wants to forget."

Kate chuckled. "There were times she was *so* funny. Remember the face she used to make when she'd get gas but couldn't burp? She'd throw her little arms out to the side, make fists, turn and stick out her tongue." Kate imitated Ur and it made Jaq laugh.

"That's pretty good. You look like Yoda with a bellyache. Say, how about a sip of water?"

Kate turned to grab the Thermos. The Jeep hit a stone and began to list. Both of them looked beyond the edge of the road and glimpsed eternity. It was over in a second as the truck thumped a second time and settled back onto the roadbed.

"Jesus," Jaq said hoarsely, "that was close. I think I'll hug the uphill side a little tighter."

"Maybe you should pay more attention to the road."

"Maybe you should go screw yourself." Jaq's fingers tightened around the steering wheel. *God, Jaq, you're an asshole.* "Hey, I'm sorry, I *am* paying attention. It's just that there's a lot of debris. I don't think they've graded this thing since Labor Day. We'll just have to take our time."

"Take all the time you want. Boy, I still can't get used to these mountain roads without guardrails. Back East they put guardrails above a ditch that's two feet deep. What is that drop off? Two *thousand* feet?"

"Yeah, about two thousand. But it's still only the first two feet that matter."

Kate grinned. "Want that water?"

"Sure, thanks. And tighten that seat belt. If we go over, I want them to be able to identify you." They both laughed nervously and remained very still as the truck picked its way around loose rock for the next five miles.

As the road wound higher and higher, Trail Creek turned into a small, silver thread. Sunlight dripped down the steep flanks of the foothills like butterscotch. Snow had dusted the ground and made the deep green fir and pine stand out in bold relief. Outcroppings of gray granite defined the border between the brown earth and the light blue, flawless sky.

Finally, the road flattened. Jaq exhaled loudly. "Made it!"

"Jaq? Let's quit a little on the early side today and take the highway back to Ketchum. I don't want to creep back down this road in the dark."

"Done," said Jaq, as the Jeep plunged into a dense forest of fir that flanked the road.

Soon a wide basin replaced the woods. To their right a small stream, containing a healthy population of brook trout, wound through a meadow of black grass and willow. Since the water was too small to support big fish, they did not stop, not even to wet a line. But Kate kept a sharp eye out nonetheless, alert for the first sign of prey.

Kate bounced off the seat. "Brookie, brookie!" she shouted. "Maybe it's a good omen."

"Just maybe it is," Jaq said, grinning.

"Yup. We're gonna slam 'em!" They were going fishing.

As they sped over the washboard of the dirt road, they bounced lightly on their seats. The day stretched its limbs and rose to greet the earth, washing the basin with the limpid morning light of the mountains. Ruddy peaks towered over foothills thick with sage. A crop of dry grass and bright yellow willow bark cradled the creek. Late autumn rippled, purple and brown. Kate turned off the heater and rolled down the window a few tentative inches. Cool air rushed in and spilled over their faces. It was like licking an icicle freshly snapped from a frozen gutter.

"Some tunes?" Jaq asked. "I'm feeling a little friskier."

Kate nodded and grabbed a cassette out of the cubby box. The pure hollow sound of a flute, supported by the soft beat of the timpani, filled the cab. "I do so love Mozart," Kate said.

"If only *we* had a flute that was magic and could lead her back," Jaq said. Kate's eyes filled with tears. "I'm sorry," Jaq said and reached to pop the tape out.

"No," Kate said, grabbing his hand. "Let me just flip it and we'll start over."

"Yup. Let's start over."

Rounding a corner guarded on the left by a large sandstone outcrop, they hit pavement once again. Dead ahead lay the Big Lost Mountains. Massive and white in all seasons, they rose a mile up and out of the valley floor. The truck's tires sang on the asphalt.

"Sing, goddess, the wrath of Achilles," Jaq said, as if prompted.

"What?" Kate said.

"First line of the *Iliad*. Sort of."

"What made you think of that?" Kate asked.

"The Lost Mountains. They remind me of the walls of Troy." For some reason, Jaq shuddered. He didn't feel chilled but he asked Kate to close the window anyway.

"Why didn't you become a classicist?" Kate asked.

"So I could meet you on Wall Street," Jaq said.

Kate picked a finger. "If you hadn't met me—"

Jaq laid a hand lightly on Kate's arm. "There's a passage in the *Iliad*. Priam enters the camp of the Greeks to retrieve Hector's body. Achilles offers him food, but Priam, consumed by grief, refuses. Achilles tells Priam that he mourned for his friend Patroclus, but reminds the king that the business of living demands attention."

Kate grabbed Jaq's hand and kissed the tips of his fingers. Neither of them said another word. Fifteen minutes later they reached the outskirts of Mackay.

◙ ◉ ◙

The town was a typical Western whistle stop, without the whistle. A dozen or so frame buildings comprised its critical mass. A motel welcomed sportsmen whose enthusiasm had outlasted daylight. A restaurant offered beer and whiskey, hamburgers and cheeseburgers.

Jaq turned right at the only traffic light and drove behind town, past the rodeo grounds, until they reached a gate that allowed access to the river. Kate hopped out of the truck to let them through.

"Come on, Jaq!" Kate stamped her foot lightly, then secured the gate with a small piece of wire.

"Jesus, Jaq. Where were you? A thousand miles away?" Kate asked.

"No. More like twenty. Or maybe three thousand years." Kate cocked her head and silently regarded Jaq for a moment. "There was something about the Lost's ridgeline back there. It was as if I could see Trojans glaring down at me." He shrugged. "Silly. Anyway, sorry. We're burning daylight."

Jaq killed the engine at the river's edge. He dropped the rear hatch and pulled out the rod cases, waders and boots, while Kate spread a tarp on the ground to keep their feet dry while they changed.

Next came the ritual of putting the rods up. To Jaq it had always had the feel of a sacrament. The rod case, a short aluminum cylinder, was unscrewed slowly. Not because any damage could be done to the equipment, but just because it felt right. Then the rod, encased in felt and tied fast with a cord, was lifted out of the tube. Each section, butt, mid and tippet, occupied its proper sleeve. Sensuous was the word that came closest to the feeling of pulling the sections out. Slick graphite or fiberglass or bamboo, they slid smoothly and effortlessly from the bag. Finally, the sections were joined together.

"Where shall we try?" asked Kate as they headed toward the sound of the roaring river, beating against boulders like a battle drum.

"I'd like to nymph in the deep run by the old mine shaft, near the sluice. But first, we might loosen up a little in the riffle water below it, up around the next bend."

Short stubble crunched underfoot and they made good time. Willows flanked them on the left, cottonwoods on the right. Soon the cottonwoods claimed the riverbank entirely, until at last the stand of trees ended abruptly, giving way to a large field that stretched far upriver toward the Lost Mountains, looming chilly and white. The low slant of the winter sun defined precise angles on every object.

Kate and Jaq paused in front of a large log extending fifteen feet into the water, which should have provided cover for big fish. But ice complicated the casting and covered the prime part of the hole. Twenty yards upstream the water became shallower and the river wider and clear of ice.

"The fish will be smaller in that riffle water, but it might be a good place to start," Kate said.

"Yeah. Let's try it. We can loosen up, smooth out some kinks and find the range in our casting. Besides, I feel sort of rusty. I think I need to stick a fish just to get my timing back."

"Me, too. Even if they're just little guys up ahead, the skunk will be off the deck if we land one."

Cautiously and quietly, they walked upriver along the bank. Stopping at the bottom of the run, Jaq laid down the dry fly rod, a small seven-foot bamboo that Kate had given him as a wedding present, and held onto the larger, graphite rod he would use for nymphs.

Moving together, though not exactly in unison, Jaq being the quicker and Kate the more deliberate fisherman, they waded fifty yards upriver, consuming the better part of an hour. Each stuck a dozen fish of twelve to fifteen inches and landed nearly half of those.

By noon, the air temperature had climbed above fifty degrees. Warming their backs as it moved slowly across a crackling blue sky, the sun was exploding on the surface of the Lost, shooting bits of itself in all directions.

"Got the 'schmutz' off?" Jaq asked.

"I'll say!" Kate replied, grinning.

"Good. Then why don't you go get the dry-fly rod we left on the bank downstream, and I'll scout up ahead for 'bucket jaws.'"

"Done!"

◙ ◉ ◙

Kate quartered cross-stream to the far bank, which at that point was really a beach of worn stones made from what had been the river's bottom during spring runoff.

Kate squatted and ran her hand over the surface of a large rock. Already warmed by the sun, it was like a loaf of freshly baked bread. The water danced and splashed and rumbled in its channel. Kate squinted as she glanced at a sky that remained unstained by even a single cloud. Sun, sky, river, rocks. Fire, air, water, earth. So simple, she thought.

A loud, deep boom rolled across the surface of the Lost. The sound, followed immediately by a tremendous splash, made Kate jump. She thought that perhaps a huge cottonwood had toppled into the river. In fact, a great hunk of ice had broken loose under the combined assault of current and heat. *Ice.* Her thoughts were swept for an instant to the edge of a large frozen lake. The image was completely unconnected to anything in her experience.

Then, the image evanesced. She was standing on the bank of the Lost River. Shaking herself in an attempt to shed idle thoughts, she popped up and walked, more swiftly now, stumbling from time to time on the odd stone.

Lying on a tuft of dried grass, Jaq's bamboo rod rose every so often when a puff of wind would blow through the dead stalks. The cane was a light caramel color, shot through with dark, thin veins. *Pretty thing.*

Its motion made a delicate, rattling sound, carrying Kate's mind back to the dry whispers she had heard on Ur's baby monitor when Ur was alive. Then memory morphed into the succession of days and nights that she had listened to the child's labored breathing.

A rush of air brushed her cheek. A voice called. A woman's voice, she thought. A raspy rattle answered. She saw a gust of wind lift the cane rod through the dry grass. The voice called again, more urgently this time. Kate's stomach tightened.

"Kate? Kate! Are you all right?"

Spinning her around gently, Jaq looked at her full in the face. Her skin, naturally fair, was silvery white. And her eyes were blazing cobalt, but fathoms deep and far away. "Kate. Jesus. Are you okay? Are you sick?"

She blinked. She gulped some air. "No, I'm fine, really I am. Maybe some water. I'd like that."

"Sure. Sure." Jaq opened his orange rucksack hurriedly and grabbed a thermos. He poured her a cup, right to the brim. His hands were unsteady and a dollop of water sloshed onto the back of his hand.

Kate managed a couple of tentative sips. "Thanks, pal."

"You're welcome." Jaq wiped the back of his hand on his waders. "What happened, Kate?"

For a moment, she sat quietly. Then she shrugged. "I don't know." A slice of silence slipped between them.

The wind blew a sudden gust, nearly lifting Kate's cap off her head. "Damn wind," she said as she pulled her hat down over her forehead, "I sure hope it doesn't come up. It's been perfect so far for casting."

Jaq grabbed the bamboo rod and put his other hand in Kate's as they began to walk back upstream. He felt a slight tug. Softly, she spoke to him. "Jaq?"

"Yes. What is it?"

Kate lowered her lovely blue eyes. "Something did happen back there." Kate exhaled. "It's silly, but … I heard a sound, a boom, like ice cracking. You know how creepy that is."

He nodded. "A piece broke off when I was scouting up ahead and it startled me so badly I almost fell in the goddamned river."

"That started it, I think."

"Started what?"

"Shhh! Just listen. I had this … I don't know what to call it. Not a vision or anything. It was kind of a mental image. Yes, that's it. I was standing at the edge of a frozen lake and I was frightened. Then a gust of wind came up and blew your little bamboo rod around in the grass. It made a dry, kind of raspy, rattling sound. You know, the way Ur used to breathe." Kate picked at a finger. "Jaq?"

"Yeah?"

"Did you happen to turn on Ur's baby monitor recently?" Kate asked. "I mean, were you fooling around with it or anything?"

"What's this all—"

"Did you?" Kate asked more insistently.

"No. Why?"

"Because this morning, after you left, I thought I heard the sound of her breathing on the monitor. Just for a few moments."

"Okay. Maybe you turned it on by mistake. The sounds on the monitor are probably explainable, and the fly rod made the same sound when the wind struck it. So what?" Jaq said.

"Well, then I heard this voice. An old woman's voice, I think. And then I heard you calling my name." Kate rubbed her forehead. "I don't know."

"Why do you keep that thing on your night table anyway?"

"Oh, screw you," Kate said. "Why did you keep those frigging green booties?"

"How do you know about the booties?" Jaq asked. "When did you ever get a chance to see them? They were destroyed at the hospital."

"For some reason they were the first thing I noticed when I came to, after the C-section. But what do you mean they were destroyed? They were sticking out of your jacket pocket when I picked you up," Kate said.

Jaq grabbed her sleeve. "Something weird happened to me this morning, too." Jaq proceeded to relate his experience to Kate. "And then Tia was shaking me. She startled me. And we, uh, talked."

"Jaq?"

"It wasn't a pleasant conversation. But I really didn't try to instigate anything." Kate narrowed her eyes. "Honest. Anyway, I thought I'd gone nuts when she pointed out the booties. I made up some lame excuse for wearing them. But, honestly, I really believe they came from that house. I'm sure the pair I wore at the hospital was dumped in a burn bag.

"Then I had this feeling of something really dangerous about Tia. I was actually frightened. Her skin turned very dark and took on an odd sheen. Hard and brittle looking, but sort of shiny. Kind of like—"

"A big black widow." Kate moved close to Jaq. "The kiss. The slick wet palp. Probing. The reek of pheromones," Kate said, whispering the sibilants.

"Come on, Kate. Cut that out."

Kate shrugged. "Fine. Bunch o' nonsense, huh? So let's drop it. I'm sure you're wrong about the booties being burned and, after last night, after talking about Ur, who could blame either one of us for letting the power of suggestion grab our imaginations by the gonads." She pulled at the brim of her cap. "Besides, I want to go stick me 'bucket jaws.'"

"You're probably right about our imaginations." Jaq smiled. "Or maybe I was having the DTs." Kate punched him on the arm. "Anyway, a school's holding in the deep channel up near the old bridge."

"Well, then, let's go. We're just standing around here—"

"Burning daylight!"

◎ ◉ ◎

They walked briskly along the narrow bank, flanked by bare, dark cottonwoods and the icy river. A small cloud that had dared to stray into the clean, blue space above blotted out the sun. Their skin cooled unpleasantly, and they both looked skyward and frowned. And then, just as suddenly as it had intruded, the tiny cloud moved on. They were laughing now. Time was wasting and it *was* a beautiful day.

Slipping around a border of ice that had sprung seemingly from solid rock, they clambered up the outcrop where Jaq had watched the fish working. Catching sight of three or four huge rainbow, Kate sucked in a sharp breath and stepped forward.

"Kate, get down—" The pod burst apart in a metallic flash, sun glinting off of their silver scales.

"Oh, no, I scared them off. I'm sorry," said Kate. "Well, it's getting late anyway. Want to head back? We couldn't have had a better day."

"You? You want to quit early?" Jaq said.

Leaning over, she closed her eyes and kissed him lightly on the mouth. She parted her lips slightly and her tongue flicked out and brushed against Jaq's teeth. Flashing a broad, toothy smile, Jaq began to fumble with the shoulder straps holding up Kate's waders. Kate grabbed a handful of hair on each side of Jaq's head. She pulled him close to her, kissed his cheek and chewed his ear, blowing into it softly between kisses. They looked around and walked to a little clearing among some willows directly behind them.

Everything seemed better than it probably was. The Neoprene spread beneath them felt softer, the day warmer. Boring its way through a thin patch of high clouds, the sun felt as if it were melting the cells of Jaq's body like pockets of honey in a comb and, too quickly, the hot liquid seemed to flow between him and Kate.

"Phew!" was about all Jaq could manage.

"Holy moly," was Kate's profound reply.

And then. "I love you."

"I love you, too." Who spoke first? Did it matter? They dozed for seconds that seemed like hours, until a gust of chill wind spanked their flanks.

Both of them were quiet for a moment. A breeze stirred the awns of the dried grass that surrounded them, making a light, papery, rattling sound. Kate gripped Jaq's hand.

And the breeze bore an acrid aroma. On the high prairie the wind would scatter fine particles of dust that smelled as if they had been baked. Breathing deeply, Jaq drank in the scent of flint. It made his eyes flare. Jaq thought of Ilium, the plains of Troy, and imagined it may have smelled the same three millennia ago in that dry, bright corner of the world. Of course, the sea must have tinged the air with salt. Yet, when the breeze fell and the sun scorched the soil, the Greeks and the Trojans, even the gods, must have tasted flint.

Jaq turned and looked to the east, to the Lost Mountains looming over the high plateau. Chalk white, bare and brittle, they became the walls and towers of Troy. And Jaq started as he stared. For along the ridge he thought he saw figures staring down. But who? And at whom? At Hector being dragged through the dust? *Hector? No. They're looking at me.*

"Jaq? Jaq!" Kate said. "Lost again?" Kate asked.

"Yes. I mean, no! Just frozen stiff." Kate stared at him but did not say a word.

Jaq frowned. "Well, actually, remember I said earlier that the ridgeline of the Lost reminded me of the walls of Troy. It's ... it's as if there were someone or something, or things, staring down on me. Achilles killed Hector beneath those walls in single combat. The Greeks often called a hero's finest moments in battle Aristeia." Jaq took a deep breath and looked directly into Kate's face. "I feel as if there's a battle I've been waiting to face all of my life. And it frightens me."

"Me, too," Kate said. She touched him lightly on the arm. "I mean, I'm cold, too." Without another word, they dressed and stepped out from behind the willows and onto an ice-free bank at the head of the flat water where Kate had scattered the school.

Upstream the water moved faster, tumbling over rocks that had piled up just below a small scruffy island covered with weeds and willow. Directly opposite the widest part of the island, the Lost had cut deeply into the bank, a holding place for large trout.

Jaq gasped audibly. Kate, who had been stretching and enjoying the pleasant offering of warmth from the sun, jumped at the sound. "Jesus! Are you all right? I mean, this *Iliad* stuff …."

"Yes, I'm okay. But, I just saw something. I think it was a fish. I mean, of course it was a fish. What else could it be?"

"How should I know? You saw it. I didn't," Kate said peevishly.

"I suppose I did. But the fish was so big and it was bright and it was—I don't really know how to describe the colors. Let's go up and have a look."

They slid into knee-deep water, wade-able right up to the hole. "Wait," Kate said. She turned and took a couple of steps back toward the bank, stretched and grabbed Jaq's bamboo. "Pretty silly going up there unarmed," she said, and then, fighting the current, headed upstream with a mechanical, rolling gait.

Suddenly, Kate stopped dead. She blinked.

"Did you see it?" Jaq whispered.

"Yeah." Kate swallowed hard. "Yeah. It's a fish all right, Jaq. But, crikey!"

"Shhh!"

"Sorry." Kate lowered her voice. "It's so—brilliant."

"Strip off some line and start shootin'."

"You saw it. You fish it," Kate said.

Jaq took the rod gently and examined the tiny dry fly tied to the tippet. He shook his head. "This'll never work. The Betis hatch has stopped."

But Kate just stared straight at him. "No. Go ahead and use it, Jaq. It doesn't really make any difference which fly you use. That fish is here for you to catch."

"No. I suppose it doesn't. Everything today has been so goddamned strange. Well ....." He shook himself and stepped up a few feet to get position on his fish. The four-weight line couldn't cast very far and he was closer to his target than he would have liked. Turning to Kate, he began to protest. "Kate, maybe we should go back for a bigger rod. I'm awfully close and I might spook it."

"Jaq. Cast."

He took a deep breath and made a few false casts to measure the distance. The fish was still feeding regularly, every thirty seconds or so. Making one final, false cast, Jaq shot the light line at his target. His arm melded with the bamboo rod and his wrist flicked in perfect time with the line. Beyond the point where technique becomes art, he sensed beauty. The fly landed softly in the seam between current and eddy, just above his fish. It floated naturally, without a hint of drag.

Instead of rolling, his trout stuck its fishy snout out of the water. Flashing argentine and purple in the sun, it sipped the fly delicately. So absorbed was Jaq in the scene, he actually forgot to set the hook. No matter. His trout sounded and hooked itself.

"Hit 'em, Jaq. Rip lips," he heard Kate shouting. 'Oh, right,' said his brain to his arm. Up it jerked, setting the imbedded hook deeper still, and the fish was off upstream on a run that made his reel sing. Jaq had had his index finger and thumb resting lightly on the spool and the line came off the reel with such speed that it actually burned his flesh.

At that moment, she decided to leap, shooting up through the sparkling, shimmering surface of the stream. Her sides flashed in the sun-- silver, deep pink and violet. Jaq watched, jaw unhinged, as the fish hung in midair, suspended for what seemed like a whole sackfull of seconds. Then, in a graceful arc, she pointed her snout toward the water and plunged back into the icy cold of the stream.

She leapt so many times that Jaq stopped counting. Dancing and twisting in the sun, she seemed to draw energy from it. With each jump she grew brighter, until Jaq thought he might faint from watching her. Abruptly, she sounded, surging upstream and then down, with and against the current, without effort, as if she might run forever. And yet, she would stop every time the backing looked as if it was going to run out.

In his hands, Jaq felt not only the mass of his fish straining against him, but he sensed its strength and its unbounded joy as well. Then she stopped. She stopped jumping and she stopped running and pushed her nose above the current in a sign of exhaustion. Jaq reeled furiously. But everything was moving too slowly. His side began to ache, then throb. He thought she would never reach them.

"Hurry! Hurry!" Kate was saying. Breathing fast and breathing hard, Jaq began to sweat. He abandoned the reel crank and began to strip line.

When at last the fish came within reach, Jaq slid his hand underneath her. Where mottled green should have been on her head and back were silver scales. Her sides were splashed with rose. Inset into her flanks, the median line pulsed deep purple.

Both anglers remained silent, the only noise the playful rush of the smaller, shallower water on the far side of the island. Jaq handed his rod to Kate and unclipped a pair of forceps from his vest. Gently, he grasped the hook and slid it from the trout's upper lip. She did not bleed.

Jaq's voice shook. "She looks fine, don't you think?"

"Yes. Yes. Just tired, that's all," Kate said. "I think she'll be okay. Plunge her?"

"No. I'm afraid to do that. She's exhausted." Placing his hands under her belly, he faced the fish upstream to allow fresh water to flush through her gills.

After several minutes, the fish had not recovered at all. In fact, her respiration had slowed. Cautiously, Jaq removed his left hand from her underside to see if she was playing possum. But she just rolled to one side, gasping rapidly.

Almost frantic now, Jaq began to move her back and forth in an effort to flush more fresh water over her gills. "Please. Please live!" he cried. The fish began to quiver. She was dying. Jaq knew it. He had landed enough fish to know the signs. At that moment, the cloudbank that had been slowly moving in from the west shrouded the sun. The air quickly turned chill and a raw wind sprang up. The river, which had been like a shimmering sheet of Mylar, turned a duller, though no less fantastic, hue, like running quicksilver.

The fish shuddered again, violently this time, and Jaq started to cry. "Please, no," he moaned. Drops of rain began to fall. And, as they struck the surface of the stream, they exploded into splashes of scarlet. Jaq's tears struck the trout and they turned blood red, as they splattered her flesh.

"Give her to me," Kate said softly.

"But I ... what's happening, Kate? Christ, what is going on here?"

"Just give her to me." Kate's voice sounded more insistent. She held out her hands. Jaq's own hands were shaking in syncopation with the fish's death throes. Carefully, he placed it in Kate's outstretched palms. The rain and his tears continued to fall. They were streaming now, in fact. Red. Red. Blood. Blood. Splat. Splatter. Slowly, but not so subtly, the trout's color had changed, growing duller, losing its luster and vibrancy.

Cradling the fish gently in her hands, Kate placed it back into the stream. A gust of wind rattled the line of the bamboo rod in its guides. Kate turned, for a moment, toward the sound, then focused her attention back on the fish. Imperceptibly, its coloration began to change, to brighten, flashing fire, health and life. Soon the fish was moving its tail with vigor, shining brightly beneath the quicksilver surface of the stream. Rain, clean and crystal clear, was now striking the surface of the river regularly. With one smooth motion, Kate let go of the fish and slowly it swam upstream and away.

She made one last, spectacular leap, bursting through the surface of the Lost, flashing with more radiance and light under those leaden skies than she had in full sun. And then she vanished.

Without speaking a word, they turned and dove into each other's eyes. The rain had turned to sleet and was now coming down quite hard. Kate looked up. "We'd better get out of here," she said hoarsely. "I think winter has arrived."

"Yeah, sure," Jaq said. And then added, "Thanks," in a choked whisper. She smiled and shook her head a few times. Whether in humble refusal or bewilderment, Jaq did not know.

A huge bolt of lightning cracked directly above their heads, followed by an enormous thunderclap. "Let's get out of here. Get out of this water FAST!" Kate cried. Gripping one another's forearms, they moved swiftly across the headwater of the pond and scrambled onto the far bank.

They began to jog. As they passed the sluice, they stopped and in a flash scooped up their gear. Another bolt of lightning cracked overhead. It was snowing hard now. They sprinted back downriver and within ten minutes they had reached the truck. Quickly they doffed their waders and stowed their gear, then roared off towards town. They were in such a rush that they almost forgot to secure the gate guarding the property behind them.

"Hey, Jaq?" Kate said as they approached the intersection with Highway 93, "we *are* going to bag Trail Ridge Road and take the long way back, aren't we?"

Jaq tapped the wheel lightly and blew a blast of air between his lips. "You bet. It's tough enough making it over the pass on a clear day. In this storm and in the dark, we'd go vertical for sure." Hanging a hard right, they shot south down the highway.

Reaching over with her left arm, Kate grabbed a handful of Jaq's hair and began to work it between her fingers. "Hey, cut that out," Jaq said, smiling.

"Thanks," Kate said.

They rode for miles without speaking. Not from diffidence, nor lack of things to talk of, but merely from a deep tiredness. Coming down off the plateau, they turned north toward Ketchum on Highway 75. As gray faded to purple that snapped to black, Kate dozed off and did not wake up until they rolled up their driveway, the tires crunching through three inches of fresh powder. Snowflakes drifted into and out of the glare of the headlights. Jaq killed the engine and stretched.

"Oh, my gosh," Kate said hoarsely. "I didn't mean for you to—"

Jaq placed two fingers on her lips. "The silence is sweet," he said quietly. "But most of all it feels good to stop moving. I can still feel my legs fighting the current."

"Well, let's fight the last twenty feet to the door," Kate said.

Two hours later, they lay side-by-side in bed, sharing their warmth. "Amazing how a good glass of red wine or two rallies the body and the mind," Jaq said.

"Jaq?" she said softly.

"Yes?" All evening their conversation had been of fish and flies, water and weather.

"Jaq, I wonder where she is right now?"

"Who? She? You mean Ur?" *Of course, she means Ur.*

"No. No. I mean I wonder that, too. But no. The fish. *That* fish. God, she was gorgeous."

"Yes, she was. I think I understand the parable about the fish feeding five thousand now. Those fish fed souls."

"Why, Jaq, what a nice thought. You'll have to remember to tell Father Nick about it." Kate picked at a finger. "Jaq?"

"What?" He had dozed off and sounded slightly annoyed.

"But where do you think she *is*, Jaq?"

It bothered him, too. He wanted very badly to see that fish again. He stretched his arms behind his head. "I don't know. I wish I did." He paused. "Kate?"

"Yes?"

"What in hell *did* happen today? Your little episode with the baby monitor—"

"We agreed was explainable," Kate said.

"But Tia—"

"It was dark."

Jaq sighed. "But what about the blood? What about the sleet that turned to blood as it hit the water while we were trying to revive that fish? You saw it, didn't you?"

"Yes. We both did. So?" Kate asked.

"Consensus. It means that something happened that was more than just our minds playing tricks," Jaq said.

"Tomorrow. Maybe we'll figure it out tomorrow," Kate said. She buried her nose in his hair and kissed him lightly on the back of the head. Soon they were both breathing slowly and deeply, rocked gently to sleep by the memory of the river's motion that remained in their legs and bodies.

◎ ◉ ◎

Somewhere, well upstream of Mackay, a fish cut its wake through the water, leaving sets of smooth ripples that spread diagonally and behind her, their surface tension disturbed only by snowflakes that vanished almost as soon as they touched the water. At last she reached the horizon, for the horizon did not recede for her, and, if such a thing can be imagined, made one great, magnificent leap, flashing rose and purple and silver, illuminating the snow crystals that swirled about, and hurtled herself toward infinity.

◙ ◉ ◙

CHAPTER 4

Jaq set his razor down and looked into the mirror. Directly behind him, Kate stood cradling a mug in her hands. "Pu-Erh Cambric, sir. I hope the tea is to your liking."

Jaq took a sip and licked a dollop of foam off of his upper lip. "Adequate," he said.

"Thank you, sir. Shall I draw your bath?" Kate said, broadening the "a".

"Getting in with me this morning?" Jaq asked, raising an eyebrow.

"You're late, sir," Kate said, as she turned the shower key.

"And you're right," he said, stretching an arm behind his back and puckering his lips.

"Anything else, sir?"

"No, that will be all."

"Very good, sir." Kate turned and walked out the door.

Jaq smiled and hopped into the shower, all steaming and gleaming glass and brass, and in three minutes he was out. Kate had returned with a cup of coffee and was sitting in an easy chair, staring at a spot on the floor.

"What's so interesting about green tile?" Jaq asked.

"Oh, nothing. I mean *precisely* nothing. It's the empty space that interests me."

Jaq turned his attention to the floor. He remembered Ur lying on her back on top of a patch of lamb's wool, making scratchy breathing sounds, staring at the ceiling and moving her legs and arms in a herky-jerky motion. She always seemed to have enjoyed herself, though they could never be sure. She would "motor" for hours while her parents would shower and shave, powder and cream, always being careful to step around her. Now they simply walked across the floor through empty space. "Yeah. I know what you're talking about," he said.

Kate frowned.

"Hey," Jaq said, "you sure you're okay? Want me to stay home today? Being the first Christmas and all, it might be kind of rough at times. For both of us."

Adopting a brave smile, she shook her head. "Nope. We both have a lot to do. And, of course, there's the party."

"You really sure? Most suicides occur at Christmastime, you know," he teased.

"Why, Jaq. What a cheerful thought. No, don't worry about me. Stoics don't kill themselves. At least, not if their emotions are holding the blade. Nope, I just cry on the toilet. Besides, if I flip, I'll take you out first," Kate said.

"First? You mean you'd do a double murder-suicide? Wow! Too bad they don't have a tabloid in Ketchum. Imagine the headline: 'Christmas Crushed Wife Kills Hubby-Self.' They'd talk about it around here for years." He paused. "Say, if you really do get it in your head to do it, let's go back to New York so it'll make the *Post*."

Kate laughed heartily. "Jaq, you're nuts. Come on, get moving." Jaq slapped on some clothes and hustled to the door. "Now don't forget to remind Faddle about the party."

"Okay," said Jaq, "no problem. I need to talk with him today, anyway. And I might invite the two kids. Vinnie and Clara."

"Great. And Father Nick. Don't forget to stop by the church and remind him." Nicholas Beele was the priest at the local Catholic church. Although a Jesuit by training, neither Kate nor Jaq was quite sure what he was by inclination.

"Sure. I wouldn't miss that stop for anything," Jaq said.

"I'll bet you wouldn't," Kate said. Both of the boys enjoyed having a glass of scotch—or two, or three. She would often find them several sheets to the wind, arguing Homer, or Horace, or epistemology, in Nick's study.

"Only one scotch for you guys. Okay? I don't want you both spacing the party."

Jaq raised his right hand. "Promise."

"I've heard that before. Just don't be late."

He crossed his heart.

They kissed and he was off.

◙ ◉ ◙

Kate heard the door of Jaq's old '52 pickup rattle shut and she heard the engine growl. She waved to him from the window and he gave his truck's horn a cranky little toot; then she watched and waited until the two tiny red tail lights disappeared around the first bend in the driveway.

Kate sat for awhile on the edge of their bed and soaked in the soft amber light that filtered through the louvered shutters from the bathroom. She reached for her watch to reset the alarm for six-thirty and noticed a faint, intermittent red glow within the drawer of the table. It shocked her awake. Hair pricked up on her arms. She hesitated, then reached for the handle and opened the drawer.

Ur's monitor blipped and blinked away, tiny red dots shooting across the display with the same irregularity that had characterized the baby's breathing while she had been alive. Yet, she heard no sound. No raspy gurgle that had emphasized the fact that every breath was a struggle. Kate turned the monitor over in her hand. "Damn," she mumbled, "I must have forgotten to turn it off. What *is* wrong with me?"

As she was about to flip the switch, she thought she heard a scratching sound, dry and hard like dead branches scraping rock. Or like the little cane rod, lifted by the wind off of the dead grass on the high prairie. She held the monitor up close to her ear. Then it began again, though it was faint and seemed far away. She hunched her shoulders to throw off a chill and wished she had let Jaq stay home. Get a grip on yourself, she thought.

Setting the monitor back onto the nightstand, she resolved to go to Ur's room to check it out. *Check what out?* She and Jaq had both heard bumps in the night and run to Ur's room in hopes of finding a tiny apparition. They never had and probably never would. As Jaq had often remarked, there was no longer any magic in the world.

Crossing the walkway to her daughter's bedroom, Kate stole a glance into the living area below. Light from the kitchen intruded upon the darkness, but reluctantly, casting long, dull shadows onto the carpet, then fading to black just below the ceiling. The large chandelier that hung there was made from a tangle of carved and polished wood, its lines seductive to the eye. Like some great arachnid, it seemed to swing by its own silk over the dim, cavernous space below. Kate's stomach tightened. Maybe she had taken Jaq's talk of spiders a little too literally, she thought. Or lightly.

Shaking off the suggestion, Kate walked into Ur's room and reached for the light switch. Pure silence greeted her. They had cleared out all of Ur's furniture after she had died. All that remained was a rocking chair, where Kate used to hold Ur and feed her through a G-tube, straight into her stomach. The chair sat quite still now, opposite the door, in a space framed by a bow window. She crossed to the bathroom and peeked in. The room shone pure white, with an accent in rose and light blue, in stillness.

Kate sat down in the rocker and reached for the transmitter, which sat on a bench seat below the bow window. A small sound caught her attention. Kate cocked her head, then started badly as a fist of dormant aspen branches brushed against the windowpanes, raking her nerves raw. Fear fanned her anger and she opened the window and snapped off the offending twig. *Too bad it had been a branch.* Loss began to compete with her other emotions. *Too bad it hadn't been Ur. Too goddamned bad there was no magic in the world.*

Kate breathed deeply. The act helped check the assault of emotion on her reason. She grabbed the transmitter to switch it off. Her eyes flared and her hands shook a little. It had never been turned on. And then she began to cry. Whether from fear or sorrow, she could not tell. Holding her arms around herself, she sobbed, uncontrollably and bitterly. Sobbed until the first light of dawn turned the eastern sky from gray to pale rose. Sobbed until there were no tears left to cry.

◙ ◉ ◙

The old Chevy crunched to a stop in the dry powder that had accumulated during the night. A few bright snowflakes drifted through the pale, yellow beams of the headlights. Jaq killed the engine and sat back for a moment. He thought of the nights his dad would come home from work and take him for a ride around the block before supper in his very cool, very dark blue 1950 Dodge panel truck. In the winter, the snowflakes would dance the same dance in the front of the headlights. The journeys had been thrilling and seemingly endless, as if they had gone not in a small circle, but to the moon and back.

When they moved to Idaho, Jaq bought his own vintage pickup and had taken Ur for a ride. He was never quite sure whether or not she had enjoyed herself. It was always difficult to tell, since she never smiled. And the jostling of the cab on its ancient springs had promptly put her to sleep. Jaq smiled. But it had made her cheeks, plump from the steroids that controlled her seizures, shake in counterpoint.

Shaking himself, Jaq locked up the truck, as if there were anything worth stealing in the old heap, and gave the left front tire a solid, affectionate kick, sending soft powder flying in a fine spray. Something solid shot high in the air off the toe of his boot and rebounded off of the door. He stooped down and picked up a small coin. Gently blowing off the snow, he saw that it was a 1992 penny, probably the same one he had tossed the other day. Bad pennies keep turning up, he thought blackly. He hurled the coin down the street.

At that very early hour, the office was empty. Even Tia wouldn't be there. Pitch black was punctuated by bits of green light on the CRTs, like so many fireflies frozen at an instant in time. Leaning against the doorjamb, he was tempted to stand awhile and soak in the silence and the darkness. But the penny nagged him.

Jaq frowned and made for his desk. He reached for the charts sitting atop his Bloomberg and set to work recording the previous day's price action in futures. In fact, there had been little action in anything that month. Next year's crops were tucked in for the winter beneath a blanket of soil and snow, while last year's sat in silos. Stocks were somnolent. Except for LODESTAR, a penny stock that he traded. Tax selling was over for the year. Bonds were boring. Jaq yawned. Only Juice was rockin' and rollin'. Boy, was it ever. *What had Clara done?* He decided not to peek at his trading blotter, diligently returning to recording the tedious, meaningless highs and lows in other markets.

◙ ◉ ◙

By the time Jaq had finished updating his charts, the office was bright and busy. He swiveled his chair in the direction of Faddle's office, remembering that he had unfinished business. It seemed as if he'd assembled quite an itinerary for the day.

Clara's workstation lay in his line of sight. She sat talking to Vinnie. His hands were moving in meaningful synchrony with the inflection in his voice. Clara's brows were tightly knit. Jaq had been so absorbed he hadn't heard them come in. He decided to investigate. Besides, he needed to talk to Clara about Juice.

"So, what's up?" Jaq asked. "You guys discovered a cure for cancer or what?"

"Nah," Vinnie said, running his hands through his thick, black hair. "We're saving that job for next week."

Clara giggled.

This is serious, after all. "Clara," Jaq said darkly, "what did we do with Juice?" At once her manner became completely businesslike, deadly serious. Jaq liked that. An ability to switch emotional and intellectual gears quickly, an ability to dissociate, would help her trade.

"Well, you see, we didn't do anything. Vinnie has this idea about Juice, about the charts—"

"So, who's trading the position, Clara? You or Vinnie?"

Clara averted her gaze momentarily, then lifted her chin, looked Jaq straight in the eye and announced, "I am."

"Ay, I'm sorry, Mister q. I better go find some stuff to hand out or something."

Vinnie turned to exit but Jaq reached out and grabbed him by the collar. "No, you stay here. A good trader should consider all input. That's relevant, that is."

"Ay, all right! I'm definitely relevant."

"Good, Vinnie. That's nice to hear."

Clara rushed to Vinnie's aid. "Really, his analysis is, well, cunning. He thinks we should hold."

"I agree," said Jaq. "You know that. But it's your position. What do you think?" She was silent. "What do you feel?"

"I still want to sell. But—"

"Fine. Then do it."

Jaq started toward Faddle's office then, as if remembering something, he turned to Vinnie.

"So, what's your method, Vinnie? Point and figure, support and resistance, candles?"

"Nah. That stuff is silly. It's all, uh, flat."

"Flat?"

"Yeah. You know, two-dimensional."

"Oh." Jaq folded his arms across his chest. *This is different.* "So what do you do, solve differential equations in your head?"

"Yeah. Sort of." The kid really meant it. "I look at price and volume and time and a few other things. You know. And, uh, poof."

"Poof, what?"

"You know."

"No, I don't."

"Well, I see patterns. Like equations that kind of pop out of large groups of numbers."

"Jaq," Clara said, "he can identify large *groups* of things." She bit her lip. "You know, like in *Rainman.* You remember the way Dustin Hoffman was able to 'see' exactly how many matches had been dumped out. Four hundred fifty-one or something. He was, oh, what's the term?"

"An idiot savant," Jaq said.

"Not politically correct, but yes, that's it," Clara said.

"You can do that, Vinnie?"

"Nah," Vinnie said, turning down the corners of his mouth and wrinkling his nose. "Two hundred matches, maybe. But not four hundred. I'm not that big an idiot."

Jaq wasn't quite sure what he had there, but he knew it might be awesome. "Vinnie, we'll talk later. Clara, sell the Juice."

Jaq disappeared into John Faddle's office.

◎ ◉ ◎

"Hey, I'm sorry," Vinnie said. "Do you think he's really angry?"

"I don't know. I think he's just a little annoyed. Or maybe he just wants me to understand that this is serious."

"And do you?"

"Yes, of course I do," she shot back. "He's trying to teach me to trade and he's letting me do it with his own money. Vinnie, he thinks I'm good, or can be. He thinks I can make it in New York."

"Yeah, and what do you think?"

Clara dug her fingers into the arms of her chair until their tips turned white. "Think? What do I think? I don't think, pal. I *know* I can make it."

Vinnie raised his hands. "Whoa! Geez." But Clara didn't move a single muscle. Vinnie shoved his hands into his pockets. "All right. You know, huh? Well, trading isn't about knowledge. It's about educated guessing. Probability in a game played with dice that you can't see, that you can only feel. And the fact is, if you're good, you'll be wrong almost as often as you're right. But sometimes failure is the key to success. It grows guts. Do you think you can fail? Can you handle it?"

"I won't fail!" Clara had raised her voice, and the whole office turned to listen.

"You're scared," Vinnie said softly.

Clara's eyes began to fill with tears. She turned away from Vinnie. "Jesus, don't fucking cry," she whispered to herself.

"What'd you say?"

Clara turned back to face Vinnie. "I said, 'I won't fail.' Like you. I won't end up handing out stupid reports. Like you. A clerk. I won't end up wiping some asshole's shoes." Vinnie's face crimsoned. Clara's eyes fixed on his, and she covered her mouth.

"Fuck you," he whispered and turned away.

Clara jumped up and touched Vinnie lightly on the arm. "Please. I'm sorry. I have to talk to you."

"Don't you understand English?"

"Sure I do. But I don't understand what's happening to me."

"Me, me, me," Vinnie said. His face was still bright red. "That's all you think about. Your stinking self. That's probably all you ever thought about. Well ...." Vinnie's voice trailed off. He snapped his fingers in agitation. "Well, like I said. Fuck you."

Clara cast a furtive glance at a nearby screen and saw that there were only twenty minutes left until juice opened. She covered her eyes for a moment. Turning back toward Vinnie, she squeezed his arm tightly. Their eyes met. "Okay. Fuck me," she said.

Vinnie raised an eyebrow.

"Damn," she whispered to herself, "I'm off my game."

"What was that?" Vinnie asked.

"Uh, nothing."

"You're having quite a conversation with yourself this morning."

"Look, I mean, fuck *me*. Okay?"

Vinnie's eyes brightened and the corners of his mouth rose ever so slightly.

"Come on," she said. "Let's go outside."

"Outside? It's freezing," Vinnie said.

"Good. We both need to cool off a little." She led him by the arm out through the front door. They stood off to the side of the porch in the blue shadows. The cold air must have acted like a shot of adrenaline for, closing her eyes, Clara grabbed Vinnie by the skull and kissed him hard on the mouth. Vinnie started to kiss her back, but Clara broke it off. "Vinnie, I'm really sorry about what I said to you in there.

"Do you know what actually happened in St. Louis?" Vinnie asked.

"The story is that some broker, Edison, I think was his name, rode you mercilessly. They say he even made you shine his shoes." Clara shrugged.

"Yeah, Edison rode me about everything. My hair. Called me 'greaser'. Called me 'wop' and 'guinea'. He even broke my balls about my shoes." Clara looked down at Vinnie's engineer boots. "You like 'em?"

"Well, yeah. Sure." Clara said.

Vinnie smiled. "Anyway, one night, I brought him a cup of coffee. He swiveled around in his seat to grab it and bumped into my arm. A little bit slopped over the rim and fell right onto his freshly shined shoes. He tells me,

'Wipe it off, Wop.' I'm getting pretty pissed but I do as he says. Then he tells me that I did such a good job that maybe he'd let me wipe his ass.

"I lost it. Silly thing but it hit a button. Next thing I'm screaming, 'You fucking cocksucker, I'm gonna break your fucking head!' This guy was the consummate prick and was always careful to break balls when there was a crowd. Well, we were alone and I thought he was going to piss his pants. 'Botta boom, botta fucking bing. I'll squash your fucking head like a fucking melon!' I'm screaming.

"Then I hear a voice. 'Vinnie, get into my office,' Levine was saying. We'd forgotten about Levine." Vinnie chuckled softly. "Everybody seems to do that. Then Edison says, "I want him fired. I want his guinea ass out of here today." Levine tells him to shut up and the next day we're both on our way to Sun Valley. That's it." Vinnie shrugged.

"Oh, Vinnie. I *am* so sorry about what I said." She touched him lightly on the arm. "I was scared. Like I was scared just then when you started to kiss me back. I'm not used to it." Vinnie grinned broadly and Clara blushed. "That's not what I mean. Exactly, that is. I'm not used to being unsure of myself. Do you see what I mean? I don't *know* if I can trade.

"And you. I don't know what, but there's something about you that I like. I mean *really* like." Clara wrapped her arms around her shoulders. "It's your mind. I want to know more and I'm not sure you'll let me." She straightened herself. "That's it."

Vinnie chuckled. "Yeah, I understand real good. You're afraid of failure. And me? I know I could be the best technical analyst on The Street. I know I care about you." He shook his head and laughed. "But everybody always said I was a fuck-up. My parents, my teachers. Everybody. I'm afraid to *succeed*. Some pair we are, huh?"

"Maybe. It's sure a start, anyway." They were both quiet for a moment. "Aren't you going to kiss me?" Clara asked.

"I already did. Sort of. Besides, Juice opens in five and they're not gonna hold the bell for us. First things first, I say."

"Me, too. Maybe we've got something in common after all. As I said, it sure is a start." They raced back through the door, slamming it behind them with a crash.

◎ ◉ ◙

Faddle-hunched over his desk like a bear pondering a salmon, poring over a mass of reports and printouts. Other than the large space he occupied, there was nothing extraordinary about his appearance. All of John's suits were a dullish blue-gray. Both of them. Black wingtips, forever in need of a shine, provided the perfect accessory to hair that looked five days overdue for a cut; the unkempt crop sat atop a head that was smallish and accentuated his bulk. Thick black glasses sat slightly askew a blunt nose and framed eyes of gray-green that were chilly in their flatness.

"Hey, John. Got a minute?"

Faddle jerked his head up. "Huh? Oh. Jaq. Sure, yeah! Siddown!" Faddle said, in a booming baritone. "Sure, siddown, siddown!"

Jaq settled himself into one of two metal-frame, Naugahyde, institutional chairs that faced Faddle's equally austere desk. He smiled and shook his head.

"Goddammit, what's so funny?"

"Nothing. Nothing's funny. I just like the shit out of you, John. What you see, or what you hear, is definitely what you get. There's not a devious bone in your whole goddamned body."

"Course not! Course not. Why hide anything? What you sow, you reap. Good 'n' bad. That's my motto. What you sow, you reap. Pure 'n' simple."

"Why, John. The scriptures. I didn't know you were religious."

"I'm not. What gave you that silly idea? Religion's a lot o' nonsense." Faddle's scratched his cheek. Then, jabbing his finger on the desk blotter for emphasis, "But that doesn't mean those apostles and prophets and what not couldn't dash off a snappy saying or two in a pinch. 'As ye sow so shall ye reap.' Kinda zippy, don't ya think? Say, speaking of snappy, have you seen Vijay's daily sheet?" Vijay Bladanaputablatarana was Coogan's equity analyst in New York. "Vinnie!" Faddle shouted.

Jaq reminded himself that keeping the conversation with Faddle on point, let alone convincing him to cooperate with Levine, was going to require extraordinary effort. Dealing with Faddle was like herding buffalo. It could be done, but it was very dangerous. "Vijay's on vacation, John," Jaq said.

Vinnie stuck his head cautiously into the office.

"Vacation?" Faddle said softly.

"Vinnie, it's okay," Jaq said. Vinnie retreated.

"Imagine, the little bastard tries to creep away on vacation." Faddle picked up the receiver on the New York hoot.

"John, put the phone down. The guy hasn't taken any time off since he started here. And that was nearly four years ago."

"That's right! And I haven't taken any time off either." Faddle had bluff-charged and Jaq knew it. Maybe this wouldn't be so hard after all. "Fact is," Faddle said, his voice softening, "I haven't taken any time off in twenty years."

"Maybe that's the problem."

Faddle blinked. "What problem?"

"Screaming, yelling all the time. Some time off might do you some good." Jaq cleared his throat. "John," he said, "there *are* other things that you do besides work?"

Faddle stared at a small lamp set in the corner of his desk. "Yeah. Oh, sure, of course," he said quietly. "Yeah!" he repeated. "I eat and sleep. Three square meals, early to bed, early to rise. That's my motto. Early to bed, early to rise. Who said that anyway?" Faddle doubled up his chin. "Ben Franklin, wasn't it?"

"Yeah, that's right."

"Ambitious son of a bitch, wasn't he? Got his picture on the old C-note."

"John, for Christ's sake, shut up."

"What?" Faddle blinked dully.

"John, we're talking about something important."

"Yeah, sure we are," Faddle said. But there was a puzzled look on his face that indicated he had no idea what he was agreeing to. Then he rallied. "Sure we are. We're talking about hard work."

"No, John. We're talking about somebody getting their ass fired."

"Oh, don't worry, Jaq, I'd never fire Vijay. Get him fired that is. Doesn't actually work for me, you know." Faddle chuckled. "Why, I couldn't stand the thought of him and that big brood of his out on the streets."

"I know that, John. But I'm not here to talk about Vijay. I'm here to talk about you."

Faddle's features hardened. "Me? Say, has this got something to do with that bullshit the other day in Levine's office? That's right! Now I remember! You were there, weren't you?" Faddle pounded his first so hard on the table that the little lamp leapt an inch in the air and fell off the edge and into the Jaq's lap. "So you think I'm churning, do you? You and that little shit!"

"Jesus, John." Jaq set the lamp back on the table. "I don't think you're churning, and neither does Levine."

"Well, I should hope not. My accounts have always made money. And I mean good money." Faddle's face flared bright burgundy. "Goddammit, Jaq—"

"John, just shut up for a minute," Jaq said, with an authority in his voice that stopped Faddle cold. Jaq had not used that voice for a very long time. But he would need more than just authority to haul Faddle in. He needed to find some way to connect with the big broker. Jaq took a moment to set the lamp back onto Faddle's desk and noticed a price tag on its base. It read, 'W. T. Grant, $2.49'. *How do you herd buffalo? Diversion.* Jaq gave Faddle a quizzical look. "W. T. Grant?"

"Huh? Whadda you mean? Company went bankrupt years ago."

"The lamp. You bought it at Grant's for two and a half bucks. When did you buy this thing, anyway? When Eisenhower was President?"

"Naw. Kennedy." Reaching across the desk, he touched the small maroon cardboard shade delicately with his fat fingers. To Jaq there was something poignant about the way the giant lavished attention on the tiny relic. "Bought it when I was a freshman at Minot State. I can still remember the day. I was so excited. Minot was like …." Faddle's eyes fogged and he bit his lower lip. "It was like Paris. Or New York! And Grant's was probably the biggest store I'd ever been in. Yeah. Biggest ever. I suppose that was one of the happiest days of my life. Everything was new, everything represented a possibility. And you know what?"

"No, what?"

"I've held onto that feeling ever since. Kept it stuffed in my pocket all these years. And every day I squeeze it in my fist to light my fires. Get what I mean, don't you?"

Jaq nodded. "Sure. Kind of like an ember."

"Yeah. That's it. In a nutshell, as they say. In a nutshell."

"Did you always know you were going to be a broker? Did you know it that first day in Minot?" Jaq asked.

"Hell, no. Fact is, I started out with the idea of being a speech therapist."

"Speech therapist?" Jaq squeaked. "How'd you ever end up in this business?"

"Well, my dad died before the end of my freshman year. He was a wheat farmer, like most everybody else in North Dakota, I guess. His shirt got caught in a combine. Tore his whole arm off. It was a Saturday afternoon, and he was out at the barn working on the damned thing alone. Stupid, to work on it alone. He must've passed out from shock and he just bled to death."

"Jesus, John," Jaq whispered. "Did you have to quit school?"

"No goddamned way I was quitting school. My mother wouldn't have let me even if I'd wanted to. We rented out our acreage and I took a job in a local brokerage office. See, there was this big sign in the window that said, 'Help Wanted—Office Boy.'" Faddle grinned. "Then I saw what all those fellas were making at Merrill and I kind of liked the snappy atmosphere around the place.

"Besides, there wasn't much money in speech therapy. Still ...." His voice trailed off. Faddle was quiet for a moment. "Damn shame for those kids I might've helped, but life isn't always fair. I guess you know that as well as anyone."

"Yeah, I guess I do," Jaq said. The image of Ur's deadpan expression stung him. But Jaq had a reason for sitting in Faddle's office. "John, whatever made you think about speech therapy?"

"That's easy." Faddle leaned back in his chair and folded his hands across his chest. "When I was a kid I stuttered."

Jaq's lips parted and his jaw dropped a notch. "You? *You* stuttered?"

"Yep! Kids used to make fun o' me. Called me F-F-F-F-Faddle and stuff like that. Anyway, in fifth grade this teacher grabbed me and said it was time that I learned to speak properly. She remade me. She was very disappointed when I dropped speech at Minot." Faddle paused, and then, leaning over his desk, lowered his voice to a whisper. "Tell you a secret, though," he said, his eyes twinkling. "She didn't cure me one hundred percent."

"What do you mean?"

"Ever notice how I repeat phrases?"

"Sure," Jaq said. *And the clichés.* "How could I *not* notice?"

"That's my vestigial stutter. It's my pressure valve. Keeps me from falling apart. Linguistically, that is." Faddle laughed and Jaq laughed with him. "It's a fact." Faddle nodded his head for emphasis. As if he needed to emphasize anything.

"I guess the life I'm leading now is one huge pressure valve. Or maybe I've just run away," Jaq said.

"I'll have to admit, your lifestyle's a little odd." Faddle cleared his throat. He shifted in his chair and the springs and bearings squeaked and groaned under the pressure. "You know what I mean. Fishing and skiing and trading all those goddamned goofy stocks and commodities and all of that crap that you trade."

"John, the only penny stock I trade is LODESTAR."

"Goddamned company that wants to make airplanes or spaceships or whatever out of glass." Faddle shook his head. "But if you *had* run away, no one would blame you. After Ur and all." Faddle said her name gently.

Jaq sat quietly for a moment.

"Jaq, I'm sorry. I didn't mean—"

"No, no. I was thinking about your dad and how he bled to death, and it reminded me of the day Ur was born. I was in a panic inside but I put on the green scrubs all by myself and walked into the operating room. They sat me in a chair right by Kate's head and away from the action at the other end of the table." Jaq smiled weakly. "I was aware of this blur of green fabric out of the corner of my eye, but I couldn't help myself from focusing on Kate. Her cheek muscles were flaccid, and her jaw line was relaxed. Her hair fell across her forehead and lay in a mass at the base of her skull, just like when she slept.

Except some deep tension bunched the skin of her lids and spilled out of the corner of her eye in this tiny fan of folds.

"And from her right ear dangled a small gold earring that I'd given to her when we'd learned we were pregnant. A pair of golden pigs with wings had seemed appropriate. We'd tried for ten years to have a kid, you know."

"No, I didn't," Faddle remarked quietly.

Jaq shrugged. "Anyway, I thought maybe pigs *could* fly. Then I saw this still mass of flesh, smeared with blood. It was Ur."

"Maybe we've got more in common than just a pressure valve," Faddle said. Then his face lit up. "Say, why don't you throw in with me. Give up all that penny stock bullshit and throw in with me."

"No, thanks, John. I appreciate it, I really do. I'm flattered, but no thanks."

"Aw, come on. I need someone like you anyway. I'll do stocks and you do bonds." Faddle was swaying back and forth in his chair like a kid at the circus. "And Rock would be so goddamned excited he'd shit." Rock was Lawrence "Rock" Adriano, Chairman, President, CEO and just about anything else that mattered at Coogan.

"No, he wouldn't," Jaq said sullenly, shaking his head. "He wants me back in New York. 'Just like the old days,' he's always saying. John, the only reason Rock wants me back, will put up with me, is because I'll make Coogan, make *him,* more money. No, I think I'll just stick with my goofy lifestyle for the time being. Right now I need the outlet." Jaq paused for a moment, then exhaled audibly, as if to emphasize his point. "At least you and I have pressure valves. That's more than you can say for Levine." Jaq held his breath.

"Levine? What in hell are you talking about? What's he got to do with anything?"

"Plenty. That's why I'm here. Remember?"

"I thought I settled all of that the other day. And *we* just settled it right here! You said that you didn't think I was churning and neither did Levine," Faddle said.

"That's right. But you're on the edge, John. It could look like you're churning to a regulator. One of the little people from the NASD, with their black glasses and their calculators. And, then, John, if they think they've found something, *anything* that doesn't quite fit, the lawyers show up. Then it's an inquisition. And we both know how inquisitions always end up."

Faddle weakly shook his head. "And meanwhile, all the managers, all the leeches that live off your gross, are having a shit fit about this."

"If Levine gets fired again, it won't be my fault," Faddle said, sitting up in his chair. "No, sir. Listen, I haven't said one goddamned thing about this churning thing. That's all between Levine and his bosses. No, sir! I haven't said one goddamned word! Oh, and they've asked me about it. Bet your bottom dollar on that. Yes, sir! Bet your bottom dollar on it." Faddle was repeating himself and he was sweating. "'What do you want us to do, John, about Levine? He seems to think you're churning, John,' they say. Well, bullshit! I DON'T CHURN!"

"For Christ's sake, we know that! I've already told you that twice. And Levine is actually trying to *help* you by looking at your trading blotters. But Coogan can't afford the bad press. It couldn't afford fines; and most of all it can't afford to lose you. So, back the fuck off! Please." Jaq had shot his bolt.

Faddle was chewing his lower lip. His eyes were beady and small drops of sweat sat along his hairline, patiently awaiting gravity's inevitable tug. "All right," he said at last. "I guess I'm smart enough to change a little without hurting my clients or my business."

Jaq got up. His job was finished. Then he remembered one last thing. "And, John?" he said, lowering his voice.

"What?" Faddle said in a tone that indicated he was out of favors.

"Get that bunch of jerk-offs that supposedly run your retail system off Levine's back."

Faddle wrapped his huge hand around the armrest of his chair and squeezed. "Goddamn it, Jaq, I never put them *on* his back. If they want to break his balls that's *his* problem and that's *his* fault. He's been a goddamned troublemaker for years."

"No, the problem is he's been trying to do his job and he's been playing by the rules for years and those slimy bastards have been shaving the same rules for their own fucking profit."

"That may be so, that may be so. But you make your own bed and you have to lie in it. Yes, sir. Make your bed and lie in it, I say."

"No, John. Levine didn't create this situation. Neither did you, for that matter. But you sure as hell can do something about it. Now, you've agreed to change your style." Faddle began to protest, but Jaq held up his hand and cut him short. "You agreed, John." Faddle slumped back in his chair. "You know, you and Levine are just two sides of the same coin."

Faddle raised his eyebrows the slightest fraction of an inch. "Yeah? How do you figure?"

"Because you're both consumed by your jobs and both of you care about doing them well. In a sense, you're both highly moral."

"Who the hell's saying I'm immoral? Goddammit, I want to know who thinks that!"

"Nobody. Nobody's saying you're a crook." Jaq lowered his voice and paused for effect. "Yet." The word sat there like a lump of fresh, wet dough, pregnant with potential.

"W-what did you mean, yet?" Faddle was actually stuttering. "No!" Faddle roared. "I've not done a single thing wrong."

"But that isn't the point. That's what I've been trying to tell—"

"I don't give a goddamn." No stutter. "Might makes right? Is that it? Well, right makes might, I say. If they come for me, I'll show 'em." For several long seconds, the air held Faddle's words like the ghostly imprint of some Big Bang.

"All right, John," Jaq said at last. "You show 'em. When the shit hits the fan, you show 'em John. If anyone can, you can. Just do me a favor and call those managers, those *peckerheads,* off Levine's case."

"That's none of my—"

"Bullshit! It *is* your business, John. It's *our* business," Jaq said.

"Aw, come on, Jaq. They'll leave Levine alone. I mean, rough him up a little, maybe. Nothing serious. No, sir. Nothin' serious at all."

"Good. You just make sure that nothing happens."

"Or what?" Faddle smiled, but it was not convincing.

"If you won't protect him, I will. Remember that." The two men looked at each other with an odd mixture of hardness and sorrow. Faddle mumbled something incomprehensible.

"Oh, and Kate and I are having a party this evening," Jaq said, as he opened the door. "We're celebrating Winter Solstice. We'd like you to come."

"Hmm? Naw. I've got work to do. What with Bladawata on vacation and all. Goddamned little Paki bastard."

"Indian."

"Whatever."

"Come on, John. Cut the crap. Don't sulk on me now. Sit on the bottom like some big old, buck Brown. Besides, Kate won't stand for it. You really want to have to deal with her if you bail out?"

Faddle smiled wanly and shook his head. "Course not. Course not. See you at, when?"

"Sun sets at four thirty-seven. Say four."

"Okay." Faddle's phone rang. "Yes, Mrs. Beanspea. Good morning." Faddle's voice tumbled into the receiver like a keg of molasses. "Let's see now. Equity in your account is—"

◙ ◉ ◙

Closing the door firmly but quietly behind him, Jaq slumped against it, drawing strength from the smooth hardness that fixed him in space.

"Jaq." A voice startled him. Brenda, the stolid, competent office secretary stared at him with an empty expression. Like her clothes that hung in straight lines from shoulder to calf, Brenda lacked any interesting contours.

"Yes, Brenda?"

"It's Kate. Line 6," she said flatly.

Jaq usually talked to Kate at least a half dozen times a day. Always had. As he reached for the receiver, Brenda spoke again with the slightest inflection in her voice. "She sounds upset." The world rocked. *This must be serious.* "Kate," he said. He could hear his voice betraying worry.

"Hi," she said hoarsely. The line hissed with the sound of soft static.

"You all right?"

"Yeah, I just wanted to um—" She sniffled, trying in vain to collect the remnants of spent bodily fluids. "Um, I—" She breathed deeply. "I just wanted to remind you that—" She stopped, sobbing. "That I love you, Jaq." The dam broke.

"I love you, too," Jaq said softly. He resisted the urge to hang up and hurry home. They had learned to help each other at a distance after Ur had died. Jaq settled himself slowly into his chair. "What's wrong, babe?"

"Oh, um, nothing. I, uh, just wanted to remind you to pick up another little drum at Indian Joe's store. I think we're short of instruments. I didn't, uh, want anyone to feel left out."

"Sure, no problem." Jaq paused. "And so that's why you're crying, because you were freaked that Father Nick might not have a drum to pound when the sun goes down?"

Sniffling, Kate cleared her nose and exhaled a heavy, staccato breath. "No," she said, her voice rippling with a throaty chuckle. "Of course not. It's Ur."

"What do you mean, 'it's Ur'?"

Once again, Kate inhaled hard, dragging her breath through a few seconds of silence. "I think she's in trouble."

"What do you mean she's in trouble? She's dead," Jaq said carefully.

"I don't know. Call it intuition, but I have this feeling. Monday on the river was so damned strange. I tried pretty hard to deny it, I guess. Anyway, remember I told you about my little episode with Ur's baby monitor? Well, it was on again this morning."

"What do you mean, it was on? Who left it on?" Jaq asked, raising his voice.

"I'm trying to tell you! Look. The monitor isn't important. I guess I forgot to turn it off. Anyway, the same raspy sounds were coming from it. Oooh!" Jaq could feel Kate shiver. "So I went to investigate."

"And?"

"And there was an aspen branch that must have snapped in the storm the other night scraping against the window."

"So?"

"Exactly. So I sat down in her rocker and grabbed the transmitter to shut it off once and for all. You know. Well, it *was* switched off."

"I'm coming home right away," Jaq said.

"No."

"Like hell. I'll—"

"No!" Kate said. "There's something up, and it has to do with Ur. I *know* it. Call it mother's fucking intuition or whatever."

Jaq frowned deeply and ran his hand over the top of his head. "So what should we do?"

"Are you still going to see Father Nick? To make sure he's coming to the Solstice party?" Kate asked.

"Sure. But you know and I know that I'm really going to drink scotch and bullshit."

"Right. Well, could you ask him about all this? I mean everything. The monitor, Tia, the Fish. The… wherever it was you went. Everything."

Jaq felt the hairs stick straight up on his arms, then groaned. "He'll think we're nuts. Why don't you ask him yourself?"

"Believe me, I will. Tonight. But you'll have more time to give him some background. Especially about the other day on the river. I can't forget the blood. The rain and the tears. We *both* saw that."

"Do you think he's an exorcist or something?" Jaq asked.

"I goddamned well hope so," Kate said.

"Okay. I'll ask him."

"Thanks. And one more thing? Remember, don't you guys drink too much scotch." Kate laughed a gurgling laugh.

"Yes, dear. I love you, too."

"I love you," Kate said softly.

◙ ◉ ◙

Just as softly, Jaq heard the receiver of her phone settle back onto its base. For an instant, a flood of thoughts burst through the thin dike that separated Jaq from his memories. He closed his eyes and imagined his own hand running over an empty space that contained contour, but not mass. His hand recalled the texture and shape of Ur's tiny body. It recalled the surface of her skin, smooth and elastic, and her hair, like copper corn silk and smelling of delicate baby shampoo from her evening bath.

How could Ur be 'in trouble'? She was dead. He had put her into the mortician's wagon himself. Screaming descending minor fourths, the phone sat strangled in Jaq's hand. He hung the damned thing up. Plastic smacked against plastic with an authoritative crack.

Shutting his eyes and swallowing hard, Jaq felt decidedly chilly. In fact, his hands went ice cold. When he opened his eyes, whomever did he see slinking stealthily through a crack in the front door but Tia. It was highly unusual for her to be late for work.

"Good morning, Tia," he said in a voice that sounded unnaturally loud; but no one noticed. The trading room was now in full swing. Phones were beeping and thrumming, Xeroxes whirring, papers shuffling.

Tia, however, had heard. She turned toward him quite naturally, smiled and said, "Ah, good morning to you." Natural, thought Jaq, for anybody but Tia.

"Half day?" Jaq asked cautiously. Tia shook her full, dark head of hair and flashed a smile, her strong white teeth gleaming under the flickering fluorescents. This was the type of encounter he was supposed to avoid. A row between him and Tia would only upset Kate. Jaq could smell danger but decided to press. "Well, then, what kept you?"

Tia's smile faded. She shook her head again and shrugged. "Nothing important." Pausing, her face brightened, as if she had suddenly seized a rare insect in a tiny net. "I was just—hanging around. Yes, just hanging around."

"Why? What were you waiting for?" A memory flickered inside Jaq's head. The memory was black and shiny and chitinous. He swallowed hard.

"Opportunity," Tia said flatly.

"Opportunity?" Jaq said.

Tia's eyes spit shrapnel. "Yeah, that's right. You know, what you and people like you have had all your lives and failed to appreciate."

"Welcome back, Tia."

"Huh?"

"Don't forget. Four o'clock this afternoon. Kate is so looking forward to your coming."

"Oh," Tia said smiling, in that scalding, scolding tone of which only women are capable when they are in complete control of their anger. "I wouldn't dream of missing the 'opportunity.'"

◙ ◉ ◙

Jaq breathed a sigh of relief. The encounter with Tia hadn't turned out badly, but it left him with an uneasy feeling. He checked the time on his Bloomberg screen. 11:00 AM. The party began at four and he still had a lot to do.

Jaq shoved his charts aside and headed for the door. Clara intercepted him. On and off all morning he had been wondering what she had done and when she would report to him. It was his money, but it was her job.

"You leaving?" she asked.

"Yes. I'm finished here and I have to run a couple of errands for Kate," he said, shrugging on his coat.

"Don't you want to know what happened in Juice?"

"Sure. I've wanted to know all morning," Jaq said. But it's your job to tell me, not mine to ask. Results are just facts." Clara was quiet. "So, how'd we do?"

"Well, okay, I think." Good, thought Jaq. He didn't think Clara had ever been unsure about anything in her life. "I mean, the call for Juice was eight cents lower so I put in a market order to sell on the opening."

"And were you filled?"

"Was I! Down two cents! Locals in the trading pit slurped it up and then it traded up twenty cents. Jesus, I thought I'd die."

"Well, you didn't and you traded on your conviction. So far you did all the right things."

"Really?"

"Yeah, really."

"Jeez. Well, anyway, Vinnie came over and I told him he'd been right. And he gave me a look like, 'So what else is new?' Boy, I really wanted to smack him. But then he said that while he felt pretty good about price direction on the opening, he hadn't studied Juice long enough to be certain about the time factor. That is, you know, how long it would stay up once it rose." Clara blushed deep crimson. Jaq pretended not to notice. "Anyway, guess what? It dropped! The price dropped. It's down thirty cents!"

"So you're feeling better now?"

"Yeah, lots. Really, I thought I'd shit my pants when I was filled on the opening and it shot up like a missile."

"Well, Clara, I'm glad you didn't." Jaq grinned and Clara smiled back.

"Nice job, really. Say, Kate and I would love you two to come over this afternoon and—"

Vinnie had wandered over whistling the old 'orange juice on ice is nice' jingle. "Ay, Anita Bryant," he said to Clara, "what gives?"

"Say, Vinnie," Jaq said, "I'd like to talk to you a little more about your, uh, theories."

Vinnie smiled broadly and pumped his right arm. "Sure thing. Any time."

"How about tonight?" Vinnie's smile faded, and he shot a glance at Clara. It was obvious they had a date. "We're having sort of a party," Jaq said. "We're celebrating the Winter Solstice."

Vinnie smiled an uncomprehending smile. "The shortest day of the year, Vinnie," Clara prompted.

"Oh, yeah, sure." He paused. "Why?"

"Because, Vinnie," Jaq said, "we're pagans."

"Jeez, you're not gonna kill any animals or anything, are you? I mean, I don't wanna get busted."

"Ay, no problem," Jaq said, grinning. "The goat in the stew is dead." Clara giggled.

"Okay, okay. I'm in. What time? Midnight?" Vinnie asked.

"No, this afternoon. Four o'clock. Sunset."

Vinnie turned to Clara. "Okay?"

"Sure," Clara said, "We'd love to. See you at four."

◙ ◉ ◙

CHAPTER 5

———

On the front steps, cold air shot straight up Jaq's nose and behind his eyeballs, so exhilarating that he felt as if his brain had taken a direct hit. He figured he'd done all right that morning. Faddle. Clara. He paused for a moment to repeat Clara's name over in his mind and imagine what Ur might have been like. *Ur. What is going on?* Jaq shook himself, then hopped to the sidewalk and hung a right, heading for the Indian's.

He'd even managed to avoid a row with Tia. Almost giddy, Jaq bent down, picked up a handful of snow and greedily stuffed it into his mouth. Pursing his lips, cheeks bulging, he let the snow melt slowly, trickling drop by icy drop down the back of his throat. Jaq began to chew what was left. It was cold and it made his teeth hurt, but somehow that felt good. Then he heard an unpleasant crunch. Quickly he spat out the remaining snow into the palm of his hand. "Son of a bitch," he said. It was the same penny he had tossed earlier and he cocked his arm, intending to let it fly as far as possible. But for no good reason, he shoved it into his pants pocket.

Despite the bad penny turning up, Jaq felt aired out. He exhaled slowly and watched as his breath condensed into a light brume. The sky was bright blue and clear. Looking west over the bell tower of Louie's Restaurant to the top of Mt. Baldy, he could discern the tiny black forms of skiers. The slopes, with their white snow and animate specks, looked like the head of an old dog with fleas.

Shaking himself like a happy mutt, he sprinted across the street and hopped onto a raised wooden sidewalk that fronted a row of stores on East

Avenue. The window of the last shop announced in simple signage: Indian Joe's Native American Crafts.

Another sign hung from the door: Out to Lunch. Joe rarely left the store, but often hung out the sign at odd hours. Jaq grinned and stepped in to the faint sound of tom-toms.

◎ ◉ ◎

Joe snorted, "I'm closed for lunch." He was smoking and studying a Vegas scratch sheet.

"Still eating Kools, Joe?" Jaq asked.

Joe regarded him impassively. "Indian Joe to you, paleface."

"Technically, I'm a man of color. On the one drop theory," Jaq said.

"Oh, yeah, that's right. Something about your grandfather having been a Chaldean. You and *Marduk* Beele, the two wacky Iraqis."

"Yeah, that's right," Jaq said. "By the way, I've always meant to ask you, what's with the 'Indian' thing?"

Joe shrugged. "Tourists check out my sign, walk in and then don't know whether to call my stuff Indian or Native American. They get uncomfortable because they feel guilty, but they don't know why they feel that way. So they buy more. Simple." Joe took a drag on his cigarette and blew the smoke in Jaq's direction. "And by the way, why don't you get off my back about the cigs?"

Jaq waved off the thick cloud of nicotine. "Because they're bad for you. Haven't you heard? And Kools are the worst."

"Yeah?" the Indian said, raising his eyebrows. He put the cigarette back in his mouth and took the longest, deepest drag Jaq had ever seen anyone take. The ash was a good inch and a half long before Joe released the cigarette from lip lock. Then he blew out the smoke in irregular bursts. After the last wisp had cleared his teeth, he leveled his gaze at Jaq. "Smoke signals," he said. "Know what it means?" Jaq shook his head. "It means 'Fuck off.' Say, come 'ere, will ya?"

Perched on a stool behind a pine bench, he turned the scratch sheet so that Jaq could read it. Randomly distributed over the surface of the counter were deep black impact craters from hot cigarette droppings, mixed with hieroglyphics recording lines on ball games long past. The Indian was of medium height but of robust build, with an immense barrel chest. His hands looked as if they could crack walnuts. "Tell me what you think," he said, the words launched from his broad, flat face, dark-bronzed, with high cheekbones framed by jet black hair that was laced with coarse strands of gray. "Well," Joe said, a slight irritation in his voice, "what do you think?"

"I think you ought to stop smoking. It'll kill you."

"Shit. It hasn't killed me yet. Besides, I'll never die." Joe gave the pack of Kools a light tap with the pencil stub he held delicately between the thumb and forefinger of his left hand. "Not from these things, anyway."

"Yeah? How old are you, anyway?"

"Four hundred and twenty-six." Jaq laughed. "Think I'm full of shit, don't you?"

"Sure, of course I do."

"Four hundred and twenty-six thousand." Jaq shook his head and rolled his eyes. Shrugging and taking another puff, then flicking the ash onto the floor behind him, the Indian returned to his scratch sheets. "I've got Mississippi State over Iowa, plus 13 in the Poulan Weed-Eater tonight, and the Rangers over the Devils minus a goal and a half. What do you think?"

Chewing on his lip, Jaq asked, "The Rangers at the Garden?"

"Yeah."

"I like the bets. In fact, lay a hundred for me on the Rangers."

"New Yorker," Joe mumbled. He marked the bets then looked up from his sheets. "I'll call it in later." Cocking his head, the Indian stared straight at Jaq, his onyx eyes swirling like a dark and dangerous pool. "You've had visions," Joe said.

"About the Rangers?" Jaq croaked. A terrible thirst gripped him. The air in the store smelled faintly of flint and earth. It stung his nostrils.

"No," Joe said, "not about the Rangers. Although if that ever happens, don't forget to call me. I could've used some help last weekend. Dropped a grand." The Indian shifted his bulk, and the pine stool squeaked beneath him like a small animal caught in a trap. "But I'm not talking about hunches. I'm talking about seeing, *really* seeing, through the barriers that separate 'here' from 'elsewhere.' How was it?"

"Scary." Jaq swallowed hard. "How'd you know?"

"Your eyes."

"They were so blue. Such a deep, rich blue," Jaq said, in a whisper.

The Indian appeared confused. "Ur's eyes," Jaq said. The Indian nodded. Jaq could feel his larynx tighten. "I parted her lids after she died, and before the coroner came to the house. Her eyes actually startled me."

"Well, yours tell me that you've been 'elsewhere.'" Joe took a drag on his cigarette. "Death has been your companion for some time. I think he's finally getting around to inviting you over to his place." Jaq shivered. "Does that frighten you?"

"Yes," Jaq said.

"Have you told Kate about this?"

"Yes."

"Does she believe you?" the Indian asked.

"I think so. She's had visions as well. Sort of."

The Indian bit his lip and then chain lit another Kool. "Is she frightened also?"

"Yes, but not for herself. She thinks Ur is in some kind of trouble."

"Are you frightened for Ur, too?"

"No. I don't sense that she's in any kind of danger, really. I mean, she's dead. I'm frightened for myself. A little. Selfish prick, huh?"

"No. You can't choose the time and place to confirm your courage." Turning his palms upward, Joe shrugged. "It just happens. Besides, even most of those classical heroes you love to yap about got happy feet at some point."

"And you think this place, death's place, will be 'elsewhere.'" Jaq's voice quavered.

"Death's abode is also that of birth, of creation."

"That's comforting," Jaq said sarcastically.

"It's meant to be."

Jaq averted his gaze and stared at the floor.

"Comforting, but no guarantee of safety," Joe continued. "The abode of death is where you've always expected it to be, but it may hold surprises."

"And what is that supposed to mean?"

Waving his hand, the Indian coughed and coughed, turning a deep maroon. He kept waving. But he wasn't waving Jaq off, he was waving for breath. Jaq had been through the drill before and waited patiently for the fit to run its course. At last the Indian cleared his throat mightily and spat into a wastebasket located strategically next to his stool.

"You okay?" the Indian asked.

"Am *I* okay?"

Joe grinned. "So, what did you come in for today?"

Taking the hint, Jaq changed gears and said simply, "A drum. We're short a drum for the party tonight. Or maybe a whistle or a flute. You *do* remember the Winter Solstice party we're having?"

"Sure. Let's see," the Indian said, turning to face his display shelves. All the other Native crafts stores Jaq had seen were a jumble of items—moccasins, toy hatchets, drums, t-shirts. But Joe's place possessed order. On the floor and off to the side, in a window nook away from the main traffic pattern of the shop, lay a half dozen ceremonial rugs of beautifully dressed hide, stitched around the edges in leather or beadwork and offset carefully, one on top of the other. In the middle of the party wall stood an enormous pine cabinet, unstained and glowing, with a patina that reflected years of sunlight and human touch.

There were dozens of drawers set into the face of the cabinet. Each drawer had a platform, eight inches to a foot square, that served to display one example of the type of items contained within—bone whistles, clay flutes, possible sacks and silver finger cymbals.

"Joe?" The Indian jerked his head around to face Jaq.

"Why only one of a kind on each shelf? I mean, couldn't you sell more of this stuff if people could see all of it? Touch it? I mean, it's a basic rule of retailing. Show 'em, suck 'em in, then shaft 'em."

The Indian laughed heartily. "That's right. But my merchandise is to be bought, not sold. What's important are the decisions people make. The choices we make affect our own timeline and the timelines of everyone and everything else."

"Say, when did you become a philosopher, anyway?" Jaq asked.

"Always have been. Hadn't you noticed?" The Indian coughed. "Anyway, back to your question. Every particle, which means, of course, every *thing* composed of particles, exists, theoretically, in multiple 'possible' states. Observation, interaction, collapses the possible states to a single 'reality.'"

"Jesus, now you're a physicist!"

"Physicist, philosopher, same difference." Joe squinted as the smoke from his cigarette began to swirl around his left eye. "Anyway, each item displayed represents only one of many possible purchases. The act of choice collapses them into an acquisition. This," the Indian said, sweeping his arm in a grand arc across the wall occupied by the display, "is my 'quantum cabinet.' It is a metaphor."

"Fuck," Jaq swore softly. "Joe?"

"Yeah?"

"I love ya," Jaq said.

The Indian sighed. "I know."

"Could you choose for me? Would that spoil it?"

"Of course not. That's a choice also. I'd be happy to. Honored." Climbing a step stool, Joe examined his options. "Winter Solstice, huh? Shortest day of the year. The sun realizes he needs to spend a little more time on the job and night decides to give the old boy a pass. Light and darkness. Those two are powerful medicine."

Once again, Jaq's throat went dry. His nostrils stung. "Say," he rasped, "think I could open a window?"

"The window is open," Joe said, pointing to the bay on the opposite wall. Jaq swallowed hard and snuck a glance.

He noticed Nick standing across East Avenue. More precisely, he saw the Reverend Father Nicholas Marduk Beele of the Society of Jesus. Marduk was a family name. His grandparents, like Jaq's own grandfather, had been Chaldean, or Mesopotamian, as Nick preferred. Mesopotamia, Beele said, happened to be one of those words that captured the essence of what it described. It was, intellectually, onomatopoeic.

It struck Jaq that Beele, more frequently than would happen by pure coincidence, was exactly where he ought to be. Staring straight ahead, with graceful movements and perfect aplomb, Father Nick stepped off the curb and walked through the traffic. While he maintained a direct path toward the Indian's, he and the cars simply missed one another. Not a single vehicle honked.

While the tom toms beat furiously, the Indian continued to rummage, though with great care it seemed to Jaq, through the cabinet. "Here to pay up?" Joe asked, his back still turned. "You owe a 'honeybee'. Just drop it on the counter."

"Actually, no. I saw Jaq, and he and I have an appointment."

"That what you call boozing these days?" Jaq's mouth was still dry and he licked his lips at the suggestion.

Beele ignored the comment. "Let the hundred ride."

"On?"

"The Devils," Nick said, his voice stroking the noun. "Assuming the spread hasn't changed."

"It hasn't." With great care, Joe withdrew two pair of silver Blackfoot finger cymbals and climbed back down.

Admiring the pieces, Jaq blew a brittle whistle. "Wrap 'em up," he said hoarsely.

Joe placed each item in a wad of double tissue and stuffed them into a paper sack. Clutching the bag, Jaq was startled by the effect of the crackling paper and rustling tissue disturbing the stillness that had settled on the store.

"Forty bucks," Joe said. He pocketed the two twenties.

"Thanks," Jaq said. "For the instruments and the, um, insight. Sure you won't come this afternoon?"

"No, but thanks anyway. And thank Kate. I've got too much dough on Mississippi State. I wouldn't enjoy myself. I'd be running to the TV every five minutes and that wouldn't be very polite." Jaq started to protest, but Joe cut him off. "Besides, I'm going away for a couple of days."

"Indeed?" Beele said.

"Yeah, indeed."

"Where?" Jaq asked with a strong sense of apprehension that surprised him.

The Indian's face faintly suggested a smile. "Elsewhere," he said, "where else?"

"Sure," Jaq said and, with Father Nick, walked out the front door to the beat of Blackfoot war drums. But he knew that he wasn't "sure" at all.

◙ ◉ ◙

CHAPTER 6

———

Jaq hopped off the wooden sidewalk and stepped up to the curb. "Let's go up to the light. We wouldn't want to get a ticket for jaywalking, now would we?" Beele said.

In silence the two men walked up to the corner. "You look as if you'd seen a—ghost," Nick said, with a subtle exhalation of breath and delicate emphasis on the sibilant 's' that sent a shiver through Jaq. "Or did I put my mascara on crooked?" He laughed at his own joke in a voice of some perfect pitch between bass and baritone that wrapped the listener in a thick wad of sound.

Jaq laughed along with the priest, but quickly his laugh settled into a strong smile. As it did, he regarded the priest with care. Lean flesh fit a frame that stretched to something well over six feet. His face, naturally dark complected, was like a knife blade, and his eyes, bright green, were its edge. His hair, mustache and goatee were closely cropped, bright and black, flecked with a few renegade strands of silver.

Nick dressed lightly. Cold never seemed to bother him. He wore a tweed sportcoat and goatskin gloves. There was nothing unusual in this except that Nick always wore gloves, even indoors. Jaq had never seen him take them off.

"How'd you do that?" Jaq asked at last.

"Do what?"

"Do what?!" Jaq said, waving his hand in the direction from which they had come. Nick remained impassive. "Cross the street, for Christ's sake, while I was in the shop."

Nick put his hand to his chin. "Well, I merely placed one foot in front of the other. Simple, bipedal, upright locomotion."

Jaq felt his nerves fray. So he inhaled the cold air deeply and felt his frustration carried off by his breath. The pair had stopped in front of a path that led to the rectory of the Father de Smet R.C. Church. Barely a few paces up a lovely stone walk stood the place that would offer them a delicious hour of retreat from the world and things worldly, save their precious scotch. But his sense of calm and pure anticipation evaporated. None other than the Reverend Bildad Proud intercepted them. Jaq groaned aloud.

Nick smiled, wickedly, Jaq thought, and greeted the Evangelist. "Well, well, my dear Reverend Proud. And how is our brother today?"

Jaq winced.

"Very well. Very well, indeed, praise the Lord! And *our* brother in Christ?" Proud asked.

"Well indeed, sir, thank you."

Proud patted the tips of his pudgy fingers. "Yes, brothers in Christ. But Cain and Abel were brothers as well. Does the Pope still rule in Rome?"

"Indeed. And we remain his shepherds, ministering to those in need and trying, when we are able, to do good works," Beele replied, smiling slyly.

"Ah," Proud said, "but good works are not the keys to the kingdom. No, Father, they are not. It is only through grace that we are saved, not good works."

"Well, then," Father Nick said gently, "perhaps you are in luck, for as far as I can tell, you have always assiduously avoided good works." Proud's face, soft and puffy, flushed like a hemorrhoid. "Or did I mistake your meaning?"

Proud turned away from Nick and smiled at Jaq with teeth stained yellow and streaked brown from the caffeine that constituted the Reverend's only vice. Or so he claimed. "You see, Jaq, it's not whether you've paid the price of admission but whether or not you hold the ticket."

On an impulse, Jaq thrust his hand into his pants pocket. Slowly, he withdrew his hand and found his fingers pinching Lincoln's face. "I'm not sure you can have one without the other."

"Excuse me?"

"Will this do?" Jaq asked.

Proud's eyes narrowed and he cocked his head, like a bird trying to secure a proper perspective. "Give unto Caesar," he whispered.

"Or Charon," Jaq said, his mind snatching the strange metaphor that had just popped into his head.

Proud clenched his pudgy fists. "Don't trifle. I'm speaking of grace."

"Grace? Did you know Kate's mother?" Jaq asked.

But Proud had become distracted by a few of his flock strolling past. "Good morning, ladies! I'll be down directly." He turned back to face Jaq, but looked as if he'd lost his place.

"Kate? Yes, Kate! And how is your lovely wife?"

Jaq's mind was soaked by the image of Proud leering at Kate through the car window. That his wife's name could be formed inside of that mouth struck Jaq as a true blasphemy. "Fine," he said, simply.

"Ahh," Proud sighed, trying to sound sad and grave. "Of course it must still be difficult for the both of you after the death of your daughter. We all think of you and pray for you. Perhaps you two might join us at Bible study," Proud said, gesturing after the ladies who had passed by, "so that we might minister to your hurt." Proud stroked his flabby neck. "I know! We'll study Jairus' daughter in Mark."

"I'm sorry, I …." Jaq began.

"Hasn't the Padre shared the story with you? Why, even more reason to join us! You might find the air refreshing. Rome's has become stale over the years, I fear." Proud took a step toward Jaq. Jaq retreated. "The Lord raised Jairus' daughter from the dead!"

"Did he?" Nick said.

"Were you there?" Proud asked, a tiny blob of spittle forming at the corner of his mouth.

Nick raised an eyebrow and rubbed the palm of his glove. "No one was allowed in, if you'll recall. Save Peter and James and John."

Proud wheeled around to face Jaq and cleared his throat. "Well, well, then. What's in the bag? Christmas presents for Kate?"

Proud was not devoid of talents. The abrupt change of subject shifted Jaq's mood. "Ah, no," he said. "Actually, they're instruments." Jaq retrieved the tiny copper cymbals and slapped them together, producing a lovely tinkling sound. He smiled. "They're for a party we are having this afternoon. It's at our home. And I don't think you've ever been, have you?"

"Why, why no. I haven't."

"No, of course you haven't. An oversight on our part. Not very thoughtful of us, after all this time. Would you care to come?"

Proud's face expanded with a smile that made him look like a grotesque parade balloon. "Why, yes! Praise God, I would. How kind of you. I never thought. Well, the Lord does work his wonders in mysterious ways. A Christmas party, you say?"

"No, I didn't say that," Jaq replied, allowing a troubled expression to cross his face. "Actually, it's a party to celebrate the Winter Solstice. We're pagans, you know."

Proud's pudgy face collapsed. Jaq looked at Nick, back at Proud and laughed. "I'm sorry. I didn't mean the Father and I. I meant Kate and I. Kate and I are pagans. Ever since Ur died." Proud's lips peeled back over his teeth like those of a corpse going into a state of rigor mortis. "But don't worry," Jaq continued, "not everyone there will be a pagan. The Levines will be there and they're practicing Jews and, of course, there will be Father Nick. He's a Christian, so you'll be safe."

"Ahhhhh!" Proud screeched. "Blasphemy! Pagans. Sun worship. I've prayed for you and that wife of yours over the loss of your child. I see now that I was wrong." Proud took a step toward Jaq. "It's just as well the both of you are childless. Demon spawn, that's what that little creature would have been. What was her name? Ur! Ur of the Chaldees, of Ishtar. Of Satan!"

Jaq turned such deep crimson that his face went almost black. Dropping his package and thrusting his hands out, he grabbed Bildad Proud by the collar. "You son of a bitch," was all he could spit out. Jaq realized right then and there that he was going to break the fat man's neck.

"Jaq!" Father Nick's voice boomed. "Let him go." Breathing heavily and sweating, Jaq dropped his hands.

Relief washed over Proud's features. "Yes, demon spawn," he hissed, his courage returning.

With a movement so fast Jaq could not follow it with his eye, Father Nick's hand lashed out and grabbed Proud by his forearm. "I suggest," Nick said quietly, "that you apologize." Nick's goatskin glove stretched tighter and tighter as he squeezed the preacher's arm. "That was an unloving and an unchristian thing to say about a helpless child. Apologize!"

Proud didn't make a sound. Then Jaq saw a large dark stain spread from the preacher's crotch and down his leg. He was wetting his pants. With the slightest flick of his wrist, Nick released Bildad Proud and sent him staggering backwards.

Somehow Proud managed to maintain his balance. His jaw hung slack and a fat red tongue rested on his lower lip. A quizzical expression crossed his face. Peering over his many chins, he glimpsed the dark stain on his trousers and understood what had happened.

Gasping, he looked up at Nick. "You!" he croaked, pointing at the priest.

Nick raised his left hand and held up the index and middle fingers. Proud's eyes grew wide and he bared his teeth, but no word, no sound came from his mouth. He turned and hurried away.

◙ ◉ ◙

"You dropped your package." Absently, Jaq scooped up the sack. "Let's go in and have that drink," Beele said, placing his hand on Jaq's shoulder. Jaq closed his eyes and let the pressure of Beele's hand seep into his flesh.

Together, they made their way to the priest's study on a path that wound through a garden and around the split-timber church, its steeple fashioned from stripped logs. Within the tower hung a bell, rung by hand and by Beele day and night to announce the hours of prayer: Lauds, Vespers and all of the minor hours. Father Nick did not need much sleep.

A bluestone walkway wound through a wild profusion of bushes and shrubs, some native, all dry-land plants. Only the desiccated, vestigial branches of last year's growth could be seen now above the shallow, white blanket of the previous night's snowfall. Here and there a red or yellow branch of willow would brighten the bleakness of winter.

Entering the study of the parish cottage through a door of unpainted pine plank, Jaq set his parka and package on a small wooden bench and crossed a Persian carpet. Something of an expert on Oriental rugs, Nick, despite his modest income, had amassed a collection that filled all the floors of the parish house. The rug in his study, however, was his prize. It had been woven, Beele claimed, by Zoroaster himself and was dyed uniquely black and white, the two shades of the rug representing the opposing forces of good and evil.

Viewed from a fixed spot and at a distance, the design had always exhibited the complexity common to most Persians. But as Jaq crossed the carpet, he happened to glance down and saw its patterns begin subtly to move and shift. Borders between black and white blurred. Perspective became an interactive process between observer and observed. He realized that he had a question for Nick.

Sinking into a cavernous maroon leather armchair, Jaq luxuriated for a moment in the firm yet supple feel of the thing, allowing the turmoil of the past few days to settle. Jaq closed his eyes and inhaled deeply. "My God! The smell of cedarwood and old books is absolutely intoxicating."

"That was the idea," the priest said, sitting opposite behind a large, simple desk of cedar.

Jaq peeked at the Persian. "Um, speaking of ideas, you once called that rug your 'quantum carpet.' Did you know that the Indian calls his display the 'quantum cabinet'?"

"That's where I got the idea," Nick said. "You must know, of course, that the Indian and I have shared many hours together and I admit he has taught me a great deal. Especially about point of view, about shades of gray." Nick gestured at the carpet. "Gray, you see, is not the favorite color of the Christian orthodoxy."

"Yes, I know," Jaq said, trying very hard not to think about Bildad Proud. "By the way, speaking of the Indian, I had no idea you bet. I mean, we've talked about nearly everything else but sports."

"God plays dice, Einstein notwithstanding, so why shouldn't his shepherd? In fact, I believe that God would prefer to bet sports. There's an element of free will about athletic contests. He loses the advantage of the house."

"Heresy!"

"Well, what else would one expect from a Jesuit?"

For a few seconds they remained quiet, regarding one another. "Well!" Nick said at last, "how about that glass of scotch?"

"Yeah," Jaq said, smiling weakly. Then, in a stronger, brighter tone, "Yes, of course. It's about time."

Carefully, the priest retrieved a small brass key from the side pocket of his sport coat, delicately fitted key to lock in a small cabinet built into the bookcase, and opened the cupboard door with great solemnity.

"Say, Nick, Lagavulin's pretty good whiskey, but does it deserve being stored under lock and key?"

"Ah," Nick said, "but on my small income it *is* truly rare." Jaq wanted to shrink into his shorts, but Nick, the perfect host, quickly added, "And besides, I fear the cleaning lady has taken a hit or two."

Jaq studied the room he had seen tens of times. Except for the rug, only two red leather chairs faced one another across the simple cedar desk. But bookshelves of oak, floor to ceiling, lined the wall behind Nick, as well as the entire east wall to his left. The west wall was largely occupied by a big bow window which, along with two smaller paned windows flanking the entrance and facing south, provided the study with a great deal of light, even in deepest winter.

While the priest poured, Jaq soaked in the warmth and quiet, while he stared between his feet at the Persian. Patterns suddenly began to dance and shift. Jaq felt himself being drawn in and he did not resist. The sensation was intoxicating.

"Jaq!" He heard a voice call him back. "Don't stray too long from us, now. It is dangerous without a proper guide."

"Hmm? Oh, of course. I'm sorry, I was just …."

"I know precisely what was happening and where you were going. It is an enormous temptation."

Jaq smiled feebly. "And you are here to protect me from temptation. I guess that is your job, after all."

"Not entirely." He handed Jaq his scotch. "Cheers!" the priest cried.

Jaq eyed Nick suspiciously. "Cheers," he echoed, raising his glass. Jaq savored the smoky flavor of burning peat, as well as the tiniest hint of iodine, washing over his tongue. Warm, spidery creatures skittered to his extremities. His head buzzed, while he felt his nerves cool.

"Do you mind if I smoke?" Nick asked.

"Of course not! Pipe smoke and old books, cedar and scotch ..."

"An olfactory apotheosis!"

The pipe was fashioned from briar, of sturdy bulldog design, blackened at the top from long use. With one gloved hand caressing the bowl, the priest lifted the pipe to his lips. With the other hand, it appeared to Jaq as if he simply flicked thumb against index finger, producing a jet of blue fire. Puffs of smoke drifted across the room. Then Beele blew gently on his hand, and the flame vanished.

Jaq sat rigidly, his mouth slightly agape.

"My goodness," Nick said, "are you all right? You haven't stolen a glance at that damned carpet again and gotten lost now, have you?"

Jaq shook his head. "Nick? How'd you do *that*?"

The priest sighed and a thin smile stretched his lips. "Really, this is becoming tiresome. You are a man with acute powers of observation and a keen intelligence. And yet you persist in producing a steady stream of silly questions. 'Nick, how'd you cross the street? Nick, how'd you light your pipe?'" The smile faded, replaced by a look of concern. "Are you quite sure you're all right?"

Jaq took a large swig of scotch. The alcohol burned his throat and he had to catch his breath. "Yeah," he rasped, "I'm okay. But c'mon Nick, cut the crap. Where're the matches?"

"Ah, that. Well, it's a simple magician's trick. Nothing more."

"Magician?"

"Want to see me pull a rabbit out of a hat?" Nick asked. The priest looked around as if in search of something and, at last, exclaimed in a very theatrical manner, "Alas, no hat."

"Seriously, cut it out, Nick. What's really going on? You're telling me you're a magician?"

"Quite. But an amateur, really," Nick replied, elegantly emphasizing the hard "t" in amateur.

Jaq pondered the priest's inflection for a moment. It was easy to see why some parishioners were put off by him. "Some ama*teur*," Jaq said, flinging the priest's pronunciation back at him.

Nick laughed heartily. Picking up his pipe, Nick produced a pack of matches from the side pocket of his sport coat and relit the tobacco. A cloud of smoke drifted upward and filled the room with its pungent aroma.

"Any particular reason for using matches?" Jaq asked.

"Well, I don't want to become a bore. Besides, if I were to do the trick again you might figure it out. Really, I'm not all that good."

"I doubt that," Jaq said sullenly.

Nick shrugged. A small silence fell upon the two of them. "You look strained," Nick offered gently.

Jaq squeezed his eyes shut for a moment. "I guess I am. A lot's been happening. And that incident with Proud didn't help matters. Jesus! I really thought for a moment that I was going to kill the son of a bitch."

"You were."

"Well, then, I should thank you."

"Hardly. I'm an ordained priest. I couldn't exactly stand around and let you commit a mortal sin, now could I? But, tell me, what *has* been happening?"

Jaq downed a large draught of whisky, draining the crystal. "Mind if I have another? This might take awhile."

Extracting the cork with that ever-promising squeak! pop!, the priest refilled Jaq's glass and then topped off his own. "Well then, let's have it," Nick said. Carefully, methodically, but with great economy, Jaq recounted the events of the past three days. Impassively, the priest listened to his story. Once, Jaq thought, he had seen Nick's green eyes flash when he had spoken of the spider, but he hadn't been sure.

"And that's all?" Nick said, when Jaq had finished.

"Is that all? Hell, I'd think that was plenty."

"Yes, of course, you're right. It's more than enough. Too much, really, after what you and Kate have been through this past year." Nick paused to sip his scotch. "Tell me, what are you thinking about right now?"

"Ur. It's always Ur. Well, not always."

"I think I understand. If it were always Ur, you'd go mad."

"If I haven't already. These past few days the feelings have come back stronger than ever. Grieving's like that, I guess."

"Yes, it is. But what feelings, specifically?"

"Hurt. Raw hurt. I was thinking …."

"Go on."

"No, it's a silly thought."

"I beg your pardon?" Nick said politely.

"I said—Oh, hell, I suppose I can say silly things in front of you. We're good enough friends, aren't we?" He heard the pleading in his voice.

"Of course we are. Say what you damned well please."

"Well, I was thinking of Amfortas and the knights of the Grail. He had a wound in his side that tormented him and wouldn't heal. And the damned thing wouldn't kill him either. That's how it is thinking about Ur."

"And, so," Nick said, "do you think some hero, some Parsifal, will come along to slay poor, mad Klingsor and bring you redemption and peace?"

"Of course not."

"And why not?"

"Salvation? Redemption? From what? By whom?" Jaq said, his voice damp with bitterness.

Nick appeared stung. "Salvation is a large idea, I'll admit. And maybe an outdated one. Justice is much preferred these days. A good, old-fashioned settling of accounts."

"Hey, I'm sorry." Jaq bit his lip. "Salvation is sort of your job, isn't it?"

"No, it is *precisely* my job," Nick said.

The intonation in Nick's voice seemed to slice the wound in Jaq's side. "Okay! Then fucking save us, will you?"

Nick closed his eyes and shook his head. "No. That's not what I was driving at."

"I'm sorry, I—"

Nick ignored him. "Let's start with little beliefs."

Jaq cleared his throat and shifted in his chair. "Such as?"

"Knights with pure souls, the souls of children. Or, perhaps, children with the courage of knights. Which was Parsifal, anyway? Perhaps both, but a knight in any case who fought devils and dragons."

For a moment, Jaq felt terribly sad. "Fight devils and dragons? But there is no magic left in the world. I wish there were."

"Magic? Who's talking about magic?"

"Why, you were, just a few moment ago," Jaq said. "Look, it's just that sometimes I wish I could shut my eyes and when I'd open them I'd be with Ur."

"Perhaps there is no magic. But there is what some might call 'fantasy'," Nick said.

Jaq sank back, just a bit, into his chair. "All this talk of dragons and devils. Are you an exorcist or something? I mean—" Jaq coughed. "You are a Jesuit after all."

"You did suggest the analogy of Amfortas. But perhaps I ought to explain myself." Nick spread his arms wide. "Tell me, just what is it that philosophers believe about the nature of reality?"

"I'm sorry, I thought you said you were going to explain *yourself*," Jaq said.

"Indeed, but you've claimed from time to time to be a philosopher. So I'm simply employing Socrates' method," Nick said.

"Indeed," Jaq said sourly. The priest remained impassive and Jaq shifted, somewhat uncomfortably, in his chair. "Okay, then. There are the empiricists, Locke, Hume and the boys, who believe that the world is exactly as we perceive it. The rationalists, on the other hand, citing illusions and dreams and whatnot, believe that we can only rely on what we conceive in our conscious minds. 'Cogito ergo sum'. Good old Descartes. Some of their stuff got a bit silly. Leibniz' 'monads' and all."

"Do you think so?" Nick asked. "I thought 'illusions' were on the short list of things you needed explained." Jaq merely grimaced. "No need to become petulant. So, what is it, I'd like to know, that *you* believe?"

Jaq sipped his scotch. "Well, it's obvious that there are limits to our *perceptions*. We see in only three dimensions, hear only a limited range of frequencies. Our biology orders our world. Oh, we've been very clever. We've invented thinking machines to do our math for us, devices to magnify objects too far away or too small to be captured by normal vision. We've peered beyond visible light into the infrared and the x-ray, measured changes in air pressure that we can't hear. We've even conceived of dimensions we can't experience. But no matter how hard we try, our immediate experience is confined to four. The rest is indirect.

"Even though that holistic organization may not accurately represent 'reality', it represents an organization of data *by* the mind for the benefit of the observer."

"Kant is very dear to your heart, isn't he?"

"Well … why, yes. I suppose he is."

"So you're satisfied that the world, the 'true' nature of things, while unfolding before us, is, essentially, opaque to our minds and static. That is, immutable," Nick said.

"I'm sorry, I …." Jaq sensed a trap being set and stepped aside.

"All right, then. At the Indian's today, you bought those lovely silver cymbals from his 'quantum cabinet.'"

"A silly metaphor. Charming, but silly."

"Do you think so?"

"Well, it *is* a bit off the mark from the role of choice or observation or decoherence, or whatever you want to call it, in real quantum theory," Jaq said.

"*Real* quantum theory?" Nick stroked the bowl of his pipe with a gloved hand. "But, then, everything is a metaphor, isn't it? You and I, sitting here talking, watching one another, in three dimensions and in living, though limited, color, is a metaphor. Especially if you believe in the organization of the world of phenomena by the mind proposed by your dear Immanuel Kant. Rutherford's depiction of the atom as a miniature solar system was a metaphor, but it got the job done. Even the equations of Einstein and Bohr, if I were able to grasp them, are mathematical metaphors. So let's not toss metaphor off so lightly."

"Wait. I'm a bit lost," Jaq said.

"You wanted to know precisely if your 'visions' were valid. Or were they merely 'appearances', in the form of illusions, in the Cartesian sense. You, I think, and Kate especially, fear for your daughter, which seems even sillier than the Indian's 'quantum cabinet', since we all know that Ur is dead.

"You asked if I believe in devils and dragons. I'm trying to help us answer your question in terms that will make sense to you, since you prefer philosophical arguments."

Nick lit his pipe. "We are talking about the nature of reality and the role of choice and chance in shaping reality, as represented by quantum theory. Quantum theory in as accurate, yet simple, a way as you and I can understand it. We are talking about the connection between observer and observed."

Nick slammed his glass on the desk, sending droplets of liquor flying into the air. And, almost in affirmation, the slanting rays of the weak December sun caught the spray of scotch that shot out of the tumbler, suspending the liquid there for an instant, refracting a spectrum of colors that went beneath red and beyond blue. "Observation *can* and *does* affect reality, not merely catalogue and synthesize it. Choice affects reality. Whether in the mundane but beautiful way that Frost spoke of as a 'road not taken', or in the multi-universe world of poor, mad Hugh Everett, with its myriad timelines. Or in the simple, or maybe not so simple, 'double slit' experiment, where turning a photon detector on or off at one of the two slits changes a single photon *magically* into either a particle or a wave.

"Kant didn't, couldn't, have thought through the feedback mechanism implicit in observation nor understood it in the way we do today. But!" Nick raised a gloved finger. "But, the concept had been grasped before Kant by one of those poor, weird, mystical rationalists."

"By?"

"Come, come, Jaq. You do seem quite strung out. Here, have another swallow." Nick poured two fingers of scotch into Jaq's glass. Obligingly, he sipped, threw his head back and swallowed hard. The fiery liquid felt good as it trickled down his throat, igniting at last in the pit of his stomach.

"Of course," Jaq said. "Bishop George Berkeley."

"Yes. And what did Berkeley say?"

"Basically, he said that God exists."

"Dammit, Jaq. Shall we discuss epistemology or would you rather draw a picture with crayons?"

Jaq leaned forward and set his glass down with a smack on Nick's desk. "Okay. He asserted," Jaq began, "that matter, the 'real' world, was exactly as we perceived it. In that regard he was like the empiricists. But he denied that 'matter' had an existence separate and distinct from the perceiving mind. He thought that existence itself was a function of being perceived by some mind. He said, *esse est percipi*— to be is to be perceived, trumping Descartes' *cogito ergo sum*. He claimed that every*thing*, since it must exist in a mind, and since the human mind was too limited to conceive all phenomena, must exist in God's mind or be perceived by God, and, therefore, since our own consciousness affirms existence itself, God, in fact, must exist." Jaq burped softly.

The lowering sun illuminated the lower part of Nick's face. His eyes were left in darkness and the effect softened his appearance. The priest smiled a kind smile.

"Old Berkeley is considered to have thrown together a pretty snappy argument for God, you know," Jaq said.

"Although he was not the first," Nick said. "Brahma, it is believed by the Hindus, would fall asleep and his dream would embrace the reality that we inhabit, though the specific acts of creation were left to another. Then he would awaken and the world would be destroyed, only to be recreated in his next dream."

"And how long would he sleep," Jaq asked, surprising himself by asking a question to which the answer interested him very little.

"Some reckon a few million human years. Some say four hundred thousand, give or take," Nick said. "Why?"

"Nothing." Jaq sat quietly for a moment. "But, of course, you run into the problem of infinite regression. Who perceives God?"

"Himself."

"And, we 'perceive' ourselves. So, is consciousness identical to God? Are you saying that we're all gods?"

"Yes, in a sense we are."

"But you're suggesting something more, aren't you? Are you saying that you believe we can alter reality by observing selectively? Not just the path or spin of some isolated photon, but the macroscopic world itself? I mean, c'mon, Nick. Sure, there's a valid mathematical argument for multiple universes and, okay, macroscopic objects do have wave functions. But aren't you taking Berkeley a bit too far?"

"Remember, it's just a metaphor." Nick smiled, but it was unconvincing. "Look, you said that you wished there was magic in the world."

Jaq dipped a finger into his scotch and ran it around the edge of the crystal, producing a pleasing, mellow hum. "Maybe we're all gods in the sense that we alter the world line of reality by participating in it. But are you claiming that *we* can, *I* can, create a separate reality? Mind over matter? Fantasy by thinking it? Pure knights and demons?"

"We're all gods, in a sense, but some have abilities that, shall we say, are *superior*."

"Do you have that ability?" Jaq leaned forward. "Do you? Could you create a reality in which Ur didn't die? Could you?"

"I do not and I could not. But you, or Kate, may have the gift." Nick drained his scotch. "Or curse." Jaq sat motionless on the edge of his seat. "You don't look skeptical enough. Don't I sound like a fool to you?"

"Last week I would have said yes."

"And what, specifically, happened to change your mind?"

"What happened? What didn't," Jaq said, slamming his glass on the priest's desk. "The fish, the baby monitor, Tia …."

"Ah, yes, Tia," Nick said absently. "Very open-minded. Charming girl, charming. Tell me again about Tia." Jaq recounted the incident in his office, the metamorphosis, the black, shiny, chitinous skin. "Is there anything else that you've failed to tell me? That you've forgotten?"

"No. Wait! How could I forget?" And Jaq told Nick about the green surgical slippers. "I never brought them home from the hospital after Ur was born. At least I don't think I did."

Nick's eyes brightened, but the green fire was cold and hard. A silence which lasted for some minutes embraced the pair. At last, Jaq pressed the priest. "What *do* you think?"

"I'm not at all sure. Perhaps it's all pure coincidence. Cartesian 'appearances'. Hallucinations. But there may be danger. And I think I may be able to help, if it comes to that."

"Comes to what?" Jaq ran a finger under the collar of his shirt. His neck was damp with sweat.

"Once the boundaries of everyday sense are breached, possibilities of only infinitesimal probability are capable of multiplying danger—and opportunity."

Although the priest's voice sounded cool and rational, a subtlety in the inflection, the words themselves—danger and opportunity—made the small hairs on Jaq's arms and at the nape of his neck stand straight up. "You're serious, aren't you?"

"Magic is *not* gone from the world," Nick said softly. "Don't believe it." The priest settled deeply into the embrace of his great red leather armchair, as if fully spent. "Although it's not 'magic,' really. It's a point of view."

Reaching across the desk, Nick retrieved his old bulldog pipe. Cradling it in his left hand, he brought his right to rest over the bowl and snapped his index finger, causing a bright jet of blue flame to erupt, seemingly from his thumb. He puffed hard, three times, igniting the tobacco.

Jaq blinked and shook his head. "You mean 'magic' like that?" he said cynically.

Nick chuckled deeply. "No. That was a trick. Real 'magic' requires imagination. And will." The priest pointed the stem of his pipe at Jaq. "But you possess the key catalyst. Motive."

"Motive?"

"Salvation. Save the child and save yourself. Heal the wound and close the hole in your soul," Nick said.

"Goddamn me and my infernal hurt! What about my daughter?"

"As I said, she may be in danger. She may need your help."

Jaq felt a surge. Heart expanded, blood vessels dilated to the bursting point. His throat thickened and he found it hard to swallow. "That's what Kate thinks," Jaq croaked. "That she's in trouble. What do you *really* believe? Dammit, Nick!"

Although Jaq sounded desperate, the priest merely shrugged. "As I said, I'm not sure. I believe that your point of view, and Kate's, may be valid. But as for myself, I need more evidence."

"Evidence," Jaq said, slumping back into his chair.

Smiling slyly, the priest picked up the cork and slammed it back into the bottle's neck. It made a satisfying squeak, announcing closure. The sound helped Jaq relax a bit. "What I do know," Nick said, "is that you'll miss your own party if you don't get moving. It's nearly three."

"I forgot about the time. Jesus! You're right. I've got to go." Then he paused. "Jesus," he repeated. But, this time the word was inflected as a question, not an expletive.

"Yes?"

"Um, nothing. Look, could you come a little early? We could use the help and I know that Kate will have some questions. She put me up to all of this."

"I'm sure she did," Nick said. "And I'm equally sure her questions will be more direct."

"Indeed," Jaq said, smiling.

The priest laughed heartily. "I'll think on what you've said and try to give what guidance I can."

"Is that what you are? A guide?" Jaq asked.

"In a sense, yes. That's what we do in the Society."

"And you're asking Kate and me to follow?" Jaq's flush had cooled. He felt his breath spilling slowly and evenly into and out of his lungs.

"I'm not a leader. I'm simply for hire."

"And the price?"

"For you and Kate? Just the asking."

Jaq started to ask the question, but Nick stopped him, holding up both gloved hands. "Later," he said in a tone that discouraged disagreement. "I'll see you at … ?"

"Three-thirty?"

The priest nodded.

Jaq rose and glanced at the carpet. The design was fractal, each pattern repeated again and again, at smaller scale and in exquisite detail. Images, sounds, smells assaulted him. A flat, empty desert baking in bright, white heat. A cold frozen lake. A bright quick-silvery stream, so much like the Lost the previous day when they'd caught the fish. Yet different. Fingers sank into the flesh of his arm and guided him away from the confusion.

Pale, golden light seeped through the windows of the study and motes of dust drifted lazily about in the glow. "Yes," Jaq said aloud. "Thank you. Three-thirty, then."

"Take care, my dear Jaq. Reality can be—deceptive," Nick said, his voice trailing off the final word, like a boat slipping out of a cove in a dead calm.

Without another word, Jaq picked up his package and walked out into the crisp, chill air of a late afternoon in December. After he had negotiated a few paces down the walkway, he realized that he had left the door open. He turned and saw the priest's lank figure draped in his chair. Then the door swung shut and he heard the latch click. Somehow, nothing seemed to surprise him anymore.

◙ ◉ ◙

CHAPTER 7

Jaq's head began to hurt something fierce. A double espresso checked the pounding inside his skull but failed to check a slippery sense of reality. On the road home he seemed to regret everything from the day that had held promise. The attempt to reconcile Levine and Faddle, the scotch he had so looked forward to and now made his head ache.

Jaq cranked down the window. The icy air of the Idaho desert raked his cheeks with its bony fingers. He thought of Clara and Vinnie. Promise replaced regret and fatigue.

Jaq killed the engine in front of his house, a log structure of Adirondack design, built on a bench and surrounded by Ponderosa and spruce that exploded up the hillside in a thick mat, then gave way to scrub once again. He grabbed Joe's bag of instruments and bolted for the kitchen.

Racing past Jaq, Kate brushed his cheek with a kiss. "Hi, sweetie," she said, "would you turn down that pot of wine on the stove?"

"Why are you cooking wine, for Christ's sake?"

"It's not cooking, it's mulling."

"Mulling?"

"This is a pagan party. So, well, what did the old Druids drink? I don't know. Mulled wine is medieval, but that's about as close as I could get. And I've got a five-liter keg of German beer and—"

"Okay, okay." Jaq grabbed her. "C'mere." He kissed her hard. "You okay?"

She breathed a deep sigh, raised her chin, and managed a straight, thin-lipped smile. "Yes, I am."

"Really?"

"No, not really. But I'll manage."

"That's not good enough."

"Well, for now it'll have to be. We're doing a party. We've got people coming." She leaned back in his arms and picked at her finger. "Did you talk to Nick?"

"Yes, sure. You know that's where I've been."

"Well, I *wasn't* sure. You don't smell like a burning peat bog."

"Of course not. I was responsible. I exercised discretion, self-control—"

"Burning! Oh, my gosh. Jaq, turn down that wine." Kate bolted for the stove. Carefully opening the oven door, she peered inside. "That was close. Just a little fat." She siphoned off some drippings with a basting syringe, then turned down the heat.

"Jee-sus!" Jaq said. "That smells great. What is it?"

"Roast mutton."

"Mutton? You mean lamb, don't you?"

"No, mutton. I ordered it through Atkinson's. They had to get it from Twin Falls. More authentic, you know."

"Like mulled wine."

"Yes. Like mulled wine."

"You know, Kate, if I wanted a glass of water, you'd probably go outside and dig a well. What other authentic creations can we expect this evening?"

"Well, a coarse, seven-grain bread to go with the mutton. People can make little sandwiches if they like. And there's sautéed cabbage, with juniper berries and root vegetables—parsnips and turnips and carrots—steamed in wine and sage. That's for the vegetarians. Tia won't eat the mutton."

"Why didn't you make her a roast tofu loaf?"

"Oh, shut up, Jaq. Do me a favor, will you? Pull the tray of fruit and Stilton out of the fridge and set them on the counter." She paused. "Jaq?" she said softly, her voice rippling at the edges.

"Yeah?"

"You said you talked to Nick. What did he say? You know, about all the things that have happened the past couple of days. Did you tell him about the monitor?"

"Yes, I did. I told him everything."

"And?"

"He agreed with you, I think. He believes something may be wrong."

"With Ur?"

"Possibly."

"And what about you?"

Jaq leaned against the large, green granite work island. The stone felt cool and soothing as he worked his palms over its surface. "I really don't know, Kate. I guess I don't have a feel, an instinct for it, the way you do. Remember, your connection to her is more direct. I'm just a man. I have to operate at a distance."

"*Is.* You said is."

"What?"

"You said, that my connection *is* more direct. You used the present tense. You didn't say *was.*"

Jaq frowned.

"Did Nick say anything else?"

"He said he might be able to help."

"How?" Kate asked excitedly.

Jaq shrugged, then straightened up. "Magic."

"Fucking *what?*"

"Look, it's complicated. You can ask him yourself when he gets here."

Kate picked up a fork and twirled it in her fingers. "When's that?"

"A few minutes early. Three-thirty. Maybe quarter to four. He said he'd like to help you. Get ready for the party, that is."

Kate glanced at the clock on the microwave. "Oh, shit. It's almost three-thirty. Jaq! Run upstairs and change, or wash, or whatever, and get right back down here. I need you to set out the plates and glassware."

"Aye, sir!" Jaq saluted. When he reached the landing above the living area, a patch of green in an unfamiliar spot caught his eye. A pair of goofy reindeer heads atop long red stockings stared back at him from beneath a length of Christmas roping, strung above the mouth of their great stone fireplace. *Kate's done it.* He'd snapped at her when she'd suggested the idea of decorating the house. He didn't want to celebrate. Not yet. He hadn't the guts. But Kate was a determined lady.

More roping draped the windows of the great room. Scattered about were splashes of red and green and gold. Candlesticks, ashtrays and other gewgaws, understated but obvious. The north wall, however, opposite all of the glass, was empty. Before Ur, a Christmas tree would have stood there. Kate had spared him that.

"Kate!" he shouted.

"Whaaat!" she called back from the kitchen. And then, "What, what, what," as she stormed into the living room.

"The monitor? Did you put it back?" Jaq asked.

"Yes, inside my bed table. Why?"

"Oh, nothing. I just wanted to have a look. Maybe Nick should as well, when he gets here."

She bit her lip. "Not that he's an exorcist or anything, but yeah, I was going to ask him to do that."

"Exorcist," Jaq said quietly. He shook his head. "I guess Jesuits'll do that to you."

"I don't know, but I'll show you what pissed off wives'll do if you don't haul it." She started back to the kitchen.

"Kate? I like the, uh, the roping and all. Nice touch."

"Thanks." She looked at her feet. "But you're not going to get all hang-dog on me are you?"

"No. Promise. It's very pretty. Cheerful, really." Kate's eyes flashed and her face brightened. "And do you know how pretty *you* are when you're happy?"

"No, I don't, really. But if you think *this* stuff is pretty, imagine how absolutely gorgeous a tree would be. There. Right over there on that bare old, white wall next to the landing."

"Sorry," he said, softly. "Please. Not just yet. Not this year."

"Maybe next?" Kate's tone tweaked but did not push.

Jaq stood at the doorway to their bedroom. "Yes. Maybe next year," he said.

◎ ◉ ◙

For a moment, Kate stared at the blank spot on the wall where a Christmas tree might have been. "Empty spaces," she whispered. On the day Ur died, the house had been full of them. All of the places where she had lain on her fleece, had bathed, had slept, had been fed. Empty spaces that would be filled in, not by grand events, but by the small circumstances of living. Holes, really, that life would reclaim.

Leaning against the kitchen doorjamb, Kate crossed her arms and set her jaw. Poor Jaq, she thought. He often spoke of a hole in his side, a hurt. Perhaps he needed to hang on to the holes for a while.

To Kate, it seemed as if there were a cord that connected her to Ur. Right now that cord, just like the one that killed her daughter, was stretched taut. It pulled at her belly. Right now she needed a drink.

Retreating into the kitchen, Kate removed a crystal goblet from a bank of birch cupboards and set it down on the granite counter, making a solid, reassuring "clink." Glass insets in the cabinets scattered gold and rose light, reflected off the silvery, snow-covered hills. Filling the glass to the brim with Bordeaux, she listened carefully to the sound of the running liquid. Holding the glass aloft, she smiled to herself as the incident light in the kitchen made the wine glow. Then, she shuddered at the thought of Ur's some kind of blind, some kind of deaf body, wracked by spasms, a tiny hole in her tiny belly where the food went in. "The senses can also be hell," she said aloud.

Raising the glass to her lips, she took a large mouthful of wine, wonderfully dry, almost cottony. She tilted her head back and swallowed hard. A warm glow that stopped just short of burning spread across her stomach.

She began to giggle. At what? She hadn't a clue. At herself, perhaps? At her frenzy to finish what was already done? At the silly Solstice party they were giving, with its drums and whistles? It didn't matter. There had been times since Ur died when she never thought she would laugh again.

Taking another small sip of wine, she leaned back against the counter, cradling the glass in her left hand, cradling herself in her arms. She gazed out the window and across the valley at the ridge opposite, now orange at its summit.

The valley bottom lay in deep purple shadow. Surveying the kitchen, she saw that everything was ready, everything in order. She had done a good job.

A clanking sound startled her. The pot of parsnips and turnips was steaming away. "Oh, my gosh," she said aloud and rushed to turn down the gas.

Gingerly, she lifted the lid off of the large stew pot. Steam spewed out, bathing her face in a delicately scented vapor that held great promise for the simple vegetable dish. If only they hadn't overcooked. Lifting a fork from the stack of silverware that lay nearby, she softly pierced the flesh of a turnip hunk. The fork met the slightest resistance and she breathed a sigh of relief. Then her euphoria evaporated. *It's just a goddamned pot of vegetables.*

She glanced at the clock. Three-fifty. The front door chimes split the quiet second. Desperately, she hoped it was Father Beele. Purposely leaving the parsnips uncovered, she hurried to the door.

The priest flashed his familiar smile, a hard smile that did not engage his own eyes entirely. Smiling broadly, Kate hoped that her relief and her expectation showed on her face. "Please come in. May I take your jacket or gloves or something?"

"Yes, thank you. My scarf, if you please. Otherwise I'll be quite comfortable." Beele had changed from his tweeds into a black blazer. Underneath he wore a buff corduroy shirt. "Is something wrong?" Beele asked. "I hope the jeans aren't too informal."

"Oh, no. Sorry. I didn't mean to stare. Actually, you look pretty spiffy. It's just ...." Kate's eyes widened. She shrugged. "It's just that you don't look very, uh, clerical. But it's very nice. It's—"

Nick lifted his hand. "Thank you for the compliment. Even an ancient bachelor can be flattered." They smiled at one another and were silent.

"I thought I heard the bell. Say, Nick!" Slowly they both turned their heads toward Jaq. "Hey, what's going on here? Am I being set up or something?"

"No," Nick said. "Your wife was just flirting with me."

"That's right. I told him he looks awfully spiffy. And, Jaq, just look at *you*."

Jaq was wearing faded navy corduroys, a belt with a buckle that had long since lost its brass, and an old Bean flannel that looked as if it might have once been red. "What's wrong?" Jaq asked honestly.

"Never mind," Kate said, shaking her head. "Oh, I'm sorry, Nick. Let me have your scarf. And may I take your gloves?"

"No, thank you," Beele said. "I never take them off."

"Come to think of it, you don't. Would it be rude of me to ask why?" Kate said.

"Not at all. Rather, it would be quite characteristic. Inquisitive and direct."

"Watch it, Kate. He's probably setting you up," Jaq said.

"Which is quite like *you*, my dear Jaq. Circumspect to a fault," Beele said.

Jaq laughed. "I think I've been insulted."

"Not at all, merely described. But back to your question, Kate. I have a skin condition on my hands that is quite painful and even more unsightly. I take the gloves off only at night and in privacy." Nick smiled at them both. "Now you know. You've often wondered, Jaq, but never asked."

Jaq opened his mouth to reply but stopped, feeling oddly uncomfortable.

"Do you doubt me, Thomas?" Nick asked, and at that raised his left hand, then touched it with his right as if he were going to lift off the glove.

"No, please, we believe you," Kate said, shooting a quick glance at Jaq. She stood, twisting Beele's scarf in her hands. "Um, at the risk of being direct again, may we talk about Ur?"

"Of course. But your other guests arrive at four?" Kate nodded. "Then may I suggest we wait until after the party."

"But you believe us?" Kate said.

"Ye-e-ss."

"And you *will* help?"

"Yes. But there simply isn't time right now to do Ur—justice."

"I'm not sure there'll ever be time for that ....No! To hell with the guests and the—"

At once a cacophony of alarms erupted in the kitchen and in sequence. "Oh, damn!" Kate stamped her foot. "All right. All right! Later, then." And she bolted. "Say," Kate shouted over her shoulder, "I was having a glass of wine. Could I coax you boys into joining me?"

"You're not only bright and lovely, but you are clairvoyant as well!" Beele cried. "I'll pour."

In the kitchen, Kate began to bark orders. Jaq was instructed to set out the plates and flatware on the serving counter. Beele's job was to fetch the crystal. Kate poured the parsnips, hot and steaming, into a serving dish.

"Now, where's the cover?" she muttered to herself and began to rummage through the cabinets. "There it is," she said. Reflected in the cabinet glass, she saw Beele snatch a large yellow hunk of turnip and pop it into his mouth. Kate started to cry out, but it was too late. Involuntarily, Kate clenched her teeth.

But Beele simply chewed away, a small smile of satisfaction playing at the corners of his mouth. He saw Kate staring and swallowed hard. "Oh, I'm so sorry. It really is terribly rude of me. Picking away at your creations and with my fingers, no less."

"Oh, no, not at all. I was just ... Wasn't that turnip just a *little* on the warm side?"

The serving dish sat pumping out copious quantities of steam. "Ah, yes. Actually I, um, picked one off the top and it was a most agreeable temperature." Kate cocked her head and stared. "Well, a little warm perhaps, but marvelous nevertheless."

"Good."

"Yes, um, marvelous. Did I detect a hint of—"

"Sage."

"Yes. That's it, of course. Sage. A favorite of mine, and good for the mind. Did you know that?"

Kate nodded.

"Yes, well. I do so love the root vegetables. They spend all of their time beneath the earth, hidden from the light, where it is dark and damp and warm. Chthonic creatures." Nick picked up a large parsnip, holding it delicately between his fingers.

"Looks phallic to me," Jaq said.

"Yes, I suppose it does," Nick said. "And, if we allow the metaphor to complete itself, it is a most incestuous vegetable."

"My God, Nick!" Kate said.

"Do I surprise you?"

"Actually, no. That's what's so astonishing. She raised her glass. "Anyway, thanks for your help. Cheers," she said simply.

Cheers all around. But none of them looked entirely certain of the sentiment.

◙ ◉ ◙

The door chimes rang. The Levines had arrived with their two boys, David and Daniel. Levine looked a bit sheepish. "I hope it's okay," he said, glancing at the twins, "but we couldn't find a baby—"

The boys grimaced, but Sarah plunged right in. "We thought they might find the party educational."

"And we hope so, too," Kate said.

"Yeah," Jaq said. "And if you guys get bored you can watch my new fifty-inch monster TV."

"Cool!" David cried.

"Yeah, cool," Daniel agreed. "But sometimes grown-ups are about as entertaining as it gets." Kate and Jaq both laughed and took the Levines' coats.

Punctual to a fault, the Levines led the cascade of guests that poured through the door in irregular bursts over the next ten minutes. After the Levines came Tia, then Faddle. Vinnie and Clara roared up the driveway on his Harley. Greetings were exchanged, conversations begun but never finished, questions asked but never answered.

"Hi, Frankie," Jaq said. Frances Howard, divorced and childless, owned a flower shop in town and lived above it in a loft. Kate loved flowers, loved all plants for that matter, and had opened herself up to the dark, pretty, slightly built woman.

"Uh, boy, phew! You wouldn't believe the traffic in town I almost didn't get out of the store there was this customer and yeah oh thanks Jaq, where's Kate? I hope I'm not late I …."

Jaq planted a kiss on the cheek, undeterred by an omnipresent cigarette that dangled, unlit, from the corner of her mouth. He had never seen her smoke, but she claimed she liked the look. Something about Bette Davis.

"Kate had to get back in the kitchen. Would you care for a drink?" Jaq asked.

"Sure of course why not but I'll help myself if you don't mind. She's in the kitchen? Good, yes, I'll help myself thanks for taking my gloves here …." and Frankie wandered off in the direction of the kitchen, yammering all the while. "Boy, this is really a great idea, a Solstice party I've never been to one I wonder what it really means and I guess … Kate!" she shrieked, and her voice became lost in the general din.

As Jaq was hanging Frankie's jacket neatly among the other coats, he began to wonder if Dana, Ur's nurse, had forgotten the party, or, more likely, whether they had signed her the wrong time. 'Signed' because Dana was profoundly deaf. But he didn't have long to worry, for he saw Dana's car pulling up the driveway. Jaq stepped outside to greet her. Crisp air, cooling now at altitude by the second, scrubbed him clean. "Come on," he signed, "it's going fast. The sun." He flashed a grin.

"Okay," Dana signed. "But don't worry, there's time."

Striding up to Jaq, she bent over and gave him a hug. He felt the air seep from his lungs. At something over six feet, large-boned and muscular, Dana towered above him. Blue eyes flashed beneath a big tangle of yellow hair that framed a smile that was even bigger, set in sandy skin studded with freckles.

On their way to the kitchen, as they passed the staircase, Dana stopped. "May I?" she signed.

"Of course."

Dana would always ask to see Ur's room. One day they wanted to know what she found so interesting about an empty nursery. "Nothing," she had 'said'. Kate and Jaq had asked her if she believed in ghosts. "It depends on what you mean by 'ghosts.' You see, the soul never dies." They had asked if she was religious. "No, just observant." They had left it at that.

Jaq waited patiently for Dana at the base of the stairs. As she descended, he noticed that she seemed perplexed. "Find something?"

"I'm not sure." Jaq decided to press the issue and tell her about the baby monitor, but lost his chance.

"Dana!" Kate cried, her voice already a little throaty from the wine. She did not always sign. The two hugged warmly. Jaq shrugged, and together they joined the crowd.

"Okay, gang!" Jaq clapped his hands. "Everyone out onto the porch. Take your drinks and pick up an instrument on your way out." In a chorus of laughs and grunts and mutterings, they assembled on the deck. Kate and Jaq made the rounds and filled their glasses.

"What do we do now?" Tia asked, her tone carrying a petulant edge.

"Well, whatever you feel like, really," Jaq said, shrugging. "Sing, chant, recite, dance, whatever."

"Ah, more than that, Jaq," Beele said. "This ceremony is not without precedent, you know."

"So you've done this before?" Tia said. "I'm surprised you haven't been excommunicated, defrocked."

"Perhaps one day I shall be. I'm a Jesuit, after all." Beele drowned the fire in Tia's eyes with a smile as warm as the snow that lay piled up around the porch. "It is a fact," the priest continued, "that most of our sacred holidays fall curiously, perhaps perilously, close to the dates of important pagan celebrations. The Winter Solstice and Christmastime are paired."

"Seems to me," Tia said, having recovered her courage, "that just proves that religion is a commodity like any other and was packaged to make it saleable to the masses."

"I am a simple priest and neither an historian nor an ideologue and don't know whether all of these dates and festivals coincide by chance or by choice. I do know that the celebration of *this* particular day pales, in the pagan calendar, by comparison with its midsummer counterpart. And yet it is a celebration indicative of both humility and hope.

"Mother Earth, at Winter Solstice, allows the sun only a few brief hours of life and then swallows it whole at the horizon. Perhaps she devours her lover." The priest paused. "Or maybe she mocks her son, turning her face away from him. But the Solstice also sends a message of hope, because we know that tomorrow we will receive just a little more heat and light; that the cycle begins all over again.

"So lift your glasses and drink to the sun's return. Bang and blow your instruments. Perhaps we can work a little magic and delay the sun's inevitable demise this evening." Jaq thought Nick shot him a brief, piercing glance. He turned to catch Kate's attention but found her standing perfectly still, wide-eyed and focused on the priest. Then, all at once, and yet, not at all together, the group cheered and drank, then banged and blew a weird cacophony of sounds. The sun hung just over the distant hills, wrapped in a thin pink haze.

Dana caressed her drum, as if thankful for its vibrations. Levine appeared less frightened of the world around him. Faddle, who had been among the last to arrive and had been uncharacteristically laconic, stopped fidgeting. Vinnie and Clara, as if sharing the powerful metaphor of Earth and Sun, moved closer together. Frankie stopped yammering like Popeye and then, suddenly, took the unlit cigarette from her mouth and shoved it into her pants pocket. Even Tia's defiant gaze softened. The deep blue of the mountains, and the sky, reddish pink at the horizon, silver above, reminded Jaq of the fish. Kate gasped and as their eyes met, he understood they were sharing the same thoughts.

The "music" grew louder and louder and then, quite unexpectedly, Beele clapped his hands. "I think it would be appropriate if we allowed our hosts to complete the sun's journey. Kate, if you please."

Kate looked around a bit nervously and then began to blow softly on her clay whistle. The star pulsed purplish for a few seconds, rocked gently and then continued its course, though more slowly, it seemed. There were a few murmurs of 'lovely' and 'sweet', but Jaq felt they were directed more at Kate's melancholy playing rather than at the subtle change that he had witnessed in the setting sun.

Kate let the flute fall from her lips. "Jaq?" was all Nick said. While Jaq was unsure what the priest expected of him, neither was he sure what he expected of himself, although the demand pressed painfully against his side. He lifted the small silver cymbals in his fingers and began to tap them in an odd but insistent syncopation. Slowly, the sun doubled in size, and the fiery tongues that ringed its circumference licked the twilight sky greedily. It halted its descent and hung, suspended over the purple hills. Minutes passed. Or were they hours?

"Enough!" Beele roared, his hands raised and his palms pressed together as if in prayer. "Let the sun go. You can't hold onto it forever. All things have their own private destiny." At that, the sun disappeared over the high horizon in a final flash of pink prominences.

◙ ◉ ◙

"Now," Beele said, "let's move indoors. Kate has prepared a most savory meal of ancient favorites. I can attest to that, since I will admit that I surreptitiously sampled some of them while helping her in the kitchen before your arrival."

Dutifully, and somewhat dazed, they all filed in. Kate and Jaq were the last to leave the deck, in front of Nick. They paused and regarded him pointedly. "Yeah, we know," Kate said. "Later."

The priest simply inclined his head and stepped inside.

"Ay, Father," Vinnie said, then slurped some wine. "What in hell was going on out there?"

Beele raised an eyebrow.

"Aw, I'm really sorry, Father, I—"

"Whatever are you sorry about, Vincent?"

"You know, saying hell and all. Swearing."

Beele laughed aloud. "Oh, Vincent, these are the 1990s, not the 1890s."

"I know. But back in my old school in Brooklyn it was like the 1390s. One time there was this nun and I said—" At that moment, Vinnie noticed the two Levine boys listening intently off to the side.

"Daniel. David," Sarah Levine said, rather sternly. "Why don't you go downstairs and watch Jaq's new TV?"

"Aw, Mom!" the boys cried in unison.

"It would be a good socialization process for the boys to remain here," Beele said, smiling kindly and rubbing Daniel on the head.

"I don't know, Father," Vinnie said. "I might not be the right role model for these guys."

The boys' faces fell. "I think you'd be exemplary," Beele replied. The boys' faces brightened. Sarah Levine appeared unsure. Daniel and David eyed her expectantly.

"Well, all right," she said at last, shook her head and walked away.

The boys, who had been holding their collective breaths, exhaled loudly and low-fived. "Okay, so—" David looked at Daniel.

"Vinnie?" Daniel said tentatively.

"Vinnie's good. Or Vincent," Vinnie said, then cleared his throat.

"Okay, then, Vinnie. So tell us about Brooklyn!" David said. "We were born there, you know."

"Of course I know! Remember, that's where your father hired me at Coogan."

"Sure, we know that, but we left when we were really young so we don't remember much about the place," Daniel said.

"That's right," David said, "so what about the nunnery?"

Both Beele and Vinnie stifled a pair of smiles. "It was a school," Vinnie corrected. "Anyway, I swore, 'damn' or 'hell' or something, and the nun hears me and 'Botta Boom!' smacks me right across the side of the head. Hit me over the right ear and I couldn't hear anything out of it for a month."

"What's 'Botta Boom'?" Daniel asked.

"It's when you give somebody a chop with your right hand," Vinnie explained, making a jabbing motion with his fist. The boys flinched.

"What if you hit them with your left?" David asked.

"That's 'Botta Bing'" Vinnie said, smiling. "C'mon. What's wrong with you guys? I thought you said you were from Brooklyn." The Levine twins looked chagrined. "Anyway, about a week later, Sister calls on me. I sat in the back corner, and she's on my bad side now. "Besides," Vinnie lowered his voice, "I'm staring out the window at the trees." Beele gave him a sharp look. "Ailanthus. You know, the tree that grows in Brooklyn."

Beele nodded. "Yes, Vincent, of course I know it. They call it the 'Tree of Heaven,' after all, don't they?"

Vinnie brightened, as if admitted to a state of grace. "That's right! Anyway, I wasn't goofing off. I was thinking about how its habit is expressed as a fractal." Vinnie paused and scanned the group that had collected around him. Mostly, he was met by blank stares. "Well, a fractal is like when the smaller pieces of something look just like the bigger pieces. Like the whole thing's put together that way."

"Sure," Frankie said, "of course, it's simple, it's like those cute Russian Gorbie dolls that nest. Each one is smaller than the following, except I guess you mean that they'd all have to look the same."

With his face molded into a serious and thoughtful expression, Vinnie nodded. "Yeah, that's pretty close. I mean, not exactly, but I think you got the idea. Anyway, Sister Mary Elizabeth I think it was, comes up behind me and—"

"Botta Bing!" the twins shouted.

"That's right," Vinnie said, smiling. "She smacks me on my left ear and then I couldn't hear anything at all for a month and my grades all stunk so then my father beat me. Ay, you can understand, I'm kind of careful nowadays about what I say to priests and nuns."

The flesh of Beele's face sagged. The lids of his eyes drooped and with them his gaze turned a soft, pale green. Jaq wished to dig out his deepest hurts and pour them into the priest. Jaq had seen that expression somewhere before. Then Beele's face flexed and his gaze hardened. "I guess your father was one son of a bitch," he said.

Vinnie flinched. "Yeah, I guess he was at that," he said softly.

"But," Beele continued, "your feelings about your father are your business and, besides, we're getting off track. You asked me a question about what happened out there, I believe."

Vinnie nodded.

"Well, nothing extraordinary, I should think. We all drank some wine, banged some drums, blew some whistles and acted a little silly. Then, the sun went down."

"Yes," Clara said, "that's accurate. But 'then' lasted a very long time."

"Yessiree," Faddle agreed. "You hit the nail right on the head. Yessir, right on the head. Why, the sun hung over that hill for five minutes if it hung there for a second."

"Five minutes? Try ten!" Sarah Levine cried.

"How 'bout half an hour? I mean it could've been forever for all I know I mean it seemed as if—" and Frankie's account was drowned out by a general babble. Even Dana was signing furiously. Only Tia was silent, as she stared malevolently at the priest. He stared back with a flat expression.

At last Beele held up his arms and admonished everyone to quiet down. The kitchen fell silent. "What time is it now?"

Jaq looked at the microwave, others checked their watches. "Four forty-five," was answered in consensus, if not in unison.

"When was the sun supposed to have set?" Beele asked.

"Four thirty-five," Jaq said.

"And how long have we been in here, in the kitchen?"

"Ten minutes or so," Levine answered.

"So, it *seems* that the sun set on schedule. It *seems* that appearances can be deceiving."

"Or that particular points of view can diverge radically from the consensus," Jaq said, quietly.

Beele smiled. "Yes, or that our common sense notions of reality may differ from alternative explanations."

"Enough, already," Sarah Levine said. "I've got a splitting headache from listening to such stuff."

"And probably because you're hungry as well," said Kate. "Enough is right. Fill your glasses and line up at the counter."

"You're quite right, Kate. We could speculate for hours," said Beele.

"Maybe you could, but I couldn't," Faddle boomed. "I like facts. Yessir, just facts. Not wooly-headed gobbledy nonsense. And the fact is I'm starved. Could eat a horse. Eat a horse for a fact." Faddle laughed aloud at his own simple play on words.

"Will a leg of mutton do?" Kate asked.

"From the size of you, Mister Faddle, even Jesus might have had a rough go of it stretching this mutton leg," Beele said. "Feeding the five thousand, I'll venture, was a snap." Everyone laughed and lined up. Even Tia managed a faint smirk.

Jaq tugged lightly at Beele's sleeve. "Nick, back there, when Vinnie mentioned his father, you …."

"Yes?"

"I'm sorry, I just mean—" Jaq began.

"You mean you were surprised by my empathy?" the priest suggested.

"Well, you are kind of a tough nut, you know. I mean, very rational," Jaq said.

Nick laid a gloved hand gently on Jaq's shoulder. "For some of us, the only way to our hearts is through our brains. I think you, especially, understand that. But that doesn't mean we lack heart. The route our feelings take is simply a bit less direct."

"Kate and I were talking about something like that the other morning. About being Stoic," Jaq said. "She said that I was a Stoic by inclination."

"And she?"

"By choice," Jaq replied.

"A very perceptive lady. In either case, it means not letting your feelings control your actions. It doesn't mean feelings are absent," Nick said. "And it implies acceptance of the good along with the bad. And that dinner looks very good to me. Come along, Jaq. I think we've had enough speculation for the moment and it's time to get on with the business of living."

"Homer," Jaq whispered.

"Pardon me?" Nick said.

Jaq smiled. "I said, let's eat."

People piled plates with food, with mutton and parsnips and turnips and poached pike and large hunks of dense, dark bread. Wine and music, playful Prokofiev and pagan Peer Gynt, flowed.

Plates were cleaned and refilled and cleaned again. People gravitated to relative acquaintances rather than relative strangers. Clara and Vinnie talked with Levine about the market and gossiped about some of the big shots back in New York. Sarah and Frankie yammered away about plants, one's avocation, the other's vocation and the passion of both. Dana, self-conscious, had volunteered, over Kate's objection, to retire to the kitchen to clean up.

The hosts floated. Kate joined the two ladies. Jaq, as he was taking a sip of claret, noticed that things were heating up in the little knot formed by Faddle, Beele and Tia. *This isn't good.* Then he smiled. *But it might be interesting.*

"… bullshit!" Tia had just concluded.

"Well, if it's such a bad idea, how come it's lasted for ten thousand years? Hell, come to think of it, more like a couple o' million. That's unless you believe all of that creationist crap." Faddle shot an uneasy glance at Beele.

"I'm sorry," Jaq said. "I'm interrupting. What was it you were saying was a bad idea, John?"

The big man scratched his cheek. He thumped his fist against his forehead. With passion, he chugged what was left of his wine. "Oh, yeah!"

Kate had wandered over. "Would you like a refill, John?" she asked.

"Gee, thanks." Faddle handed his cup to Kate. "I was just saying that men had run things for, well, for a helluva long time and if it had been such a rotten idea, like most other rotten ideas, it would've died of natural causes."

"Well, it's dying now and good riddance," Tia said. "Males have dominated by sheer brute force, that's all."

"It's hard to admit, but I have to agree with you, Tia. Might often makes right," Jaq said. Tia began to protest but Jaq held up his free hand. "I said the reasons were valid, *objectively*. That doesn't justify them from an ethical standpoint." Tia's expression turned sour, and she simply shrugged.

"If you'll excuse me," Beele said.

"I'm sorry, Nick," said Kate. "Do you need a refill?"

"No. No thank you. I just wanted to talk to your friend, uh ...."

"Frankie."

"Yes, Frankie. I've caught snatches of their conversation. They're talking about one of my passions. Plants. Which seem, by the way, to have done a better job than their parasitic brethren in the animal kingdom of defining roles for the sexes." And Beele slipped off.

Kate turned back to the group and tried weakly to pick up the stranded thread of the conversation. "I have to agree with you, Jaq. Might *did* make right. And good riddance. I'm glad we're living in the twentieth century."

Kate smiled what Jaq thought to be a very motherly smile. "Well, then," he said, "it seems as if we're building some kind of consexus." Jaq covered his mouth and burped softly. "How about a refill, Kate?"

"It's consensus. Jaq, maybe you've—"

"You know, Kate," Tia said, glaring malevolently, "I think it's a good thing your boy, Jaq, is living in the twentieth century. Not the tenth. I'm sorry to say, he wouldn't have made the cut."

"He would, too," Kate shot back. Her cheeks glowed pink from the wine and she moved closer to Jaq.

"Now, don't take it personally," Tia said, "but Jaq's, well, just sort of puny." Jaq doubled his chin and looked himself over self-consciously.

"He is not!" Kate said, smacking Jaq on the chest a couple of times with the palm of her hand. "Not exactly."

"Now Faddle here is pretty good stock." She followed Kate's lead and chucked the big broker in the chest with her fist. The smile on her face was replaced with a look of uncertainty. Tia shook her head. "No, he's too much of a brute. Probably not bright enough."

Faddle's eyebrows crawled over the tops of his glasses. "Now, hold your horses. Just hold your horses—"

"Easy, John," Jaq said. Jaq decided it was time to throw water on the whole gang. "We're all just having some fun. I mean, Tia might be a little cracked, but she's entitled to her opinion."

"You're all cracked," Faddle said. "Men are bigger, stronger, faster and probably smarter, too." Although he didn't sound as if he really believed the smarter part, both women joined forces in a flurry of objections.

"Hold on, hold on. Like Jaq said, everyone's entitled to their opinion. Men are superior and will run the show for some time to come. Some time to come." Faddle closed with an emphatic nod followed by a huge slurp of wine.

"Okay, tough guy," Tia said. "I don't think you're any of those things. Except bigger, and that's more of a handicap from what I can see." She poked him lightly in the belly. Her finger seemed to meet unexpected resistance and her eyes flared in surprise.

Faddle chuckled. "Okay. Whaddaya wanna do? Box?"

"No. Indian wrestle. Right here, right now," Tia said.

"Done!" Faddle said and he began to clear a space in the center of the room.

"Wait a minute—" Kate said.

"It's okay," Jaq said. "We'll keep an eye on them. Nobody'll get hurt. Nothing will get busted. I promise."

Kate rolled her eyes and shrugged. The rest of the guests were staring now at the big broker.

"May I have your attention," Jaq said. "John and Tia are going to have a bout to determine once and for all the question of the superiority of the male sex. It will be one fall." Slowly, everyone formed a circle around the contestants who were facing one another, toe to toe, right hands clasping right forearms. Jaq said simply, "Begin."

For a few moments Faddle and Tia measured one another. Faddle, despite the copious quantity of wine he had consumed, moved deliberately. Tia had removed her sweater and the tank top beneath revealed the results of her regimen at the gym. Shoulders, biceps and forearms rippled as she squeezed Faddle's right hand, testing her opponent.

Beele had sidled over to Jaq and whispered, though not so quietly that he could not be overheard, "This contest is certainly a fine example of the human penchant for escalation of conflict."

"Do me a favor," Jaq said, "and help me make sure it doesn't escalate out of control."

"Alas, I am merely a simple parish priest."

The two combatants remained locked, searching for a small advantage. Faddle found it first. With a powerful pull, he dragged Tia toward him and landed her with an unpleasant thump onto her rump. "Ha ha!" he cried. Looking down at Tia, he added somewhat graciously, "Well done, well done. My, you're stronger than most of the fellas I used to wrestle at good ol' Minot State. Here, let me help you up."

He offered her his hand, but she swatted it away. "I can help myself up."

"Gee whiz, no need to get sore. After all, it was your idea and I did win fair and square. You all saw. Fair and square."

"Oh, go to hell!" Tia said, tears welling up in her eyes.

Faddle appeared confused and embarrassed. "Well, uh, go to hell yourself," was all he could manage, standing over Tia, arms agape, blinking uncomprehendingly.

Tia jumped up and walked quickly to the powder room. The crowd parted to let her pass.

"Well," Kate said, turning to Jaq, "great card, Don King." Jaq fidgeted with his wine goblet. Everyone remained silent.

"Like I said," Faddle mumbled at last, "I guess that decided the question of male superiority. Strength-wise, at least." He looked down at his feet and shuffled them on the rug. The party was broken and no one knew how to fix it.

Dana stepped into the center of the carpet. She began to sign. "She's saying, 'You're full of hot air, Mr. Faddle, and I'd like to let it out of you. One fall,'" Kate said.

"Aw, come on," Faddle said. "This won't prove anything. She'd land on her duff just like poor old Tia. I don't want anyone to get hurt."

"Yes," Jaq said. "I agree with John. Let's just drop it, okay?" His grin, met by Kate's icy expression, faded quickly.

"No," Kate said, "let's not drop it. Let's see who gets dropped."

"But, Kate—"

"You had your turn, Jaq. Now I'm the promoter and I say the match is on. Have at 'im, Dana, you've got a lot of ladies counting on you." All of the women cheered.

Jaq turned to Beele for help. Beele simply raised an eyebrow.

The two contestants squared off, toe to toe, testing one another. Suddenly, Dana's fingers gripped Faddle's forearm like a steel vice. His eyes widened. With one swift and graceful movement, she pulled Faddle toward her while bending one knee. Then, exploding upward, she flung the three-hundred pound man into the air and over her shoulder. He landed behind her with a thud that shook the house.

He didn't stir. Jaq rushed to his side. *Oh, Jesus, she's fucking killed him.* "John, John, you okay?" he said. Everyone crowded around nervously. Everyone but Dana. She stood to the side and watched impassively. Then, Faddle gasped. His eyes fluttered and opened. He gasped again, then coughed. "Judas Priest," he rasped. "Guess I had the wind knocked out of me. First time I've been out of air in years. How about some water?"

"Sure. Sure thing," Jaq said and rushed to the kitchen to fetch a glass. John Faddle struggled up onto his elbows and eyed Dana. "You won, fair 'n' square. Fair 'n' square. Where'd you learn to fight like that?"

"I had eight brothers," Dana signed, "all bigger than me. Never lost a scrap after I turned about sixteen. Besides, your balance is lousy."

Kate began to translate. "She said—"

But Faddle cut her off. "I know what she said. So my balance is lousy, huh?"

Dana nodded. "I can teach you how to fix that," she signed. "But I'll still whip you."

Faddle began to sign, "I'll take you up on your offer. But don't be so sure about who'll be the whuppee."

Dana grinned and offered him her hand. Struggling to his feet, the big broker stood there for a moment and stared at Dana, holding her hand. He pressed gently and she squeezed back.

"How did you know what she was saying?" Kate asked.

Faddle chuckled. "Ask Jaq. I told him the whole story this morning." Then he let loose a gigantic laugh. "Well, what're ya all standin' around for? This is a party. And a pagan party at that. We ate, we drank, and we fought. What the hell'd you expect? He swiveled his head around, blinking above a large, clownish smile. " Say, where's Tia? I'd like to toast her." Faddle waved off the water that Jaq had brought and grabbed his wine instead. "She's one hell of a lady!"

"I just saw her slip out the door," Clara said.

"Let me see if I can catch her," Kate said.

"No, I'll go," Jaq said.

"Jaq, I don't think that's such a good—"

Jaq rubbed Kate's arm, "I started this whole thing."

Kate managed a faint smile. "Very Stoic."

"Yeah, isn't it."

◙ ◉ ◙

Jaq drew a deep breath. The clear night air assaulted his skin and his senses like a shower of fine, dry snow. He shivered, peering out from the front porch and into the dim white light that spilled across the driveway. Straining to see within the faint shadows beyond, he heard shoes scuffing the gravel and caught a flicker of movement.

Jogging toward Tia, Jaq called to her, but she did not acknowledge him. Looking up for a brief moment, he thought that more stars blazed, and more brightly, than he had ever seen. "Tia," he called again as he approached the dark figure in the driveway. But she stood silently, with her back turned to him, rummaging through her pockets, apparently for her keys.

"Tia, for cryin' out loud," Jaq said, his breath freezing in front of his face. "Look, I'm sorry. We didn't mean it …. Oh, hell. We all meant it. Even you. Besides, guess what? Dana dropped Faddle on his butt. So you won. You know. You, plural, won."

Tia had stopped rummaging. Jaq placed his hand lightly on her elbow. "Please come back. Won't you, Tia? I—" As she turned, a small, strangled "Aaaarrrhh …." rose, high pitched and raspy, from his throat.

Two orbs, like beads of black glass, stared back at him. Two sharp fangs touched, making a dry, clicking sound. Within the maw, the maxilla and labium glistened. *Click! Click!* Jaq tried to move but could not. *Click! Click!* A few photons from the garage floodlights flickered on the surface of Her eyes, then disappeared, drowned in their depths. Jaq felt himself being swallowed up by the blackness, by the eyes, by the wet maw. *Click! Click!* A palpus quivered and floated through the icy stillness of the night, feeling for his face.

Breaking free of his fear, he ran for the front steps, but caught his toe on the first riser and fell awkwardly. The corner of the step drove deeply into his side. He winced and let out a dry gasp, but clambered quickly up to the landing. Wheeling around with his hand raised as if he could protect himself from Her, Jaq saw only the taillights of Tia's car receding into the night. He sat for a moment, catching his breath. He wiped his forehead, damp with sweat, with his sleeve, swallowed and drew fresh, cold air in through his nostrils. He thought he could smell his own fear. Closing his eyes, he saw reflected off the backs of his own eyelids the hard, horny head, the onyx orbs, flat, expressionless, absent emotion.

Jaq shuddered, shook himself and rose. Tia's car had disappeared around the bend. The stars seemed less bright now. *Get a grip, get a grip!* He felt a sharp pain and winced. Looking down, he saw that his shirt had been torn slightly over his ribs. Jaq touched the damp spot with the tips of his fingers. "Just a scrape," he whispered aloud.

◙ ◉ ◙

"It seems Tia's gone home," Jaq said as he shut the door with some effort.

"Is everything all right?" Clara asked.

"Of course, everything's not all right," Kate said, though with no hint of rebuke in her voice. "Jaq, what—" Kate began, then stopped when she noticed the tear in Jaq's shirt. But Jaq stopped her with a look.

"Damn it all," Faddle said. "It's my fault for sure. I'm sorry, Kate. Guess I'd better be going."

"No, John, it's not your fault at all," Kate said gently, walking up to the big man and touching him on the arm.

"Who knows about fault?" Sarah Levine said. "But John's right about going. The boys have school tomorrow." Sarah gave Kate a hug.

Jaq took her cue. "Yes, well, I'll get your coats." An antiphonal chorus followed of, "Yes, I'd better be going too."

Jaq turned to hand Sarah Levine her coat, but she had become distracted by Frankie as they tried to answer the age-old question of what to do with poinsettias when the holiday season was over.

Levine tugged at Jaq's sleeve. "May I speak with you for a moment?" he said, apparently sensing his opportunity.

"Of course." Jaq had avoided discussing his conversation with Faddle. He was still trying to figure out whether he had convinced Faddle to cooperate.

Pulling Jaq away from the crush at the front door, Levine led him over to the fireplace, glanced around furtively and then just hung his head.

Jaq waited. "What in hell is wrong?" he said at last.

The little man looked up, his face looking as if it were going to crack into a thousand pieces. "They fired me," he croaked. "The bastards fired me. They finally did it. No place left to send me, they said. They laughed. He laughed, I mean. He, he …." Levine started to hyperventilate.

Quickly, Jaq grabbed the water he had brought earlier for Faddle. "Here, drink this." Levine shook his head. In fact, Levine was shaking all over. "Drink it. Please." Levine drank, took a breath, and quieted down.

"Now, tell me," Jaq said, "*exactly* what's happened."

Levine caught his breath again. "Rooney called me." Rooney ran Coogan's retail brokerage system. "He said they'd met today."

"Who are *they*?"

"The retail managers. All the big shots back in New York. He said they'd had it with my bullshit. They'd given me enough chances and that screwing with Faddle was the last straw." Levine paused, then began again excitedly, but in a hoarse whisper. "I thought you said you'd talk to Faddle. I thought you said he'd stop. Dammit, Jaq, you promised me."

"No, Levine. I told you I'd try. And the conversation didn't go well at all."

Levine bit his lower lip and his eyes glazed over. "Rooney laughed at me. I begged him, I guess. But he laughed at me, the son of a bitch."

Jaq was watching an identity disintegrate before his eyes. "So, the prick laughed at you."

"Huh?"

"Rooney. He laughed at you?" Jaq felt his throat and chest thicken, as his blood began to race through his body. Levine nodded. "Did Rooney tell you to leave, to physically remove yourself from the office?"

"No. He said it was Christmas and just to show me how generous he was, I could stay until New Year's Eve."

"Good. Then just keep going to work as if nothing has happened. Okay?" Jaq said.

Levine hesitated. "Are you sure about this?"

"No. But I've got an idea and it's got a chance."

"But what am I going to tell Sarah? What am I going to do?" Levine asked.

"Don't tell her anything."

"Well, then, what are *you* going to do?" Levine asked, his voice quiet but frantic. "Will you talk to John again?"

"No. Screw John. Look, you relax and let me handle it from here."

Levine began to speak, but then caught himself. He nodded and went to break Sarah away from Frankie and Beele.

"So, you see," Beele was saying, "I seem to have no rapport whatsoever with my houseplants." He sighed and his face assumed a look of utter desolation. But his eyes were laughing. "They all simply up and die. And their deaths are not of the quick, painless variety. They are slow and wasting."

"I find that hard to believe. Your garden is so abundant," Frankie said. She was speaking calmly and evenly. She shoved an unlit cigarette into her pocket. "Tell you what. Maybe I'll drop by some afternoon and see what we can do about that one brown thumb you have. The indoor one."

Beele's ears flushed deep purple, but only for a moment. "Thank you, that would be very nice," he said. "Do you like opera?" he asked rather abruptly.

"I really don't know," Frankie said.

"Are you open this Saturday? The Metropolitan broadcasts here in the afternoon."

"We're closing early, actually. A respite from the Christmas rush," Frankie said.

"Well, then?"

Kate saw Vinnie and Clara out. "I hope this hasn't been too much of a drag for you guys."

"Ay, no way," Vinnie said, cheerfully. "You nuts?" Vinnie's face flushed deep red. "I'm sorry, Mrs. q. I mean, you know, I had a great time."

"I know what you mean, Vinnie."

His face brightened. "Yeah? Well, this was great. I mean, when do you get to see the sun stop and Faddle get thrown on his butt, all in the same day? Besides, this house ... Fugettaboutit. Where'd you two figure it out?"

"Well, um, it's Art Nouveau, actually."

"It's organic."

"I beg your pardon."

"Like something alive. Or dead, that's been alive. Look at your doors!

All of the corners are curved, like flower blossoms or the brain or the gut. If organisms were linear, everything would bump into a right angle and clog the works."

Kate laughed lightheartedly. "I can see why Jaq likes you so much. You two certainly do think alike."

"Ay, all right!" Vinnie said. Then he gave Kate a sober look. "Exactly, how's that?"

Kate paused. "Um, well, kind of different. Kind of scrambled."

"Yeah? Awright. Ay." Vinnie gave his hands a soft clap then snapped his arms a couple of times, straight from the shoulders.

"Anyway, why don't you two come over on Christmas Eve? We always leave the door open. I'd love to give you both a personal tour of the house," Kate said.

"Put my name down," Vinnie said.

Clara nodded eagerly and smiled. "Great."

Vinnie and Clara left and Frankie was right behind them. As Beele went to fetch her jacket, she leaned over to Kate and whispered, "Is Nick one of those priests who can get married?"

Kate's head snapped up and she whispered back an emphatic "No. He's Roman Catholic. You're thinking of Episcopalian."

"No," Frankie said, "I wasn't thinking of anything in particular. I was more like wondering." Beele helped Frankie with her jacket. "Well, 'bye then," Frankie said, not taking her eyes off of Beele for a moment, as she linked her arm in Dana's.

Faddle and the Levines collided at the front door. "Gee, Mr. Faddle," Daniel said, "you were great!"

"How do you figure? I got whipped."

"Only once," David said, "and you slipped. I saw it!"

"No, she whipped me fair 'n' square," Faddle said.

"Maybe," Daniel said, "but you'll beat her next year. Beat 'em both! Botta Boom!"

"Botta Bing!" Daniel echoed. "I think you're probably the bravest fellow in Ketchum. No offense, Mr. q., Mr. Beele."

"No offense," they both replied, smiling.

"Bravest for sure," David said, "next to our dad."

"Yes, Faddle said quietly, "your father is very brave."

Levine averted his gaze. "We'd best be going," he said hoarsely. "Thank you Jaq. Thank you, Kate." And with that he hustled his family out the door.

Faddle gave Kate a warm hug, but his "goodbye" was gruff and his smile was forced. "John still seems awfully upset," Kate said as she shut the door.

"I had a long talk with him today and asked him to get the slime back in New York off Levine's back. He wasn't very cooperative." Jaq paused. "What I didn't tell him is that Levine got canned today."

"Oh, *no*, Jaq. Does Sarah know?" Kate asked.

"No. And I've told Levine not to tell her. I've got an idea, and if it works he won't have to. Regardless," Jaq said, "John has some responsibility here and I told him so this morning. Obviously, he didn't care much for my opinion. Anyway, I'm going to call Rock."

"Good id—" Kate gasped. "Jaq. Oh, my gosh! What happened?" A small dark stain sat on Jaq's shirt.

Jaq peered over his chin and touched the spot lightly with his finger. "Geez. Um, well, when I went for Tia, I actually did find her. And, um, she turned into …." He puffed out his cheeks and exhaled softly. "She looked like that spider thing again. It scared the hell out of me and I started to run and tripped on the stairs and hit the corner of a step. Dumb, huh?"

"No, Jaq. Not at all. Quite understandable under the circumstances," Beele said. He was leaning against the door with his fingers in his pockets and his thumbs wrapped around his belt.

"Dammit, Nick," Kate said, stamping her foot. "What in hell is going on?"

"Kate, take it easy," Jaq said, touching Kate lightly on the shoulder.

Kate pulled away. "Take it easy, bullshit. 'Quite understandable under the circumstances', he says. Look, for two days we've been hallucinating our brains out. Standing in a rain of blood, having *appliances*, for Christ's sake, turn themselves on and off, catching magic fish …. *Now*, Tia turns into a fucking spider again. Meanwhile, you two sit around drinking scotch and bullshitting about the meaning of life. Boys, I've waited patiently, very patiently, all day for an explanation."

Jaq hung his head.

"And dammit, Jaq, don't go looking all hang-dog on me. You told me that you've known your whole life there's a battle you'll have to fight, and it frightens you. Well, Ur is in trouble and we're going to help her. So, strap it on, Hector, because I think this is the big one you've been waiting for."

Looking back up and into Kate's face, Jaq chuckled softly. "Well, Nick, are you going to tell us what's going on, or do you want her to start on *you*?"

"Very well." Beele withdrew his hands from his pockets. "Western culture has been driven by a belief in the fundamental duality of mind and body. Or, perhaps more broadly, thought and matter. In Eastern philosophy, the world, 'reality' has been compared to a dance where the actors are interchangeable and process governs appearance."

"Not another philosophy lecture, please," Kate said angrily. "Jaq told me before you came that you said there is still 'magic' in the world. What the hell does that mean?"

"You said you wanted to know what was going on," Beele said in a tone that was flat and hard.

"Okay. Okay." Kate closed her eyes and clenched her fists.

"We saw the sun 'dance' earlier, when it held its position above the horizon," Beele said.

"That was no illusion?" Kate said.

"Correct. Illusion is often mistaken for the inability to provide a satisfactory explanation for a perception."

"Then that's why there was a consensus as to what happened out on the deck," Jaq said. "No one's senses were tricked."

"That's right. What we all saw was quite real, only quite different from anything we have been taught to expect. It was a reflection," Beele said.

"Reflection of what?" Jaq said.

"Eastern religions speak, quite beautifully, of the 'Infinite,' the sum of all parts of the universe, as a 'net of jewels', where each entity, each being, is not only connected to every other but reflects and affects every 'other' and is reflected and affected, in turn."

"That's not 'magic'," Kate said, "that's physics. I took enough in college to understand that. That's called decoherence, okay? Okay! So where's the magic?"

"Sometimes the mind, *a* mind, can create an entire reality. Sometimes we can see, or affect, a reality that is separate from our everyday experience," Beele answered.

"So you're telling me the sun that set wasn't 'our' sun? You're telling me that the baby monitor is picking up signals from outer space?" Kate said.

"Another space, possibly," Nick said.

"Fine. Another space. Whatever." Kate thrust her hands into her pockets and began to rock from side to side.

"In Tia, Jaq, you 'saw' one aspect of what may threaten your child," Beele said.

"My God," Kate said. "*Threatens* my child?"

"*May* threaten your child," Beele said.

"So, Ur is alive?" Kate asked.

"No. Not in the sense we are alive in this world."

Kate ran her hand through her hair. "How do you know this shit, anyway? What *do* you know?"

"What I just told you. And what you know yourself. You have 'heard' sounds from this other place. Jaq has seen a reflection in Tia of what may threaten Ur."

"You're telling me that some Black Widow has my baby?" She stepped toward Beele and grabbed him by the arms, digging her fingers deeply into his flesh. "We've got to do something," she said hoarsely.

Gently, Beele pried her hands open and held them in his. "We shall, when and if it comes to that. But for now I don't believe anything is going to happen."

"But how can you know—"

"Trust me. Please, Kate. You must let me think about all of this."

Kate stared into Beele's face for a long moment, then closed her eyes and nodded. "But you promise you will come for us if you think there's danger?"

"I'll send for you," Beele said.

"Send for us? Where—" Jaq began to ask.

"It will be obvious." Beele opened the front door. "But I sincerely believe that there is no immediate danger. Now," he said, "it's late and we've all had enough adventure for one day. At least, I have. I'm a very old man, you know." Beele stepped through the front entrance.

Kate opened her mouth as if to protest, then stopped herself, saying simply, "Are you, really?"

Throwing back his head, the priest let loose a tremendous laugh that seemed to crack the frozen night air and bounced down the steps.

"I have a headache," Kate said.

"I don't doubt it," Jaq said.

"I mean, what the fuck is up with him?" Kate picked her finger. "But what choice do we have? Besides, I do trust him, at some deep, important level."

"Me, too. But he's holding something back."

Kate looked straight into Jaq's eyes. "Sometimes he scares me."

Jaq thought of Beele and Bildad Proud and felt his guts tighten. "Want to talk?" Jaq asked. "I mean there's so much—"

"No. What I *want* to do is grab a flashlight, run outside and scream Ur's name until I find her. Or she finds us." Kate touched the stain on Jaq's shirt. "And clean that up."

Jaq nodded. "I'm sorry," Kate said. "I'm just so confused right now. Can't talk if you can't think. Maybe tomorrow, when I've had a chance to sort things out a bit. I'm going to bed."

"You go on ahead then. I'll be right up. I'm going to call Rock."

"At this hour? Can't it wait until tomorrow?"

"No. It can't. Levine's my friend. So is Faddle, for that matter. Tomorrow may be too late." Jaq kissed Kate lightly on the mouth and sent her upstairs.

◙ ◉ ◙

Walking into the library, Jaq adjusted the dimmer so that the floods cast a soft glow. He had wanted to talk, but Kate clearly had not. Feelings were not always in phase, especially when the focus of those feelings was Ur. Edgy and rubbed raw, Jaq went to the kitchen to pour himself another glass of wine, but the taste turned sour in his mouth and the wine made his temples throb. He poured the claret down the sink and rinsed the bitterness from his mouth with a handful of cold water.

Settling himself into one of the library's armchairs, he stared for a moment at the ceiling, painted a rich, cobalt blue. The color reminded him of Ur's eyes and Jaq began to hurt somewhere deep inside, in the place where Ur had been torn from him as she had been ripped from Kate's belly, head bowed, bloody, breathless …. He touched the spot. It was moist and sticky with blood where he had fallen. Slowly, the image of Ur's body faded. The ache in his side began to subside but did not disappear. Rather, it cooed softly. There was nothing he could do about that. But there was something he could do.

He lifted the phone from its base and punched in Rock Adriano's home phone number. He glanced at the clock on his bookshelf. Eight forty-five. Ten forty-five back East. Real Time. Rock would be up until at least midnight before crashing on the couch for two or three hours sleep.

"Hello!" a voice at the other end challenged.

"Rock!" Jaq said cheerfully.

"Jaq!" How are you, man?"

"Not screening your calls tonight, Rock?"

"I need the calls for diversion. I'm reading a bunch of fucking memos from a bunch of slavering branch managers about I don't know the fuck what. Jesus, this job blows, you know that?"

"I can imagine. That's why I'm out *here*."

"Yeah, well …. Say, Jaq, you're not calling to tell me you're coming back, are you?"

"No."

"Aw, c'mon! It'd be great. Just like old times. I'll capitalize a little sub and you and I'd trade whatever we want."

"Who's going to run Coogan if you quit?"

"Who gives a fuck? I'll appoint one of these cocksuckers who write all of this corporate crap."

"Rock, you're good for the company doing what you're doing now."

"Good? But I'd be great. *We'd* be great, trading," Rock said.

"No, we wouldn't, Rock. We were good. Real good. But we weren't the best. Right now, you are the best at what you do."

"Yeah, but—"

"Look, Rock, I didn't call to talk about that shit anyway," Jaq said.

"I'm sorry, Jaq," Rock said.

"No, Rock, *I'm* sorry. Maybe we can talk about your idea some other time."

Rock's voice suddenly brightened. "You mean it? You mean you'll come back to New York?"

"No, I wouldn't leave Idaho. But we don't have to be in the same room to trade. Don't have to be on the same continent anymore, for that matter," Jaq said.

"I guess." Rock paused for a moment. "But there are a few things I'd need to take care of first. You know, I can't just turn the whole goddamned company over to some idiot tomorrow. And, of course, I'll have to keep my hand in it for a while."

Jaq waited patiently until his old buddy was about spent. "Rock, that all sounds reasonable. But, uh, that's not exactly why I called."

"Oh, sure. What's on your mind? Everything all right? How's Kate?"

"She's fine. We both are. But *just*," Jaq answered.

"Yeah, it sucks," Rock said, in a gruff tone. A few seconds of silence passed between two old friends.

"Anyway," Jaq said at last, "I'm calling about Levine."

"What? Aw, shit, Jaq, what's the problem now?"

"He's been fired."

"When?" Rock asked.

"Today. You didn't know?"

"No. Maybe it's in one of these fucking memos," Rock said.

"But you knew he was in trouble? On thin ice?"

"Sure. That little bastard has been on thin ice since he started here."

"Then you've heard about his problems with Faddle?" Jaq asked.

"No. But wait a minute. I hope he's not fucking with Faddle," Rock said.

"Well, let me fill you in."

After Jaq had finished, Adriano asked cautiously, "So, you think there might be a problem? With John?"

"No, actually, I don't. I think Faddle's square. I think all of his trades are on the level. And so does Levine. The point is, you can't afford *not* to conduct an internal review of his business," Jaq said.

"But all of his trades are clean. You said you think so yourself."

"Right. Tell that to a bunch of regulators and then to a jury filled with people who think we trade on insider information when we get it out of the *Wall Street Journal*," Jaq said.

"I suppose you're right. But why'd Rooney sack him?"

"Simple. C'mon, Rock. First, Rooney hates him. Hates him, particularly, because you've always protected him. Second—Aw, c'mon, Rock. Second, what do all those scavengers get? Ten percent of Faddle's gross. You can figure it out from there."

"Well, fuck them!" Rock said. Levine irritates me as much as the next guy. Maybe more. But if those cocksuckers are fucking with the company—"

"Right. So?"

"So, what do *you* think I should do from here?" Rock asked.

Jaq realized that Rock knew the answer, but he also knew that Rock needed reassurance. "Well, first, reinstate Levine. Second, inform Faddle that the firm is going to do an audit."

"Oh, shit, Jaq. He'll flip!"

"Yeah, I know. So, fly him to New York and kiss his ass. Big time. Finally, well, do what you want with Rooney and his pals. They're a bunch of snot-fuck-cumsuckers if you ask me," Jaq said.

Rock's voice boomed with laughter at the other end of the line. "Jesus, it's good to hear you again, Jaq. You're the best!" Then Adriano fell silent. "You know," he said, softly and slowly, "they really were fucking with the company for their own stinking gain. They violated Rule 101, Jaq. Your rule. 'Don't count your compensation.' Make the right decisions and the wheat'll be there. They were *fucking* with the company. They weren't doing their jobs."

"No, they weren't. And Levine was. Always has in his own pain-in-the-ass way."

"Yeah, that's right, he has." Adriano paused. "Well, fuck them!"

"Right," Jaq said. "Goodnight, Rock."

"Yeah, sure, thanks, goodnight," Rock mumbled. "Fuck them," Jaq heard as the connection clicked off. Jaq smiled. The Raging Dago was loose, and Jaq knew he would not want to be Rooney. Especially tomorrow. No, he corrected himself, make that tonight. Jaq knew Adriano. Rooney would be answering his phone right about *now*.

When Jaq slipped between the sheets next to Kate, he felt a rush. He felt competent, useful. Perhaps he *should* think about going into a venture with Rock. Maybe move back to New York? No. Not that.

His flush of excitement cooled quickly and he listened for Kate's breathing. It was slow, deep and regular. How could she sleep after all that had happened? Then he remembered. When Ur was alive, sleep had been their only refuge from reality.

Propping himself up onto his elbow, the events of the past few days streamed through his mind. Jaq craned his neck to take a peek at Kate's nightstand. There were no flashing lights. He slipped back down onto his pillow, closed his eyes and let his mind chase a single thought. Nothing. Maybe Beele was right, maybe everything would be okay. Maybe nothing would happen.

◙ ◉ ◙

CHAPTER 8

And nothing had happened. That was Jaq's first consciousness thought. And it was Christmas Eve. Jaq rolled onto his back, stretched and smiled, soaking in the silence. Following the Solstice party, he and Kate had braced themselves for blinking baby monitors, arachnid horrors and storms of blood. But nothing had happened, as Beele had suspected.

A worrisome thought intruded upon Jaq's state of delicious complacency. Why hadn't Adriano called him? What was going on? Neither Levine, nor Faddle, nor anyone else had mentioned a thing to him. As suddenly as it had presented itself, Jaq dismissed the problem. It could wait. Today was Christmas Eve and tomorrow was Christmas Day, and he decided right then and there that he was going to enjoy them both thoroughly.

Jaq slipped from between the covers, careful not to disturb Kate, and walked quietly into their dressing room. The glass block window glowed violet and rose. He grabbed an old pair of sweats and was struck by a smell so pungent, so evocative, that it seemed to lift him out of his body and back through time. He lifted a pinch of fine brown dust off the fabric. Cedar! His dresser drawers were lined with cedar, just like the closet in his Grandma Jen's bedroom. As a boy, he would shut himself up in that closet, shutting out people and light so there was nothing in the whole world but himself and that bitter, biting, acrid smell.

Jaq lay back on the floor, stretched and watched as the violet and rose filtering through the glass blocks gave way to a lighter, brighter blue. He smiled. Grandma Jen. She was an old Yankee and *she* knew how to keep Christmas. Puddings and pies and gravies and roasted things. All vanilla and cinnamon and nutmeg—and onions. Onions baking, onions boiling, onions roasting.

All at once, Jaq was hungry. Springing up, he crept quietly to the kitchen, thinking all the while of mashed potatoes and goose and gravy and tons and tons of moist stuffing covered in great clouds of vapor that smelled of sage and butter. He resigned himself at last to a cambric tea and a handful of tiny, terribly healthy cookies loaded with walnuts and dates and honey, which Kate had baked the day before to tide them over till they made the *real* things. Killer cardiac Christmas cookies.

Jaq boiled some water, then poured it carefully over the loose leaves scattered in the large basket of the teapot and replaced the lid to let it steep. He leaned against the green granite counter and thought once again of his Grandma's closet and his Grandma's kitchen. The former a place of possibilities, the latter of certainties. Both were safe places. Had Ur ever felt safe? Did she now? Like so many of his thoughts and questions about Ur, he could not hold onto them and they disappeared like water poured upon sand, leaving only a damp spot. Jaq lifted his shirt and touched his ribs where he had fallen. They were still sore, though a light scab now covered the lesion.

Jaq snatched up his cambric, stuffed a handful of Kate's oh-so-healthy cookies into his pocket and strolled out onto the deck. While the morning was bright and sunny, the weather having turned unseasonably warm again the previous afternoon, it was still December in the northern Rockies and Jaq was seized by an involuntary shiver. But a shot of hot tea warmed him, and he settled comfortably into a deck chair that faced the Pioneers.

The sky and mountains were the same as when the sun had halted two days before. Not exactly the same, he thought. No longer violet and rose, it was now an early morning sky that had lightened to a pale, eggshell blue. Several very large pines framed the moon. Seemingly out of place in the morning sky, the setting moon tickled his brain. For perhaps a quarter of an hour, Jaq watched as the waning gibbous, suspended like a broken communion wafer against a blue wash, appeared to move down and away toward the high horizon.

When the moon was about three fingers above the hills, it grew brighter and the sky turned a deeper, richer blue. Morning was waxing. Jaq found himself staring out of a window. Just able to wrap his fingers around the molding of the sill, he stood on his toes and peered over its top. A pale moon hung in a clear, blue sky, suspended over the low hills of his native Berkshires. A breeze stirred the leaves of a pair of old maples that framed the window.

The warm wind blew through the window and brushed against Jaq's cheek. He was in his Grandma Kattie's house, which stood on a corner at the top of a steep hill, cradled as in the crook of an arm by shade trees. Jaq stood in the sleeping parlor that opened directly onto the main living room, where the windows pulsed like preternatural furnaces with the cool light of dawn.

Jaq looked out of the window again and saw that the moon was now just a short distance above the soft hills that defined that horizon. Leaves rustled, then faded, at the margins of his private picture and he watched while the jagged teeth of the Pioneer Mountains raked the pearly flanks of the waning gibbous.

And then he remembered that his Grandma Kattie had told him on that day long ago, that his Grandpa Louie had done something which was called dying, and was *in* the moon. That's where dead people went, she had asserted. *In* the moon.

All at once he was struck by a smell. A dense, warm smell. It was Grandma Kattie's perfume, *Evening in Paris*. A cheap, dime store fragrance, it had been hers nonetheless. And there was something else. The scent was mixed with the most delicate tincture of cedar and cinnamon.

A murmuring, a flux in the atmosphere really, broke the stillness of the mountain morning. Turning toward the sound, he saw seated on a wooden bench at the far end of the deck, Grandma Jen and Grandma Kattie.

Jaq scrambled back up and nearly over the top of his chair. Quickly, though, relief replaced panic, as when something precious is thought to be lost and then found a moment later in another pocket. Jaq inhaled deeply and, once again, smelled cedar and perfume. For an instant the thought crossed his mind that he was finally losing it. Then he relaxed his grip on the chair. They were, after all, though long dead, his two grandmas who sat on his outdoor deck in Idaho. He felt safe with Jen and Kattie. He always had.

"Well, I'll be damned," Jaq whispered to himself. He cocked his head, as if a different angle would give him the flash of insight that would explain the presence of the two spirits seated across from him.

Though their forms shimmered slightly, they appeared to Jaq exactly as he remembered them. Both had been big women with muscular forearms, the result of heavy housework. The hair on their heads was gray, short and set with an emphatic permanent wave. Both wore glasses with wire rims and both wore dresses of cotton covered with a small print. Grannie Jen's was a pink print on a white field and Grandma Kattie's was white on navy blue.

Grandma Kattie's whole face seemed to laugh. Grannie Jen had always looked the more serious of the two. But her eyes would twinkle when she'd crack a smile, although that was about all she'd ever offer—the tiniest crack of a smile.

His grandmothers just sat there holding hands and murmuring. Suddenly, Jaq wanted very much to talk to them. "Grams!" he said in a clear voice. But they did not notice. "Grams!" he said again, this time more loudly. Both grandmothers turned their heads and their faces broke out in enormous smiles. Even Grannie Jen's.

Jaq took a step toward them, but they held up their hands and he retreated to his chair. "I miss you," he said. They smiled and spoke, but he could not understand them.

"Where did you come from?" Jaq was not sure but he thought he saw them turn their heads in the direction of the setting moon.

Then, their images began to pulse erratically and fade. "No, don't go! Not yet!" he shouted.

Just before the last sinuous ripples of their forms vanished, he thought, *just* thought, he heard them say, "He's a good boy."

◙ ◉ ◙

"Who are you talking to out there, Jaq?"

Startled, he took a moment to refocus his senses. Of course, the voice belonged to Kate, familiar and safe as well. But the abrupt cognitive shift jolted him and he began to laugh. It was terribly infectious for Kate joined in and they couldn't stop. Finally, Jaq composed himself. "Why," he choked, "I was talking to my grandmothers. You know. Jen and Kattie."

Upon hearing Jaq's answer, Kate began laughing even harder. Driven by

Kate, Jaq abandoned himself to the impulse, until at last he lay on the deck holding his sore ribs.

"You, um, said you were talking to your grandmothers? Out here?" Kate said, wiping away the tears streaming down her cheeks.

"Yeah." Jaq swallowed hard. "That's right."

Kate's smile faded and her jaw hardened. "Well, then, Jaq, that's not funny!"

Lying flat on his back, arms splayed, Jaq's mouth puckered as if he had just sucked on something terribly sour. Springing off the deck, he began to brush the frost from his hair and sweats. "We-e-ll," he said, "it sure seemed funny to you at the time."

"Hey, I'm sorry." Kate planted a kiss on his cheek. "Good morning. It's just that I didn't realize you were speaking, you know, metaphorically. I think it's good for you to talk with your dead grannies or yourself or anyone else you like. I think it's healthy."

"Thanks, but I wasn't having an imaginary conversation. They were sitting right over there on that bench."

"Oh, c'mon, Jaq. I thought all that spooky stuff was over. Behind us."

"I was thinking the same thing myself when I got up this morning. It's as if everything that's been happening was just a weird dream. But I didn't really connect them with all of that. They were just sitting there, holding hands and chatting."

Kate, impassive as Grannie Jen, simply stood there with her arms folded. "Okay," she said at last, "so what did they say, anyway?"

"I don't know. It was as if I was watching TV and the reception was bad. "But, hey!" Jaq snapped his fingers. "Just before they blipped out, I heard them, or one of them, I'm not sure, say, 'He's a good boy!' How about that?"

Kate chuckled. "How about that? I'll tell you how about that." She gave Jaq a smack on the chest. "That's the silliest thing I've ever heard. You? A good boy? Say, were your grandmas crackers before they checked out?"

Jaq feigned a pout. "They most certainly were not. In fact, they were considered *very* discerning ladies."

"Not discerning enough, if you ask me. You sure must have pulled the wool over their eyes," Kate said.

Jaq slipped his arm inside Kate's robe and wrapped it around her waist. He could feel her body through the light flannel nightgown. He kissed her on the mouth. "I sure would like *you* to pull the wool over *my* eyes," he said in a low voice.

Kate reached up and rubbed Jaq's shoulders. "Would you mind making me a cup of coffee—first?"

"Done," Jaq said.

As they were walking back into the house, Kate stopped for a moment and turned back toward the bench. "Your grandmothers," was all she said.

"Yep."

Kate shook her head and sighed. "I'll make the coffee."

After they had left the deck, if anyone had been there to notice, they would have seen the moon sit on the horizon for a very long time. And they might have almost said that it rocked slightly, like a small child, excited in anticipation of the fulfillment of desire.

◙ ◉ ◙

"I'll grind," Jaq said, as he opened the freezer door to face an array of bags filled with coffee beans, patiently awaiting their fate.

"Indeed," Kate said, dropping her voice an octave.

Jaq chuckled at Kate's imitation of Beele. She stood aside as he loaded the beans in the grinder, her eyes darting from his hands to his face, which was puckered now and focused on the simple task at hand. "Wha'cha lookin' at?" he asked.

She wrapped her long, slender arms around his chest and rested her head on his back. "Hey," he said.

"Hey, yourself." Cool, blue light bathed the room; the spare light of north facing spaces.

Slowly and deliberately Jaq slipped his arms inside Kate's bathrobe. Gently, he ran his hands up and down over the flannel that covered her, as soft and sensuous as her back beneath was lean and hard. Then he kissed her gently. Behind them the grinder whined away. Kate tore off Jaq's sweats. He kicked off his shoes and lifted her onto the green granite.

Kate whispered, "On the counter?"

"Sure. We've never done it on the counter."

Jaq clambered up and lay down beside her. "I always like to open one present on Christmas Eve."

"And I like stocking stuffers," Kate said, her words emerging from a low, throaty growl. She grabbed his ears and pulled his face down to hers and kissed him hard ….

He was awakened out of a light doze by something that felt like fine sand striking his calves. "What's that?" Jaq asked.

Kate's only reply was a soft groan.

Craning his neck over his left shoulder, Jaq's eyes snapped open in shock as he saw the coffee grinder spewing its contents in all directions, covering everything with a brown grit as it sat there singing its idiot tune.

"Shit!" was all Jaq could manage as he leapt off of the counter to shut the damned machine off. When he hit the floor, the slick coffee grounds took his feet out from under him and he landed hard on his right hip.

Kate sat straight up. "Crikey!" she echoed and quickly leaned forward to shut the grinder off. Kate surveyed the damage. Coffee was everywhere: on the granite, on the wood floors, on the cabinets, *in* the cabinets. Below her sat Jaq, planted on his rump. She began to giggle.

"Real funny," Jaq said as he raised himself off the floor. His hands were brown with coffee grounds.

"I'm sorry." Kate tried, without success, to stifle a laugh.

"That's okay," he said, and then, with one swift movement, rubbed his palms down and across her cheeks, leaving two long, brown, clownish stains.

"Jaq, stop that!" Kate threw herself off the counter and would have repeated Jaq's slip if he hadn't caught her. "Thanks." She cleared her throat. "Well, this should only take you three or four hours to clean up."

"For me to—" The front doorbell interrupted Jaq's protest. "Jesus! Who's that?"

"I don't know. We invited practically everybody over the other night. Go answer it."

"Jaq, grind the coffee, Jaq, clean up the mess. Jaq, answer the door. What is this?"

"Jaq! I have to run to the bathroom. Go! Answer the door." Kate dashed off.

Jaq threw on his sweats and shoes. The bell rang again, this time more insistently. When he caught sight of Frankie through the glass, he winced as he braced for her relentless monologue. But it was Christmas Eve day, after all. "Hello!" he said with a smile.

"Good morning, Jaq. Merry Christmas. I hope it's not too early," Frankie said.

"No, I'm an early riser." Jaq grinned again, but this time the smile was not for Frankie. "I've been, um, up for hours. And Kate's in the bathroom. She'll be right out."

"My goodness," Frankie said as she surveyed the kitchen. "Whatever on earth, Jaq, have you done?"

"I was making coffee." *And making love to my wife on the kitchen counter and, for that matter, talking to my dead grandmas. How about that?* And how about Frankie, the Princess of Parataxis? She was punctuating her sentences.

"I can see you were making coffee. But making coffee *what*, is the question," Frankie asked.

Jaq shrugged his shoulders and thrust his hands into his pockets. "Making it spray all over," he said, affecting a close-mouthed smirk.

"Well, then, I must congratulate you on a brilliant result. Do you suppose that you might like to take a crack at making coffee brew?" Frankie said.

"Brilliant idea."

"Good. So why don't you get your little grinder and chop up some more beans and I'll clean up the mess."

Jaq thrust his hands more deeply into his pockets and stared at the floor.

"Selfish, aren't we?" she said and punctuated her remark with a sharp tap of her index finger on Jaq's shoulder. "Now we know your dirty little secret."

"You, too?" he said.

Frankie nodded.

Jaq sighed. "I'll admit I was looking forward to cranking up the vac and dragging the curtain cleaner across the floor." Jaq began to make a back-and-forth motion with his arm.

"You like to sweep out garages, too?"

"Especially garages," Jaq said.

"Garages," Frankie repeated. Both of them stared out across the kitchen, each lost, most likely, in their own private mess.

"Kate!" Frankie threw her arms up in the air and the girls exchanged hugs.

"What have you guys been talking about?" Kate asked.

"Oh, we've been fighting over who gets to clean up," Jaq said.

"Fine. Then I'll elect to be a non-combatant," Kate said.

Soon the kitchen was filled with the sounds of vacuums sucking, grinders grinding and teakettles whistling. At last Jaq leaned against the counter, grinning stupidly, and surveyed the result.

"Put some cookies on a plate, would you please, Jaq?" Kate said. "I'll pour the coffee for Frankie and me, and you can finish your tea, or whatever you call that dishwater you drink."

Almost as soon as they sat down at the kitchen table, Kate jumped halfway out of her seat. "Oh, my gosh! It's almost seven, Frankie. Shouldn't you be—"

"No, that's all right," Frankie said, laying a hand on Kate's and guiding her gently back into her chair. "I don't open 'til eight this morning. I really busted my butt the last couple of days so I'd be able to close early. All I need to do is have Walter deliver all the Christmas bouquets, poinsettias, wreaths and what not, and take care of a few walk-ins."

"Does that mean you'll be coming over later on?" Jaq asked.

"Oooh, no, I won't." Frankie's hand reached instinctively for her pocket, then stopped. Instead, her fingers began to trace small circles around the lip of her coffee cup. "I've, um, a date."

"A date?" Kate and Jaq said simultaneously.

Frankie nodded.

"You mean a date-date?" Jaq said.

"Like a guy date, date-date?" Kate said.

"Well, yes, as a matter of fact. I mean, no. Actually—" Frankie took a deep breath. "Actually, it *is* a guy. Although 'guy' is not at all the right word. He's hardly that. He's a man. Yes. Definitely, he's a man. But, well, no, it's not a romantic date, date-date, if you see what I mean." Frankie stopped and looked at them with a hopeful expression.

There was a long, thoughtful silence that followed. Jaq had noticed the way Frankie looked at Beele as she was leaving the Solstice party. He didn't like the idea one bit. It crossed his mind for an instant that this was one of those paternal experiences he would never have with Ur. "Okay, who is it?" he asked at last.

Frankie squared her shoulders and lifted her chin. "If you must know, it's Nick Beele."

"Beele?!" Kate and Jaq shouted in unison.

Frankie flinched but stood her ground. "Yes," she said, "that's right. He's invited me over to his rectory, or whatever you call it, later this morning to listen to opera."

"Opera?" they cried.

"Yes. I don't know anything at all about it, but it sounds very interesting. Nick, I mean Father Beele, is going to introduce me to the Metropolitan Opera."

"It all sounds very nice," Kate said, "but what's really going on here, Frankie? You were asking all kinds of questions the other night about what sort of priest Nick is." Kate grabbed Frankie's hand. "We just don't want you to get hurt." Kate dropped Frankie's hand. "Oh, shit. That sounds trite, but it's true."

"But I love him."

"Love him? You just met him, for Christ's sake, Frankie," Jaq said.

"But, Jaq, that's how love is sometimes, isn't it? I mean, sort of like a miracle." Frankie snapped her fingers.

Jaq and Kate exchanged a pair of delicate glances. "You're right. Of course you're right," Kate said. "But you know, as well as I do, that love isn't that simple. It involves obligation. And I'm not sure Beele can—"

"Stop, Kate. You're being awfully thoughtful. Both of you are. But I'm just going to have to let this thing run its course."

Kate sighed. "Well, then, please remember that we warned you. He's a little odd."

"I know. That's probably why I like him so much. I'm a little odd myself." Kate picked at her finger and mumbled something. Jaq rolled his eyes. Frankie ignored them both. "But, you know, I've felt just a teeny bit more normal these past couple of days."

"I noticed," Jaq said.

"Really?" Frankie chirped brightly. "Yes, well, I've thought a great deal about this. My babbling or verbal neurosis, or whatever you want to call it, began right after my dad died. Every idea that came into my head just had to come straight out of my mouth. No thought was private or well considered. Why this was so I still do not know." Frankie handed Kate an unlit Tareyton, which she produced from the side pocket of her jacket. "By the way, Kate, would you mind chucking this for me?"

"Sure. Are you sure, uh …."

Frankie shrugged. "I guess I just don't need to sleep with my teddy bear anymore." She cradled her coffee cup in her hands and stared deeply into it.

The doorbell chimed. "Do you mind?" Kate said, laying her hand on Jaq's arm.

"'Course not," Jaq said. Again, the chimes rang—once, twice—three times!—sounding impatient. "Okay, okay," he muttered as he trotted to the door. He stopped when he caught sight of John Faddle.

Although the big broker had never been what could be described as well groomed, today he was positively unkempt. Sticking up randomly were several spikes of hair, clearly slept on and clearly unwashed. Pale green irises floated in a gelatinous pulp. He stood on the other side of the large, glass front door in a trench coat with his fists clenched.

"John!" Jaq said, laying his hand on the door latch. "What a surprise. Um, Merry Christmas."

"Open the goddamned door!" Faddle bellowed.

"Who's that yelling?" Kate shouted from the kitchen.

"Oh, it's just Faddle. We're horsing around, that's all."

Faddle growled and raised his fist as if he were about to put it through the plate that separated them.

"John, don't even *think* about it. Kate would kill you." The broker blinked and lowered his hand. Jaq stepped out onto the porch. "Now, John, what's the problem?"

"The problem? You know what the goddamned problem is. Aarghh!" Faddle gurgled and turned away.

"John, c'mon. Seriously. You look like shit. What in hell happened?"

"He canned me."

"Canned you? Who?"

"Rock."

"Himself?"

"Yeah. Called me at the office last night and goddamned canned me."

"He actually said you were fired?"

Faddle blinked and moved his shoulders about in a series of small shrugs. "Well, no, he, uh, actually …."

"What exactly did he say to you, John?"

"I wasn't being a very good listener at the time, I guess." There was a silence. "Actually, he told me I was being put on probation while the firm examined the trading activity in my accounts."

"So? I told you the other day that the climate's changed. You're big, so you're visible. It's the price you pay for success."

"But they're questioning my integrity!"

"They're asking questions about your business. But nobody's saying anything about your intent. Not Rock, not me, not Levine. How many times do I have to tell you that?"

"Then you don't think Rock believes …." Faddle's features relaxed.

"No, I know he doesn't. Didn't he ask you to come to New York? See him. Spend some time. Relax. On the firm?"

"Well, yeah, I guess he … Say! How the hell'd you know that?"

"I knew because I suggested it to Rock," Jaq said.

"I knew all along that the maggots'd never do it. I'm too juicy a carcass. Too juicy. So, it *was* you." Faddle made a fist and raised his hand. Jaq had had enough. He put his palm on the big man's chest. "John, stop acting like a fucking kid. I called Rock. Called him the other night after the party, when Levine told me *he'd* been canned. Not put on probation, John. Fired."

"Who? Who fired him?"

"Who. Who. You sound like a fucking owl, John." Faddle's features fell. "I'm sorry, John, I wasn't breaking your balls." Faddle waved Jaq off. "But who in hell do you think fired Levine? The maggots, of course."

Faddle chewed on his lip and lowered his gaze toward the ground. "I didn't actually think they'd ...."

"No. That's the problem, John. You didn't fucking think at all. You haven't been thinking all along. So start. I told you the other day that I wouldn't stand by and let them fuck with Levine. I warned you, John. *You* could've done something about it, but you didn't. You were too busy worrying about your precious fucking reputation. 'How dare anyone question John Faddle?' Bullshit. The bigger you are, the more shots they take. Go back to New York, John. Spend some time there and watch what goes on. They learn how to slit throats in the mailroom. You want to do something about your reputation? Defend it."

Faddle blinked. "Sure. Can't cry over spilt milk," he said softly. "Sorry I was thinking about hitting you. Bye." Faddle brushed past Jaq and shuffled down the steps.

"John," Jaq said. "Come on in. Have some coffee." Faddle stared blankly at him. "Have some bourbon? It's Christmas Eve."

"Hmm? Oh, yeah. Merry Christmas, Jaq." Faddle walked to his car, then he walked back to the porch. "The maggots fired Levine?" he said loudly.

At that precise moment, Kate and Frankie walked out of the house. "John!" Frankie cried. She put her hands on her hips. "You look like shit. Did you say something about the Levines?" Faddle blinked. "You men do get unnerved over the oddest things. You probably didn't sleep a wink trying to decide what to get your boss for a gift. Poinsettias won't do of course. Not for Hanukkah!

But I have just the thing. Follow me down to the shop. I have a lovely blue orchid and I can set it off with some baby's breath."

"Baby's breath," Faddle echoed weakly and got into his car, a battered, white '71 Toyota.

A faint smile played on Jaq's lips. The big broker had been able to think about someone other than himself. Astonishing. Could it be that such things as redemption and salvation were possible? And twice in one day?

Kate twisted her long fingers around Jaq's forearm. "What was that all about?"

Jaq explained quickly. "Remember, Beele told us nothing was going to happen. Nothing *bad*, anyway. So far, he's right on the mark. And look at the change in Ms. Frances Howard. No babbling. She's even taking up opera."

"Two miracles?" Kate said.

"It *is* Christmas," Jaq said, flapping his arms against his sides.

"Maybe a little magic?" Kate picked at her finger.

"Maybe a little salvation," Jaq said. "At least they're headed in the right direction."

"Speaking of direction, how about heading back to the kitchen? I'm starved," Kate said.

"Me, too. Want me to whip up an omelet while you shower?" Jaq asked.

"Sounds great. Onions, tomatoes?"

"Cheddar, mushrooms?"

"Perfect. Call me," Kate said.

"Hurry."

"Don't I always?"

Jaq made a face. And for the rest of the morning they passed the time engaged in the very pleasant, very mundane, rituals of Christmas. Walnuts were crushed, dates chopped, flour sifted and carols played—and sung—all the while. Yes, Jaq thought to himself around noon, Beele was right. Nothing has happened at all. Nothing *bad*, at any rate.

◙ ◉ ◙

The two of them spent the early hours of the afternoon preparing a traditional Christmas Eve supper of kibbneh and tabouleh and baba ghanoush. It was Jaq's grandfather Louie, after all, the man in the moon, who had been Chaldean.

Around three o'clock the door chimes rang once again. Nothing had happened all afternoon. Nothing at all. "Do you mind?" Jaq held up his hands, displaying a pair of palms covered with wet burghul wheat.

"If you insist," Kate said, tossing her apron on the counter.

"Thanks, sweetie!" he called after her. Then Jaq heard a squeal, and it was a happy squeal.

"Jaq! Come here!" Kate's voice pealed irresistibly, like a silver bell. Jaq wiped his hands and scooted to the door.

Standing on the front porch were Kate and Frankie's man, Walter Johnson. Between them they held a fir tree, measuring seven or eight feet in height. All of the branches extending from the trunk snaked sinuously, giving the tree the appearance of motion. With perfect symmetry, the apical bud corkscrewed heavenward.

Jaq's mouth dropped. He pointed at the tree.

Walter pursed his lips. "It's a little different. Yuh-huh."

"Different?!" Jaq said.

Walter smiled a wide, toothless smile. Walter was old, yet, remarkably, the skin of his cheeks was smooth, except for deep wrinkles at the corners of his eyes, which were a pale, watery blue. Walter always looked as if he had just wept for joy.

"Different, but this here *is* a Christmas tree. Specifically, a Douglas fir," Walter qualified, hissing his sibilants. "Strange'un, I'll grant ya that." Walter shrugged and flashed gum.

Jaq swallowed hard. It struck him that the idea of having a Christmas tree wasn't at all as sad as it had been the year before. Last Christmas had simply been too soon. Still ….

"Oh, Jaq," Kate was saying, her face lit up by an enormous grin, "guess who sent it? Father Beele! Isn't that right, Walter?"

Walter nodded. "Cut it down hisself."

"Isn't that wonderful?" Jaq screwed up his face. Kate threw the expression right back at him. "Pick up the trunk, sweetie, and, Walter, would you hold the top."

"Yesss, ma'am," Walter whistled over his gums.

"Walter? You said Father Nick cut this down himself?" Jaq asked.

"Yep. Up to Mackay way, by the Lost, I think he said."

"Looks as if he's better at growing things than he is at chopping them down. There's a deep gash just below the bottom branches." Walter peered over the top of the fir tree and Kate moved to Jaq's side. "We'll need to saw the bottom clean, anyway. If you want, Kate, I can cut just above the gash."

"Oooh, no!" Kate said. "That would make it way too short. Besides, it gives the tree ... personality."

"I think this tree has plenty of personality already," Jaq said. "It looks like a bushy corkscrew."

"No, it's just a tree that happened to have come out a little differently." Kate smiled weakly.

"Come on now! Don't *you* start getting maudlin on *me*. Not when I'm beginning to warm up to the idea."

Kate took a deep breath and exhaled loudly. "You're right. You're right. I'll run and get the stand while you boys haul it in. And please be careful."

Within minutes, the bay windows of the great room were reflecting a large mass of green rather than a flat, blank expanse of white wall.

"Nice job, fellas. Mr. Johnson, may I get you a drink? A little Christmas cheer?"

"Seein's it's my last delivery, don't mind if I do. You wouldn't have a little Black Jack, would ya?" He held up two fingers horizontally.

"Certainly, Mr. Johnson. Some red wine, Jaq?" He grinned.

Standing in a semicircle in front of the fir, they raised their glasses to it, to a job well done, and to each other. But Walter stopped abruptly as he was tossing back his shot of Jack, raising an eyebrow.

The doorbell rang again and Kate answered. "Dana! Come in, come in! We've just put up the most wonderful present from Father Beele." Signing away, both at the same time, about the marvelous tree, Jaq and Kate stopped when they saw Dana's jaw drop.

"What's wrong?" Kate asked.

"How did you get that tree inside?" Dana signed.

Kate laughed and turned toward the tree. "What do you mean? Jaq and Mr. Johnson simply carried it …." The twisting top now reached a good twelve feet up the wall.

Walter took a deep breath and set down what remained of his bourbon. As he did, he eyed it suspiciously. "I best be goin'. The shop needs to be closed up and Ms. Frankie, she'll be gone over to Mr. Beeles's by now. Merry Christmas," he muttered as he hurried to the door. "Oh, and the Father said that there was a message in the tree, though I didn't see no note."

For some minutes after Walter's departure, Kate and Jaq and Dana stood and stared at the tree. "Regardless, it *did* come through the front door and here it *is*," Kate said at last. "So, let's decorate it. I only hope we have enough lights."

"I don't think so, Kate. If I remember correctly, we only have three and a half or four miles."

"Funny boy. Dana, do you want to stay and help?" Kate asked. Dana averted her gaze for a moment. "You don't have to, you know." Dana rubbed a knuckle. "Is something on your mind?"

"I was wondering if John Faddle was coming," she signed.

Jaq and Kate looked at one another. "Actually, he was here this morning," Jaq said.

"Oh."

Kate walked over and touched her friend lightly on the arm, and Dana looked down into Kate's eyes.

"Dana. I don't believe he's had a very good day. He's probably back in his apartment. I think that he would feel a whole hell of a lot better if you were to drop by." Then Kate raised her hands and signed, "Go to him." It actually came out, "Run to him." Dana squeezed Kate's hands, smiled at Jaq, and bolted out of the house. Kate and Jaq shouted, "Merry Christmas", but Dana's back was turned.

"She certainly is in a hurry," Kate said.

"Maybe she's really horny."

"Oh, stop it, Jaq," Kate said, smacking him lightly with the back of her hand. "Dana? Really, Jaq."

"Yeah, maybe *especially* Dana. I mean, just because you've never seen Dana with a man. Just because she's big."

"Okay, I'm sorry." Kate bowed. "I was being thoughtless, embracing a stereotype."

Jaq moved to Kate's side and spread his arms. "Say, how about embracing *this* stereotype?"

"A hug? *You* want a hug?"

Jaq smiled and shrugged. "I'm trying."

Kate wrapped her long arms around his shoulders and squeezed hard. "Jaq, you're not stereotypical of anything."

"Nor are you, my dear." He kissed her on the cheek.

"Nor was she," Kate said.

"Nor is that tree." He took a big gulp of wine. "So, let's make it what it was meant to be, a Christmas tree."

"That's what *we* want it to be," Kate said. "It may have had other ideas." Kate picked at a finger.

"Don't they always?" They both were silent for a moment. "Let's decorate it and see if it looks happy being a Christmas tree," Jaq said.

"Our Christmas tree," Kate said. "I'll go get the goodies." Kate began to bolt for the basement where the lights and ornaments had been tightly and safely packed away.

"Kate? We ought to give it some water first."

"Oh, my gosh! You're right. I'll get a bucket."

Jaq crawled under the large lower branches and into the tree. Kate slid a watering can along the floor and held up the big boughs.

"Done?" Kate asked. "My arms are about to break."

"Almost."

"Crikey!" Kate exclaimed. "I'm not sure it really needs more water. We might have to cut a hole in the roof."

Jaq rolled out from under the thick branches and gazed upward. "Jesus," he said, softly. "Well, at least we won't have to get the ladder out to top it with the star." The apical branch now reached almost to the upstairs landing, easily fourteen feet off the great room floor. Jaq pressed his face against a fat branch.

"Jaq, what on earth …."

"I was just looking at the tree real close up. Every branch is twisted. Even the needles spiral."

"A helical hemlock," Kate said, cheerfully.

"Cute. But remember, Walter told us it was—"

"A Deoxyribonucleic Douglas, then," Kate said.

"Or a fractal fir."

"Fractal fir. I like that." Kate's face folded into a frown. She set the empty watering can on the floor. "It's starting again, Jaq. First your grannies and now this tree. I'm not sure I like all of this. "Kate took a deep breath. "Did you see that note Walter mentioned?"

Jaq shook his head. "He said message."

"Okay, *message*. Anyway, Beele—"

"Beele said everything was going to be okay. He said nothing would happen."

"He said he *thought* nothing would happen," Kate replied in a low voice.

Jaq gazed upward again. "Maybe it just *looks* bigger against the bare wall."

"Maybe you're right," Kate said. But her tone sounded unconvinced.

"Let's finish watering it," Jaq said, as he slid beneath the branches. Scrunching himself closer to the base, he dipped two fingers over the edge of the stand and felt the water within a half-inch of the top. "Hey! It's perfect," he said.

Then the gash on the fir's trunk caught his eye. Deep and jagged, it oozed thick, fresh sap. "Boy, Nick sure did miss with that first swipe."

"I want to see," Kate said.

"It's not really all that interesting."

"Then why are *you* staring at it?" Kate crawled alongside him. "I'm curious. Where is … Oooh. But it doesn't look as if it was made by an axe."

"No, it seems almost like a puncture wound. Odd …." Jaq said quietly.

Kate stretched her arm out and touched the spot tentatively with her finger. Large globs of sap began to flow from the hole, streaming over her fingers and dripping into the well. Then the sap turned bright red and spilled over her hand. They both jumped back, squirting out from under the tree, and sat on the floor staring at Kate's arm.

"Blood," Kate whispered. "Like that day on the Lost."

"Jesus Christ. He could have used the fucking telephone if he wanted to send us a message."

Kate's hand shook terribly.

Jaq sprang to his feet, pulling Kate to a standing position. "Let's go," he said simply.

"Go? Go where?"

"The Lost, of course. That's where this came from."

"Now?" Kate said. "How do we know Beele's up there? I mean—"

Jaq put his hand on her cheek. "You wanted answers? I think you're about to get them. Nobody said they'd make sense. And if this isn't magic …." Jaq lowered his hand and rubbed a few small drops of blood between his fingers.

Kate wiped her cheek and stared at the red streaks on her palm. "Do you think she's there? The fish, I mean," Kate whispered.

"Something's up there. Go wash up and I'll grab some warm things. It'll be cold."

"But, Jaq, it's almost two o'clock. It'll be nearly dark by the time we get there."

"Good. Best time for spooks."

"Jaq?" Kate held his hand. "Do you think we'll find her?"

"Do you think Ur's still in trouble?"

Kate shut her eyes for a moment. "Yes, I do," she said in a matter of fact tone.

Minutes later Jaq found Kate at the front door, scribbling away.

"What're you doing?" he asked.

"Leaving a note for Vinnie and Clara. We invited them over. It would be rude if they showed up and found an empty house. I asked them to wait."

"It might be a long wait," Jaq said.

Kate set her jaw and stuck the note to the inside of the glass on the front door.

In minutes, they were roaring up Trail Ridge Road, racing to reach Mackay before the sun dropped below the horizon.

◙ ◉ ◙

I think you can slow down now, "Kate said, as the truck bore down on Mackay's single traffic light.

"You're right." Jaq took a deep breath. "I just want to make it upriver before dark."

"We've still got plenty of time. It's only three-thirty," Kate said.

"Three-thirty. But it's getting dusky," Jaq said. To the east, the summits of the Lost Range were the only features still brightly lit, glowing red-orange.

Jaq drove behind the rodeo grounds to the edge of the river, then killed the engine. For a few moments they sat quietly. Tiny flakes of snow, blown southward out of a tight pack of black- bottom clouds, drifted out of the dusk and through the twin cones of pale light that washed across the pasture. Just as the beams of his dad's old panel truck had pierced the darkness and splashed a thousand bits of chiseled ice that had fired Jaq's tiny imagination. He thought of the ride he'd given Ur in his own old Chevy.

"Looks like the leading edge of that squall has arrived," Jaq said, killing the lights.

Kate rested her head against Jaq's shoulder and squeezed. "I'm glad that Ur was born in winter and felt snowflakes melt on her face," Kate said.

"Thanks for the tree," Jaq said hoarsely.

"Thank Beele."

"But you forced the issue."

"It was ready to be forced, Jaq." She kissed him on the cheek and grabbed his hand. For a while, the only sound was the muted crunch of their boots through thin snow, punctuating the deep sostenuto of the river.

Soon, cottonwoods, tall and black, nudged them gently toward the narrow path that paralleled the Lost. Storm clouds floated in a flaccid blue sky, draping the thin, red line that traced the peaks of the Big Lost Range. The river valley itself, set between the mountains and foothills, as if in a pair of cupped hands, grew dimmer.

Jaq squinted through the snow shower. "There's the sluice. Let's go."

They trotted up to the tail water of the pond that backed up against the low concrete dam. Jaq peered across the calm surface of the pool, broken only by the dimples left by snowflakes.

"Maybe this was a dumb idea. Maybe we should just go home. Vinnie and Clara—"

"No," Kate said and smiled. "We haven't hit the horizon yet. Let's just go up to the next bend, beyond the island."

"That's a funny thing to say. We haven't hit the horizon." Jaq peered over his right shoulder and up at the high, ruddy rampart of the Lost Range, vacant now. "You know, it really is getting dark."

Kate followed his gaze. "Scared?"

"Well, no …. Hell, yes, I'm scared.

"Me too," Kate said firmly.

"Mother's intuition?"

"Damned right."

The willows grew thick, opposite the little island above the pond. Kate and Jaq had to drop down to the rocky beach, which was fairly wide at that point, for it was winter and the water was low. Another cottonwood stand sat just upriver of the island and Jaq, in the lead, clambered around the willows to higher ground.

While the snow had stopped, the onrushing gloom made it all the more difficult to see. All that remained visible now were the snow-covered bank and the tops of the trees, like so many black fingers poking the gloaming vault of the sky.

"Jaq, look." A red ember pulsed among the thick stand of trees. Slowly and in silence, they moved toward the glow. At the base of a large, solitary cottonwood, red light flared, reflecting off pale skin. Two eyes bored into the blackness, catching Jaq's gaze and Kate's in their own, then winked out as the ember cooled. Kate's fingers dug deeply into Jaq's bicep. "It *must* be Nick!"

"Mother's intuition?" Jaq swallowed hard, but found it difficult. He was just about out of spit.

"'Seek and ye shall find,'" a familiar voice called. "Isn't that the quaint phrase?" Seated before them, a thin smile on his lips, was Father Nicholas Marduk Beele. And not.

Beele was wearing boots of black leather with high, soft tops, into which were tucked a pair of loose-fitting pants. A jacket of deep purple sat on his shoulders. And, of course, there were the gloves.

Beele's beard and moustache came to a subtle but definite point, giving his naturally sharp features a keener edge. But the eyes were exactly the same, flashing green fire.

He set down his pipe. "Nick! What is all this talk about Nick?"

"It's your name," Jaq said flatly.

"Yes, one of them, anyway." Beele tssked. "You know perfectly well who it is, *what* it is, that you see before you. I've had many names. Beelzebub, Satan, Lucifer. I was always especially fond of Lucifer. At least, that is, until people began using it to name their pets. I'm sorry, one must draw the line somewhere."

"Goddammit, Nick!" Kate stamped her foot. "We've had about enough of this." Kate marched directly up to Beele. "No, I've had *precisely*, as you would say, enough of this. You drag us up here—"

"You came of your own free will."

"Sure. Right." Kate cleared her throat. "Look, you nearly frightened the two of us out of our wits. Why didn't you just call us up, like anybody else?"

"I'm not anybody else."

"Well, you're dressed like, like—I don't know what you're dressed up like. But it looks silly. And you expect us to believe—"

"I don't expect anything of you, Kate. And even if I did, my expectations don't really count for very much. It's *your* expectations that matter," Beele said.

Kate rubbed her temples. "Dammit, Nick, I don't need philosophizing right now. I need answers. Okay, you are Nicholas Beele. And you most certainly are our friend. It's time for you to level with us."

"Yes, I am Nicholas Beele, your friend. I am also what you see here before you. Call me what you will. And I am others that you, or perhaps even I, do not know. The best I have yet been able to accomplish is to keep my various selves, the warring, fractious faces that I choose, or am forced to adopt by circumstance, in balance."

"Nick!" Kate's voice discharged again like a cannon. "I think you're also known as the Great Deceiver."

The green fire in Beele's eyes was damped. "Perhaps I should come to the point."

"Yes, please do," Kate said, the muscles bulging around her jaw line. "Come to the fucking point."

"I believe we can help one another. You see, my mother, Tiamat, has been raging and ravaging her way across the universe for untold eons. She is the creator, more correctly, the creatrix, but she is also a destroyer. It's time to put a stop to her."

"Ravaging?" Jaq said.

"She interferes."

Jaq regarded Beele carefully for a moment. "But I thought Tiamat was slain by her son, Marduk, in the old Creation Epic."

"My dear Jaq, the Epic is not a history but, perhaps, a prophecy. It may be the future, but it is certainly not the past."

"So, if I understand you, you want us to help you kill your mom."

"Don't attempt to trifle with me, young man."

Jaq felt his guts loosen and stepped back. He understood now how Proud had felt.

"All right, Nick," Kate said, holding her ground. "And what will you do for us?" The pleading tone in her voice could not be concealed. Kate looked as if she might faint waiting for his answer.

Beele's lips stretched slowly into a smile. But it was not a cruel smile. "You're very brave, Kate. Do you know that? Very brave and very bright. You know exactly what it is that I may do for you. Your child, Ur, is captive of a most vile, heinous, selfish being, who has taken—what shall I call it? Her immortal soul? A highly inaccurate and antiquated concept, but it will do. I believe you get my drift?"

Kate nodded. "Why has this *Tiamat* done this to Ur, and to us?"

Beele shrugged. "You'll have the opportunity to ask her yourself if you decide to accept my pact of mutual assistance."

"So, we make a deal with the Devil?" Kate asked.

"I believe the histories have always been severely biased and consistently exaggerated."

Jaq closed his eyes and rubbed the bridge of his nose between his thumb and forefinger. "Okay. Let me get this fucking-A straight. My daughter, Ur, my real daughter, her own self, not that bag of ashes that lies buried back East, has been abducted by a creature, the she-bitch Creatrix of the universe, by the name of Tiamat. You'll help us find and rescue Ur in return for our help in killing Tiamat."

Beele nodded.

"Fuck this," Jaq said and turned downriver.

"Wait, Jaq, please," Kate said. "If you *are* Satan, why would you need our help at all?"

Beele sighed. "As I've mentioned, my powers and my purpose, I might add, have been misrepresented."

"Then what is your purpose on *this* expedition?" Kate asked.

"I will be your guide. And advisor, I might add. However, I must admit to you that I, myself, am not entirely clear concerning the specifics. You see, I have some small abilities at prognostication. But, alas, like most seers I cannot divine my own destiny. For if I did, of course, I might change my own actions and that, in its turn, would affect all other outcomes, rendering my powers useless." Beele raised his palms in a sign of helplessness that was not entirely convincing.

"Okay. Where is it exactly that you're going to guide us?" Jaq asked.

"Well, my dear Jaq, since we are intending to rescue your daughter who is, corporeally speaking, dead, we must go where it is you have always believed all dead people must go. The moon."

"Oh, come on now, Beele. We all know it's just a ball of dirt and rocks," Jaq said coolly.

"Yes, that's quite true of that moon rising above the Lost even now. But we haven't been to that manifestation of the moon that is in your mind, in your imagination, the place where the dead go." Beele paused. "Don't you recall, Jaq, that afternoon when we discussed the universe as a place of infinite possibilities and agreed that the mind itself was capable of actualizing reality?"

"We agreed over a bottle of scotch in the comfort of your study. But this is different, Nick. You're trying to tell me that we're going to take a trip, riding on the back of one of my fantasies."

"Precisely," Nick hissed through his teeth, giving the sibilants an eerie stress.

"Bullshit! Kate, let's go home. It's getting late. Nick, go home and put on some jammies." And, once again, he turned on his heel to head back to the truck.

"No, wait!" Kate grabbed Jaq's arm. "I don't give a damn about quantum physics. I don't give a damn about epistemology, and I don't give a damn whether or not Nicholas Beele is dressed up like a pirate. I do know that Ur is in trouble, and if *he* holds the key to her rescue, I'm going to use him."

"Excellent. It's all settled then." Beele spread his arms as if in an embrace and laid his hands gently on Kate and Jaq. Jaq eyed the gray gloves nervously. "Now let's see …." Beele stepped back and placed his hands on his chin. "You seem to be dressed adequately."

"Adequately for what?" Kate asked.

"A lunar expedition, of course. It gets a bit chilly."

"Chilly?" Jaq said. "Why, it's hundreds of degrees below zero at night, and during the day the temperature hits the boiling point."

"Not on your moon, Jaq. There will be an atmosphere. Otherwise, how could you survive?" Beele said, clearly relishing the problems posed by his rhetorical question.

"Jaq, can the logic." Kate stared at Beele. "Okay. You said you were our guide. Guide!"

Beele nodded. "You're right as usual, Kate. We've not much time. You will lead us there."

"I thought you were the guide," she said.

"Actually, my capacity is more advisory. You will lead us. And, by the way, you, Jaq, must get us back."

"But how—" Jaq began.

"In good time. Kate?" Beele made a low bow.

"But where? Which way?"

"Ah, I *am* sorry. I believe this is where I may be of some small assistance." Walking over to the tree, Beele appeared to slip off a glove. Jaq couldn't be sure. Beele's back was turned. Then he lifted a large bolt of fabric and unrolled it at the base of the old cottonwood.

Jaq gasped softly.

"What is it?" Kate asked.

"I think it's a rug from Nick's study. He calls it his 'quantum carpet' and I think it's the magic we've been looking for."

Kate began to speak, but Beele had walked back to where they stood and handed her Ur's baby monitor. "I'm sorry. Perhaps I should have asked, though I *am* known as something of a thief."

Kate took the monitor, her hand trembling. "Of souls?" she said.

"No," Nick said firmly. "That would be my mother."

Kate's hand stopped shaking and she reached with her other, free hand to turn on the monitor.

"That won't be necessary," Beele said and, at that, a light, raspy sound began to flow from the little radio. Yet the sound was not an analog. It was precise, as if Kate were holding Ur herself. Kate ran to the carpet and simply stood there, clutching the monitor.

"Come, Jaq," Nick said, moving to Kate's side. "Allow me," he said, and gently took the monitor from Kate and put it into a small pouch strapped to his side.

"Kate," Jaq said. He handed her a coin.

"What's this?" she asked.

"Just a bad penny I've been trying to lose. Maybe it's not so bad after all. Maybe it wasn't meant to be lost," Jaq said.

Kate glanced at it. "Ninety-two," she whispered and thrust it in her pocket. Jaq kissed her hard.

Then Beele stooped and touched the base of the old cottonwood. Instantly, it began to ooze. First sap, then bright red blood flowed out of the tree and spilled across the ground. Beele stretched out the same gloved hand and flicked his thumb. At once the blood burst into flames which shot upward and engulfed the trunk.

"Oh, shit!" Jaq cried.

"No, no, Jaq," Kate said. "Feel it? There's no heat."

"Knock and the door shall open unto you," Beele said.

"Ur!" Kate cried, as she rushed furiously into the flames.

Beele gestured and Jaq leapt into the blaze.

◙ ◉ ◙

The door blew open. "Ay! Joyeux Noel!" Vinnie and Clara had arrived.

"Merry Christmas!" Clara said. They were both lit. Not beer and shots or bottle of wine lit, but happily, pleasantly, lit nonetheless.

Clara closed the door. "Vinnie, they left a note." The good cheer spread across their faces vanished. "Gee. I was really looking forward to a little Christmas party. We always had one at home on Christmas Eve."

"I was looking forward to it too. We *never* had one at home on Christmas Eve. The old man was always loaded." Vinnie sighed. "Fugettaboutit. We'll do just like Mrs. q says in the note and make ourselves at home until—Marone! Look at that tree. What'd they do? Pry the roof off and drop it in with a crane?"

"And what the heck is that on the bottom branch? An ornament or a pilot light?"

At that precise moment, the base of the tree erupted in flames.

"Jesus H. Christ! Where's the fire extinguisher?"

"No, wait," Clara said, her hands trembling as she clung to Vinnie's shirt. "There's no heat coming from the fire. Only light."

Three figures, like ghostly traces on film, stepped into the blaze. They disappeared and the flames were damped.

"Oh, my God, Vinnie, did you see that? Shouldn't we call the police or something?"

"No," Vinnie whispered. "No," he said again, this time more firmly. "Let's wait right here. Just like Mrs. q said in the—Hey, wait!" Vinnie stepped up to the tree and surveyed it, then took Clara's hand and climbed the stairs to the landing above. He lifted a small envelope from the apical branch. "What is this, a treasure hunt or something?" Vinnie's eyes scanned the card rapidly.

"What's it say?" Clara asked.

He handed her the note. "It's from Father Beele. It says we're supposed to meet Mr. and Mrs. q tomorrow afternoon near a sluice on the Lost, just north of Mackay." Vinnie paused thoughtfully. "What's a sluice?"

"Kind of like a dam." Vinnie nodded slowly. "Remember the other night," Clara said, "when the sun seemed to hang over the hills forever? And what we just saw. Maybe there's a connection."

"No maybe about it," Vinnie said. He grabbed a branch of the fir and studied it closely. "This is a very complicated fractal."

"Fractal?"

"Fractional dimension. Remember the other night Frankie and I were talking about fractals. Well, most trees can be represented mathematically as dimensions between one and two. But the dimension of this one is slightly less than three."

"Slightly less than three? How—" Clara began.

"I'll explain. But this other stuff …." Vinnie pulled at his pompadour. "I don't know. But I do know one thing." He smiled. "I'm going up to Mackay tomorrow."

"*We're* going to Mackay," Clara said.

Vinnie cocked his head and gave Clara a quizzical look. She simply smiled and took his hand in hers.

◙ ◉ ◙

CHAPTER 9

Jaq landed un-serendipitously on a hard, flat surface. The force of the impact drove his teeth through the soft tissue on the inside of his cheek. Ignoring the astringent, metallic taste of his own blood, he pushed himself up onto his knees. Soft blue light pulsed from fixed points on the four walls of a room. *A room or a lair?* A shiver ran up Jaq's back. "Kate!" he shouted. "Nick!"

"Jaq! In here."

He bolted through a small doorway and into a room several times the size of the first. It, too, glowed blue, but more brightly. Nick was kneeling on the floor beside Kate, who sat with her head between her legs.

"You okay, honey?" Jaq asked, touching her hair with the tips of his fingers.

"Yeah." Raising her head, she breathed deeply. "And you?"

"Fine."

Kate cupped Jaq's cheek gently in her hand. Yes, he thought, I'm fine. He looked her full in the face. Her eyes had always been such a bottomless blue. But now they reflected the striking luminescence on the walls. *Like Ur's eyes.*

"Well," Nick said, "this display of mutual concern is very touching, but we really don't have all that much time."

"Yes, I know," Kate said. "I heard."

"Heard what?" Jaq asked.

"Dry breathing. That scratching sound again. How could you not?" Kate said.

Jaq shrugged uncomfortably. "I guess I was totally absorbed in that place we traveled through. It was so beautiful it almost hurt. Thousands of bits of brilliantly colored glass. Jewels maybe? Reflecting one another." Jaq offered up a sheepish smile as penance.

"God damn you, Jaq." Kate sprang to her feet. "Lost in your own private dream." Jaq sucked on the abrasion inside his cheek. "You're selfish, that's what you are. Next thing, you and Beelzebub here will start discussing shadows on a cave wall," Kate said, gesturing around the room.

"I'm sorry. Really, I didn't hear anything."

"Kate," Nick said, "since Ur died, have you both felt the same feelings at the same time and in the same way?"

Kate picked at a finger in silence. "I'm sorry," she said.

"Good. That's settled," Nick said, though Jaq felt quite certain it was not. "Remember, we all, *all of us,* bring something unique and of value to this quest. Let's treat one another as if we were different senses of the same body. 'Three in one,' if you'll excuse the metaphor. So let's be moving."

"Fine. But where to?" Jaq asked.

"More to the point, Nick," Kate said, "where *are* we?"

"Elsewhere. Where else?" Out of a dark corner and into the blue glow walked the Indian.

"Joe!" Jaq said.

"Joe, what are *you* doing here?" Kate asked in a husky, hushed tone, her eyes opened wide.

"Let's just say I'm the welcoming committee. So, welcome."

"To?" Jaq asked.

"Hey, c'mon, kid. I think it's about time for you to stop playing games. Nick's already told you. Right?" The priest nodded.

"Say, by the way, Nick. You got any flame left in that mitt of yours?" The Indian snagged a Kool from the pocket of his shirt and shoved it between his teeth. The priest rolled his eyes and snapped his fingers. A jet of flame erupted from Beele's thumb and the Indian craned his neck to light the cigarette. Pursing his lips, he took a long, deep drag. "Thanks. Anyway, as I was saying, welcome to the moon. Your moon, Jaq. Luna. This is *your* dream. Or, more precisely, your idea."

"Okay," Jaq said, shutting his eyes tightly for a moment. "Then are you coming with us, too?"

"Nope. As I said, I'm a one-man welcoming committee. Think of me as a doorkeeper." The group started at the sound of a door rattling open above and behind them. A bright bolt of yellowish light tumbled down a set of stairs. "I've gotta go," the Indian said.

"Wait. Where—" Jaq checked himself. He just couldn't handle the Indian's wise-ass reply another time. "I mean, *when* will we see you again?"

"When you leave, of course. I have to lock up behind you." With that, the Indian disappeared, not just into the gloom but, it seemed, through the wall as well. Maybe there is magic left in the world after all, Jaq thought.

◙ ◉ ◙

Down the stairs came two small figures. "Jaq. Kate," Nick called, sharply but quietly. They pressed themselves against the side of the staircase and within its shadow.

"Did you hear something?" one of them asked.

"Yeah. You scared?" the other asked in a voice that was overly loud.

"Dare ya!" said the first.

"Double dare!" They raced down the stairs. Out lashed Beele's hands with a speed that was too quick for Jaq to follow, but he seized them with the gentle touch of a lion carrying its cubs and set them on the floor. One of them opened his mouth, but Beele intercepted his intention by placing a finger to his own lips.

"Danny!" Kate exclaimed.

"David," Jaq said.

Beele hushed them and frowned.

"Danny, Dave," Jaq said in a whisper. "What are you guys doing here?"

"Shouldn't we be asking *you* that question?" the one who looked like Daniel asked. The sophistication of the reply surprised Jaq. The boys *looked* like the Levines' teenagers, but they were the size of seven year olds.

"Daniel—" Kate began.

"My name's Bing, I'll have you know, and my brother is Boom."

Kate scratched her nose. "Well, my name is Kate and this is Jaq. And I get the feeling you know who this fellow is."

"It's not as if we've met before or anything like that," Boom said. "But we've heard plenty of stories about him. Old Nick, we call him."

"And he sure does fit the description. Except, say! Where're your horns and tail?" Bing asked.

Beele chuckled. "An unnecessary embellishment, if not a gross exaggeration, meant to frighten people. But I can see it would take more than an old legend to scare you boys."

"You've sure got that right," Bing said. "It takes more than some silly old story to scare us."

"Yeah," Boom said. "A whole lot more. Fact is, nothing much scares us. So watch it, Mr. Nick. No funny business or Botta Boom!"

"Botta Bing!" his brother cried in counterpoint.

Beele raised his palms. "I can assure you both that I have not the slightest intention of engaging in any funny business." The boys puffed their chests, but their self-satisfaction lasted only a second.

"Bi-i-ing! Bo-o-om!" a woman's voice called. "I've got customers coming in and you've got a job." Bing and Boom exchanged glances and squirmed.

"Perhaps you boys should complete your errand," Beele said.

"You're not kidding," Boom said. They turned to go, but Beele stopped them.

"I must ask a favor, however. I know your mother, Haras. But I don't wish our sudden appearance to alarm her. Would you be so kind as to announce us, but with discretion, and only when no one else is present?"

"Sure thing," Boom said.

"Remember, inform your mother only when she is quite alone."

"No problem," Bing agreed. They charged toward the corner where the Indian had disappeared.

Several empty pails stood alongside large storage casks. Boom uncovered one of the barrels, while Bing fetched a ladle off of the wall. Carefully, almost reverently, Bing scooped out a heavy, white substance while Boom held the pails.

After they had filled two buckets to the brim, Bing covered the cask. Halfway up the steps, the boys stole a glance at Beele. He gave them a knowing wink.

"Why don't we just go upstairs and announce ourselves and get the hell out of here?" Jaq asked.

"As if I couldn't already guess," Kate said.

"I'm sure you would be guessing correctly, Kate. I am not especially welcome here."

"No, I should say not," Kate said, "if you're remembered as Old Nick, with horns and a tail."

Beele closed his eyes and stroked the bridge of his nose with his thumb and index finger. "Ah, it's all so tiresome. But that's how she, Tiamat, that is, has fashioned me. To be an object of fear and loathing."

"Well, if that was her intent, she botched the job," Kate said firmly.

"Thank you. Actually, she wished to set me up as a kind of negative paradigm. Something to be—avoided."

"Nice mom," Jaq said.

"Quite." Beele sighed. "You see, whenever I come here—and I do visit on an irregular basis for the place has a certain restorative effect on me—it seems that something bad always happens to these people. On my last visit—" Beele was cut short as the door at the head of the stairs closed and once again, a soft blue light soaked the cellar, pulsing from various points on the walls.

"Nick?" a woman whispered.

"We're directly below you," Beele said.

"We? Who's we? My god, there's not more than one of you now, is there?"

"Certainly not." Beele was grinning, as he stepped out from the shadow of the staircase and motioned to Kate and Jaq to follow.

The woman's eyes widened. She looked exactly like Sarah Levine, though like Bing and Boom, was half her size. Bright, black eyes were set in a broad face that was tough but kind. Her large, loose-fitting dress was of the same strange material as her children's. Shining dull silver, it exhibited the texture of steel wool.

"I see you've brought along some of the Biguns," the woman said. "I guess they're from Mir."

"Mir?" Kate said.

"Earth," Beele said. "It's what the inhabitants here call your world. But I've entirely forgotten my manners."

"Manners? Just come clean, Mr. Nick Beele. The last time you were here it was trouble enough. Now there are three of you."

"It's all quite simple, really. You see, Haras, Tiamat has abducted, Ur, the young daughter of these two people, Jaq and Kate. They have come to rescue her, and I am here to be of whatever small assistance I am capable," Beele said.

"So she's at it again," Haras said.

"Again? You mean she's done this before?" Kate said.

"Has she done this before? *Why* she does it, god only knows. But she never keeps them for long."

"This time is different. The child has been gone for over a year, thirteen cycles of Mir."

Haras chewed on her lip. "That *is* different. And perhaps that explains why everything's started to turn on its head around here."

"What do you mean, everything's started to turn on its head?" Kate asked.

"Come. I'll explain," Haras said. At the head of the stairs, Haras turned around. "Follow me and don't stray off. If they should see you two—well, I don't know. And if they should see *him*? I won't be responsible."

Haras led them into a spacious, low-ceilinged room, lit by several large wall torches. A shiny white, greasy-looking substance covered their ends, burning with a clear, bright flame. All about lay utensils: spoons and ladles and large pots. In the center of the room a huge stone box belched heat while on top, crocks made of dark gray stone, porous and pock-marked, bubbled away. Curiously, there were no cooking smells.

They followed Haras through the kitchen to a doorway that was protected by a drape of the same material as the clothes that Haras wore. Jaq rubbed the cloth between his fingers. "What is the—" But before he could finish he was pitched headlong onto the floor, breaking the fall with his palms.

"What the heck—" Nuzzling up alongside him was an animal that looked very much like a sheep, but its body seemed far too fat and round to be carried by its spindly little legs, and its face was more gracile. "Beh! Beh!" it cried in a reedy, high-pitched voice.

Haras chuckled deeply. "He likes you already. They usually don't take to strangers right away."

"Wonderful," Jaq said glumly.

"And your question is answered in the bargain. We make all of our cloth from Lamikin's fleece."

"Beh! Beh!" the Lamikin fluted.

"Lamikin," Jaq said. "Very cute." He and the sheep looked one another in the eye.

"Cute? Their real name is Baran. But cute's just what Lamikin is."

Jaq struggled to his feet and flexed his hands a couple of times. They were scraped raw and bleeding a little.

"Let me see those," Haras said. She winced. "Not to worry. Sit at the table." Haras was fussing over him. He liked that.

She brought a small pot and lifted the lid gently. Within it, a blob emitted the fantastic blue light of the sconces in the cellar. Haras scooped up two fingers full and slowly spread it over the abrasions. Jaq felt a tingling, as a marvelous warmth spread through his hands and up his arms.

"What is this stuff?" Jaq asked.

"Sudsy floors. They're little beasts. It's their poops that're good for you."

"Sudsy—" Jaq snapped his fingers. "*Pseudomonas fluorescens*! It's a little bug that eats oil."

"Oil? Sudsies eat Kleb," Haras said. She pointed to the tallow-like substance that was burning with a bright white flame in the center of the table, the same flame that burned on the wall torches.

Jaq dipped his fingers into the side of the pot. It had a greasy feel when he rubbed it between his fingers, but lacked odor.

"Taste it if you like," Haras said. "Sudsy floors eat it, we eat it, even Lamikin eats it. Sometimes. If there's no Greeb."

Jaq touched the tip of his finger to his tongue. It had no taste.

Kate laid a hand on Jaq's arm. "This place is sucking me in too, but—"

"Yes, we must go," Jaq said politely to Haras.

"Haras," Nick said. "If you'd be so kind, we will need provisions."

Haras tsked. "You'll need provisions, but you'll need your strength right now." She disappeared behind a curtain, all the while muttering, "… all skin and bones. She's so pretty, but skin and bones. I'll fix that."

"She's awfully nice," Jaq said.

"I think we've made our first friend," Kate added. "Which, I gather, is more than can be said for you."

"Hardly. You mistake her entirely. Actually, we are quite fond of one another. It's just that she—well, she loves to break my balls," Beele said, rolling the "r" in "break" with great flair. He cleared his throat nervously. "I do hope you'll pardon the turn of phrase, Kate, I—"

"Stop," Kate said. "But I have a question. You've been here before. But the Indian said that this was Jaq's dream. Dreams don't have pasts."

"That's correct, they don't. However, if you will remember, Joe corrected himself. He said that this was Jaq's *idea*. There is a difference. Jaq's mind has contributed details, and some very important details I must emphasize, to the particular reality we are occupying. And once he has actualized this reality, the past seems to fill itself in and the future unfolds on its own."

"Well, then, if he thinks about pink unicorns, will we encounter pink unicorns?" Kate asked.

"No. This is about his consciousness, not his imagination. He is constrained. Everything is. It's as if Jaq were given a box of crayons and told to—pardon the expression—color this world. He has a choice *of*, but is limited *to*, the colors in the box. Do you see?"

"So no pink unicorns?" Kate said with a small smile.

Beele chuckled. "No, I'm afraid not." Then his features darkened. "If only the creatures you will encounter were as gentle as pink unicorns."

Kate started to ask another question, but they were interrupted by Haras, who blew into the room carrying three steaming bowls. "There. Eat!" Set before them was the same white substance that burned away in the candle pot. However, it looked as if it had sprouted purple moles. "Now, I'll go pack your supplies and then you can tell me what gives, Mr. Nick Beele."

"What are these?" Kate asked, poking at the purple chunks.

"They're Greeb. Lamikins love them. It's what they eat. We only take them on special occasions." Haras shot Beele a cross glance and harumphed. "And I suppose this occasion is as special as any."

Delicately, Kate picked a Greeb out of her serving bowl and took a tiny, tentative bite. Her eyes widened. "Mushrooms. Delicious!"

"Mushrooms. Of course," Jaq said. "Greeb. And Kleb is Russian for bread and Mir means world and Luna—"

"So it seems as if the Russkies colonized the moon first in your pea brain," Kate said.

Jaq all of a sudden felt very self-conscious. In fact, he felt thoroughly embarrassed. Awkwardly, he picked up a morsel of Greeb, then felt something nuzzling his leg. Lamikin looked up at him with large, expressionless eyes. Jaq gave it the Greeb, and Lamikin gobbled the hunk greedily.

"Let them eat in peace!" Haras gave the animal a smack. Lamikin bleated sharply and charged past Bing and Boom, who had burst through the curtain.

"Krenk says he wants to see you right away!" Bing said.

"Yes. He's back. Everyone's back," Boom said.

"And they're hungry," Bing said.

"And they're thirsty," Boom said. "We told them we'd help, but they want you."

"Where is your father?" Haras asked.

"He's still putting up the Lamikins," Bing said.

A very large, very ugly head thrust itself into the room from behind the Lamikin-wool curtain. "There you are!" it cried and thrust itself farther into the room. The head was attached to a body that was shorter than Haras's, but the moon-man's arms were nearly as big as Jaq's thighs.

As soon as the creature saw the trio at the table, he pulled up. His mouth dropped open. His eyes widened. Then they narrowed. "And you!" he growled, pointing at Beele. "We'll see about this," he said as he turned and raced out the door. "Boys! Come 'ere! Come 'ere!"

"Oh dear, Krenk!" Haras cried, scrambling after him.

Kate began to laugh. She tried to stop. She held her breath for a few seconds, but that only made her snort, which sounded so absurd she began to laugh some more. Throwing her head back, she let go a long, low whistle. "My. That was exhilarating," she said.

"Indeed," Beele said.

"Indeed, shit," Jaq said. "A half hour ago, Kate, you were ready to kill the both of us for taking this whole crazy business as anything less than deadly serious. Now you're feeling exhilarated. And five minutes ago, for Christ's sake, you were sitting here discussing epistefuckingmology with Nick. You've been crucifying me for that. What in hell's gotten into you?"

"Hey, look, this is hard for both of us," she said, rubbing Jaq's hand. "It's just that I feel, I don't know, more at peace now. Or something. Maybe it's that this is all so strange and all so real at the same time. Our friend, Nick Beele, the *priest*, is Satan. Or says he is." Kate cast a quick glance in Beele's direction, but he remained impassive. She shrugged. "But we still trust him as our friend. This place we've found ourselves in is quite impossible, but very real. I guess I just don't believe that we can force outcomes anymore. So I'm going to let go, to let it happen."

"That doesn't sound like you at all, Kate. Fatalistic. *Deterministic*," Jaq said.

"Hardly. It's actually quite Stoic. If we've been dealt only one set of crayons that doesn't mean we can't choose the colors. Nope. I'm gonna just let it happen. When the time comes, I know we'll make the right choices."

Jaq thought that he saw Nick raise an eyebrow. He couldn't be sure. "Well, I'm sorry for being cranky," he said.

Shouts and loud cries erupted from the bar. Haras's tiny body described an outline against the drape that screened off the kitchen. "Haras has been kind enough to offer us her hospitality. We don't need her protection," Beele said. "Come along. It is, in fact, time to 'let it happen.'"

"Let us through," shouted a voice that Jaq recognized as Krenk's.

"This is *my* tavern. It is *my* home. And they are *my* guests. You should stand back now, Krenk, or you'll wish you had," Haras said.

"Okay, boys," Krenk bellowed. "I hate to do this to a woman but—"

Beele drew the curtain back sharply. "Do what to a woman?" The 'boys' froze. "Do what to a woman?" he asked again in a low, rumbling voice.

Kate and Jaq peered over Beele's shoulders. The tavern's main room was a low-ceilinged affair with a profusion of wall sconces glowing blue, and long, low tables set with Kleb candles. A dozen men and a few women were milling about. All were the same height as Krenk and Haras. Some possessed Krenk's robust build. Others, like Haras, were more gracile.

Beele stepped into the room and strode over to a long, green granite bar. Kate and Jaq followed. While they suffered angry looks, no one said a word. The crowd parted quietly.

"Madame Haras," Beele said with great flair. "Three Peevo, if you please."

Haras strode to the bar through the crowd and found Krenk partly blocking her path. "Are you stuck or something?" Haras followed her question with a resounding smack to Krenk's chest.

"Say! What the—" Krenk began.

Haras set down three mugs and a jar with great care on the polished green stone. Alongside she placed a small pot. Then she proceeded to fill each mug about three-quarters full of Kleb.

Kate lifted the lid quite carefully off the pot. It glowed bright blue. Beele gestured to her to mix them. "So you take a pinch of sudsy floors and drop it into the Kleb and—presto! Peevo," she said, sounding very pleased with herself.

"Yes," Haras said. "Kleb feeds the Sudsies and they feed the soil and soil feeds the Greeb and the Greeb feed Lamikins."

"Not these, they won't," a voice rumbled menacingly from the direction of the tavern's entrance. There were gasps. "Dead as doornails. Dead for sure," said the man, who was carrying two dead Lamikins, one under each arm. Kate and Jaq exchanged a look of cautious recognition. They had spotted yet another familiar landmark in an unfamiliar land. All seventy-seven inches and three hundred pounds of him. But John Faddle was, at that very moment, back in Ketchum, Idaho.

Without a word, everyone drew back. The big man set the animals down gently on the bar. For a time he just stared at the two lifeless forms, all four legs stiff and fully extended. Their mouths and ears and snouts were filled with dust.

Krenk and a few of his followers crept toward the bar. Krenk started shouting. "It's him's done it!" Krenk pointed a thick, crooked finger at Beele.

"Last time, he blocked us off from Velikovsky and we almost starved. And now this. Well, I won't let him do it again." With tremendous speed for a person so thickly muscled, his right arm shot out. Upward flew a mallet aimed straight for Beele's head. No one had time to shout a warning. But faster than Krenk, faster than anything Jaq had ever seen, Beele's hands flicked out and caught the weapon within an inch of his face. Slowly, Beele squeezed his fingers around the stone head and it crumbled in his hands. Beele's eyes spit green fire and his lips writhed into a crooked smile. Krenk went white. He cringed and closed his eyes.

"Enough!" the big man shouted. He reached out and seized the naked shaft of the sledge. "We do not treat guests this way in Old Spall."

"They're not my guests," Krenk said, his voice shaking.

"No? Then they're my guests." The big fellow punctuated his claim by lowering his fist with a thud on the bar.

"Thank you," Beele said quietly.

"I'm Eldaf," the man said to Jaq and Kate.

Kate looked at Jaq and raised her eyebrows, then extended her hand. "I'm Kate. And this is my husband, Jaq."

Eldaf took Kate's hand and nodded at Jaq. "Well, what brings you here?" Eldaf paused and shot a glance at Beele. "This time."

"It seems Tiamat's got their child. Their daughter," Haras said.

"I didn't ask you," Eldaf said.

"No, but I answered. So don't get fresh with me," Haras scolded. Eldaf could not keep his eyes from smiling.

"Begging your pardon," a soft voice piped up out of the crowd. It belonged to a dwarfish moon-man.

Haras glared at him. "So, what is it, Sepp?"

Sepp addressed Kate. "As you've likely been told, this all has happened before. Away they go, for a week or a few, and back they come good as new. The problem is, her attention does seem to wander a bit while she's got them. And if she's distracted, there can be hell to pay."

"Distracts her? What do you mean? What happens?" Jaq asked.

"Well, like the last time Beelzebub come," Sepp said, pointing at Nick.

"She'd just taken Elspeth, here." Sepp indicated a slightly built woman with blonde hair.

"Did she hurt you?" Jaq asked.

"No. At least not that I remember," Elspeth said. "I was only an infant, after all. But as far as I know, I'm right as rain. Whatever rain is." Elspeth laughed and her voice made a beautiful tinkling sound, like a sun shower striking wind chimes.

Kate leaned back against the bar and exhaled slowly. "Yes. I guess you are all right."

"Why should she be *distracted*? She's the Creatrix. Isn't she omniscient?" Jaq asked.

Beele shook his head. "If Tiamat exercises her power, rather than simply being aware of possibilities, she chooses and alters events in a very specific way."

"Sounds like pink unicorns to me," Jaq grumbled. There was something wrong, ever so slightly wrong, with Nick's explanation. "All right. What happened the last time she took a child?"

Eldaf cleared his throat. "Things slip. Tiamat helps regulate things. Borders mostly. Boundaries. She and hers stay on her side. We on ours."

"Hers? Her what?" Kate asked.

"She has a legion. A kind of palace guard to protect her. Though it's anyone's guess what she needs protecting from," Eldaf said. "Anyway, every so often, if she's not paying attention, one of hers will wander over to our side."

"And then?" Jaq asked.

"Oh, we just shoo them back. But last time Old Nick visited, there were a few skirmishes. Nobody hurt. But worse, there was a terrible quake and it sealed off the entrance to Velikovsky."

"Krenk shouted something about Velikovsky just before he tried to bash Beele's head in," Jaq said. "Just what is Velikovsky?"

"It's a comet," Beele said.

"A big ball of ice and hydrocarbons," Kate said.

Nick nodded. "They mine Velikovsky for food, and it is a source of water that supplements the underground grottos."

"But like I said," Krenk said, sneering, "we almost starved."

"Almost," Beele hissed. "I blew a hole through the rubble before I left."

"You did?" Krenk cried.

"Yes," Beele said flatly. Krenk scratched his chin.

"Okay, okay," Kate said. She had her hands behind her, gripping the edge of the bar tightly. "What's that all have to do with Tiamat and her obsession with kidnapping children?"

"Girls. She kidnaps girls," Haras said.

"Okay, girls. So what does this have to do with *my* little girl? With Ur?"

"I don't know," Eldaf said. "Maybe nothing. It's just that we've been having problems at the boundaries."

"Like before?" Kate asked.

"Yes. But worse. Now her Banshees are killing things. These two Lamikins. Next? Who knows? But maybe it has nothing to do with your child. We've had these problems for over a year and, as you know, Tiamat only keeps the children for a short while."

"That's what I've been trying to tell you," Haras said. "They lost their daughter over a year ago." A smattering of whispers wove through the crowd.

"And now that he's here, and *them*," Krenk said, stepping forward, "all hell could break loose and we'd be done for. So maybe you three'd be best leavin' now." Krenk paused. "No offense."

"My dear Krenk. That is precisely what we can*not* do. We must attempt to rescue the child," Beele said.

"Rescue her? Why? The old girl'll give her back. Always has," Sepp said.

"This time the circumstances are different. Not only is the girl from Mir, which is, you will agree, unprecedented, but the child died and *then* was abducted." There were gasps and shouts of "the witch," and, "the poor babe."

"Crikey," Krenk said. "So Tiamat's taken her little ghostie?"

"Indeed. So you see, there is nowhere for Tiamat to return Ur *to*. We must rescue the child or you will lose your world, Old Spall. And there is more. The universe itself may dissolve if Tiamat's attention is turned away from it for too long," Beele concluded.

Cocking his head, Jaq narrowed his eyes slightly, studying Beele's face. "We must leave, but first, may we impose on you for that Kleb and Peevo."

"Boys," Haras said, "go get their provisions." Bing and Boom disappeared into the kitchen.

"More importantly, we shall be in need of a guide," Beele said.

"Guide? What for?" Eldaf asked. "You know your way around here quite well, I should think."

"Ye-e-e-s, well, I should. But it has been quite some time since my last visit." Jaq knew that Beele was lying. This moon, Jaq's moon, was just that much different from the one Nick had known on his last visit. *Besides the Devil's supposed to lie. It's what he's good at.*

Eldaf scratched his head. "I suppose I could get you there. Point you in the right direction, anyway."

"No. You need every able-bodied man here if things get tight," Beele said.

"We'll go! We'll go!" Bing and Boom shouted, running up to Beele and handing him a sack filled with Kleb and Peevo.

"You will not," Haras said, grabbing them both by the shoulders.

"Your mother is right. It's far too dangerous."

"But we're not afraid. If we run into some old Sand Banshee, Botta Bing!" shouted Bing.

"Botta Boom!" yelled Boom.

"I'm sure you're both very brave," Beele said.

"Hardly chips off the old block, then," Krenk said.

Beele shot him a cold glance and Krenk averted his gaze. "You are very much needed here. Old Spall depends upon your family for its food and drink." The boys looked down at their boots. Nick tousled their hair.

"I'll show you the way," said Elspeth in a small, clear voice. "I've been there, after all."

"You will not. I will," growled another from somewhere close by and deep within the pile of people that surrounded the bar. "So make way." There were sniggers. Out of the crowd stepped a man who was a full head shorter than the rest. His legs bowed unnaturally and his crooked spine twisted his torso away from his hips. His hands were gnarled and his fingers crooked. But his arms were thicker by half again than Krenk's.

"I am Kak Zhal," he said with great dignity. More sniggers, mostly from

Krenk's claque. "I am Elspeth's father. Or stepfather. Never had a child of my own blood. But I've loved Elspeth as my own. So I know what a parent feels and I'd like to help you both. You seem all right to me. Even for Biguns. Beggin' your pardon, Eldaf."

Eldaf smiled.

"We'd be pleased to have your help," Kate said.

"I suppose we could afford to lose old Kak Zhal," Krenk said. "Nick hisself admitted we need only 'able bodied' men here." Krenk and his gang broke into laughter.

Kak Zhal moved toward Krenk and picked up the haft of the mallet that Eldaf had discarded onto the floor and broke it in two. And then he broke it in half again. Krenk grumbled and retreated a step. Defiantly, Kak Zhal threw the four pieces of bone onto the floor and thrust out his chest as best he could. "I'll admit I'm a little off standard on the 'bodied' side, but I'm 'able' as any. And if you've ever any doubt, boys, I'll be happy to satisfy your curiosity. Well, then, shall we leave?"

"We must," Beele said. "And now."

Eldaf stepped forward. "Good luck to you. I fear, from what you've said, we need you to succeed."

"We shall," Beele said. "But not without difficulty. Guard this place well, Eldaf. And keep well. Before this is over, we may need your help, too."

Nicholas Beele parted the curtain guarding the entrance to the bar, and the four stepped out into the lunar night.

◎ ◉ ◎

CHAPTER 10

———

Kate and Jaq gasped and grasped one another. The frigid atmosphere made it feel like a plunge into a glacial lake in the high Rockies.

Beele turned at the sound.

"It's okay," said Jaq. He thought he saw Nick smile, then continue on with Kak Zhal.

Kate and Jaq hung back. A small sliver of light passed from behind the curtain that served as the entrance to the bar and fell on Kate's face. Jaq gave her a soft, lingering kiss. She hugged him. "This is it," she said.

"Yup. Good luck to us," Jaq said.

"To us all," Kate said, her voice husky.

Beele and Kak Zhal were a good fifty meters ahead. "We'd better move," Jaq said. But the regolith, the layer of soil that covered the surface of Luna, was thick and very soft. With every step they sank, as if trying to run on a squashy beach. Jaq stumbled over a rock and went down face first into the dirt, stirring up a cloud of dust.

"Oooh! Are you okay?" Jaq was coughing and spitting dirt. The lunar dust was quite fine, and Jaq looked like a sugared cruller. "My, you're having quite the time with your feet tonight, aren't you?"

For an instant, Jaq felt cranky, but shook it off. "Yeah. I guess I am."

They trudged along for a few minutes. "God," Kate said at last, "it is *dark* here. Aren't there supposed to be stars or something?"

They both looked up and noticed the thinnest ribbon of light twinkling above their heads. "Nice going, Jaq. One measly line of stars. Couldn't you have dreamt up a whole sky-full?" Back toward the tavern, they could make out several entrances that were betrayed by slivers of blue or whitish light. "It is kind of cozy looking." In the distance, a Lamikin bleated.

"Yeah," Jaq said. "Like a Christmas scene."

"Well, it is Christmas, after all."

"Yes. I guess it is. Merry Christmas."

"I hope so. Merry Christmas," Kate said.

They walked on in silence and in darkness for a few minutes, then they thought they saw Beele and Kak Zhal disappear. Panicking, they picked up their pace. Groping around a rock wall, they turned a corner and emerged from the dim defile to find Beele and Kak Zhal waiting.

Spread before them was a vast plain as white as bone, flanked by a range of mountains that rose in stepped fashion for what appeared to be miles up and into the sky.

Overhead the stars sparkled, as if a drape of black velvet had been pricked full of holes and now was yielding, rupturing at a billion different points, illuminating the landscape.

"Kak Zhal, does my memory fail me, or do we proceed to the right and over those low hills? Beele asked.

"Right you are, sir. To the right. Ha!" Kak Zhal said. With a queer rolling gait, moving for all he was worth on the pylons that served as legs, Kak Zhal set off in the van. After a few paces, Jaq stopped to catch a glimpse of Old Spall, but it was hidden by the large cornerstone of rock that formed one side of the entrance to the canyon. All else was black as asphalt that had cooled and set.

"C'mon, Jaq," Kate said. "Not much to see back there."

"And we've a lot to do yet out there. Somewhere."

"If that somewhere is anything like this—" Kate swept her arm in an arc that covered the mountains and the plain and the sky. "It's—Do you remember when I saw Ur for the first time in the Special Care Nursery?"

"And you said you never would have thought she'd be so pretty," Jaq said.

"Yeah. And the fish. Now this. How can any of those things be connected with something evil?"

"I dunno." Jaq's stomach twisted into a knot. "But we're going to find Ur and we're going to save her. And I'm taking down Tiamat if I have to."

"Maybe that's Nick's job," Kate said.

Jaq shook his head. "If it was, why did he bring us along? No. I think it's for me to do, if I can."

"You can. We can," Kate said.

"Well, anyway, I'm scared." Jaq gulped a draught of frigid air. "When I was about three, this big kid chased me with a knife. It was just a little jackknife, but it looked pretty damned big to me. After that, I never liked to fight." He stared down at his feet and kicked some dust about.

Kate picked at a finger. "Did you ever run away?"

"Sometimes."

"Did you ever win a fight?" Kate asked.

"Yup. When I stood my ground and it really mattered."

"Well, I guess this one matters more than anything we've ever done." Kate squeezed his hand hard.

"Aren't you scared? Jaq asked.

"No. But I have a feeling I'm going to be before this is over. So let's move. We're burnin' starlight."

Jaq laughed. "Yeah. Let's find Ur."

◙ ◉ ◙

Slowly but steadily the group made its way, though the way was not as smooth as it had looked when they emerged from the canyon entrance to Old Spall. Large boulders were strewn about the floor of the plain. The starlight shone equally bright in all directions and when it struck the ground, it fell across the landscape like a light wash, failing to cast shadows and throw obstacles into relief. Distances were deceiving.

Jaq tripped. "Goddammit!"

"You okay?" Kate asked.

"Yes. It's just such damned slow going." Jaq paused. "I'm sorry. I'm just on edge, I guess."

"Good. But save it for Tiamat."

After a time, they began to feel their feet and their bodies acquire a rhythm and pace that was in harmony with the landscape. They took their eyes off their feet and focused them on the stark beauty that surrounded them, making the grinding passage of time more bearable.

Hours passed. Nothing stirred in the deep lunar night, only the soft 'poof' of their footfalls.

"Kate? Did you hear that?" Jaq asked.

"What?"

"Kind of a scratching—no, a scuffing sound."

She listened, then shook her head.

"I suppose it was just my imagination," Jaq said.

"Well, if any place can feed the imagination, it's this one." She grabbed Jaq's arm. "Wait. Maybe you're right. I thought I heard voices. And laughing. Giggling, actually."

"Is there a problem?" Nick asked.

"Uh, no," Kate said. "I mean, I don't know exactly. We thought we heard something behind us. I thought I heard laughter." Nick eyed her flatly.

"If there is somethin' behind us and it means us harm, it wouldn't be laughin'," Kak Zhal said. "Fact is, out here what would harm us is no laughin' matter."

"Kak Zhal is right. The dangers out here are deadly serious," Nick said. "And if I overheard you correctly, this place can be very fertile ground for the imagination."

"Maybe you're right," Kate said. "*Probably* you're right. But remember, Nick, this is Jaq's dream. There may be some surprises in store, even for you."

Jaq regarded Nick intently, but did not notice any reaction to Kate's remark.

Kak Zhal looked up at Nick with a puzzled expression. "What's she sayin'? His *dream*?"

"It's a bit complicated, I'm afraid," Nick said.

"Well, if I'm anything, it's *un*complicated. So I'll not bother about it. And Mrs. Kate, don't you worry, there's nothin' here'll take me unawares. So dream on, Mr. Jaq! Dream one for me too." Kak Zhal laughed heartily.

Low hills lay in the distance. To their left, massive peaks, as high as any on Earth, etched a jagged horizon line. The noises, the sniggerings, had vanished as

Old Spall had, into the blackness. Soon the hills surrounded them completely and the mountains vanished as they entered a narrow valley and stood at the base of a hill that no longer looked so very low.

"Phew," Kak Zhal said. "Here at last and thankful of it."

"Where at last?" Jaq said.

"Why, where else? The bottom of the hill we've been aimin' at. Good thing, too. My legs is about blowed out. Will be soon. So up we go." Kak Zhal started to scramble up the steep incline.

"Wait!" Kate cried. "Can we rest a bit?"

"If we stop, we might fall dead asleep and this ain't a good place to do that. Not with Sand Banshees and all runnin' loose," Kak Zhal replied.

"Sand Banshees." Kate blew out hard. "Right." She put her head down and followed.

For several hundred yards they crawled across loose scree. "What is this stuff? This rotten rock," Kate called ahead. "God. It's like trying to climb over marbles."

Jaq stopped and coughed. "Breccia." Jaq caught his breath. "Stuff that fuses when a meteor hits."

Kak Zhal turned and sat down, digging his heels into the scree. "Good eye, Mr. Jaq. And breccia'll break ya, if ya use her for grips. Ha!"

"My, what fun having one's own Mr. Science on expedition. This certainly is turning out to be an intellectually enlightening journey. A veritable Chautauqua. Lessons in lunar geology from Jaq and sonnets from our guide. What next?" Nick stretched his gloved hand. "I would suggest that you splay your fingers for better traction and climb using your legs."

As they neared the summit, they all began to increase their speed, but Jaq halted for a moment. Far down the slope, perhaps fifty meters or so, a few small pieces of loose rock tumbled towards the bottom. Were they still being followed? Had they ever been? Jaq squinted and scanned the valley floor. Nothing. The only sound was the whoosh! pfoof! of boots above him. He turned and scrambled up the slope.

"Up we go," Kak Zhal barked cheerfully, extending a hand to Jaq and literally lifting him off his feet and onto a small plateau.

"Whooo!" Jaq said. "Thank you." He gave his pants and shirt a brisk brush. "Well, Nick, perhaps you can tell us what it is we've gained."

"Why, elevation, my dear Jaq."

Kate moved to Jaq's side and wrapped her hands around his arm. "And what a magnificent elevation it is."

To their left lay an extension of the bone white plain they had just crossed. To their right rose the lunar massif they had followed. Details were not visible on the peaks, which were captured in silhouette against a brilliant background of stars: blue stars, white stars, orange, red and golden yellow stars. They stood there silently holding hands on the narrow rim of what appeared to be a gigantic crater.

"Well, this is as good a place as any to hunker down. I could use some rest," Kak Zhal said. "And I expect you could too, being Biguns an' all. As for Ol' Nick here, he'll have to tell us if it's rest he needs or no. For I'll be blowed if I know what stuff he's made of."

Nick had remained quiet all the while, staring out across the valley floor that lay ahead of them.

"Nick?" Kate said.

"Hmm? Oh, yes. Rest is quite in order. Quite. And contrary to what you may believe, my dear fellow, I need it as much as anyone. Need it, in fact, as much as I need some sustenance. Need it almost as much as I need a good big swallow of Peevo. And if everyone is agreeable, I would suggest we bivouac beneath that steep rock face up ahead. The position is superior."

"Well, I'm not agreeable," Kate said. "Ur is in trouble."

"Trouble, yes, but immediate danger, no. I know my mother well enough, and there is no clear sign that she is doing anything more at the moment than fiddling."

"Fiddling?" Kate said, throwing the word back at Beele with an angry edge.

"An unfortunate choice of words. Forgive me. But in any event, none of us will be of much good to Ur if we are famished and exhausted." Kate picked at her finger but said nothing.

While Kak Zhal led the way to the cliff face, Nick remained behind for a few moments and gazed out over the crater rim. Kate, Jaq and Kak Zhal dropped to the ground, propping themselves up against the cliff like rag dolls lined up against the wall of a child's bedroom. Nick gave everyone a good, long swallow of Peevo and then broke off and distributed some dried Kleb. Kate sniffed at her small hunk and wrinkled her nose.

"Sudsies' cousins, 'dirty floors,' are a desiccant. Think of the Kleb as a fine Limburger," Nick said. Rather tentatively, Kate took a nibble then devoured the rest greedily.

Jaq found the ache draining from the muscles in his legs and back, and he actually felt as if he was warming up. Was it the mildly narcotic effect of the Peevo? No matter. He remembered that he had a lot of questions.

But Kate beat him to it. "Nick? Which way are we heading? Not that it matters. I suppose I should ask how far do we have to go?"

Nick ignored the second question. "The sun would set to our left over those mountains, so I supposed that could be called the West. Therefore, as you may deduce, we have been walking in a northerly direction."

"And how cold is it, really?" Jaq asked.

"Freezing. Zero Celsius, that is. But the complete lack of humidity in the atmosphere makes it *seem* warmer, much like our air at home."

"Zero?" Jaq squeaked.

"Don't be alarmed. Sleep well. Peevo equilibrates the metabolism, unlike alcohol. Although I must admit I would most dearly love a dram of scotch right now." Nick sighed.

Jaq was about to ask another question, but Kate was half a word ahead and charging. "Kak Zhal, what is a Sand Banshee?"

"Well, like you heard, they're sort of a Praetorian Guard. Whatever in hell a Praetorian is. But first off, they're sillycants."

"Sillycants?"

"Yep. Or 'liths.' Call 'em what you like. They's things made of sand 'n' dirt 'n' rocks and the like. Anyways, one minute there's nothin' there and the next they just whirl up out of the ground. Whirl up and make the most mournful sound, like lost souls. Mostly they've been no bother. A good whack with a broom'll take care of 'em. But lately—" Kak Zhal coughed.

"Lately, what?" Kate said.

"Lately, they've been hardening up like. Takes a good whack with a cleaver or sledge to bring 'em down. Still, they're not much problem unless there's a pack of 'em. That's why Eldaf and the others is patrollin'. If anyone can stop ", it's Eldaf. Still, if there's too many …. But then there's Anad as well."

"Who's Anad?" Kate said. She stifled a big yawn with her sleeve.

"The other Bigun hereabouts. She and Eldaf's from New Spall, is where."

"New Spa … ah-ah—" Kate began. Another yawn erupted.

"Enough questions for now, kids," Nick said. Kate nodded, her eyes half closed already. "I'll stand watch. Sleep well." And with that Kate was out, breathing deeply. Kak Zhal winked at Nick, scratched his beard, then pulled his Lamikin cap down over his eyes. In minutes, he was snoring heavily.

Jaq scooted over to Kate and settled himself up close beside her. She stirred, moaning softly, but did not awaken.

While Jaq's body was tired, he felt surprisingly alert. "Nick, if you'd like, I'll take the first watch. I'm not really all that bushed."

"You don't *think* you're tired. You will be. Besides, I don't need sleep. Not now, at any rate."

"But I thought you said you needed rest just like everyone else."

"Rest, yes. Sleep, no."

"What you said before was a half truth, then, which brings me to my next question," Jaq said.

"Which is, why did I lie back at Old Spall?" Nick drew his feet up and set his hands casually on his knees. "The villagers were correct that my mother is the cause of their current troubles. But not because she has been distracted." Nick turned his head and stared out over the crater below.

"Go on, please."

Shutting his eyes, Nick pinched his nose between his forefingers and cleared his throat. "The villagers believe that Tiamat is God and her mind, her attention, is the glue that holds everything together. They are wrong. She is the Creatrix, but she is not God. Her mind actualized the universe as we know it, but it does not maintain it. Rather she, along with her creations, is involved in the ongoing actualization of reality. Some may affect that reality more than others, as you are doing even now. A few possess the gift. Or the curse."

Jaq started to interrupt, but Nick waved him off. "It is not important how you do it. But to get back to your original question, I lied to the people at Old Spall about my forgetting the way because they would never understand what I have just told you. No, rather, they would never *believe* it. And belief is a much more difficult thing to change than understanding. Of course I didn't forget the way to Tiamat's lair; I quite simply do not know it, since this place is just that much different from the one I do remember."

"How different? What about Sarah, or Haras, and the twins and—"

"There have been slight changes, but they are mostly cosmetic. Besides, doppelgangers are not all that uncommon. In any event, you are chiefly responsible for the subtle differences. But returning to the question of my mother being distracted, there is no harm in their believing that either, for in one sense they are right. She *cannot* go on as she is. Her time is finished. However, they believe that she must return her attention to the task of maintaining the order of the world as they know it. The real issue is, she can*not* be allowed to continue to participate in the process of unfolding that reality. She must not be allowed."

"Why not?" Jaq asked anxiously.

"Because she meddles overly and she has immense powers. And she is evil," Beele whispered. "No, let me correct myself. I do not believe that she truly *is* evil. But she has done evil things."

"To you?"

"Yes, to me, and now to your child. She must not be allowed."

"What evil things?" Jaq clenched his fists and started to rise. "We have to go." Nick stayed him gently, placing his hand on Jaq's shoulder. Nick's touch did not bother Jaq. Rather, it was comforting. Jaq eyed Nick's glove. "Then, this journey is highly personal," Jaq said.

"As it is for you."

Jaq felt an enormous surge of anger, though its object was not completely clear to him. "You're damned right it's personal. And you're telling me that you don't know where Ur is. You don't know where to find her."

"Not exactly."

"Not exactly!" Jaq swept his arm in a large arc. "This is one big, dark, barren fucking place, Nick. I mean, "not exactly" could be anywhere."

"I wasn't saying I couldn't find Ur. *Not exactly*. Don't you see the difference? I know this place and I know my mother and we will find Ur."

"Great. Great! You suck us into this *expedition*. You say you'll be our guide, then you tell me you're blind," Jaq said.

"The blind have other senses. And, yes, I said I would be your guide, not your savior. You're responsible for that. Both of you are."

"Both." Jaq kicked at some stones. "Does Kate—Of course she knows this is all fucked up. She was a banshee back in Idaho, and now she's just going to 'let it happen.'"

"Jaq," Nick said in a low voice, rubbing his gloved hands, one against the other, "we will succeed in this."

Something in Nick's eyes, some sorrow, grabbed Jaq. For a moment, he felt as if he wanted to lay his head on Nick's chest. Then he stiffened. He felt terribly confused, by Nick's explanations and by Nick's demand that they trust him. "I need a break." Jaq rose to his feet.

"Jaq—"

"Don't worry. I'm not storming off. I just need to take a leak." In search of some small privacy, Jaq made for the big rocks that stood at the top of the talus slope. Nick moved away quietly and stood at the crater's rim, motionless, peering into the blackness below.

◙ ◉ ◙

CHAPTER 11

———

Jaq's boots made sharp, scratching sounds and Nick turned his attention from the valley floor. Their eyes met. Nick made a motion that Jaq should hurry. Jaq ducked behind some big boulders, which sat at the head of the massif that dominated the crater, and noticed a narrow trail that wound down and behind the cliffs. Perhaps it was a natural feature. Or maybe it had been made by Lamikins. Or Sand Banshees. Jaq felt the hair prick up on his arms, but his fear was overcome by curiosity.

The talus slope that defined the edge of the great plain below stretched, seemingly without limits, ahead of and behind him. Jaq craned his neck and the elevation of the sheer rock face overhanging him made him sway on his heels. His hands shot out and grabbed the rock wall for support.

A light sweat broke underneath his collar. "Steady," he said aloud, as if the sound of his own voice would give him a shot of courage. Again he spoke, warding off unseen and unknown predators. "There. Just a few paces down and across the slope the path takes a turn. Perfect."

Though his eyes had adjusted to the darkness, Jaq continued cautiously with short steps, shuffling here and there where the terrain seemed uncertain.

Rounding the shallow corner, Jaq regained his composure and his bladder regained the initiative. The denouement was sweet. Jaq sighed, his thighs tingling as his stomach muscles relaxed. Jaq zipped up then rubbed his hands lightly in the dust that lay at his feet.

The physical relief he felt seemed to spread. Maybe Nick was all right after all. Yet, would he and Kate have gone on this seemingly preposterous quest if Nick had said he'd help, but had told them he wasn't at all certain how much help he could really offer. Jaq's face puckered. Or perhaps Beele had lied all along, was still lying. Maybe he had dragged them along to help *him*, to be sacrificed in some insane grudge match with his mom.

Jaq closed his eyes and rubbed them hard with his fingers, thrust his hands into the pockets of his down vest and peered down the trail. A few meters farther it turned again. Below him, the empty plain stretched to meet another range of mountains. Several stars burst above the jagged ridgeline, half a dozen blobs of light, thick yellow throbbing orange amd electric blue that snapped and sizzled, popped and pulsed.

Jaq knew, absolutely knew, that there must be more of them grouped in the cluster. He would be able to view them *all* just around the next bend. No, he would glimpse them. Nick had said to hurry and he was right, of course.

Rounding the corner, Jaq let out a gasp. Perhaps a dozen stars strung themselves out in a dazzling line of light and smack in their center pulsed a massive red giant.

"Jesus," Jaq swore quietly. "I wish Kate were here." *I wonder if Ur has seen this?* He stepped back to gain a better vantage. But he had been so absorbed that he didn't see that the trail itself ended in a knife-edge that ran across the top of the talus slope and the cliffs behind him fell away sharply, guarding a shallow cirque.

Jaq pitched backward down a steep incline. Managing to turn onto his belly, he tried to dig his fingers into a surface that had turned to soft sand. Above, he saw the patch of starry night sky receding. Desperately, he began to kick and claw, but this only made him spin and tumble. "Oh, shit!" Face first, he slid into the black throat of the cirque.

◙ ◉ ◙

There were no birds, nor even the stirring of a breeze, to awaken her. Kate stretched and opened an eye, then rolled to face Kak Zhal. His back had slipped off of the rocks he had used to brace himself and he slept, lying supine and fully extended, which wasn't much. His chest heaved mightily as he drew in, then blew out, air in great bursts. "Just like Ur," Kate said to no one in particular. She rested her head in her hand and studied his twisted torso, his gnarled hands and his face, like some rumpled, ripe tropical fruit, all bumps and knots and convolutions, mashed in here and there for good measure. "You were dealt a rotten hand, weren't you, friend?" she whispered again. "Just like Ur."

Why had he come? Because he knew what it meant to lose a child? Certainly. But Kak Zhal was also trying to prove his own worth. To himself more than to the boors at the tavern. Kate knew that Jaq also had mixed motives for making this journey. Oh, of course, he would have done it simply to save Ur. Yet, a few days before, on the Lost, he had alluded to some silly, personal war he needed to wage. What had he called it? Aristeia. Single combat. And then there was his admission of fear just after they had left Old Spall. Why was it so important for men to prove, or maybe it was to discover, their courage? Men. Kate reached behind her back to touch *her* man.

She sat straight up. "Where's Jaq?" Kate shouted. "Nick!" she called loudly, waking Kak Zhal. But Nick, standing on the crater rim, did not move. Voices, apparently, did not carry well in the thin lunar atmosphere.

"What's all the yelling about?" Kak Zhal grunted, as he struggled to a seated position.

"Nick!" Kate called again, running to him. He turned slowly and Kate stopped short.

Nick studied her with the eyes of a blind man. Distant, searching, focused elsewhere. "Yes," he said quietly.

"Where's Jaq?" Kate asked bluntly.

"He needed to relieve himself." Nick's gaze snapped into focus. "However, he has been gone overly long."

"Overly long? Well, then, what the hell have you been waiting for? Let's go find him."

Nick held up a hand. "I sense no danger."

"Boy, that's a relief." Kate drummed her fingers against her thighs. "Nick? What's the problem? I mean, ever since we got here you've been fixated on that valley floor."

Nick ignored Kate's question. "Kak Zhal. I had expected to find Hades out there." He pointed to a spot far up the valley floor and in the direction they had been heading.

"Well, ya had a right to. Used to be there. But the dead must be getting jumpy. Seems like they've wandered off."

"Indeed. Do you know by chance where they've wandered off *to*?" Nick asked.

"Yep. That's why ya brought me along, ain't it? Eldaf and some of the boys seen 'em milling about, driftin' in the direction of the Styx."

Nick frowned. "How long will it take us, Kak Zhal? On foot?"

"Quarter day. Quarter night. Same difference."

"Three or four earth days, then, Kate," Nick said, inviting her back into the conversation.

"Three or four days! What about Ur?" Kate said.

"She's not the problem. The problem is that the sun will be up in less than two earth days."

"Then we'll have to go to ground," Kak Zhal said. "If I'd known we was in such a hurry—"

"What in hell is he saying?" Kate cried.

"While the long lunar nights are habitable, the days are not," Nick said.

"What did you mean, 'she's not the problem'? Dammit, Nick, what's going on? Ur's in trouble, and back at the tavern you tell us we have to eat. Then we have to leave. Then we have to rest. I mean, is she in danger or isn't she?"

"I don't know what mother's up to. Although I'm quite certain it's no good. However, the danger to Ur, while proximate, is not immediate as is the danger to you. The environment here—"

Kate walked directly up to Beele. "You don't know what your mother's up to. You don't sense that Ur is in any danger. Maybe that's because you just don't know." Kate gripped Beele by the shoulders. "You don't know where Ur is, do you?"

"Not exactly. But Kate, Kak Zhal here has given me—"

"Nick, give me the baby monitor."

"Kate, it won't—"

"Give it to me!"

Beele withdrew the device from his pack and handed it to Kate. It was silent. She fumbled with the dials, but still there was no sound.

"I'm sorry. It is an artifact of your child's. It helped us get here, that's all," Beele said.

Kate handed the monitor back to Beele. "No. If you knew where Ur was and you had all of the Devil's supposed magic powers, why would you have brought us along? Why would you have asked us, unless we provided something you didn't have?" Kate closed her eyes for a moment and exhaled slowly. "I'm not angry, Nick. Ur is in this place and we couldn't have gotten here without you. I do trust you, but I don't want to be bull-shitted. So is there anything, really, that you *can* do for us. For Ur?"

Nick raised his arms. "Out with you!" His voice boomed, even in the thin lunar air. "Out, I said." Nick's voice was softer this time, yet deep and dangerous. Nothing stirred. He stretched his arms and two jets of blue flame erupted from the tips of his fingers, stretching across the full twenty meters of ledge where they'd bivouacked. Kate and Kak Zhal jumped. The air seemed to sizzle even after he called the fire back within himself.

"Jesus," Kate said. "Remind me to stand back the next time you light your pipe."

"Now show yourselves or I'll fry you both where you stand!" Nick said. Out from behind two large boulders stepped Botta Bing and Botta Boom.

"So Jaq was right, you two guys *were* following us," Kate said.

Bing eyed Nick warily, then stuck out his chest. "Yup. It was us for sure."

"But it's not nice to go creeping around behind people's backs," Kate said. "And it's dangerous besides."

"We're sorry," Boom said. "But we want to help."

"That's right," Bing said. "We're brave as anybody. Brave as our dad. Almost."

Nick's eyes were drawn to a spot behind the boys and at the top of the talus slope. He raised an eyebrow.

Kate walked over and knelt beside the two children, putting her hands on their shoulders. "I know you guys are brave and we appreciate what you're trying to do. But we need to get across that valley, and fast. I doubt there's much you can do to help us in that."

"But—" Bing began.

"Besides, I'm sure your mother's worried sick," Kak Zhal said.

"I don't know about their mother, but their father certainly has been." Enivel approached slowly, regarding the boys with both anger and concern.

Casting their eyes downward, the two boys mumbled, "We're sorry," and scuffed some dirt.

"Your apologies are all very well, but let me tell you both, when I get you back to Old Spall—"

"But Dad, we can't go back. We have to help them," Bing said.

"That's right. Especially after what Krenk said about you back at the tavern, after Kate and Jaq and Kak Zhal and Ol' Nick left," Boom said glumly.

"What did they say, if I may inquire?" Nick asked.

"They said Dad should have gone with you. That he wouldn't be missed, even if something happened to him, 'cause he wasn't much good for anything anyway. And then Krenk …. Let me tell you, soon as I'm big enough, Botta Bing!"

"Yeah, Botta Boom!"

The faintest rumbling from within the steep rock walls of the crater shook the ground. "What was that?" Kate said.

Nick ignored Kate's question. "What did Krenk say, Bing?"

"He said Dad should go, but wouldn't, 'cause he was a coward."

"Boys," Nick said firmly, "what Krenk and his fellows have said, or ever will say for that matter, is rubbish. It is patently false. And you are brave young men as well. Unfortunately, bravery will not solve our problem."

"That it won't," Kak Zhal said. "What we need is wings. And that's not likely unless Old Nick here could sprout a pair and we could ride him like a Dust Bat."

Nick sniffed. "I'm afraid sprouting wings is not in my repertoire. Any more than I could grow horns and a tail."

"But that's just it," Bing said excitedly. "We *can* help you."

"You're saying ya can fly?" Kak Zhal said.

"No. But we can do something almost as good. Maybe better. We can take you on Rock Cats," Bing said.

"Rock Cats, is it? Next thing we'll be ridin' pink uneecorns. Whatever a uneecorn is," Kak Zhal said.

"Now, boys," Enivel said, "it's all well and good your trying to help. But I'm afraid your imaginations have run away with your good sense. You know there's no such silicant as a Rock Cat. It's just a story." Enivel turned to the rest of the group. "I'm sorry for any trouble they've caused and I'm *very* sorry for delaying you. Let's go, boys."

"But Dad—" Boom began.

"Wait, please. I don't wish to compromise your parental authority, but may we see what it was the boys were going to attempt?" Nick said, gesturing vaguely at the vertical rock wall.

Enivel shrugged uncomfortably. "I don't see what good it will do."

"Perhaps we all shall see. Bing, Boom. If you please, and if you *can*, summon your Rock Cats," Beele said.

"Yessir! Yessir!" the boys cried.

"Botta Bing!" yelled Bing, striking his tiny fist against the rock wall.

"Botta Boom!" echoed Boom, doing the same.

The ground rumbled. "Botta Bing! Botta Boom!" they shouted again. Once more the ground shook. Then silence. Boom frowned. "It's always worked before," Bing said.

Kak Zhal's jaw dropped when the shaking stopped, making him look that much more like a gargoyle. Then a twinkle flashed in his eye. "Out of the mouths of babes," he said softly.

"Do you suppose—" Enivel began. "I mean, it's just a legend."

"But legends have a basis in fact." For a moment, Kate regarded the two small boys, and Nick in his funny outfit, and the crumpled figure of Kak Zhal. Then she stared up at the sky blazing with brilliant, brightly colored stars. "Well, Kak Zhal, have you changed your mind about Rock Cats?" she asked.

"Dunno," Kak Zhal answered, "but I'm thinking laughter is the missin' ingredient here. If the stories are true, they gotta know you've a blithe spirit."

"Blithe," Kate repeated. *Who is this fellow?*

"Yup," Kak Zhal affirmed.

"I don't know." Bing sighed. "I guess I don't feel very funny at the moment."

Trudging over to the boys, Kak Zhal pressed his face close to theirs. He blew out his cheeks and crossed his eyes, all the while wiggling his ears.

"Oh, my gosh," Kate said, laughing easily. Even Nick smiled. But the boys beat them all, giggling and chortling. "Botta Bing! Botta Boom!" they cried once more, striking the cliff.

A deep rumbling swelled within the rock. As the ground began to shake, huge cracks opened up in the cliff face and all laughter ceased. Smiles vanished. Nick raised an eyebrow. Two thin cracks described the outline of an ear, then another, then two more. The surface of the rock face crumbled and two broad snouts erupted. Paws protruded at the base of the cliff; the wall ruptured and spread, forced open by two broad chests, and out thundered a pair of enormous felines. They stood over three meters tall at the shoulder and their masks bore the distinctive ears and whiskers of the terrestrial lynx. Bobbed tails twitched on their massive rumps.

The cliff face had been formed from black basalt, giving the Cats a dark and fearsome appearance. They stretched and bellowed. Kate jumped backwards. Kak Zhal and Enivel simply stood frozen in space, like the stone from which the Rock Cats had sprung.

"Don't be afraid. They won't hurt you," Bing said, as he and his brother approached the Cats.

"Bing! Boom!" Enivel's voice was thick with a parent's fear.

"It's quite all right," Nick said. The Cats knelt down so that the brothers could stroke their gravelly cheeks. They growled softly. "It appears that we have secured a means of expediting our journey."

"*We'll* have to take you, though. They'll only listen to me and Boom," Bing said.

"Quite. So it seems we must enlist you boys as drovers. If, that is, your father will permit you to accompany us," Nick said.

"Of course, but ...." Enivel laid his hands on his sons' cheeks. "Why hadn't you ever told us about the Cats?"

"We didn't think you'd believe us," Boom said.

Enivel tousled their hair. "Well, I know what you're doing is very important. To you and to the rest of us at Old Spall." Enivel paused and set his jaw. "Besides, it's the right thing to do."

Kate could only smile. *Well, well, Levine.* "Levine. Jaq. Jaq! Oh, God! Nick! What—"

"Jaq, as I said, has been gone overly long, but—"

"Overly long?" Kate was breathing rapidly and deeply. Her face glowed with perspiration, even in the cold, dry air. "We can't leave without him."

"Kak Zhal!" Nick's voice overwhelmed the vast space they occupied. "Would you be willing to assist?"

Kak Zhal nodded. "I'll find him and we'll join ya later, or sooner. But I'll find him."

"Nick, no," Kate said. "I'll go. I can't lose them both. Not Ur *and* Jaq!" Kate's hands shook terribly. She anchored them on her elbows as the tremors passed briskly through her body.

"Kate," Nick said. "You and Jaq came here for a reason. For Ur."

Kate swept the sweat from her face and wiped her hands on her vest. "Of course, you're right. Yes. Jaq and I have a responsibility …." Kate cleared her throat and stared at the ground.

Nick walked up to Kate and put his arms around her. It felt terribly strange and wonderful. No wonder Jaq loved to spend so much time with the man. No wonder they had trusted him. Kate wanted to lay in Nick's arms forever. She wished to lose herself in them. "Jaq was not meant to be lost here," he whispered. Kate was certain at that precise moment that everything would be all right.

"Masters Bing and Boom," Nick said. "If you please."

The boys touched the creatures lightly on their flanks and they knelt down. Kate and Bing climbed onto the back of one, while Nick and Boom and Enivel mounted the other. To her surprise, Kate found foot and handholds easily, for the rock had been shot through with holes where gas bubbles had been trapped when it had cooled.

"Kak Zhal," Nick said, "when you find him, use your judgment. Take him back to Old Spall if you must. There may not be time to follow us."

"Boom and I can wait here for a while," Enivel said.

"No. If we make good speed to Hades, I don't wish Master Bing to travel back alone," Beele said.

"I'll find him for sure and I'll take him back to Old Spall, if I have to and if he'll go," Kak Zhal said.

"Tell him he must," Kate said. "Tell him I can't lose them both. Kak Zhal, please ...."

Kak Zhal winked, then yawed off toward the talus slope.

◙ ◉ ◙

"Botta Bing!" Bing cried. "Botta Boom," Boom shouted. Each gave his Cat an affectionate rap behind its rocky ear and off they charged around the crater's rim, while Nick set their course.

As the liths canted their bodies toward the valley floor to hold their line, Kate pressed her face hard against her Cat's stony back and tightened her grip. Soon the ride smoothed, and she was able to raise her head. She could distinguish the subtle curvature of the lunar surface on the plains to the east. And on their edge sat the faintest line of light.

"Nick!" Kate shouted above the pounding of the creatures' feet. Nick sat casually, his right hand flexed with an easy hold on the Cat, as if he were gripping a bowling ball. "What's that light on the horizon? Is it the sun?" she asked with a twinge of anxiety.

"No, thankfully, that is not the sun. It's the first intimation of Mir. Earthrise."

Kate felt her throat tighten in anticipation and bit her lip. "How're you doing?" Kate asked Bing, who straddled the creature's great neck, laughing and talking to his Cat all the while.

"The best. This is the best!"

"Good. Then let's make tracks."

"Yes, ma'am!" Joy was written over every square inch of his small body.

"Race ya!" Bing shouted to his brother.

"Beat ya!" Boom said.

"Oh, shit," Kate muttered under her breath. The boys let the Rock Cats have their heads, and there was nothing she could do but hold on tight. As they dashed around the great arc of the crater, the Cats' feet thumped loudly in the soft soil, throwing up bits of rock and sand that stung the cheeks and eyes. Every few tens of meters, boulders of breccia would be strewn about, blocking the way. Up and over them the Rock Cats would soar, occasionally landing on one, pulverizing it in an instant beneath massive paws.

As they descended, a thick blanket of stars whooshed by overhead and they settled into silence. Quite suddenly, Nick shouted to Boom, "We must turn here and make our way down to the valley."

"Yessir," Boom said. Though his voice was calm, his face was flushed and his eyes glassy, whether from wind or dust or the fever of the chase was impossible to tell. Bing gave his Cat a light tap on its neck with his left heel, and they turned and dove in tandem over the edge.

Kate had no time to react and she began to slide down the Cat's side. She saw the massive legs of Bing's beast crushing stone beneath them and saw herself in an instant ground beneath them as well. She thought of Ur and she thought of Jaq, but not in words or images. A hand slipped inside the waist of her pants and tossed her back onto the Rock Cat. Kate felt a surge of adrenaline. "That was a tiny bit too close," she shouted.

"Please pay attention. Feel the Cat. Anticipate it."

"How about a 'heads up'," she snapped.

Nick cleared his throat. "Quite. I'm sorry. Hold on then. This may become uncomfortable."

Lurching down the talus slope, covered with loose and rotten rock, the Cats slowed. Kate thought her fingers would snap from holding on. Everyone clung to their Cat. Everyone, that is, except Nick, seated like a Rajah atop a great pachyderm.

Finally the pitch flattened as they hit the valley floor with a padded whoompf! Its color, a deep ashen gray, contrasted sharply with the lighter bone shade of the talus slope. Kate breathed an audible sigh of relief, but sucked the air right back in as they charged off again at an even greater speed.

Earthrise had retreated behind the massif. Only stars broke the blackness. Nick began shouting directions ever more frequently and, by the sound of his voice, ever more frantically. Then, as they broke onto the open plain, they caught sight of Mir, its leading cusp kissing the horizon. Gibbous, like the moon they had left behind in Idaho, it floated in a black sky. A white tracery of clouds caressed the planet's blue seas and brown continents. Tears welled up in Kate's eyes. "Will Ur be able to come home? Will she want to?" On they rode. And on and on. For hours? Days? Kate wondered.

Suddenly, Nick was shouting. "There! Over there! The Styx. Make for it, boys!" Perhaps a few Klics distant, a shining, sinuous ribbon of silver wound its way across the bone-white expanse of the valley floor.

When they reached the river, some flopped to the ground and others rubbed their arms and legs in an effort to restore circulation. Kate walked stiffly toward the Styx. She stopped and stretched, then regarded the river. Its banks, deeply undercut, made Kate think of the spring creeks back home in Idaho. But the Styx did not feed a lush, green landscape. *Green.* For a moment, she longed for the sight and the scent of green. Here there was only a stinging dry smell, almost burnt.

"Kate, look." Nick tapped her on the shoulder.

"Mmm?" Nick spun her around gently. "Oooh. I hadn't ever known that the moon had mountains that high. I'd always thought of it as all craters and low hills and plains." Looming beyond and above them, in the direction from which they had come, a great lunar range caught the reflected light of Mir. "They look like the Lost Mountains ... a little. But bigger," Kate said.

"Lovely, aren't they?" Nick said. "They are not really much higher than the Lost. But their vertical rise is far greater from this valley floor. And elevations exist on this world that are higher still. Six thousand meters and more. You see how easy it is to allow the charm of this place to completely bewitch you," Nick laughed.

"You're in excellent spirits," Kate said.

"Yes, I suppose I am. Many hours ago, I had not imagined that two children would come to our aid, and with Rock Cats, of all things. I must say I am pleased that I cannot 'see' everything. Surprise is such a marvelous human emotion. And I'm glad I possess some of the human emotions." His smile faded. "I have my mother to thank for that, even if their inclusion in my persona was altogether unintentional. So much of what she has done has had consequences entirely unforeseen by her. And, to be colloquial, it has driven her nuts." Nick smoothed his gloves over his hands.

"But now we have a problem, or at least a decision that we must make. Come." Nick walked to the confluence of two streams that fed the main river lying directly across their path.

Bing and Boom were fussing over their Cats, which lay stretched out on the ground, "purring" and "growling," the sound like rock being crushed to gravel. Their heads turned as Kate walked by, following her with eyes of dull, flat stone. *What goes on behind those eyes?* Whatever it was, the boys were able to reach it.

"What *is* this stuff?" Kate asked, referring to the silvery substance that flowed sluggishly past them. "Looks like mercury. Quicksilver. Oh, and see, there!" Kate pointed excitedly to tiny flecks of luminescent blue. "It's Peevo!" Gripped by a sudden and terrible thirst, Kate knelt and cupped her hands.

"No!"

Kate froze.

"Both of your inferences were correct. The Styx is laced with quicksilver and pseudomonas. The aspect is gorgeous, but I'm afraid, like the Lethe, which fed the mythical Styx, it would feed forgetfulness. But the loss of memory would be complete. And eternal."

"I hadn't realized how thirsty I was," Kate said absently.

"We will all have a good slug of Peevo before we continue. But *that* is the issue in question. Which of the two feeders should we follow? I simply do not know which way to go. My dilemma is no different than before, only we're a bit closer to our goal. Kate, do you have any intuition about the thing?"

Intuition? Turning to face the River Styx, Kate squinted and chewed her lip, searching for some inkling that would help them make the right choice.

"Look, there!" Enivel cried, pointing at the smaller stream that ran northeast.

"What is it?" Kate asked, seeing only the glowing orb of Mir and the silvery, sparkling Styx.

"I don't know. I've never seen anything quite like it," Enivel said.

Not ten meters from where they stood, the Fish erupted through the surface of the stream, flashing rose and purple and brilliant argentine.

"That's her!" Kate cried.

"The fish you saw on the Lost?" Nick asked.

"Yes. But the colors! They're more ... more profound here. Like 'rosy-fingered dawn' and the 'wine-dark sea,'" she whispered.

"Homer?" Nick said.

"Homer. And Jaq." Tears welled in her eyes and Kate forced a tight-lipped smile. "My heart doesn't know which direction to take. Back or forward. Oh, Jaq. Oh, Ur."

"You are Stoics, you and Jaq, are you not? So how does reason instruct you? What would Jaq do?" Nick asked.

Kate gazed directly downstream. "It instructs me in a parent's responsibility."

Rising again, the Fish traced a long, high arc and dove back into the right fork of the Styx, heading northeast across the great valley floor. "I guess that settles that," Kate said, wiping her cheeks with her sleeve.

A great noise erupted behind them. The Rock Cats, despite the attempts of Bing and Boom to settle them, were up and pawing, growling and straining. "If the fish aroused our suspicions, the Cats have confirmed them. I suggest we climb on before they abandon us," Nick said.

As soon as they were mounted, Nick gave the signal. Bing and Boom nudged the Cats, as if they needed urging, and each took an enormous leap, clearing the Styx, and dashed after the fish. Although it was by now hundreds of meters ahead, they could still make it out clearly, as its scales caught the light of Mir, reflecting it like a million mirrors.

Racing as if possessed, they soon passed the promontory that defined the end of one great plain and the beginning of another, wider still. The pace the Rock Cats forced was ferocious, yet the Fish, despite their enormous efforts, managed to maintain its distance.

After crossing countless klics of dry, flat desert, Kate discerned a difference in the landscape. Merely a suggestion at first, gradually a huge bank of vapor swelled before them. Green-gray, dense and sickly, it swirled sluggishly. The

Fish vanished into the murk. The Rock Cats charged straight ahead, but at the first whiff of the fog they tossed their heads, pulling up short and throwing everyone off and onto the ground in a great heap.

Nick scrambled to lift himself off of Enivel. "Is everyone all right? Answer, please, if you can!"

"Yes, yes," Enivel said, struggling to his feet. "But the boys!"

"We're A-OK, Dad."

Kate had had the wind knocked out of her, but the boys' curious turn of phrase focused her attention immediately. "Yes, I'm fine," she answered.

The tiny band was now all on their feet, a bit bruised perhaps, but fit. "Ladies and gentlemen," Nick said, brushing off his boots, "Masters Bing and Boom, may I welcome you to Hell."

◙ ◉ ◙

"I'll do the welcoming here, if you please!" Out of the dense, green vapor stepped a figure. The Rock Cats growled and retreated. "The gates of Hades are my domain."

Kate's eyes flared and she felt a shock course down her spine. The voice belonged to Bildad Proud.

"I would say that is a bit presumptuous," Nick said. "Hades is not mine, and certainly it is not yours to claim. The Lady Tiamat merely suffers our presence here." Nick stared at Bildad coldly.

"Ah, then. I'm afraid you've misunderstood me. Let's just say that I decide who has the privilege of entering here. That responsibility *is* my domain," Bildad said unctuously.

"And what has happened to Charon?" Nick asked.

"He's gone," Bildad said laconically, a thin smile snaking across his lips.

Nick clenched his fists and took a step forward. Bildad retreated a pace, even though the Styx, separating him from Beele, was far wider than a man could jump. But Nick Beele was no man. "Gone where?" Nick asked.

"Gone. The Lady Tiamat, praise her, praise her, just got bored with him," Bildad said, shrugging.

"Bored?" Nick said.

"Yes. I suppose that was it. Although the Lady needs no reasons for what she does."

"Often she has none. But that is beside the point. What did she do with him, man?"

Pressing his hands together and making a supplicant bow, Proud retreated another half pace. "I'm afraid she ate him. Sucked him dry, I suppose." Proud's words made Kate shudder.

"He was a good man," Nick said.

Bildad Proud, having recovered his courage, if not the advantage, stood up straight. "And whatever does goodness have to do with anything? You never will learn, Beelzebub, will you?"

A silence, thicker than the swirling vapor, choked the atmosphere. But Kate was becoming impatient. "All right, so you are the new ferryman. What is it you want?" she asked.

Proud laughed. "If you will pay the toll, you may enter."

"Toll? I'm not dead, Proud," Kate said.

"Not yet," Bildad answered.

"You're damned right about that!" Kate thrust her hands into her pockets in hopes that—*Please!* Her fingers felt a piece of smooth metal. "I'll be goddamned," she said softly.

"I beg your pardon?" Bildad said.

"Will this do?" Kate said, pulling the penny that Jaq had given her from her pocket.

Bildad squinted. "Aaargh!" Bending over, he thrust his hands into the thick muck that swirled about his feet, retrieved a rather wideish plank, and laid it over the Styx from one bank to the other. "You may come," he said.

"What happened to the boat?" Kate asked sarcastically.

Proud smirked. "Times are tough, young woman. Are you coming?"

Halfway through the five meters, Kate glanced down at the green sludge that lapped against the board. For a moment, she felt her nerve falter, then she stared straight ahead and hurriedly reached the bank. "Nick?"

"I'm sorry," Proud said, withdrawing the plank swiftly. "First, I must have his fare. The rules. They're not mine. No, no. I simply enforce them. Don't blame me. No, no. Don't blame *me.*"

"Nick!" Kate said again. Though there was no hint of panic, there was pain in her voice and on her face. Beele held up a finger.

"What about us?" Bing cried.

"You and your father have done more than enough already," Nick shouted over the noise of the river, which had begun to churn more violently.

"But we want to help!" Boom said.

"You might render one additional service. It is, of course, contingent," Nick said. "Enivel, find Kak Zhal and, if he has located Jaq, lead him here."

"He must have the fare, he—" Proud began. Beele's eyes bored directly into Proud's. Bildad Proud averted his gaze and shrank back.

"That's settled," Beele said, turning back to Enivel. "But if the sun is up, return them to Old Spall." Enivel nodded.

A light tremor shook the ground beneath their feet. The Rock Cats growled. The boys moved closer to their father.

"Nick, please, are you coming?" Kate said, more insistently.

"Him? He has no money. Disdains it, from what I know," Proud said.

"I disdain extortion," Nick said. In one enormous stride he leapt across the Styx.

"But you can't—" Bildad began.

"But I have," Nick said.

"You!" Bildad Proud raised an arm and pointed his finger straight at Nicholas Beele. "You take too many liberties. So take care."

"I shall," Beele said. And he and Kate slipped off into the thick mist.

Neither looked back, but they heard him call to Beele. "My name is Proud, but you are possessed of the pride that comes before the fall. You've no time for me now, but you will, you will."

For an instant, Kate wondered which danger was greater, the Lady that lay ahead of them, or the ferryman she hoped they were leaving behind.

◙ ◉ ◙

CHAPTER 12

———

Jaq struggled to his hands and knees and took a few shallow breaths. His lungs felt as if they had sucked in a sackfull of dust and he coughed hard. He ran his tongue over his teeth, then spat out a mouthful of gritty saliva. A sharp pain shot across the side of his head. He shut his eyes tightly and they began to water. Finally, the pain subsided. He must have struck his head on one of the boulders strewn about the bottom of the steep embankment. Jaq looked up and saw a small sliver of sky filled with stars. Rocks overhung the incline, and he decided he must have fallen into a cavern of some sort. "Nice job, Jaq," he said aloud. "Fucking dope." His head still hurt, but not as badly.

He rubbed it gingerly and turned to face a wall of blackness. In moments, his eyes adjusted to the light and black turned to pale, lifeless gray. A void with substance but without texture.

Jaq shuddered. Beele had claimed that Ur was in no immediate danger, so Jaq believed they would not abandon him, and he realized the risk to one of them taking the same sick tumble he had.

"Well, nothing else for it," he said very loudly in an effort to boost his courage, and began to scramble up the slope. Or at least he tried. And tried. But the regolith was too soft, and he simply slipped back down at each attempt.

Jaq brushed a layer of thick talcum off of his trousers. "Fuck me!" Once again, he turned to face the cave recess. He was gripped by a terrible fear that actually made him feel nauseous. As he stared at the gray vapor, he felt as if his identity would simply be smeared across the mist if he were to step forward.

"Get a grip," he said with an edge of anger. He decided to start calling out in hopes that his voice might echo off the cavern walls. At that moment, Jaq thought he heard a cry behind him and was knocked off his feet by a vicious clip below the knees.

Quickly, he sprang to his feet. Another sharp pain shot across his right temple, but it was brief and shallow. Looking down, he saw what appeared to be a sack of oats lying in the soft dirt. The sack stirred, then groaned. "Kak Zhal!" Jaq shouted, grasping his friend by his jacket and hauling him up.

Kak Zhal sputtered and coughed and spat. As he raised his head, his face lit up in a grin. "Ha, ha! Mr. Jaq! I'll be blowed. Knew I'd find you but I didn't expect to find you like this. Darned beautiful out tonight. I kinda got lost in the stars."

"Me, too. And the others?" Jaq asked anxiously.

"Went on ahead. They need to keep ahead of 'sun's up,' you see."

"Damn! I've already tried to climb out of here and I don't think we can make it out without help. And how do they expect to rescue Ur?" Jaq's voice began to rise. "*I'm* the one who has to do it!"

"Wouldn't do much good even if we could climb out," Kak Zhal said. Jaq gave Kak Zhal a puzzled look. "Problem is, they hitched a ride on Rock Cats."

Jaq scrunched up his face. "Huh?"

"Mmmm. This is how it all happened …." And Kak Zhal proceeded to tell Jaq all that had occurred since Nick discovered Bing and Boom.

"Bing and Boom. So, that's what I heard," Jaq said.

"Yup. And so ya see, we'd never catch 'em. So, we'd best make it up and out of here and back to Old Spall before sun's up or we won't be much good to anybody, roasted to a turn."

"Old Spall? Like hell. You can go back. I'm going on. Even if it kills me."

"It will, Mr. Jaq, it will." The two men stared at one another for a long time. Then Kak Zhal's eyes began to dart around. "Maybe goin' on means goin' in and not goin' up."

Jaq squinted into the gray fog, which felt like a huge elastic membrane about to wrap him like a shroud. He exhaled hard to untie the knot in his guts. Something, some*one*, was waiting for him. He could sense its presence. "Okay."

Kak Zhal began to step ahead and into the fog, but Jaq yanked him back. Kak Zhal looked up at him defiantly. "I said I'd guide you and I will."

"Thank you. But I believe we're going to have to trust my instincts here," Jaq said.

"Where you goin'?"

"I don't know, exactly." Jaq smiled at his choice of words. "But this is my reality."

"Same thing Beele said. What's that supposed to mean?" Kak Zhal asked.

"I'm not entirely sure myself, but I think I'm about to find out." He stared at his queer-looking companion for a moment. *Where in hell did I come up with him? Where in Hell, indeed.*

"Your job's done. You found me and you don't need to follow," Jaq said.

Kak Zhal shook his head. "I'm my own man here." With that he expanded his enormous chest, for he could not stretch to make his point. "And I'm *your* man in this fix. What I suffered when Elspeth was taken is little compared to what you must be feeling. I have her back. Your little—what's her name?"

"Ur."

"Queer. And beautiful. The name sounds deep and timeless," Kak Zhal said.

"I didn't know you were a philosopher."

"I'm not. But I'm a father. Even though I *took* Elspeth as my own, I'm her father just the same. And fathers rise to the occasion when there's need." Kak Zhal turned and regarded the steep slope behind them for a moment. "And there's no risin' for us in that direction, so let's move on ahead. I've got your back, Mr. Jaq."

Jaq smiled broadly. "And who better?"

◙ ◉ ◙

They plunged into fog and walked for what seemed like a long time. Seemed, because time had acquired a curiously evanescent quality. There existed a then and a now, but the connection was tenuous.

Jaq bent at the waist and massaged his calves. "Your muscles starting to give out?" Kak Zhal asked.

"No, my legs aren't tired. It's just that it feels like I've been walking, but getting nowhere."

"It's the stoppin' that gets me," Kak Zhal said, spreading his legs to steady himself. "Hoooo …! My brains are swimming like from Peevo. Whooo!" He stood in place shaking his head and smacking it lightly. "Whooo, whoop," he cooed softly.

Jaq swiveled his head in a wide arc, but the gray mist was perfectly invariant. "The geometry here doesn't feel normal. The place seems to lack—extension."

"Heh?"

"I'm sorry. I mean, it feels as if we could take a step and be back in Old Spall, or we could be back in my own world."

Kak Zhal nodded. "I feel it, too. Makes sense though."

"How—"

"You see, the moon's only so big, and there's not the room for all the dead plus all that'll die. Unless Hades is part of this world and not part of it. Kind of like a secret chamber."

"Or kind of like a wormhole. Or a black hole. Not exactly, but kind of," Jaq said.

Kak Zhal shrugged. "Don't know about all that. Place seems *un*holy, if you ask me."

Jaq felt panic grip him. They were truly lost and could not be found again. If he hadn't taken a leak—when was it? —he thought he'd piss himself.

He turned himself slowly about in what he knew was a vain attempt to gain his bearings. Slowly, because he felt terribly fragile at that moment and knew he could not let himself break. Then he felt the atmosphere thinning. Something tickled the back of his brain. He thought he knew the way. "Come on," he said.

Slowly, the gray fog began to evaporate and the place acquired detail. At once, he was gripped by an overwhelming feeling of despair, for he found himself staring at a slice of sky defining a ridgeline at the top of a steep hill. "We've gone in a fucking circle." He grabbed Kak Zhal by the shoulders. "No!" he cried. "Kak Zhal. We have to get out of here!" Jaq ran full speed at the slope and began to claw the soft regolith, all the while churning his legs as hard as he could. But he simply slid back down the slope.

"Now listen," Kak Zhal said as he dragged Jaq to his feet. "We're not gonna die. We can—"

"I don't give a damn about that. I'm probably going to die anyway. But I have to get back to Kate and Nick. I have to save Ur. I'm the only one who can. Don't you see?"

"Sure I do. I see the sky. Look." Kak Zhal pointed at the black slice beneath the cavern roof. "There's no stars at all. Only one place on the moon with a hole in the sky like that. Forget your black hole and your wormhole, this is the hole that counts for us. And it sits right over the source of the Styx!"

◙ ◉ ◙

"Jaq!" A voice, brilliant and precise, cut through the great gray mass behind them. A man sat on a plain stone bench at the base of an amphitheatre. Long, jet-black hair and a closely cropped beard framed high cheekbones and a hooked nose. The face was Asiatic, though not Oriental, the eyes large and round and pale gray.

The rest of the stadium was sparsely occupied, but every time Jaq tried to focus on a figure, it blended back into the brume. He remembered being watched that day on the river from the summits of the Lost Mountains. Involuntarily he shivered, feeling terribly exposed, almost naked.

"I've been waiting for you," the man in the front row said. He wore a white belted tunic, decorated on the sleeves and at the hem with thick stripes of purple. At his side hung a great sword. A large hole, crusted with dried gore, yawned directly above his collarbone.

Jaq swallowed hard. "You must have been waiting a long time," Jaq said. The man laughed as if he were mocking Jaq.

"Why—" Kak Zhal scowled and clenched his fists.

"No," Jaq said, placing his hand on Kak Zhal's chest. "I think I know this fellow. His name is Hector." Kak Zhal regarded Jaq skeptically and stepped back.

"Excellent!" Hector said, smiling broadly and slapping his palms against his thighs. "So, you're on a quest." Jaq nodded. "And what do you hope to find?"

"My wife, Kate, and Nick Beele, to start with," Jaq replied.

"Then you are in the right place," Hector answered. "Though the term 'place' can be somewhat ambiguous here." Hector pursed his lips and his eyes flashed.

"And I've come to rescue my daughter, Ur. But I suspect you know that," Jaq said.

"Then your cause is as noble as mine was not. Rather than die in the dust that day, I should have hacked my miserable brother, Paris, to pieces and tossed them to the Greeks in a sack." Hector's eyes lost their focus and became like a great expanse of gray sky, high and wide and impossibly thin. "I understand loss. There were so many …" Jaq waited patiently for the man to return from his private memories. "So," Hector said at last, "what is it I may do for you?"

"I hadn't thought you could do anything for me. But …." Jaq thought of the boy that had chased him with a knife. "Courage. Can you help me with that?"

"Courage," Hector repeated quietly. Jaq nodded. The man laughed again, but this time it sounded hollow. While his mouth was open, the sound seemed to come at Jaq from every direction. Then his face fell and the smile was replaced by a scowl. "Look!" Hector roared, leaping from his seat. Jaq jumped back, and even Kak Zhal recoiled.

Hector pressed close to Jaq. His complexion was deathly pale. He ran his fingers over deep abrasions that covered one side of his face. "Do these look like the marks of courage to you? I ran from Achilles, and these scars are the price paid for cowardice, when he dragged me through the dirt."

"But you stood your ground and fought. The man couldn't be killed, for Christ's sake." Hector stepped back, regarding Jaq with a look of amusement, and folded his arms. "Well, almost," Jaq said uncomfortably.

"Physical courage," the Trojan said, "is as unpredictable as it is unreliable. It can abandon you, fail you completely. Or it can show itself when fear would be a truer friend and flight the wiser course."

Hector seized Jaq's hand. "Here!" he said, stuffing Jaq's fingers into the black, encrusted hole in his neck. Jaq felt as if ice were running through his veins, up his arm and down into his bowels. Frigid fingers wrapped themselves around his heart. Hector's gaze softened and he withdrew Jaq's hand from his neck.

"But—" Jaq began quietly.

Hector placed a finger on Jaq's lips. "I can't *give* you what you ask. No one can. But I can give you something else that will prove as valuable, if, when the time comes, you find your courage."

Reaching across his chest, Hector withdrew his weapon from his belt. While the hilt and pommels were wrapped in common leather, the blade, perhaps a meter in length, was made of blue-gray iron. He swung the sword above his head, then slashed it delicately across Jaq's collarbone. Jaq winced but did not move from the spot where he stood.

Hector grinned. "A beginning, then." He snapped the fingers of his free hand against the gaping hole in his neck and handed Jaq the sword.

"Beware Trojans bearing gifts," a voice said. A man stepped down and out of the gray fog. Thin but well muscled, he had long red hair tied at the back, and a red beard, close-cropped in the fashion of Hector's. He was smiling and his brown eyes sparkled with sharp intelligence.

◙ ◉ ◙

"Nick, where are we going?" Kate asked.

"To rescue your daughter, of course. That's the point, isn't it?" Nick said.

"But I can't see a damned thing in all this murk." Nick did not reply, but slipped his hand gently into hers and squeezed it firmly.

"Thank you," she said. They walked without speaking for what seemed to her like hours, or maybe days. "Nick," she said at last, "how will we ever succeed without Jaq? I mean, this is *his* world."

"Not entirely. And sometimes help comes from the most unexpected direction."

"Direction? In this place? We could be going in circles for all we know," Kate said.

"Perhaps 'when you least expect it' would be a better turn of phrase," a voice said. Two figures faced them.

"Hello, Kate," one of them said.

"I don't know you," Kate said.

"But we know you." A woman spoke, large-boned and tall, with a massive pile of blond hair spilling over her shoulders. "I am Achilles," she said.

"Achilles? But I thought that … I mean everybody knows that—"

"Another damnable lie by that old, blind bastard. Of course, I'll have to admit that Homer could turn a phrase. But it would never have done to let posterity know that the greatest hero of Greece was a woman. Miserable old hypocrite. Women fed him, dressed him, even wiped his ass when he became too old to know one end from the other. Beh …."

"Then I suppose that your companion is Patroclus," Kate said. At Achilles' side stood a man who was far older, his hair and beard both steel gray, but still remarkably fit. Deep intelligence shone in his eyes, but he did not speak. Patroclus smiled and slipped his hand into Achilles', who squeezed it lightly.

"Now, I have something for you." Reaching into the murk, Achilles withdrew an enormous spear. Over two meters long, its shaft was fashioned from a thick branch. The point was made of metal, though whether it was bronze or iron was impossible to tell. Kate wasn't sure whether she would be able to fit her fingers around the shank, let alone lift the thing. "Take it," Achilles said firmly.

Kate bounced the spear a couple of times in her hand and, much to her surprise, found it manageable and well balanced. "Good," Achilles said, then let loose a colossal cry. "You are a warrior and well matched to your weapon."

"As you are, I trust, my dear," Patroclus said playfully.

Achilles tugged at Patroclus' hair. "Now, Kate, I must ask you a question before I let you take my dart."

"Some dart!" Kate said.

Achilles smiled. "Answer me, Kate. What is your motivation for coming here?"

"Love," she said in a strong voice.

Achilles stepped forward and gave Kate a huge hug. "Then you will prevail. Use the power in that weapon well."

"The power? I—"

"You will know how to use the power when the time comes." Achilles and Patroclus retreated into the fog.

◎ ◉ ◎

"Odysseus?" Jaq said, tentatively.

"The same. Your *boyhood* hero, if I'm not mistaken? Until, that is, you abandoned me in favor of this gloomy fellow."

"Life turned out to be a gloomier event than I had ever imagined as a boy. That's all," Jaq said sourly.

"Well, we're trying to change all of that now, aren't we?" Odysseus' eyes flashed. "What you need is a plan. Do you have one?"

"Well, actually, I haven't, um …."

Odysseus shook his head in disappointment and tsked. "First, you must know your enemy. Tiamat fancies philosophers."

"Fancies them?" Hector cried. "Is that why she has that charming collection in her nest?"

"What collection? What is he talking about?" Jaq asked.

Odysseus waved the questions off. "But she bores easily and you may be able to annoy her. Then challenge her to combat. Remember that she has little regard for anyone's intelligence other than her own, and she can lack creativity. Most importantly, when the moment comes, make her angry. No, furious. Enrage her."

"But why would I want to piss her off? She's the fucking Creatrix!" Jaq said, feeling his fear trying to crawl its way out from under his skin.

"Come on, Jaq!" Odysseus said, clapping a hand on Jaq's shoulder. "I really am beginning to worry about you. You're a Stoic, so you know that emotions are a liability. And it's well known that anger is the worst emotion possible in combat."

"That is correct. As I stated clearly in my essay, 'On Anger'—" a voice droned from higher up in the amphitheatre.

"Please, Seneca, not now!" Odysseus said rather rudely, and the figure that had begun to take shape vanished.

Jaq hung his head and fingered Hector's sword nervously. The Trojan approached and pressed his face close to Jaq's. His breath smelled of cloves and camphor that must have been stuffed into his mouth before he was set ablaze. "I've given you a weapon and he's given you the key to cracking her defenses.

Look. When you fight you must remember to think, even as she forgets. For a split second, surprise may gain you the advantage. Seize it. Attack! And when you fall upon her, hack away. Release, but cautiously, the anger you felt when your child was taken from you. If you control it, you'll win the day."

Closing his eyes, Jaq saw clearly the gaping maw and moist mandibles of Tiamat, and shuddered. Opening them, he spoke to Hector and Odysseus, his voice shaking slightly. "I just hope, when the time comes—" He took a deep breath. "I'm not a pussy about this."

The two warriors looked at one another with puzzled expressions. "I'm sorry. We've spent some time learning your history—" Hector began.

"And your lexicon. But the phrase eludes us. What do cats—" Odysseus began.

Jaq took his thumbs and index fingers and made a wedge. Hector and Odysseus both began to laugh.

"Cuneus," Seneca said solemnly.

"You doubt the courage of a female? Tiamat's hardly timid. And would you care to share this opinion with your wife, who, I believe, is quite close by?" Odysseus said.

"Well, no, I—"

"And," Hector began, pointing to his wound and laughing heartily, "if you still doubt the courage of a woman—"

◙ ◉ ◙

"Jaq!" Kate shouted, and Hector and Odysseus evanesced.

Kate thrust Achilles' spear into Nick's hands and ran to Jaq at full speed. She wrapped her arms around his shoulders and buried her face in his chest. Then she stepped away, still holding on to his arms.

"What are you doing?" Jaq asked.

"Just taking a mental snapshot, in case I lose you again in this place."

"If you lose him again, I'll find him," Kak Zhal said.

"Thank you, Kak Zhal," Kate said, stooping and planting a light kiss on his forehead. Kak Zhal scrunched up his face and turned bright red. "But how did the two of you get here so fast?"

"This place lacks extension," Kak Zhal said with an emphatic nod of the head.

Nick cleared his throat. "Indeed."

Jaq stifled a smile.

Kate's eyes flared. "Where'd you get *that*," she asked, pointing to Jaq's sword.

"It's, um, Hector's. He gave it to me."

"Hector? Oh, Jaq," Kate said, placing her hands on her hips.

Nick handed Kate her weapon.

"My sword? Where in Hell did you get that?" Jaq asked.

Kate lifted her chin and smiled, almost smugly, Jaq thought. "From Achilles. *She* gave it to me."

"Achilles? Jesus," Jaq swore softly. "A woman."

"Yeah. And what's so surprising about that?" Kate asked. "After all, it's turned out that God's a woman too." Kate smiled sweetly. "What's wrong? Starting to feel overmatched?"

"God?" Jaq mumbled. He slipped Hector's sword into his belt. "May I see the spear?" he asked brusquely.

"Of course. It's useless to anyone but me."

"Right," Jaq said.

Kate lifted an eyebrow and thrust it into Jaq's hands. His arm buckled and the weapon collapsed against his shoulder, knocking him backward. Wrapping his own hand around the shaft turned out to be nearly impossible. "I'll say this thing is useless. It might make a good doorstop. Or a crowbar."

"Let me help," Kate needled. She snatched the spear from Jaq's hand, then bounced it a few times in her own.

"All right, kids," Nick said, clapping his hands, "out of the sandbox."

"I'm sorry, Nick," Kate said. "I guess I was feeling just a bit …."

"Like a man," Jaq said, smiling.

"We've work to do," Nick said. "Jaq, we're fortunate you found us. Kate and I are no longer required to improvise."

Understanding somehow what was required of him, Jaq nodded and turned his senses without. A sound attracted his attention. Light and breathy and sweet, it behaved like a beacon. "This way," he said.

◎ ◉ ◎

Suddenly, the sound collapsed to a point. Leaning against a marble column, a ruin of some kind with the capital broken off, was a figure. Short and of medium build, with a broad forehead and a pair of large, mischievous eyes set wide, he wore black breeches and a waistcoat to match. He was playing a silver piccolo and the music was unmistakable. "Mozart!" Jaq said.

"Wolfgang Amadeus at your service," he replied with a broad smile, stepping away from the pillar and making a deep bow. "I am afraid, sir," he said, "you have me at a disadvantage."

"My name is Jaq."

"Ahh … Jaq. Of course. Jaq and Kate …."

"Yes, um, this is really an honor; however, we must be going." But Mozart wasn't listening. He was staring off into the brume.

"And Ur," Mozart whispered, his attention returning. Jaq stared at the silver flute Mozart was holding. *Perhaps ….* "Herr Jaq," Mozart continued, "I must admit I'm flattered that you recognized me but how—"

"The tune. Unmistakable," Jaq said.

"But that's impossible. It's new."

"Well, then, I guess I'd call it your 'sound,'" Jaq said.

"My sound. I like that." Mozart pursed his lips and nodded approvingly. "And I'm glad you like *it* as well. Certainly, music is of more value to the soul than anything you'd get from that depressing Hector or that slimy fellow Odysseus." Mozart shuddered at the mention of the Ithacan's name.

"I don't know about that, sir," Kak Zhal said. Mozart turned and regarded him with both surprise and skepticism. "What I mean is, they were brave fellows. They were soldiers."

"Cut-throats, really, if I may say so. They killed people. That's what *they* did. Little use of that skill here. Everyone's already dead. Hoo! Hoo!" Mozart doubled over in a fit of laughter. Jaq had to stifle a laugh himself.

Mozart straightened up, patting his forehead with a small white handkerchief. "Ah, well, me. Ahem. Um, Herr …?" he said, addressing Kak Zhal.

"Kak Zhal, your honor."

"Yes, well, Herr Kak Zhal, do you play the flute?"

"Used to. Ones made of little Lamikin bones."

"Good." Mozart handed him his instrument, which Kak Zhal accepted with great care. "Please receive this little piccolo as my gift."

"But it's been an awful long time since I played, sir. When I was a kid. If anybody'd believe I ever was one."

"What I believe is that you still have the heart of a child," Mozart said.

"That's good?" Kak Zhal asked.

"Very good. Now, I'm going to whistle a tune of mine." Mozart pursed his lips again and blew softly. Jaq clenched his fist around the hilt of Hector's sword. "Do you like it?" Mozart asked.

"Beautiful. What's it called?"

"Tamino's tune!" Jaq blurted out. Mozart smiled broadly.

"Eh? Termeeno. Hmm."

"Can you play it?" Mozart asked.

"I'll try." Out of the instrument came the loveliest music Jaq thought he had ever heard.

"You have a natural gift," Mozart said.

Kak Zhal stopped playing. "No, sir, it's not my gift, it's *your* gift that makes all the difference. Ha! Ha!" Mozart and Kak Zhal began giggling.

"Two blithe spirits," Kate said quietly. Jaq gave her a puzzled look. "Later," she said.

"Now," Mozart said, "you are to play that tune whenever you feel that you or anyone else in your band …. Band! Hoo, hoo!" The two of them began laughing again until tears were streaming down their cheeks. "Ah, me …." Mozart said at last. "Well, then, when you or any one of your party is in distress which has no other remedy, you are to play that tune."

Kak Zhal nodded emphatically. "Sir?" he asked. "Does the whistle play anything else?"

"Of course. Anything you like. Feel free to improvise. But remember, in times of great distress…."

"Yes, sir. Termeeno's tune."

Mozart grinned and vanished behind the column.

◙ ◉ ◙

"Let's go," Jaq said. He felt as if he was getting the hang of his role. Before he had taken more than a couple of steps, the mist began to thin and they found themselves stepping into a tunnel.

Jaq ran his hands over the gray basalt walls, which reflected weakly the low light of the fog behind them. No more than a few dozen paces distant, the light disappeared altogether, the rock sucking it up like a malevolent sponge. Overhead, the ceiling hung stolid and sinister.

Shuffling along silently, afraid of being tripped up by an unseen obstacle, they pressed on. Their feet made little slaps and slow slurps on the wet stone floor. Within minutes, blackness swallowed them up.

As a faint, unpleasant odor began to fill the passageway, Jaq noticed, up ahead, a section of the wall that pulsed with a pale greenish light. Rounding a sharp corner, they entered an enormous cavern. Kak Zhal coughed and Kate gagged on an odor so foul and thick, it seemed as if it could be squeezed. All over the walls, blobs of matter glowed a sickly green, some resting on rock ledges, others dripping down and off the stone in sluggish, disorganized streams of putrefaction.

Vaulted ceilings soared hundreds of meters upward, only to meet others soaring hundreds higher still. Frozen intrusions from the guts of the moon, rock fragments and clusters of boulders from its hot, early history, were strewn about. Shiny spheres, glistening green-black like obsidian gall bladders, stuck to the walls or lay on the floor. Shards were strewn about, their facets flashing like chartreuse diamonds.

"Gaw," Kak Zhal gurgled. "Now who'd ever light their dacha with 'dirty floors'?"

Nick sighed. "Mother never did have a flair for decorating."

Mother? We're close, thought Jaq.

"I don't know," Kate said, taking deep breaths through her mouth. "It stinks, but it's beautiful."

Beauty and horror. Jaq felt his side ache. "We're close," Jaq said. Nick merely shot him a casual glance. *This is my game.* Fear and anger checked one another in perfect equipoise. Fear and anger, those two ancient monsters, remnants of an earlier epoch when guts quivered like jelly, wrapped in a shiny, smooth, hard case of chitin. Jaq swallowed hard.

"Kate? What was it you just said?" Jaq asked.

"I said that this place is beautiful, even though it stinks."

"Tradeoffs," Jaq said.

"What?"

"C'mon, you're the economist. There ain't no such thing as a free lunch." So what *would* the cost be, Jaq wondered? He regarded his friends, the old and the new, Nick and Kak Zhal. He looked at his love, Kate. The hole in his side was on fire. He felt a steel curtain falling inside, the bolts fastening it in place. He felt the fire contained, his emotions damped.

Carefully, they negotiated boulders the size of Rock Cats. Littered haphazardly about the immense cavern were smaller lumps of crystalline rock and individual facets broken off from the mother stones, all glittering green against the gray basalt of the cave floor.

Craning his neck, Jaq peered beyond the steep, stepped rock walls, above the levels where the sickly green light glowed weakly. All that hung above their heads was a soaring infinity, immense and black and deathly still. Then something caught his eye. At a distance lay a large pile of the green crystals, a mat spilling from behind a gigantic boulder, which was tens of meters high. The rock was hiding something. *Maybe* …. "Over there," was all Jaq said, pointing to the massive monolith.

They were off at a sprint. Losing her footing on some loose gravel, Kate stumbled, but Nick checked her fall. 'Thanks', her eyes said, as he pulled her erect. Kak Zhal, rolling from side to side in choppy bursts, kept pace with the pack. Jaq's side burned, but the pain was exquisite.

Beyond the boulder, Jaq pulled up. Another immense crystal carpet stretched before them, verdant and shining. On the far side, perhaps a hundred meters distant, was a breach in the wall that shone like a small furnace. Soft, orange-white light spilled over the green crystals in front of it, creating a shin-deep, lime-orange glow that covered the entire field of facets, defending the access.

"Is it my imagination, or is it getting warmer?" Kate asked, wiping a thin line of perspiration from her upper lip.

"This is it," Jaq said. The hole in his side felt as if it were being drawn, sucked, toward the opening that lay at the opposite end of the field of gems.

"Bravo," Nick said. Jaq's face flushed. "But take care. Pride can be as destructive to reason as anger. Get a grip."

Jaq nodded. He understood, but could not feel, what it was that Nick was telling him. Across and over the green and orange glow, he saw only one thing. Their objective. His objective. Only a hundred meters away, across a very pretty field of stones.

"I'll take the van," Jaq said. As he took his first step, a rattling sound, like marbles being poured from a sack, stopped him. Click, click. Two at a time at first, the crystals directly in front of him began to move. Then with greater speed, the facets organized themselves into coherent forms, spheres and cylinders, short, long, thin and thick. Click, click, click. At last, and with a crash, the pieces slammed together, and directly across their path stood a stone figure almost three meters tall.

The face had no distinct features, save three shallow depressions. Eyes, blank and turned inward, and a mouth, howling from some unknown pain. The creature bent and passed its hand over the cave floor, brushing aside the crystals. Like a magnet, it drew tiny grains out of the hard sand, ground from mountains of basalt, and picked up a dull gray sword.

Everyone stood perfectly still. Then Jaq advanced one tiny, tentative step and a soft moan was heard. The sound filled the space around them and then soared upward, vanishing within the black limitless vault above their heads.

"I'll be blowed," Kak Zhal whispered. "A Sand Banshee. And one o' the Praetorian Guard at that."

Without taking his eyes off of the Banshee for even a moment, Jaq spoke over his left shoulder to Kak Zhal. "Have you fought them?"

"Yep. Not often, but some."

"Well?" Jaq said.

"Mmm," Kak Zhal said, scratching his large, potato-shaped nose.

"Come on!"

"Right. Well, the bodies are softish, but the ones I had a scrap with were made o' dirt, not diamantees like this one. Either way, their weapons're hard. They can hurt ya bad. Old Krenk took a mace on the noggin when he was young, that's why everyone thinks he's so ornery."

"Kak Zhal. Please!"

"Right. Well, they're clumsy. Course, this one, I don't know. But I'll back you up, so let's have at him."

Jaq simply nodded and stepped onto the crystal mat. All the while, the Banshee had stood perfectly still, but as soon as Jaq's foot touched the stones, it began to wail. Now the sound was louder and more menacing. It raised the hairs on Jaq's neck, but strangely, what he felt was exhilaration, not fear. Adrenaline, he reasoned. Reason. *Remember to think.*

Lunging at the Banshee with a wild yell, Jaq grabbed the hilt of Hector's sword with both hands and slashed upward at its head. The creature was anything but clumsy and parried Jaq's move. The clank of metal against stone rang out, showering them in a spray of sparks. Jaq slashed at the banshee's midsection but once again, his blow was blocked.

The crystal Banshee lunged and began to hammer Jaq. He could feel the shock of the Banshee's blows traveling up his arm in sickening waves. He fell, but quickly raised himself on one knee, holding Hector's sword in front of his face.

Then he was almost knocked over again, but by Kak Zhal, who brushed past him as he dove for the creature's leg. Wrapping his massive arms about a crystal limb, he squeezed his eyes shut and strained to snap it off. The silicant gave Kak Zhal a whack with its forearm that sent him sprawling. Jaq thought that, just maybe, he had heard a crack.

Gripping his sword with both hands, Jaq charged the Banshee, meaning to hack away at its damaged limb, but the lith proved too quick and knocked the weapon from his hand and onto the floor. *This is it.* "I love you, Kate!"

"Jaq! No!" Kate shouted and ran directly at the Banshee, holding Achilles' spear aloft.

"Kate!" Nick cried. "Slash it!" But Kate wasn't listening.

Teeth bared, holding the spear with both hands like a harpoon, Kate drove the point directly at the place that would have been the creature's heart. If it had had one. But the Banshee was too quick and sidestepped Kate's thrust. With a hideous shriek, the silicant swung its sword arm and the blade barely missed severing her head as she was knocked over by Kak Zhal.

Jaq gasped. Then out of the corner of his eye, he saw Nick raise his hands, then lower them back down. But he didn't stop to think as he sprang up and raced to retrieve his sword.

Kate lay sprawled on the ground and the Banshee advanced for the kill. But Kak Zhal, with uncanny speed, dove for its damaged limb. A loud crack echoed throughout the chamber. With one final twist and a noisy grunt, Kak Zhal snapped the Banshee's leg from its torso. It toppled, dropping its weapon. As it fell, Jaq, with one wild stroke, slashed through its midsection. Kak Zhal had been right. Its body *was* softer than its blade. And as the Banshee collapsed onto the floor, a hollow, baleful, almost sad moan went up. Stranger still, its body crumbled into facets and fragments.

"Ashes to ashes," Jaq whispered. He blinked. *Kate!* "Kate!" he cried, running to her. Kak Zhal was helping her to her feet. Jaq hugged her close.

"Almost," Kate said hoarsely. She kissed Jaq on the cheek and gently pushed him away. "But almost only counts in horseshoes."

"Eh?" Kak Zhal said.

Kate slipped her hand into Jaq's and began to laugh. "Oh, it's just another expression. But what I'd really like to express is my thanks. To you."

"Express an expression. That's a good one!" Kak Zhal said.

"And so are you," Kate said, taking one of Kak Zhal's hands in hers. He blushed, his face looking like a ripe mango.

Jaq laughed. "That's right; we couldn't have done it without you. We couldn't have done it without one another." He paused, grinning broadly, then added, "But we did *do* it!"

"Yes, you did indeed *do* it," Nick said. They had almost forgotten that he was there.

Jaq did not like the sarcasm in Nick's tone. "No thanks to you," he said sharply.

"I'm sorry. I'm afraid my powers are useless here."

"I don't know. Seems like they're pretty much useless, period," Jaq said sourly. "So far, from what I've seen, they're only good for lighting cigars."

"And frightening children," Kate said.

"My powers are no more than parlor tricks. Like making the lame walk and blind men see. But I explained all of that to you a few days ago, Jaq. You *do* remember, don't you?"

Nick was continuing to hide something, Jaq was certain of that. But when he studied his friend, he saw only empathy and kindness. And pain. Somewhere, Jaq knew he had seen that look before. "As long as our problems don't get any bigger than the one we just faced, I guess it won't matter if you simply hang around."

"Interesting turn of phrase, my dear Jaq. But I'm afraid they've grown bigger still," Beele said.

"Beg your pardon?" Kate said, chuckling. "I mean, we've more or less dispatched Tiamat's Praetorian Guard."

"Less, I'd say." Nick twirled his finger in the air, indicating that they all turn toward the tunnel entrance. Amidst a rising clatter, like a thousand locusts swarming, the field of facets was rising up into an army of silicant soldiers, all like the first.

"Crikey," Kak Zhal said softly.

Slowly, as if they knew they had time, the Guard advanced with a wailing like the sound from a thousand graves, opened at the end of the world.

"My spear!" Kate cried.

"Useless anyway," Jaq said, tightening his grip on Hector's sword while he backed away.

"That sword of yours won't do much good either against that gang, if they've all as much sand as the first one had," Kak Zhal said.

"I suggest we back away slowly," Nick said. "But we may have to retreat into the first tunnel."

"No!" Kate shouted. "I'm not going back. If I fucking die here, I'm not going back!"

"If *we* die here," Jaq said. "Nick, maybe you can't guide and maybe you can't fight, but you *did* tell us you were along as an adviser. So advise, man."

"Perhaps ...." Nick paused. "Kak Zhal?"

"Eh?" Kak Zhal's face brightened with the spark of an idea. "Of course. When we're in distress and nothing else will do is what that Mo-zart fella said." Kak Zhal withdrew the small silver flute from the pocket of his Lamikin vest. "Now let's see. If I can just remember that Termeeno's tune." Jaq whistled a few bars and Kak Zhal began to blow. Out of the instrument floated a high, insinuating, almost painfully sweet sound. At once, the Guard halted. Sword arms dropped and as Kak Zhal began to move forward, the Banshees parted, opening a path leading directly to the breach in the basalt wall.

"My spear! There it is!" Kate cried. It lay only a few meters off their path, but behind a mass of Banshees.

Kate made a move for it, but Jaq grabbed her arm. "Leave it."

"But she gave it to me for a reason," Kate said curtly.

"It won't do us much good if you're not around to toss it," Jaq said. Kate glanced at the weapon, then brushed Jaq's hand from her arm and kept walking toward the orange light.

As they passed rank after rank of stone soldiers, their shins sliced through a lime-orange glow. Occasional wails wove around the melody, and all about them was the percussive sound of crystals clicking as the Guard disintegrated. Kak Zhal kept playing, as they stepped across the threshold.

◙ ☉ ◙

CHAPTER 13

"Hello, Mother," Beele said. "I should think you'd be paying more attention to your defenses. They struck me as rather anemic." Kak Zhal stopped blowing and lowered his flute slowly to his side. Over in the corner of the cave, two figures faced one another, engaged, apparently, in deep but muted conversation. One was a small girl with a thick head of light auburn hair. The other was a spider, a gargantuan creature, at least three meters tall.

"U-u-u-ur!" Kate screamed, shattering the stillness, as she ran toward her daughter.

Tiamat tensed ever so slightly and flexed her limbs, then rushed at Kate, her long, black, horny legs scraping and clicking unpleasantly along the rock floor. Kate, her eyes focused only on Ur, slammed into the hairy tarsus of Tiamat's left foreleg. The impact sent her tumbling.

"Kate!" Jaq cried. He could feel rivulets of cold sweat trickling down his back and between his shoulder blades. As he made a move toward her, Nick checked him.

"Wait," he said, placing his hand on Jaq's shoulder.

"But, Nick, she's—"

"Please. I know my mother."

Kate held her head for a few seconds, then struggled to her hands and knees. She looked up and froze. A pair of horny fangs moved back and forth in front of a black, wet mouth, guarded by the gently quivering labial plate and the maxillae. Two sets of eyes sat on fleshy stalks, staring back at Kate. She began to crawl backward. Slowly.

"Do you make a habit of storming into someone's habitat without so much as the briefest exchange of courtesies?" the spider hissed.

Kate shifted position in an attempt to rise. "I—"

"I don't recall giving you permission to stand in my presence!"

"I, I'm sorry, I—"

"Silence! Neither do I recall giving you permission to speak. Now. Who are you?"

"I, I'm Kate. I'm called Kate."

"I didn't ask what you are called. I asked you a simple, direct question. *Who* are you?"

"I'm the girl's mother. I'm Ur's mother."

"You are confident in your answer. But then, females are, for the most part. Unlike males. Always in doubt. Nothing but obnoxious gene machines." The spider paused, sounding as if it had sighed. Kate swallowed hard. "You may get up." Cautiously, Kate rose to her feet. "So tell me, why are you here?"

"I believe I've told you," Kate said. The spider's eyestalks waved about, as if she were puzzled. "I'm her mother. I've come to take Ur home."

"*I* am her mother. I am the mother of us all. The child stays with me," the spider said. "Besides, I'm beginning to find you annoying." With that, Tiamat stretched her hairy legs, raising her horny, bloated torso another full meter off the floor, as if she were poised to strike. "And tiresome. And, I am hungry." Tiamat's fangs began to move excitedly in front of her glistening maw.

"Mother!" Nick cried, but Tiamat paid him no heed. Jaq tried to speak, but the words were locked in his throat.

Then, a high, strong voice was heard. "Stop! Stop it right now," Ur said.

Tiamat froze. Slowly, slowly the spider relaxed.

"Let her go."

Tiamat retreated from Kate, who began to move toward Ur. As she did, the spider shot out one of her palpi, blocking Kate's path.

"I think you'd better return to your friends," Ur said.

Kate began to protest. "Please," Ur said. Kate stood still for a moment, sweating profusely, her mouth open, her palms turned upward. "Please," Ur said again. Kate made her way carefully around the spider's outstretched foreleg and back to the cave entrance.

Jaq grabbed her and hugged her close. She was shaking terribly, but Jaq was not sure whether it was from fear or frustration.

"Well, Mother," Nick said, "since when did you get into the habit of taking orders from children?"

Tiamat faced Beele. "I do not take orders from children."

"Ah, but this child is different, isn't she, Mother?"

"Different? No, of course not."

"Then tell me, why has she been with you so very long? Nearly two years, Mother."

"Two years?" Tiamat shifted her position. Her legs made a nasty scratching sound on the surface of the cave floor. "What are two years to me? I've lived an eternity!"

"Perhaps nothing. But two years are a great deal of time for mortals. I'll ask you again, why have you kept her so long?"

For a moment, Tiamat maintained a reflective silence. Then she spoke. "Because she is not like the others. She is not afraid of me."

"Like the others. They were *all* afraid. Why wouldn't they be? Look at you. So you sent *them* back. Tell me, Mother. Is she giving you the answer you are looking for?"

"And what would be the question?" Tiamat hissed softly.

"Come, Mother." Beele smoothed his gloves. "'What is love?', of course. You created this universe, but you didn't know how it would unfold, what surprises it would contain. You observed love, but couldn't understand it, couldn't *feel* it. So you created me as the focus of all fears, then as an object of loathing. You thought that humans, the species *of* love, would turn to you, would adore you. But it didn't happen, did it, Mother? They'd forgotten you, so you—"

"Stop," Tiamat said.

Beele was silent. His face throbbed a deep purple. Jaq thought he saw tears well up in his friend's eyes.

It was time. Jaq stepped forward. He had a hunch. "You sent the others back, but you can't send Ur back, can you, because you killed her. Because once you involve yourself, outcomes become unpredictable." Tiamat did not speak a word in reply. Jaq thought that he might be onto something. "Well, we're taking her. *I'm* taking her," he said.

"What are these, these males you've brought with you?" Tiamat asked, turning away from Jaq and addressing Nick.

"Friends," Nick said.

"Mmm. Friends?" Tiamat waved a leg lazily in Kak Zhal's direction. "The little one. What is it called?"

Kak Zhal removed his hat. "I'm called Kak Zhal, ma'am."

"How fitting," Tiamat rasped. "Russian can capture the essence of a thing so succinctly. You are 'a pity.'" Kak Zhal bit his lip.

"You created him, Mother," Nick said coldly. "You created everything. You said so yourself."

"We all make mistakes," Tiamat said.

"Stop it," Ur said again, addressing Tiamat. "That's not nice." Tiamat skittered about to look at the child and then quickly turned back to face Jaq.

"What are *you*? The father, I suppose," Tiamat said.

"Don't you know? I thought you were omniscient," Jaq said.

"Don't be insolent."

"That wasn't my intention," Jaq lied. *Well, now we've all managed to piss her off.* "But the villagers at Old Spall said that you hold the world together. Berkeley said so too, for that matter."

"Berkeley was correct. So are the villagers," Tiamat said.

"Playing God now, Mother?" Nick said dryly.

"More than you think, my dear boy. But tell me," Tiamat said, addressing Jaq once again, "do you admire Berkeley?"

"Not especially," Jaq said. "Not until now. Not until I found out that he may have been right."

"Are you, then, a philosopher, too?"

Jaq shrugged. But his gesture merely feigned indifference, for he was trying very hard to maintain his composure. While he spoke, he kept looking at Ur. Bright auburn hair framed pure white skin. While she had his own deep-set eyes, she had her mother's broad nose. Wherever, Jaq wondered, had she gotten her thick, full lips? Like Kate's, her legs and arms were long, her hands thin and delicate.

She wore a simple gray frock that hung loosely about her body and stopped below her knees. Looking much taller than a three year old, and with more mature facial features, she had sounded older still when she had spoken. She breathed with the same raspy sound that they had never quite gotten used to. And it appeared as if she still hadn't learned to smile.

All the while, as he spoke to Tiamat, his side burned with white-hot fire. Still, he knew that he must maintain his control. He gave the bolts of his steel curtain a half turn.

"So, philosopher," Tiamat was saying, "I must tell you that I find your kind insufferable. Perhaps I will place you in my collection."

"Collection?" Jaq said.

Slowly lifting a palpus, Tiamat indicated a spot up and behind her. Until now, Jaq had paid no attention to the surroundings. He took the opportunity to observe, to gain, perhaps, some small advantage. The room was sculpted from rock that ranged in color from tan to ochre. While the grotto was not overly large, the ceiling reached fifteen or twenty meters in height and covered the room with a graceful, if irregular, arch. Behind Tiamat and Ur, a tiny silvery stream spilled from the cave wall, dancing over rocks and ledges until, at last, it collected in a small pool.

Jaq focused once again on Tiamat. She was directing his attention to a mass of webs above the source of the stream. And in the middle of each web was an object that looked as if it might once have been a man. Except now, they all hung desiccated and motionless. Jaq's mouth went dry. "Berkeley?" he asked with some difficulty.

"I did not admire him much either, despite his surprising genius. And what do you fancy, philosopher?"

"How we come to know things."

"Which is?"

Careful! "We can't experience reality directly. We simply organize it with our—"

"No! You see reality through *my* eyes. *I* support it. Without me, without my consciousness, you are blind!" she screeched.

Jaq thought she was going to eat him. *Now I've really pissed her off.* He thought he might not be able to peel his tongue off the roof of his mouth. "I understand that now."

"Splendid! So did they," Tiamat said, sweeping a horny leg across her grisly morgue. "You will fit in nicely with the rest of the old windbags."

"And Charon?" Nick asked sourly.

"He was boring me," Tiamat said.

"And Bildad—"

"Does not. Times change. *Things* change. But enough. Philosopher, what are *you* doing here?"

"I'm here for the same reason as Kate. For my daughter. I'm here to take her home," Jaq answered.

"Because he loves his daughter," Nick said in a loud voice. "Which is something you couldn't possibly comprehend." Tiamat was silent. "So I was right, wasn't I, Mother? The one thing you lack is love. Or a capacity for it."

"Sh-h-ut up," Tiamat hissed, with an especially wicked edge in her tone.

"But isn't that what we've been talking about, between ourselves, all of this time?" Ur asked. Tiamat regarded Ur again and, again, did not answer her, but turned back to Jaq instead.

"I find your answer honest enough, philosopher. So, how then do you propose to take Ur from me? By asking? I don't think so. By debating?" Tiamat glanced at her 'collection'. "I think you'd lose the argument, as did your precious Kant."

Tiamat's words surfed on top of a hint of laughter. She was toying with Jaq and he knew it. What better time, he thought, to press what small advantage he possessed. If she involved herself, she couldn't control outcomes. Not completely. That gave him a chance.

Jaq cleared his throat and took a step forward. Although he felt silly about being overly formal, he also *knew* that it was the proper thing to do. "I propose single combat," he said. "You against me. Winner takes all. Or I should say, winner takes Ur."

Tiamat hissed, but it sounded mocking to Jaq rather than threatening. "How could you possibly expect to defeat me?"

"It is not without precedent, Mother."

Tiamat's eye swiveled in Beele's direction and quivered. "Do you really think so?"

She turned her attention back to Jaq. He fingered the pommel of Hector's sword rather obviously. *Come on.* "Mm—hmm. I see you have that depressing fellow Hector's weapon. Are you a friend of his?"

"An admirer."

"Oh, dear." Tiamat shuddered in apparent disgust. "Then I should imagine Hector's final *Aristeia* is what you have in mind. It turned out badly for him, as it will for you."

"We'll see," Jaq said.

"Oh, indeed we shall!" Tiamat cried.

A flash of light blinded Jaq. He lowered his face, shielding his eyes with his forearm. When the pain in his skull subsided, he let his arm fall, only to find that he had been staring at the sun. It shone down upon a great desert that stretched flat and white to the horizon, except for one feature, a spire of dark rock, thirty meters high and ten meters wide. In the distance, he saw a human figure, very tiny at first, then growing larger and larger, running toward him. Fifty paces from where he stood, it stopped. It must have been eight feet tall.

"Achilles," Jaq whispered. Achilles, *in materia* and personified, the armor exquisite and faithful in its detail and beauty. "The helmet, set massive upon her head and crested with horse hair, shone like a star," Jaq recited almost reverently. The emotion surprised him.

"Well spoken, philosopher. Are you a poet, then, as well?"

"The verses aren't mine."

"No. But their words hold your fate, even as they recorded Hector's."

"Where's the true Achilles, then?" Jaq asked.

"Blowing old Patroclus, I'd expect. It's what he enjoys, and what she fancies. You'll be joining them soon."

Across her shoulders slung the sword with nails of silver, a bronze sword. The verses insinuated themselves into Jaq's consciousness. *Bronze!* "We'll see," Jaq said. He could feel something that he vaguely identified as courage filling him. Jaq flexed his fingers around the haft of Hector's weapon.

"We *shall* see, and so will they," Tiamat replied, pointing to a place up and behind Jaq.

A long range of bare mountains soared above them, defining the limit of the great wasteland. High atop a ridge, like one of the parapets of Ilium, stood four figures. Not Priam and Hector's family, but Jaq's own, Kate and Ur, and his friends, Nicholas Beele and Kak Zhal. Had he experienced a vision that day on the Lost, or was it a premonition? An electric shock coursed down his spine. Jaq faced Tiamat. The smell of flint and dry burnt dust stung his nostrils. "Enough talk," he said.

"As you wish." Tiamat raised her spear.

"Wait," Jaq said, realizing he had forgotten something. "My spear. Shouldn't I have a spear as well?"

"Poetic license," she said, in a wicked, grinding tone.

Jaq shrugged. "Perhaps it makes no difference." He ran his hand down the iron blade of Hector's sword. "Your weapon's a fake. It's not the spear of Peleus, Achilles' father."

"But it's just as sharp." With those words, Tiamat let out a cry that made the mountains shake. Pounding the dust of the desert plain with her massive legs, stride after stride cutting the distance between them, Tiamat bore down on Jaq. He looked behind him and up at the mountains, pasted against a white, hot sky. At that moment, all he could see was Ur. The ground shook. Jaq turned toward his adversary. Testing the measures of fear and anger within him in the balance of reason, with Tiamat no more than ten meters distant, Jaq made his decision. He ran.

Once, twice, three times they circled the great monolith, as Hector had circled a wind-blown fig tree on the plains of Troy. Jaq thought his lungs would burst and his mouth tasted of salt and dust. His down vest was drenched. Four times they circled the rock. All the while Tiamat bellowed a brain-curdling battle cry. When he thought he could run no longer, he bore down and kept his pace.

At last, five times! History was now different in its details. Foil her expectations, that was his hope. He stopped, his lungs on fire. Tiamat checked up as well. Looking her full in the face, Jaq saw that bully of his childhood standing over him with a simple jackknife. The image dissolved. He raised Hector's sword and ground his boots into the lunar dust.

"So, you've finally decided to stand and make a fight of it, philosopher? I thought I was going to have to skewer you in the back." Tiamat hefted her spear. "I don't believe I'll need *two* tosses to take you down."

Jaq was facing the mountain range now, and he could see Kate and Ur staring down. Then all he could see was a delivery room bathed in harsh white light, the doctor lifting the child's dead and bloody body from Kate's belly. Rage ignited the fire in his side, but blinded him as well. He didn't see Tiamat loose her weapon, but at the last instant he heard it, whistling through the dead, parched air, and he moved-just enough to avoid its tearing through his neck. It landed harmlessly behind him.

"Damn," Tiamat swore loudly. "Come, spear!" Tiamat barked in command. Just as Athena had returned Achilles' spear after her first cast, Tiamat's levitated off the lunar sand and shot back in a shallow arc.

Steady. As the spear flashed over Jaq's shoulder, he leapt from a crouch and, slashing upward, severed the shaft in two. The pieces fell harmlessly to the ground. Disbelief marked the features of Tiamat's face. Again Jaq glanced at his wife, daughter and friends huddled high up on the mountain ridge. The image flickered through Jaq's mind once again, the image that had haunted him for two years, of Ur's bloody body, her shoulders slumped, her chin doubled and resting in death on her tiny chest. The only rest she would know for seven months, once the doctor had revived her.

Tiamat stood facing him, blinking in disbelief. *She* who had created everything. *She* who held the world together. *She* who had taken Ur's life and, with it, all of its possibilities. That was the cruelest theft of all. "Fucking bi-i-i-tch!" Jaq screamed and, holding his sword high, charged Tiamat.

Tiamat held her eyes open, wide and unbelieving. But just before Jaq hit her, she seemed to recover and drew her own sword in defense. With Jaq's first strike, iron shattered its bronze blade. Falling backwards, she tripped and landed on her back, losing her shield. Instinctively she covered her face with an armored forearm as Jaq rained blows down on her head and shoulders. Even in his fury, he had been surprised that Tiamat's weapon had failed so quickly. Maybe there was magic left in the world after all. Maybe his sword held that magic.

But Tiamat's armor proved more durable than her sword; the bright bronze did not give way. Tiamat grabbed Jaq by the front of his shirt. For an instant, he froze, then he flipped his sword around and, with a great scream, bashed Tiamat in the middle of the face with the pommel. Pain contorted her features; then, they began to twist in rage. Anger was driving her to abandon reason. Blinded by her fury, she would be defenseless. Seizing his opportunity, Jaq lifted his sword by the hilt with both hands and prepared to drive the point down her throat. His side belched fire.

Screeching, Tiamat opened her mouth wide and suddenly Jaq found himself atop the shiny, chitinous sternum of an enormous spider, staring down its wet, greedy maw. The shock froze him for a crucial instant and she drove a fang through the thick down of his vest and between his ribs. Flailing with its palps, the creature struck Jaq on the side of the head and knocked him off of her belly.

The shock of the hard surface that broke his fall cleared his confusion. They had returned to the cave and a few meters away sat his sword. Tiamat lay helplessly on her back. She had raised her forelegs and was searching for a hold on the irregular rock ceiling. "Now!" Jaq shouted to himself as he tried to rise and rush for his weapon, but the cry paralyzed him with pain.

Over by the entrance to the lair stood Nick, quite still, powerless in this place. Kak Zhal was at his side, holding Ur's hand. Kate was sprinting toward him, screaming, "Jaq! Run!" Tiamat had righted herself and was clicking her fangs together, making a sound like bone snapping. She seemed to be in no hurry, as if she wanted to enjoy cutting him to pieces.

Jaq was able to force himself to his feet, but as he did Tiamat skittered toward him with blinding speed. "No-o-o-o!" Kate screamed, but she was too far away, as if she could help him anyway.

A fountain of blue fire flew over her shoulder. The hot compression wave nearly knocked Kate down. "Now, Jaq!" Nick was yelling as he loosed the azure flame from his hands.

The blast had hit Tiamat squarely in the sternum, blowing her off her legs and landing her on her back once again. "Yes, now, Jaq! Do it!" Kate cried.

Grabbing his weapon and gripping it firmly, to focus all of his pain and set it apart, Jaq ran straight for Tiamat. Holding the blade directly in front of him, he used the raw force of his charge to drive the point deeply into her side. Raising one last hideous screech, Tiamat shuddered involuntarily and the force of her spasm flung Jaq backward, still clutching his sword, onto the cave floor.

"Jaq!" Kate gasped. She knelt and held him by the shoulders.

"I'm okay," was all Jaq said as they both turned toward Tiamat.

As black blood gushed from the wound in her side, Tiamat's spider aspect began to dissolve. Finally, what remained, slumped against the base of the rock wall and next to the small, silver pool, was a shrunken old woman.

◙ ◉ ◙

Nick was the first to reach Kate and Jaq. "Well, we did it," Jaq said sourly, with none of the ebullience he had displayed when they had defeated the Praetorian Guard.

"Did what?" Kate said bitterly, her eyes riveted on the shriveled figure in the corner.

"That's what I mean," Jaq said. "I suppose I should thank you, Nick. I didn't think your 'powers' worked in this place."

"Neither did I. But it won't be the first time I've been wrong. Nor the last, I suspect."

"Nick," Kate said, "I think she's badly hurt. Maybe we ought to go have a look."

Nick raised an eyebrow. "Compassion? For the creature who took your child from you?"

"It is unnatural isn't it? But when I heard Ur remind her about what the two of them had been talking about during the time they'd spent together …." Kate picked at a finger. "What Tiamat did was selfish, but I don't believe she wanted to hurt Ur. In fact, I'm almost beginning to believe that she cares about her."

Kate exhaled hard and shook her head, bouncing her long blonde hair off her shoulders. Jaq was struck by its beauty. It seemed to him as it if had been so very long since he'd noticed. Jaq tried to move, but gasped loudly and ground his teeth.

"Father's hurt," Ur said.

Kate's head snapped toward Ur. "Father," was all she said, her eyes wide.

"Father," Jaq whispered.

"Let me have a look," Kate said. Carefully opening his down vest, she revealed a blood-soaked flannel shirt, torn and shredded. Beneath it, raw flesh oozed bright blood. "Oh, Jaq. Nick, we have to do something."

"Father, may I give you a kiss?" Ur asked. "Maybe it will make you feel better." The little girl walked over to Jaq, her shallow breaths rattling like dry grass. He offered his cheek and Ur applied a single, sweet kiss. She stepped back. "How was that?"

Though the wound still throbbed brutally, Jaq couldn't help chuckling. "To tell you the honest truth, Ur, it felt like a cool marshmallow." Reaching out a hand, Jaq stroked the thick, coppery hair of his daughter's head.

"What's a marshmallow?" Ur asked.

"It's something very special and very wonderful and I'll buy you a whole truckload when we get home."

"Truck," Ur repeated, as if she were turning the concept over in her mind. A flicker of recognition lit up her cobalt eyes.

Kate knelt beside her husband and daughter. Kak Zhal gave Jaq a swig of Peevo. "I think he's going to be all right, Mother." Tears welled up in Kate's eyes.

"What's wrong?" Ur asked.

Kate shook her head. "Nothing's wrong. It's just …. You called him father and you called me mother."

"Of course. That's what the two of you told Lady Tiamat."

"And you believed us?" Kate said.

"Why would you lie?"

"We would never lie to you. We never would, never did, anything we didn't think was best for you." Kate laid her hands on the cool surface of Ur's body. Tears trickled onto her cheeks.

"What's wrong, Mother?"

Kate sniffled loudly and wiped her nose with her sleeve. Ur cocked her head and looked very serious. "Ur, do you remember us?"

"No. I don't remember much at all. About before, that is. But don't feel badly, Mother. It just happened that way."

"Yes, I know. Your father and I both understand that very well. It's what's kept us going." Kate smiled at Ur, but Ur did not smile back.

A soft moan seeped from the corner of the cave where Tiamat lay. "Mother," Ur said, "we'd better go to Lady Tiamat. You said we should. I think she's hurt. Worse even than Father."

The old woman lay clutching her abdomen, fingers stained with thick, black blood. Her skin, deeply wrinkled and leathery, was a dark, nut brown color, her hair a wiry, iron gray mass. Jaq was shocked by the dichotomy between the frailty of her frame and the intensity of her eyes, bright black and without pupils. So much power in such a small package, Jaq thought. Glancing up, he saw that the webs that had held Tiamat's 'collection' were empty. And the bright orange-white light of the cave had faded to a dusky gray. Jaq shivered and squeezed the front of his parka closed.

"Well, then," Tiamat was saying, "have you gotten what you came for, Nicholas? Does it please you?"

"Yes, I suppose I've achieved my purpose, Mother. But, no, it does not please me."

"Do I detect a twinge of conscience?"

"Perhaps instinctive filial feeling. Nothing more. I did what I had to do."

"What you had to *do*. And what might that have been, sonny boy?"

"Stop you," Nick said.

"Stop *me*?"

"You created this cosmos. Couldn't you have left it at that? Look at the child. Do you think she is happy?"

Tiamat turned toward Ur, studying her. "No. I suppose not. Like you, she has an overly serious turn of mind. Although without your grim and depressing qualities."

"Thank you, Mother, for agreeing with me. So give it up. If you lack the capacity for love, accept its existence. Stop interfering."

"Interfering?!" Tiamat thundered, startling everyone. Careful, Jaq thought. There's still plenty of power left in the old bird. "Interfering," she repeated, "is what I wish to do.

"You don't have the right to wishes. They are seductive. You cannot play God."

"Play God," Tiamat said quietly. "Is that what you think I'm doing? I have existed an eternity. But God has existed an eternity of eternities. I support the fabric of *this* universe. But God supports an infinity of worlds." Tiamat studied her lair for a moment, tapping a crooked finger against her thin, leathery lips.

"Interfering," she continued. "Did you really believe that I could be conscious of creation and not resist the temptation to participate? Consciousness demands it. But you should know that. After we battled and you thought you had defeated me—"

"Thought? I blew the winds of the world into your mouth and scattered the pieces all over the worlds of your creation."

"Marduk," Jaq whispered. Kate shot him a quick glance.

"And the pieces came together again, didn't they?" Tiamat said.

"Yes. And even more filled with bitterness and spite," Nick said.

"And *you* didn't rampage? Filled with the pride of your assumed victory? The flood—"

"An exaggeration," Nick said. Kate and Jaq exchanged startled glances.

"Interference! Even God interferes. Consciousness is too seductive."

"God plays dice."

"No. Across an infinity of time, the outcomes are predictable. And boring. God places more interesting bets."

Shifting position, Tiamat grimaced in pain. Quickly and quietly, Kak Zhal shuffled to her side. Holding her by the arm, he lifted her gently, so that she might sit up. "Thank you," was all she said, and Kak Zhal returned to his place beside Ur and Kate.

"Philosopher? What do you think?" Tiamat asked, addressing Jaq with an insinuating smile.

"I think I understand a little better. Your mind holds reality together. But so do ours, each in its own small way."

"Some greater than others," Tiamat corrected, boring her black orbs into Jaq's eyes. He didn't know whether to feel fear or some measure of pride. For himself or his daughter, he wasn't sure. "Come here," Tiamat said, crooking her finger. Jaq approached with a confident step, but his feet felt as if they were made of wet sand. "I'll tell you something. That damnable Immanuel wasn't entirely wrong, I'll admit. If only he could have expressed himself better. Aaah!" Tiamat shuddered. "Listening to him was like gargling with razor blades."

"And you, my dear Kate," Tiamat said, "have you got what you came here for?"

"Yes, and no," Kate said flatly.

"You surprise me. You are uncharacteristically indecisive. Indirect."

"Not at all. I came for my daughter. But I also came to do what's best for her. I'm not sure if that's been decided."

"Ur?" Tiamat said simply, the child's name carrying the entire question.

"Mr. Beele is correct," Ur said. "Love is what you lack. But what we are doesn't have to remain fixed. It can be changed by the choices we make."

"Come with us, Ur," Kate whispered.

Beele rested his hand on Kate's arm. "But the choice is hers, isn't it. Ur's life is her own." Beele smiled gently.

"She sounds just like a child at times, and at others …."

"She is unique," Beele said. "And she may be greater than all of us as well."

"You'll stay then?" Tiamat was asking Ur. "You'll help me learn?"

"You do care for her, don't you?" Kate asked Tiamat.

"Care for her? I suppose I may have become somewhat attached to her," Tiamat answered hesitantly.

"That's a beginning," Kate said.

"So you will leave her with me? You will stay … Ur?"

"I'll think about it," Ur said. "Now, we have to leave."

"Leave? Why?" Tiamat said, her black, blank eyes bright, as if fired by her newly-found feelings of fear.

"Because we must," Ur said simply.

"But I'll die!"

"Yes, you will. But not of this wound," Ur said.

As the look on Tiamat's face phased from one of fear to one of understanding and then resignation, a loud boom sounded. The cave hall shook.

◙ ◉ ◙

CHAPTER 14

"Crikey! What's that?" Kak Zhal cried.

"I'm slipping a little, that's all," Tiamat said, a delicate smile snaking across her thin lips. "Not paying attention the way I should. Of course, I haven't been for some time now." Another quake rocked the chamber. Small fragments of rock and bits of dust fell from the cave roof.

"If you're slipping, Mother, then who—" Beele began.

"Shouldn't you have thought that through before you barged in here? What did you *think* would happen if the philosopher killed me?"

"I really didn't *think* you maintained the world, merely that you meddled."

"But you wouldn't know that, would you? We haven't really spoken these millennia," Tiamat said in a low voice.

"In any event, I did it for the child. A world corrupted would be worse than no world at all," Beele said.

"For one child. My, Kant has you by the balls too, I see! But your question, as to who will keep the world glued together, deserves an answer." Tiamat folded her hands across her chest and grinned.

Beele's face went black. "Not Bildad Proud, I hope?"

"Beh! He hasn't the grit for it. But you, young lady," Tiamat said, speaking directly to Ur, "have the grit *and* the intelligence for it. Now, I ask you again, won't you stay with me?"

Kate squeezed Jaq's hand and looked from Tiamat to Ur.

"I must go," Ur said. Kate's hand relaxed, but Jaq held on.

"Will you come back?" Tiamat asked.

"I've told you. I will think about it."

Tiamat's eyes glistened. "Well, if you do not, I thank you for the time we've spent together," she said in a hoarse whisper.

"You're welcome, ma'am," Ur said.

"Polite child," Tiamat remarked.

"Thank you!" Jaq and Kate both blurted out.

Boom! Crack! Once again the lair shook and small fissures opened in the wall behind Tiamat.

"We must leave," Beele said.

"Shouldn't we take Tiamat with us?" Kate said.

"No," Tiamat said. "It's not at all dangerous. To me, that is. I may have slipped a touch, but I have not lost my grip."

Boom!

"But ...." Kak Zhal began, as they moved to go.

"What is it?" Beele said.

"Well, it's just that it's a bit chilly in here." He began to take off his Lamikin vest. "I thought that maybe the Lady Tiamat here, being hurt and all ...."

Arresting Kak Zhal with a light touch, Nick said, "You're right, of course. And it's very kind of you. But my blood is hotter than yours." Nick knelt beside his mother and took off his purple jacket.

Laying it gently on top of her body, he began to fuss, tucking her in at the sides. She grabbed his hand. "I'll be fine. Thank you," she said. Holding his hand in hers, she studied his pearl gray gloves. "Still self-conscious about your skin condition, I see. I *am* sorry, Nicholas Marduk Beelzebub. Sorry about playing with your life for my own selfish purposes. I really wasn't aware. I tore you in half, good from bad. And I can't put you back together again. But there never really was much bad in you anyway."

"Thank you." Tears filled Beele's eyes. "I forgive you," he said.

Boom! The rock thundered.

"Go," Tiamat said.

◙ ◉ ◙

When they reached the cave entrance, which now, in the dim gray light appeared as nothing more than a black hole, Ur stopped and looked back. "So *this* is choice," she said blandly.

"What did you say?" Kate knelt beside her daughter.

"I was just talking with myself. Don't you ever do that?"

"Yes, of course we do—"

"This is a most touching domestic scene," Nick's voice snapped, "but I would suggest—" Another quake shook the cavern floor and nearly knocked them all off their feet. Small bits of dust and rock drifted down. "In fact, I *insist* we leave without delay."

Nick swept Ur up in his arms. "I realize that your future contains extraordinary possibilities. However, your legs are still rather on the short side." Gently, Nick placed his great, gloved hands around Ur's chest and hoisted her onto his shoulder.

Carefully but quickly, they made their way across the field of crystals, now pulsing putrid green. The great cavern had acquired an echo, the boom of the tremors reverberating off of the walls like the pounding of surf, the rattling noise made by the movement of facets beneath their feet vaguely suggestive of the hiss of sea foam. The cavern was reflecting itself. It felt alive.

Aftershocks were causing the rock base beneath the crystals to undulate. Jaq slipped, but Kak Zhal caught him by the hand. A rumble, then the cracking sound of rock against rock filled the space. Enormous chunks of stone hurtled down the cave walls, ricocheting off one another.

"Quickly," Nick shouted, "behind the monolith!"

As the massive stones smashed the crystals covering the floor, they made a snapping sound, like bones breaking. Jaq wasn't sure that the monolith could take the pounding, so he took Ur from Nick and cradled her in his arms. The coolness of her body stunned him. Even her kiss hadn't prepared him.

Jaq glanced at Kate and her eyes said she understood, then they darted away and flared. "My spear!" Kate cried. It lay only a few meters away and this time Jaq wasn't able to stop her. She snatched it up quickly, but as she did, a great, gray stone shot off the headwall of the cave and headed straight for her. Reflexively, she thrust at the rock with her spear point and the boulder exploded into spray of fragments.

Kate dove for the monolith and landed next to Jaq. "Remind me to thank Achilles, if I ever see her again," he said.

"Oh, you'll see her again, unless you plan on living forever," Kate said with a sardonic grin. But her smile disappeared as a large thud was felt through the floor. The van of another avalanche of rock smashed into the monolith. But the stone held, and then it grew quiet, except for a low, thrumming sound that pulsed through the cave floor and from the walls.

"What the hell's going on, Nick?" Jaq asked.

"It's Mother, of course."

"What about *Mother?*"

"I'm not at all sure. I had never actually believed she held things 'together,' until now." Nick shrugged. "In any event, I am convinced that she has not entirely lost her grip."

"Well, how fucking sure are you that we can make it across the cavern to the tunnel," Jaq said, clutching Ur more tightly.

"I think we'll make it all right," Nick said. "Somehow, though, this narrow escape may have been the least of the dangers we may face."

The tremors quieted and their only obstacles were the copious rivers of 'dirty floors' that flowed from the walls and came to rest on the cave bottom in pools of putrid sludge. As they approached the far end of the cavern, they saw that there were not one, but, rather, several tunnels that looked exactly alike. "Well?" Kate said, folding her arms.

Jaq set Ur down and folded his own arms. Somehow that seemed to relieve his irritation with Nick. "Well, I'll assume all of them lead to Hades. So I really don't believe it makes a damned bit of difference," he said and walked into the tunnel directly in front of them.

"Wait," Ur said. "It does make a difference. I believe we're trying to get back out into the open. Under the sky. A place like the one where you fought the Lady Tiamat. I can smell the outside in that one." Ur pointed to the tunnel immediately on Jaq's left. "All I could do very well as a baby was smell. But I was quite good at it. The air coming from that tunnel tickles my nose. It stings!"

Burnt, dry, smelling of flint. Jaq nodded. "Okay," he said.

The passageway was wider and considerably brighter than the one that had led them into the cave. No longer a sickly green, it shone silvery, tinged bluish-white. As they rounded the final bend, a bright flash of argentine light filled the exit.

Jaq face flushed red hot. "Come on! We've made it," he shouted, sprinting madly. Exploding out of the tunnel exit, he felt ice cold air smack him in the face. He tried to check himself, but momentum had the advantage. Whomp! Jaq slid and slid, on his face, then his side, then his bottom, until at long last he came to a stop. A vast lake of ice, shining like a huge mirror, lit by the immense blue-white orb of Mir that had since climbed high in the sky, stretched before him.

Facing the plain that extended back toward Old Spall, Jaq now saw what he thought was the Styx as only a thin silver ribbon in the far distance. He looked to his left, then to his right, and saw high rock cliffs soaring hundreds of meters, etching their jagged ridge line against a lunar sky, pale purple with earth light.

Where in Hell am I? Then, sounds. Voices. Kate was calling. And Nick. "Are you all right?" they were asking.

"Yeah, yeah. Yup," he called back as he got to his feet. Just when he thought he had righted himself, he slipped and landed on his hands and knees. "Oooh!" he heard Kate exclaim. "I'm okay. I'm okay," he shouted, struggling to his feet again and then shuffling his way gingerly to the shoreline. Nick extended a hand, as did Kate, although she was stretching, maintaining a respectful distance from the frozen lake's edge.

"Guess I got a little carried away," Jaq said, breathing heavily as he scrambled up onto the moraine that framed the ice on all sides of the cirque.

"Looks like Hell finally froze over," Kak Zhal said, gazing out over the ice.

"We will, too, if we don't keep moving," Nick said.

"Brrr!" Kate shivered. "Why *is* it so damnably cold?"

"Perhaps, in part, because Tiamat is failing," Nick answered. "Regardless, this is the deepest, coldest part of the lunar night and the sun will be rising soon on this part of Luna."

"Well, that's comforting," Kate said, her tone brightening.

"I wish it were," Nick said. "Recall how you felt while we watched Jaq's *Aristeia*." Kate nodded grimly. "While nighttime can be unpleasant, daytime can be deadly."

"That's why they built Old Spall where they did," Kak Zhal said. "We all just hole up there during the day."

"Please," Nick said, "we must move.

◙ ◉ ◙

Haltingly, the group picked its way across the talus. Except for Ur, who seemed to be enjoying herself thoroughly, hopping lightly from stone to stone. "Be careful. Don't slip," Jaq or Kate would call from time to time. But Ur paid them little attention.

"She really *does* seem to be having fun," Kate said to Jaq.

"Yeah. If only she'd smile."

Shards of sharp rock scraped their knuckles, boulders banged their knees. Kate was beginning to lag behind the group and Jaq could see the pain on her face from the effort and, most likely, from deep exhaustion as well.

"How're you doing?" Jaq asked Kate.

"Beat. Completely. I think it's all starting to catch up with me. All of it."

"Me, too. But you heard Nick." Jaq kissed her on the cheek.

"*That's* a pick-me-up," she said, though not as brightly as Jaq would have liked.

After an hour or so of painstaking progress, they arrived at the base of a promontory that extended from the rock face out onto the ice and rose a hundred meters into the air.

"We'll have to circle round. Watch your footing," Nick said.

Kate sat down on a large, flat rock. "I'm sorry. I have to rest, just for a bit," she said.

"Kate," Jaq said, "Nick explained—"

"Please. Just for a bit."

"Mother, would you like me to carry you? Just like Mr. Beele carried me? Just like you carried me for so long?"

Kate seemed to brighten. She smiled and stroked Ur's auburn hair, which shone almost like brass in the silver blue light of Mir. "I think I'm a bit large."

"And Mommy carrying you didn't turn out so well. I doubt it would turn out well for you now, Ur, if you carried *her*," Jaq said.

Kate sprang off the rock and punched Jaq lightly on the chest. "What are you saying, buster?"

"I ... Kate, I'm sorry I didn't—"

"Mother, what's sorry?" Ur asked.

"Um." Kate bit her lip. "Oh, Daddy was just being silly."

"What's silly?" Ur asked.

"Oh, it's when you don't make much sense," Kate said.

"But he actually made a great deal of sense, when I thought about it." Kate's jaw fell.

Nick stroked his beard. "It appears that you've recovered your energy, Kate. Or found more reserves. However, I've been studying the topography and it appears that we have been deposited much closer to Spall than the place where we entered Hades. If we stop for a while, I don't believe it will make that much difference. If everyone's able, though, I'd like to try and negotiate around this promontory. Perhaps there's a spot on the other side that's less exposed."

"Thank you," Kate said, and they slid around the rock.

On the far side, the promontory cut deeply into the cliffs, affording protection. As well, there was a flat rock shelf, two meters above a stony beach, large enough to accommodate the entire party, with an elevation that would provide a few precious and positive degrees of temperature gradient. "Excellent," Nick said. "This will do very nicely."

◙ ◉ ◙

"You know," Kate said, "I'm starved. I really believe I'm hungrier than I am tired."

"Now you're talkin'," Kak Zhal said. Peevo and Kleb were broken out and passed all around. Everyone had almost forgotten how long it had been, and how much they had endured, since they'd last eaten. Kleb was gobbled and Peevo swilled greedily, by everyone. Everyone, that is, except Ur.

"Aren't you hungry?" Kate asked.

"No. I don't think so," Ur said.

When they had finished their light supper, Kate turned again to Ur. "Are you tired?" she asked.

"I, I'm not sure, mother. What is—tired?"

"Ur, perhaps I can help. Do you ever feel a need to simply stop?" Nick asked.

Ur considered his question for a moment. "Yes, I do. And if that's what tired is then, yes, Mother, I *am* quite tired." Kate smiled sadly. "I'm sorry I'm different, Mother."

Gently, Kate placed her hand on the cool, slick surface of Ur's arm.

Ur regarded Nicholas Beele thoughtfully and took several raspy breaths. "Thank you for your help, um …." Ur paused, obviously turning a thought over in her mind with great care. "Father? What should I call Mr. Beele? Mr. Beele doesn't sound quite right. And what should I call our friend Kak Zhal?"

"We-e-ell," Jaq said. "How about 'uncle'? Uncle Nick and Uncle Kak Zhal."

"Uncle. *That* sounds silly. But I like it. Yes. Thank you, Uncle Nick," Ur said.

"You're welcome, Ur."

Mir had risen high enough in the sky to spill its light onto the ledge where Kak Zhal was sitting. It glinted off of the silver flute he had stuck in his vest. "Uncle Kak Zhal," Ur said, "what is that bright object in your pocket?"

"Oh," Kak Zhal said, clearly flattered by being addressed as 'uncle'. "This is a flute. I was given it by a fella by the name of Mozart."

"What does it do?" Ur asked.

"Plays music. You know, lovely sounds."

"I think I understand. Could you—*play* something, Uncle?"

Kak Zhal blushed at the word 'uncle'. Withdrawing the flute, he began to blow and out of it flowed a sweet stream of silver notes. The temperature had been dropping precipitously and magically while Kak Zhal played, what little moisture there was in the dry, lunar air precipitated out as a delicate snow shower. Earth light shone through the atmosphere, as if through a diaphanous scrim, woven from flakes of diamond.

Ur's eyes widened and she sucked in a sharp breath of air. "What is the white stuff?" Ur asked.

Kak Zhal laid the flute aside. "Schnee," he said.

"Schnee," she repeated. "Oh, please don't stop playing, Uncle. Mother, Father, look at the schnee. It's lovely, isn't it? And Uncle Kak Zhal's music is wonderful. It's perfect!"

Jaq put one arm around Kate and the other around Ur. *I'll be goddamned. We're a family.* "Yes, Ur, you're right. It certainly is perfect," he said.

While Kak Zhal played on, Kate closed her eyes and Jaq closed his. The last sounds Jaq heard were the weightless notes of Kak Zhal's flute dancing in his brain.

◙ ◉ ◙

CHAPTER 15

Kate awoke to the sound of Kak Zhal's heavy breathing. Jaq lay passed out against the south wall of the ledge. Ur and Nick had 'stopped'. Sitting erect, motionless, eyes half closed, they seemed to be in a trance. Hours had passed. Kate could tell because Mir now sat higher in the sky, illuminating the ragged ridgeline of the cirque's east wall that raked the night sky. Her bladder felt as if it were going to burst. *I haven't gone since—since Idaho!* Kate began to laugh at the incongruity of the thought, but checked herself. She was afraid she'd wet her pants.

Quietly, she rose and, grabbing Achilles' spear as a brace, descended from the ledge down to the rocky shore and surveyed the vast expanse of silver-blue ice. Laying her spear on the ground, she searched for a secluded spot. Modesty struck her as the queerest of emotions to have at that time and in that place.

Concentrating on buttoning her jeans, Kate didn't notice three figures gliding across the surface of the ice, coming from the direction of the plains that stretched back toward Old Spall. She heard a scratching sound, like grains of sand being blown against glass. For an instant, she was too frightened to lift her head.

Three figures faced her, their mouths and eyes black ovals set deeply in what appeared to be sandstone. Their expressions were mournful, lost, as if they were gripped by a terribly agony. As they advanced toward her, low, sick moans seemed to escape from their mouths. Kate's throat went absolutely dry. She tried to call out but couldn't. *Achilles' spear!* Searching about frantically, she spotted it lying not five meters away. But the silicants—*were these Sand Banshees?*—blocked her path. Backing up against a rock wall, she felt her chest tighten as the creatures closed on her.

A horrible high-pitched scream echoed off the cirque walls. A woman with thick blond hair, wearing a leather shirt and leggings and brandishing an enormous sword with a curved blade, leapt off of the rocks behind her. Falling upon the Banshees, who were no match for her size or strength, she hacked them to pieces, reducing them to a pile of gravel. When the last Banshee had been dispatched, the woman warrior turned to Kate, her eyes burning with fierce pride, the hint of a smile of satisfaction tickling her face.

"Achilles," Kate whispered breathlessly. "Thank you."

"Who is Achilles? I'm Anad." Stooping, Anad picked up Kate's spear, shooting her a hard look. "Is this your weapon?" Kate nodded. Testing the weight of the weapon, a skeptical expression crossed Anad's face. She tossed the spear to Kate, who caught it easily. The look of doubt turned to one of surprise. "Be more careful about where you leave that," Anad said.

Kate started to speak, but was interrupted by shouts. Jaq and Kak Zhal scrambled down to the shore. Nick stood silently on the edge of the ledge, his large hand resting lightly on the top of Ur's head.

When Jaq saw Anad, he pulled up short, his face expressing the question that was on his mind. "She saved me, Jaq," Kate said. "Her name is Anad."

Jaq said a simple, "Thank you."

Kak Zhal grinned from ear to cauliflower ear. "Well, well! Anad. I'll be blowed. Fancy meeting you here. Lucky, too, I expect. What's up?"

Anad smiled as the two shook hands warmly, although Kak Zhal nearly had to stand on his toes. "I could ask you the same question, you ugly old coot, but I think I know. These two must be the couple from Mir I've heard of."

"From Eldaf, I'd suppose," Kak Zhal said, in an insinuating tone.

"Yes, from Eldaf," Anad said, the smile disappearing from her face. "And others." Anad craned her neck upward and stared at the two figures on the ledge. "I know *him*. And that must be the child, Ur."

Jaq moved to his wife's side. "Kate, what happened here, anyway?"

"Well, if you must know, I had to pee and I wasn't paying attention. They came from across the lake. Sand Banshees, I guess."

"They were Sand Banshees and they did come from across the ice," Anad said. "But three are no match for me. Nor you, even, Kak Zhal."

Kak Zhal spat on the ground. "Nor thirty. But tell me, Anad, how'd ya come to be here?"

"I was prowling. That's what I do at night," she said, turning to Kate and Jaq. "It's been interesting lately, with more Sand Banshees about. Anyway, I had climbed to the top of the ridgeline across the lake and I saw movement on the ice, so I decided to investigate."

"Lucky thing," Kate said.

"And here we are," Anad said.

"And we're glad of it. Thank you again, Anad," Jaq said, stepping forward and grasping her hand. To Jaq, it felt like he'd stuck his hand into a drill press, but he stifled a grimace.

"Where are you headed?" Anad asked.

"Back to Old Spall," Kate said. She turned to Jaq. "Right?"

"No, we're going to New Spall," Jaq answered. There was no rational reason why he had said 'New Spall,' but he knew with instinctive yet apodictic certainty that was their destination.

"Ah," Anad said, in a quiet voice. "I'm from New Spall."

"Perhaps you could lead us, then," Jaq said excitedly.

Anad shook her head. "I came to *be* in New Spall, but the people of Old Spall brought me up. And Eldaf."

"Is he your brother?" Kate said.

"Lover's more like it," Kak Zhal chided.

"You …." Anad grabbed Kak Zhal by his shirt and lifted him up onto his toes.

"Please," Jaq said. "Can't you take us there?"

"I was an infant. I don't remember the place. Others, like Eldaf … How did he put it? He said he stepped out of a dream and couldn't find his way back."

"I can. I must," Jaq said. Anad shrugged.

"But there must be—Nick?" Beele remained impassive.

"I can point you in the right direction," Anad said. She smiled warmly.

"Thank you," Jaq said. Would he have the instinct to find the place? Would they survive the lunar day? Doubts and fears began to crowd his mind.

"Good. Then we should be going," Anad said. "The sun will be up soon and you'll want to travel as great a distance as possible in the darkness. And though darkness holds more dangers these days, I think you'll have no more trouble this night." She kicked at the piles of pebbles that had been Sand Banshees.

"Think again, Anad," Beele said, and pointed across the frozen lake at a horde of at least a hundred silicants, advancing slowly but steadily.

"Anad. Can you lend me your mace?" Kak Zhal asked. Anad handed him a large stone club studded with sharp fragments of bone. Testing its balance, he grinned. "This'll do."

Withdrawing the silver flute from his vest, Kak Zhal tossed it up to Ur who snatched it deftly out of the air. "Keep close watch on that, Ur. I wouldn't want to see it broke. That Mo-zart fella said to use it when nothing else would do, but I'm thinking this mace is all I'll be needing."

"Let's hope you're right, my friend," Nick said. "Ur, you remain here."

"Yes, Uncle Nick," Ur said.

Jumping from the ledge, carrying Jaq's sword, Beele joined his friends on the beach. Without a word, he passed Hector's weapon to Jaq.

"Nick," Jaq asked, "how many Sand Banshees are there?"

"A hundred, more or less."

"Spread out," Anad said.

"Wouldn't it be better to protect our flanks? You know, close ranks?" Jaq asked somewhat nervously.

"Nah," Kak Zhal said. "Anad's right. Fightin' Banshees is like harvesting Greeb."

"Make long, broad passes with your weapon. Remember, Sand Banshees' bodies are soft. But keep them at a safe distance," Nick said.

"And keep a sharp eye, for their blades're sharp," Kak Zhal added.

By now the Sand Banshees were no more than thirty meters away. They were slight, just over a meter tall. Nothing like the Praetorian Guard of Tiamat. Like the crystal liths, in place of faces sat three deep depressions where eyes and mouth should have been. Their bodies, though made of lunar dust, glowed dully in the ghostly earthlight. As they approached, their wailing rose. Within ten meters, weapons raised, they howled, then charged.

"Stick to the beach if you can," Nick shouted above the din. "The footing will be better than on the ice. Watch one another if there's a slack in your action. I'll try to cover you all."

Smashing into the defenders' weapons, the Banshees' bodies made strange scraping sounds against the metal weapons, like a mason's trowel against brick and mortar. Nick grabbed three to four silicants at a time, smashing them together, crushing their bodies like clods of earth.

At one point, the Sand Banshees swarmed away from Anad and toward Kak Zhal, perhaps sensing, in some way, his stature. "Anad!" he cried.

"Take their legs, I'll take the heads!" Anad shouted as she cut the last three Banshees facing her into pieces with a few deft swipes of her scimitar.

"Spall!" Kak Zhal roared as he and Anad charged the onrushing line of liths from opposite ends. Anad decapitated at least twenty as she rushed down the line, her sword held at shoulder height, while Kak Zhal raked their legs to dust. "Old coot, huh?" he said, passing under Anad in the middle of the thin phalanx.

Nervously, Jaq stole a glance at Kate during the action. *Magnificent.* Jaw set, eyes flashing, she was taking out the enemy in a two-fisted manner with both the butt and point of her spear. Having just mowed down a half dozen Banshees, she became careless and stepped up to the edge of the ice. With a strong lunge she swept her weapon across the bodies of several silicants, smashing them to dust. But her left foot slipped. Down she went, and ten Banshees were on her in seconds.

But Jaq was quicker and, with a grand swipe, decapitated four of them. The others he bashed to bits with the hilt of his sword.

Nick, his hands and feet covered with dust, rushed to cover Jaq as he helped Kate to her feet. "Hurt?" Jaq asked. There was a tear in the left shoulder of her shirt, surrounded by a wet blot of blood. Jaq quickly examined the wound. "Superficial. But be more careful the next time. Please."

They looked out and across the ice, and saw that there would be no next time, for the skirmish was over. Kak Zhal was mopping up, bashing the last few Banshees to powder.

The defenders collected at the base of the rock ledge. "Everyone all right?" Nick asked. "Kate?"

"Flesh wound."

"Didn't touch me, nor Anad, I'm thinkin'," Kak Zhal said. Anad nodded, confirming Kak Zhal's guess.

"Jaq? How's that side?" Nick asked.

But before he could answer, Kate's eyes widened. "Ur!" she shouted. "Are you okay?" Kate scrambled up and over the rocks to her side.

"Yes, Mother. For the moment." Everyone regarded Ur with the same question stamped on their faces. "There're more of them coming," Ur said. "Out of that cloud beyond the lake." Looking toward a huge swirl of dust out on the plains and beyond the far end of the lake, they made out small movements that could only have been Banshees.

Nick smiled wryly. "Well, whoever or *whatever* is doing this to us has planned well. Or gotten extremely lucky. The sunrise is approaching and huge thermal gradients are generated at the leading edge of the light. An enormous electrostatic charge lifts the lunar dust in a sort of cyclonic motion. Raw material for liths."

The vanguard of the approaching force could be seen advancing across the ice. "Looks larger than the first. So suck it up," Kak Zhal said.

"Nick," Kate said, "we're going to need more room to maneuver if this bunch is bigger." She picked at a finger. "Is your furnace stoked?"

"I beg your pardon?"

"I mean, do you think you might be able to throw some fire at this ice and melt it? If the lake's deep, the contour of the bottom will form a natural barrier."

"And if it's not?" Anad asked.

"Then at least we can advance and catch some breathing room."

"Indeed," Nick said with a grin. "A born tactician." Raising his arms, he seemed to gather himself for some enormous effort. Both great concentration and great strain showed in his features. Then out of his palms shot two massive jets of flame. The ice hissed and popped. Steam rose and when it cleared, they saw that they had achieved second best. The lake had been merely the depth of the thin layer of ice. Stretched before them was an extension of beach that would afford them an extra thirty meters of space and good footing.

Nick lowered his arms and frowned. Then, slowly, he led them to within five meters of the perimeter of the ice. "We'll employ the same strategy," Nick said.

"Different odds," Jaq said.

"Beh!" Kak Zhal spat. "We could beat five times what we just did."

"From the looks of it," Nick said, "we'll have to." Hundreds of silicants were spread across the ice.

"Funny," Kate croaked hoarsely, "my mouth's dry."

"Dry? I'd pee my pants if there was any juice left in me at all," Jaq said.

In an instant, the Banshees, wailing and howling, were upon them. Though the creatures were no bigger or tougher, there were simply too many. No sooner would ten go down, than another dozen would replace them. Slowly, they were driven backwards.

Soon, not ten meters separated them from the rock ledge where Jaq knew they would establish their last defense. Fierce shouts and the thundering din of rock pounding against rock erupted behind and above them. *Surrounded.* Jaq glanced over his shoulder. "The fucking cavalry!" he shouted, the skin of his face stretched to its limits by a massive grin.

Charging straight down the cliff's face, which was inclined almost to the perpendicular, were three Rock Cats. And mounted behind their great heads were Eldaf and Krenk and Enivel, with Boom and Bing, screaming for all they were worth—"Old Spall! Old Spall!"

Eldaf and Krenk split to the left and to the right when they hit the beach, circling around the five retreating defenders and hitting the Banshees first on their flanks. Trampling dozens under foot, the Rock Cats roared and pawed, smashing silicants and ice sheet alike. From astride the great creatures' backs, Krenk and Eldaf smashed the attackers with their maces, reducing them to sand and scrap.

"Never thought I'd say it, but I'm glad to see you, Krenk," Kak Zhal shouted. Krenk flashed a crooked smile.

"Anad!" Eldaf cried. "From now on, perhaps, you won't roam abroad without me. Or else you'll stay back at Old Spall like you should."

"Beh!" Anad spat while hacking four Banshees apart. Eldaf laughed. Kicking his mount in its flanks, he spurred the Cat on toward the center.

Enivel remained briefly on the natural beach below the ledge where Ur sat, watching quietly. "Bing, Boom. Off you go."

"But Dad, we want to fight," said Bing.

"Yes, we want to help," said Boom.

"You've helped enough already, calling up the Cats. And unless I miss my guess, that young lady up there's what all this commotion is about. You want to help? Guard her well."

Bing and Boom looked at one another. "We'll be serving a very useful purpose, won't we?" said Bing.

"A very *important* purpose," said Boom.

"Yes, Father," they agreed, hopping off the Rock Cat and scampering up the scree to the ledge where Ur sat.

"Eeeahh!" Enivel cried. Thundering down upon the silicants' van, he broke the Banshees' center, smashing the first several ranks in an instant. Soon, the defenders, Kate and Jaq, Nicholas Beele and the scions of Spall, Old and New, were pressing the Sand Banshees into full retreat.

"It's a grand battle, don't you think?" Bing asked Ur.

"I think it's a trick," Ur said, without looking at Bing.

"A trick? What kind of trick do you mean?" Boom said. But Ur did not answer.

The boys exchanged a confused glance and shrugged. "She's a very strange girl," Boom whispered in Bing's ear.

"This is my brother Bing," Boom said, addressing Ur. "What's your name?"

"My name's Ur."

"Don't worry," Bing said. "If the Sand Banshees get too close, we'll protect you. We'll give it to 'em good. Botta Bing!"

"Botta Boom," his brother echoed.

"I don't think they'll manage to come very close," Ur said. "But thank you. You're both very brave." Bing blushed. Boom beamed.

Above the noise of the battle, they all heard Nick shout loudly, "Damn!"

Diving out of a sky, already beginning to lighten, were two fiendish looking creatures. They had wings that spanned at least ten meters and looked to be made of separate plates. Their heads were small but ravenous.

"Dust Bats!" Krenk spat the words.

"Anad!" Nick shouted. "I'll have to take them out. Can you protect my flank?" Nick had been fighting on the extreme right of the battle line.

Anad answered with action. Bolting to Beele's side, slashing wildly, she drove back an entire phalanx of Banshees. Beele turned his fists toward the Dust Bats, unleashing two huge balls of fire. The shock wave of the first hit one of the bats squarely in the face, shattering its body up to the shoulders. But still it came.

Beele's second blast hit the other on a wing, causing it to spin out of control and crash directly into a crowd of Banshees that were threatening Krenk. At the sight of the bat, Krenk's Rock Cat went mad. Throwing Krenk from its back, it pounced on the Bat in a fury. The two creatures rolled on the ice, grinding tens of banshees beneath them as they screeched and roared with rage. Beele quickly turned to face the first Bat, hitting it in the body with several blasts.

After Anad had rushed to fill the breach left by Nick, at least thirty Sand Banshees dragged her down, raging, to the surface of the ice. Even for a warrior of her skill, she had committed herself against too many. Hearing her cries, Eldaf bolted off of his Cat and charged to her aid, brandishing his mace high and crying, "Anad! Anad!" When he had driven the silicants from her arms and legs, she sprang to her feet and fought like a mad woman, side by side with Eldaf.

The headless Dust Bat dove straight for Beele, who had been unable to slow it despite repeated volleys of fire. Eldaf's Rock Cat, racing as if from Hell itself, made for the spot where Nick stood and, just as the creature was about to smash into Beele, leapt, catching the Bat in midair and dragged it to the ground, screaming.

While the Dust Bats had been dispatched, the defenders had been compromised. With only Enivel's Rock Cat now engaging the Sand Banshees and the other two finishing off their Dust Bats, there were now simply too many silicants and it was clear that fatigue was beginning to set in.

"Drop back!" Nick cried above the howling and growling and the war cries. "We need some space." Everyone broke and sprinted ten meters to the rear. Enivel charged out of the thick of the Banshees' center and whirled his

Cat around in front of the defenders. Though they had opened up thirty meters between themselves and the Banshees, still the slower liths continued to close.

"What now?" Eldaf asked.

"I think I have an idea," Jaq said. "Nick, do you have any heat left?"

"I think so. Those Bats. Something isn't right." Nick wiped his forehead with his sleeve. Jaq had never seen him sweat. "They were too powerful." Beele took a deep breath. "But, yes, I've got fire. Why?"

"What do you get when you mix sand and heat?" Jaq asked.

"Why, glass, of course!" Kate said. Then she frowned. "But you didn't melt the Dust Bats."

"So they're called. But they're made of stronger stuff than the Sand Banshees," Nick said.

"I say we go down with honor. They're almost on us," Anad said.

"Which is why we have to give it a shot! If it fails, we'll die trying. Try to spread the flame and bathe them in the extreme heat," Jaq said.

Anad nodded and grinned broadly. "Spoken like a true New Spaller."

Nick bared his teeth, apparently summoning up some tremendous reserve, then raised his palms and, roaring, let fly a broad swath of blue fire that halted the advancing Banshees. In seconds, they had turned to statues of the most delicate glass. Throwing his flame over the top of the stationary vanguard, Nick glazed the next several ranks, leaving nothing but fragile files before them to be dispatched with ease. Falling upon the silicants, the defenders, now on the attack, smashed tens upon hundreds like crystal candlesticks.

Nick advanced grimly, loosing swath after swath of flame, until at last there were fewer than a hundred of the Banshees left on the ice. The dust storm on the plains had abated, extinguishing the supply of fresh recruits for the rock army. At last, Nick lowered his arms, shoulders slumping. Kate and Jaq rushed to his side. "Nick?" they said.

"I'm spent," Beele whispered.

Meanwhile, the Rock Cats, having ground the last of the Dust Bats into the sand and ice, loped back to join the fray. "Beele, go back. Rest. Anad 'n' I and Krenk and Kak Zhal can finish them off. Enivel!" Eldaf called, motioning for him to come over. "Off you go. Let Anad ride the beast. It'd please her. Help Kate and Jaq with Nick. He needs to rest. You go to your boys."

"No reason not to leave it to the born warriors to finish the business," Enivel said. The beast knelt, allowing him to dismount.

"Born yes, but from what I saw, Enivel, made can be as brave," Anad said, as she climbed onto the Cat.

"C'mon, Kak Zhal," Krenk said. "Ride with me."

Kak Zhal frowned. "No, thanks. Besides, I need to check on Ur. I'll go back."

"Suit yourself," Krenk said.

They charged off on their Rock Cats crying, "Spall! Spall!"

◙ ◉ ◙

When they arrived at the base of the ledge, Kate and Jaq made a move to help Nick sit down. "No, thank you, I'm fine," he said, as he slumped against the wall.

"Well," Jaq said. He began to laugh, whether from happiness or fatigue he wasn't at all sure.

"Well, well," Kate echoed, giggling.

"Well, well, well!" Enivel said, smacking his hands against his thighs. "We *beat* them!"

"Yes, Father! You are very brave," Bing said.

"You beat them!" Boom shouted.

Kak Zhal said nothing. He was looking at Ur, his head cocked, scratching the end of his nose.

"We haven't won anything, yet," Ur said. Everyone stopped laughing and stared at her. She seemed very serious. But then again, she always seemed very serious, thought Jaq.

"Ur, what do you mean we haven't won?" Kate asked.

"It was a trick," Ur said simply.

A figure slunk around the promontory. Leaning back against the rock, arms folded, it spoke. "You're unkind, child. Think of it as a *diversion*."

"My, my," Jaq said.

"You're looking pretty fit, Proud. Been working out?" Kate said.

"I beg your pardon?" A different Proud stood before them. The eyes were no longer a watery porcine blue, but deep purple and piercing. Trimmer, he wore close-fitting black pants and a leather shirt, doubtless made from Lamikin hide. Gone were the slavering jowls. The skin that stretched over his skull was a pale, pearlescent gray.

"No matter, Proud. Forget it," Kate mumbled.

"So, you created a diversion," Beele said. "It seems you created many diversions. The shift in location of Hades, the attacks by the Sand Banshees on the people of Old Spall, as well as on us, the enormous power of the Dust Bats. And all along I thought it was Tiamat 'interfering'. But why, Proud?" Beele asked. Still reclining against the rock, Beele bent a knee and carefully draped an arm over it. Color had begun to return to his face.

"To get what I came for, of course. The girl," Proud said, gesturing toward Ur and riveting his gaze on her. She stared straight back, stone-faced. "Such an unhappy little creature. I daresay she will be far better off with me."

"She'd never go with you, Proud. Your little *diversion* flopped. So why don't you just blow!" Jaq shouted.

"I must admit that I hadn't counted on reinforcements from that miserable shanty town, Old Spall. However, the battle weakened you, while I've continued to grow stronger. At least it weakened anyone of consequence." Proud shot a malevolent glance at Beele. "I believe she will go with me."

"Don't be so goddamned cocksure," Jaq said. "Ur makes her own decisions."

"Like hell," Kate said. "Maybe with Tiamat. *She* at least has some redeeming qualities. She actually cares about Ur. But she's not going with this creep!"

"Tiamat does have redeeming qualities, that is true," Proud said quietly. "Her power, primarily. Which is what I've been scavenging, as she's declined into senescence. She's slipped, and it is I who've picked up slack. But with this child, I will take *all* the power. Tiamat is weak and dying, thanks in part to you, Jaq. Give credit, I say. But I shall rule." Proud paused. "That is, *we* shall rule. Ur and I. So what do you say, child?" Proud asked, in a whisper. Ur stared at him impassively.

"Bullshit," Kate said, as she made a move toward Ur.

"No, wait, Kate," Jaq said, restraining her gently with a hand. "We have to ask Ur." She swatted his hand away. "Look, our feelings haven't always been in phase, ever since Ur was born. But we've tried to work through it." Kate stopped and picked at her finger. "We'll do as you say, but let's at least find out what Ur wants to do."

"But she's not old enough to ...." Kate stared into Jaq's eyes and then laid his hand gently back onto her arm, gripping it tightly with her own. "She's probably older than all of us put together. In some ways. All right," Kate said quietly.

"Ur?" Jaq asked. He smiled at his daughter but was not surprised when she did not smile back. *What does go on in her mind?*

Ur took a few deep, raspy breaths, looked directly at Proud and very politely said, "No, thank you, Mr. Proud. I believe I'll stay with my friends. And with my mother and father."

Bildad Proud's face darkened. His features, hardly handsome, twisted into a hideous, contorted mask. "No matter," he said. "If you won't come, I'll take you. You will learn to love me." He pushed himself off the rock and began to move for the girl.

"No-o-o-o!" Beele boomed, rising. Raising his arms, he shot a bolt of blue flame from his palms directly at Bildad Proud's chest.

But Proud deflected the blast with one of his own. The fire, though green and sickly, possessed enormous power. He shot another stream of green fire at Beele, knocking him backwards and to the ground. Proud threw his head back and roared with laughter. Taking advantage of Proud's carelessness, Beele fired, hitting him in the belly and staggering him. Angrily, Proud returned the volley, but this time Beele kept his feet.

"As you are, your power is not so great," Beele said. "You'll not be taking the child."

"Oh, but I will. And my power is sufficient to keep you at bay. Which is all I need to do for the moment. Later, when I rule with Ur, I will destroy you, Nicholas Beele. You see, your problem is, always has been, that you think solely in terms of black and white, good and evil, complete victory or defeat. I'm content to take advantage of a—stalemate."

Bildad Proud again made a move for Ur and Beele leveled a blast at him. But Proud was ready and deflected the flame, knocking Beele backward and down. "You see, even now my power is growing, and you've been weakened by your efforts on the lake. You've always been less than you'd like to believe. 'Behold, even the moon is not bright and the stars are not clean in his sight; how much less man who is maggot; and the son of man, who is a worm.'" *

Beele clenched his teeth in rage, but his strength spent, he could not move. Kate rushed to his side. "You're hurt," she said.

"He is beyond hurt. He is finished. I, on the other hand, am just beginning." Proud once again moved to mount the wall that led to the ledge and Ur. Bing and Boom stood fast and closed ranks around her. "Brave boys," Proud hissed.

"Leave my sons be," Enivel said. Together, he and Jaq rushed Proud. Flashing green fire from one hand, Proud knocked Hector's sword from Jaq's. A spout of flame erupted from the other and sent both men tumbling.

"Father!" the boys cried in fear.

But Enivel sat up. "Stay there," he said. "Stay by Ur!" Ur made a subtle move toward her own father.

Kate looked anxiously at Jaq. Though stunned, it was obvious that he was not seriously hurt. Quickly and deftly, Kate picked up Achilles' spear and charged Proud. This time he eschewed the green fire. His power was growing. With one mighty sweep of his forearm, he deflected Kate's spear, caught her across the chest and sent her sailing through the air. Hitting the rock wall opposite, her body dropped to its base and lay motionless.

Ur leapt from the ledge and ran to her mother. Kak Zhal charged after her, but his speed was no match for hers. Proud stretched out his hand to grab Ur, but missed. "Agile. And fast," he said with obvious pleasure. "We *will* make a pair."

"No, you won't. You'll come through me first," Kak Zhal growled.

"So be it, ugly little troll," Proud said.

Kak Zhal had placed himself between Bildad Proud and Ur. In front of him lay Kate's spear, just where it had fallen from her grasp when Proud had struck her. He made a move to pick it up, but Proud kicked it away. Kak Zhal spat. "No matter. I'll kill you with my bare hands."

Rushing Proud, Kak Zhal slammed into Evil. "No, Kak Zhal! The flute!" Ur cried. But Kak Zhal in his fury was beyond hearing.

The force of Kak Zhal's attack clearly surprised Proud, who was driven backward and up against the face of the promontory. Wrapping his massive arms around Proud's waist, Kak Zhal began to squeeze. Proud grimaced in pain. Evil squirmed and tried to push Kak Zhal away, but he would not budge. His eyes wide, searching, Proud reached over his head, caught hold of a large stone and with both hands and all of his strength, brought it down upon Kak Zhal's head, making a sickening sound, as if a ripe melon had been squashed. Staggering backward, Kak Zhal collapsed. Beele, still too weak to stand, eyed Proud darkly, who was leaning against the rocks, breathing heavily.

Ur ran to Kak Zhal. "No, Ur. Please, stay here," Kate said in a weak voice. Ur knelt down and touched his cheek.

Kak Zhal opened his eyes. "Did I, did I kill him? Are you safe?" he asked.

"Yes, I'm safe," she said.

"Good, good," Kak Zhal whispered.

"Oh, Uncle, you should have used the flute," Ur said, her voice shaking in syncopation with her dry breathing.

"Yes, you're right, girl. I forgot. It's yours now. Perhaps you'll remember me by it, eh?"

"I'll never forget you, Uncle," Ur said.

Kak Zhal tried to speak, but could not and exhaled his last breath, his crushed head lolling limply in Ur's tiny hands. Tears streamed down Ur's cheeks and plopped wetly onto Kak Zhal's face. "So this is loss," Ur said. She stood.

Proud pushed himself away from the rock wall. "Touching, but I think it's time for you to come with me now, girl," Proud said.

"I think not," Ur said. "You are Evil."

"No, child. Beele is evil. He is the Devil. You know that."

"No. He is man and the son of man. You said so yourself. But man is neither all good nor all bad, but both. You are *true* Evil. You are the Lie."

"What are you saying, child?"

"You are subtle. You insinuate yourself into our lives. We learn to lie to ourselves. We rationalize small evils until they consume us."

"Ah," Proud whispered. "You do know me, then."

"Yes, and you must be stopped."

"And how might *you* stop *me*? Hmm?" Proud chuckled, folding his arms and leaning back against the rock wall of the promontory.

"First, the Lie must be fixed, pinned down, or it will never be stopped," Ur said.

"And how might you do that?" Proud asked.

Walking over to where Achilles' spear had fallen, Ur stooped to pick it up. Proud laughed. "Such a large weapon for such a small girl." But his eyes widened with surprise and then fear, as Ur lifted the spear as she might have a twig. Swiftly, faster than Proud could think, she launched it with such force that it drove the point through Evil's chest and deep into the rock behind him. Black-green blood belched from his nostrils and flowed over his lips and down his chest.

The sun had risen and its rays began to spill over the east ridge of the cirque, striking the beach on which they stood. Slowly, the light's leading edge crept toward Bildad Proud. "And when the Lie at last has been fixed, it must be exposed to the light."

"No!" The word erupted from Proud's lips through a gurgling wet mass, but he could not move from the spot where Ur had pinned him to the rock. As the light of the sun struck Evil's face, beat down upon the body of the Lie, he began to burn. Skin sizzled. Then his hair exploded into flame, fire shooting skyward like a torch. His face blistered, then blackened. Eyes burst like hot grapes, fingers curled into twisted claws, until even his bones began to melt. Soon, there was nothing left of Bildad Proud but char and ash.

◙ ◉ ◙

For several moments, there was nothing to be heard, as if time had stopped. And perhaps it had.

Then, slowly, the world began to turn once again. At first, only the smell of burnt matter, only the hissing and popping of fried flesh, floated on the thin, dry air. From across the lake came the high-pitched sound of ice breaking. At last, the sun's warmth began to seep through the skin and from far off came the muffled sound of shouts and cheers.

"Father! Father!" cried Bing and Boom, running now to Enivel, who embraced them both. Bing and Boom began to weep. "You were so brave, Father," they said.

Beele shook himself and flexed his muscles, then walked to where Ur was crouched over Kak Zhal. Kneeling, Beele placed his hand on Ur's head. She locked her gaze on his. "I think I may be lost forever if I do not turn away," he said.

But he did not turn aside and, instead, cupping her face gently in his large gloved hands, he kissed her lightly on cheeks that were wet with tears and sharp with salt. At once, her ragged breathing grew quiet and her skin warmed.

"What have I done? This is no parlor trick."

Ur appeared puzzled for a moment, then very quietly said, "Thank you, Uncle Nick. And are you feeling better?"

Beele smiled broadly. "Yes. Oh, yes. Much, much better."

Ur turned to her parents. "Mother? Father? Are you both all right?" They were sitting on the beach, holding onto one another. Ur ran toward them but checked up, and she began to take deep, quiet breaths.

"My God, Jaq, listen." Jaq took Kate's hand. Ur's eyes opened wide. "Ur, what's wrong?" Kate asked in alarm.

Throwing her arms about their necks, Ur buried her head between their faces and began to breathe deeply once again, as if she were smelling an enormous, exotic flower.

"Kate, her body's warm," Jaq said.

"Mommy, Dad, I remember you."

"Ur," Kate asked, "what do you mean?" Gently, she lifted the child from her chest.

"My reason told me who you were, but not what made you special. But now I can remember. Thank you again, Uncle Nick," she said. "And I wish I could thank Uncle Kak Zhal. But he's ...." Ur's lip began to tremble and she could speak no more. Burying herself against her parents' bodies, she cried very hard and for a very long time.

Kate nuzzled Ur's hair, then pressed her face against the child's cheek, giving her daughter several soft kisses at the corners of her mouth.

Jaq could feel their hot breath mix. He almost felt ashamed of the joy he felt while his daughter wept bitterly.

At last Ur's sobs were spent. Standing erect, she wiped her face with her hand. "How do you bear loss?" she asked.

"Sometimes we wonder ourselves," Jaq said.

Kate considered her question for a moment. "It's because, on the whole, the benefits exceed the costs."

"Oh, for cryin' out loud, Kate. She's only a, a …." Jaq said, gesticulating randomly.

"I think I understand, Mommy," Ur said.

Kate smiled knowingly. "I thought you would."

Suddenly, shouts and laughter reached them from out on the thin ice, which was melting rapidly. Eldaf, Krenk and Anad were congratulating themselves on a battle hard fought and won.

As they approached the beach, the Rock Cats stopped not ten meters from the spot where Proud's carcass hung. Snarling, the Cats retreated.

"Whahoa!" Eldaf shouted as he tried to calm his Cat. When he saw Proud's body, his smile evaporated.

"What *is* that?" Anad said to no one in particular. Then the smell must have hit her. "Ugh!"

Krenk saw Kak Zhal. He loosed a high, hollow howl. "Nooo!" Although his Cat's shoulder stood a full three times Krenk's height above the beach, he jumped, landing on his hands and knees and scraping his palms badly. But he took no notice of them. He was up and running.

Throwing himself down alongside Kak Zhal's corpse, Krenk lifted his head off the rock, supporting it gently with his huge hands, as if to try to prevent any further damage from being done. "O-o-o-oh!" he wailed, softly. "I've been a mean old bastard. I knew that when I thought on what *you* were doing. And on what you did for Elspeth and for these people here. I wanted so badly to tell you I was sorry for all I'd said and done to you." Krenk fell silent and his eyes flooded with tears.

"What happened here, Beele?" Eldaf asked once again.

"Is the child safe?" Anad asked anxiously. Beele gestured toward the girl, who was standing now beside her parents, holding their hands.

"Good!" she said loudly. She looked down at Kak Zhal and put her hand to her throat.

"Are you all right?" Eldaf asked.

"My throat is thick. But I'm a warrior and so was he. And the child is safe," she said hoarsely.

Eldaf pointed to the charred scraps that clung to the promontory wall, his question clear.

"That," Beele said, "is Bildad Proud. He'd come to steal the child while we fought. But he hadn't counted on your help nor on the Rock Cats."

"The ferryman? Who killed him?" Eldaf asked.

Anad saw the spear's haft protruding from Evil's chest. "It was the woman," she said, shooting Kate an admiring glance.

"It was a woman. Or at least she will be, but it wasn't Kate. It was Ur," Beele said. Eldaf, Anad and Krenk looked at one another, their eyes wide with surprise. "We all tried to stop him. To kill him. But he was too much, even for me."

"What *was* he? What had he become?" Eldaf asked.

"He was the Untruth. He was the greatest Evil," Ur answered in a small, quiet voice.

"I think it's time we buried the dead," Jaq said, surprising himself that there was nothing else he could say, as he looked down at his friend.

Krenk sighed deeply, moved Kak Zhal's body, then cleared some loose stones off the stretch of beach where he had fallen. Driving her sword into the dirt, Anad began to loosen it and found it quite soft. Dropping to the ground, she began to scoop soil by the handful. Everyone joined in and soon the burial pit was dug.

Before they were about to place Kak Zhal into his grave, Ur stopped them. "Just a moment, please," she said. Then she placed the silver flute that Kak Zhal had given her back into his Lamikin vest pocket.

"But Ur," Kate said, "he gave it to you. It was a gift."

"No, the flute was a gift to him. He made it sing. It was part of who he was. Its music was his gift to us. I'll remember it. That's enough."

"But Ur," Jaq said, "he wanted to give you something more."

Ur faced her father. Here was this person standing before him. "He did," Ur said.

The sun had risen well above the ridgeline of the cirque's east wall, warming the atmosphere considerably. Kate and Jaq took off their down vests. "You can leave them," Beele said. "They'll be of no further use. We need to leave at once."

"Uncle Nick is right. We must go," Ur said. "Mommy and Dad, you have to get home and the door isn't always open." Jaq blinked. He stole a glance at Kate. She stared straight ahead, her jaw set in hard outline.

"Go? Where to?" Krenk asked.

"Back to Mir, of course," Eldaf said. "By way of Old Spall, unless I miss my guess."

"You miss it, Eldaf," Anad said. "They're going to Spall, but New."

A strange expression crossed Eldaf's face, as he regarded Anad silently. "Neither of us remembers much about New Spall," Eldaf said. "I think you'll find it only if it wants you to. But we can point you in the right direction, if that'll help."

"It'll help a great deal. Thanks," Jaq said.

They made their way on their Cats across an expanse of mud and rocks that had lately been covered with ice. But all that remained was a thin ribbon of liquid, flowing freely now, glinting bright silver in the sun's glare.

◙ ◉ ◙

Back on the stretch of beach where Kak Zhal was buried and what remained of Bildad Proud hung, suspended from Achilles' spear, there was a flux in the atmosphere. Tiny but perceptible. And, if anyone had been there to notice, they would have seen a phantom, rising like a wisp of smoke from the spot where Ur had struck the Lie. Thin and black and weak, but extant. As it considered what it was and who it might become, it thought that, perhaps, what little that remained was more than enough.

CHAPTER 16

When at last the spot was reached where the Styx vanished in the thick and dusty lunar soil, the sun still hung low in the sky. But the heat was merciless.

"Do you see that single tall peak in the distance?" Eldaf asked. "Beyond, there's another mountain. You can't see it from here. New Spall's close by it. Though not beyond. Not beyond. Remember that."

"Eldaf," Nick said, "are you sure you won't come? It is your home."

"No," Eldaf said, smiling sadly. "Old Spall is my home." Eldaf gestured at Anad. "But *she* might want to go with you. I think she'd like it. Think she'd like it for sure." Eldaf swallowed hard.

Anad shook her head. "No. It's back to Old Spall for me, too. Eldaf and I blooded together back there in battle. I think we've more adventures of our own to share." Slowly, she stroked her thick blonde hair.

Eldaf looked her up and down, then burst into the laughter of pure happiness. "You'll come back with me then, to Old Spall? To be my wife?"

Running her fingers through Eldaf's hair, Anad grabbed a handful. That seemed to be answer enough, for he kissed her hard. Everyone laughed and applauded. Everyone, that is, except Ur.

"Ur, don't you ever smile?" Bing asked.

Ur shrugged. "What's that?"

"Well, you know. When people are happy, they kind of … I don't know, they kind of, well, lift their lips and show their teeth. Like this." Bing flashed Ur a broad smile.

"Yes. It's easy," Boom said, grinning from ear to ear. "Try it."

Ur opened her mouth and clenched her teeth. "Is that good?" Ur asked.

"It's a beginning," Beele said.

"Eldaf?" Jaq asked. "Do you have a weapon like Anad's?"

"No. Her sword was found with her. I was found alone." Jaq handed him Hector's sword. Eldaf said nothing, but his face spoke for him. Then, in obvious high spirits, he shouted, "Enivel! Your boys are masters of the Cats. Will you lead us home?"

The boys turned their Cats then shouted to Ur, "Come back if you can. You can stay with us anytime!" Loping across the Styx, which was a mere trickle at that point, the Rock Cats soon broke into a full run, churning up clouds of dust in their wake, as they blazed back toward Old Spall.

◙ ◉ ◙

"Ur? Would you like to be our drover?" Jaq asked.

"Yes, I would," she said.

"Do you remember when I took you for a ride in my old truck?" Jaq said.

"I think so, but I believe I fell asleep."

"Well, it's your turn to take the reins. So don't fall asleep this time," Jaq said.

"No, Dad." She gave the Rock Cat a soft scratch on the top of its head, then applied a sharp kick with one leg and off they bolted.

"Whoa!" Jaq cried.

"Ur! Don't you think we ought to slow down just a little?" Kate said.

"No, Mommy. Uncle Nick's been trying to tell everyone for the longest time that we need to hurry. It's far too hot." With that, Ur gave the Cat another kick, and it leapt off of the lunar surface.

Nothing broke the blank expanse of white before them except the solitary hill in the distance. The sky was nearly as white as the sand and at the horizon's edge the air shimmered and danced.

At last the lone mountain began to spread and rise in height from the desert floor. When they finally drew alongside it, Nick asked Ur to stop the Cat. He gave Jaq and Kate a sip of Peevo, and after he had corked the skin, he told Ur to charge ahead.

Hours passed. A second peak to the south appeared and began to grow in size but, like the first, only slowly. Peevo had long been exhausted.

"Stop. Please, stop," Kate said at last, in a hoarse whisper. "I have to rest. To stop."

"But Kate ...." Nick said.

"I ... have ... to ... stop."

"Is Mommy all right?" Ur asked.

"No, she's not. She's sick. You must stop the Cat," Jaq said.

"Uncle Nick?"

"You can stop, Ur," Nick said.

Ur brought the Rock Cat to rest, then, with a gentle squeeze against its shoulder, signaled it to crouch on its haunches. Jumping off of the Cat's back, Nick helped Jaq slide Kate off the beast and into the small shadow it cast. Then Jaq collapsed beside her.

"Dad, is Mommy going to be all right?" Jaq felt too weak to answer. Ur placed her hand on Kate's cheek. "Uncle Nick," she said, "Mommy's very cold. She feels like Kak Zhal after he was hurt. Dad, are you sick, too?"

Jaq's brains felt as if they might have boiled. "I, yes ... I don't feel very well," Jaq whispered. Pulling Ur toward him, he opened his eyes as far as he was able. The lids were sore and swollen. "Ur," Jaq said, "we love you. We wanted to help you, and I think we did. And," Jaq swallowed as best he could, "we got to see you again."

"I don't want you to die. Either of you. It's not the worst thing in the world, but it's no fun, either. Dad, if I kiss Mommy, will it make her feel better? Like when I kissed your side?"

"It might."

Lightly, Ur leaned over and placed her lips against her mother's cheek. Kate stirred. Her eyes fluttered, then opened. "Ur," was all she said.

"You have to help them, Uncle Nick. You must," Ur said. Odd, but it sounded to Jaq as if it were more a command than a request. Ur glared at Nick, then walked straight up to where he stood. "Jess, you can take off your gloves."

"How did you know?" he asked in a loud voice.

"I learned a lot from the Lady Tiamat. And I've studied you since I met you. It wasn't hard to figure out." Carefully, Ur pulled at the fingers of Beele's gloves, loosening their grip on his skin, then slipped them off of his hands.

On Beele's palms and the backs of his hands were two large, ragged scars that had never completely healed. As he stared at his wounds, he began to speak. "I can feel a grinding inside, like two enormous blocks of granite being drawn to one another. Two pieces to a puzzle." Beele snapped his eyes shut as if his separate selves had at last slammed together. "There is a fit," he said. "There's work to be done, but there is a fit."

"It's a beginning, and beginnings are very important. You've said so yourself."

He wept. Tears of blood poured from his eyes. Dark blood began to flow from the wounds in his hands, dripping from the ends of his fingers and splattering in large drops onto the dry dust. Blood seeped through the side of his shirt and soaked the tops of his black boots.

Kate had regained consciousness, helped perhaps by the shadow thrown by the Cat. Jaq had buried his face in his hands, trying to relieve the pain in his skull. "Jaq, look," Kate said, in a raspy voice.

Bright flashes winked in his brain. Images swam. He blinked. The world settled onto focus. "The blood!"

Black blood turned bright red and then, as on the Lost that day, changed once again. Clear cold water flowed from the holes in Beele's hands, gushed from his side, flowed from his feet, soaking the dry dust.

"Mommy, Dad," Ur said. "Can you come? Are you able? Please, you must try. You must have a drink."

Kate and Jaq struggled the short distance to where Nick stood. Dropping to their knees, they each grabbed hold of one of Nick's hands and drank. And drank. They did not think that they would ever get enough. Neither of them *wanted* to be sated.

At last the flow slowed. Ur's parents rose, feeling refreshed and strong. "She called you something," Kate said to Nick. "She called you by another name."

"I know you!" Jaq lifted a hand and pointed at Nick. "It was just after Ur died. Someone was sitting beside me in the old truck. I put my head on his chest. I mean, that's how it felt. And I cried. Then I felt so much better. It was you, wasn't it?"

"It was I," Nick said.

Jaq dropped his arm to his side. "I don't get it. What was all that devil stuff?"

"I am also the Son of Man, as we all are, and our capacity for sin *is* original. Who I am has only now become a possibility. Ur has done that for me. As to what I am, what I was? I'm sorry...." Nick spread his arms wide. "What was I supposed to have done, after all? Walk up to people and say, 'How d'you do? I'm Jesus Christ.' They'd have thrown me into an insane asylum."

"But what about the Flood?" Jaq said. "What Tiamat said about you ... and the Flood."

"The child is Father to the man," Nick said. "I was rather unpleasant as an adolescent."

For a time, both Kate and Jaq were silent. "But you have powers, Nick. You could have *shown* people who you were," Kate said at last.

"Could I? But I just told you. I don't know yet *who* I really am. Certainly I know *what* I am, but even then, which side should I have displayed? Good or evil? Devil or Christ? I spent forty days in the wilderness talking to myself, trying to figure that one out." Beele laughed broadly. "Besides, many of my powers are only parlor tricks. You know that to be true, Jaq." Nick placed his hand on Jaq's shoulder. Jaq did not flinch. "Besides, there would have been nothing to be gained by running around waving a banner, proclaiming myself. There never is. What I needed was to be recognized. That's what my nature demanded. That is what your daughter has done."

"Then you're feeling better, Uncle Nick?" Ur said.

"Yes. Yes, Ur, as a matter of fact, I am much better. I must admit I *am* feeling a bit unsteady, like a child on new legs, unaided, for the first time. Somewhat daunted, but far more exhilarated."

"Good," Ur said. "Mommy, Dad, are you feeling much better, too?"

"Yes, we are. Much. Thank you," Kate said. Jaq smiled in agreement.

"Good. Now we need to see to the Cat. It needs to rest. It needs to return to the rock. As you can see, there's little of that around here."

"No, there isn't," Jaq said. "Deserts are—" A shock coursed across the surface of his skin. He saw his own surprise reflected in Kate's features. They were standing in a field of bright green grass.

"But how—" Kate began.

"Was it the water?' Jaq asked.

Nick turned his palms upward and shrugged. "It's your dream." A lot of help you are, once again, Jaq thought. But he checked himself, and his irritation cooled as quickly as it had flared. Nick had been a great deal of help.

"Dad, please," Ur said, "we must release the Cat."

"But Ur, we need the Cat. Perhaps now more than ever."

"It needs its rest more."

Ur walked over to the Rock Cat and scratched its cheek. Jaq moved to Ur's side and it rumbled a gravelly growl. "Nice kitty," he said nervously.

"Kitty?" Ur said. "What's kitty?"

"Well, it's a diminutive," Jaq said, thoughtfully.

"Oh, Jaq. For cryin' out loud," Kate said.

"That's what it *is*. What am I *supposed* to tell her? One minute she sounds like Plato, the next like Pollyanna. For cryin' out loud yourself."

"Dad, I don't understand what you and Mommy are talking about. What's a diminutive?"

Kate smiled and put her hands on her hips. "Well, professor?"

"Wel-l-l …." Jaq cleared his throat. "It's like, we call Nicholas, Nick, and Mother, Mommy." Jaq shot Kate a supercilious look. "Quite simple."

"I see," Ur said. "Thank you. There's so much to learn. Do you suppose it'll ever stop?" All three adults shook their heads no. "Good. Because it's fun. It's work, but it's fun."

Ur stood beside the head of the great silicant beast, appearing very small. "Kitty," she said softly. "I like that. It's a funny word. Sort of like 'uncle.' Kitty," she repeated. The Cat made a purring noise. Ur whispered into the beast's ear.

She scratched its face. It rose and, stretching its massive limbs, turned and loped across the plain. When it reached the horizon, it leapt high and disappeared.

"Dad. Don't look so concerned. Everything will be fine. Besides, I told you, Kitty needs to rest. And I believe Kitty and the other Cats did all they could do for us. It's up to us now."

"Or up to me," Jaq said. He surveyed in silence the verdant expanse that embraced them. A delicate blue ceiling draped softly overhead. "Look!" Jaq said. But when he started to point at the sky, he winced. "This damned side. I'd nearly forgotten about it, the pain in my head was so bad." Jaq gasped when he tested his range of motion again.

"Uncle Nick's water might help," Ur said.

Nick examined his hands. There were scars, but they were smooth and hard. "I'm afraid I can't, Ur. Besides, it wasn't really anything I *did*. It happened."

"Your shirt's still wet, Uncle Nick."

"So it is!" Unfastening the strings that secured his shirt at the chest, Nick took it off and held it out to Jaq.

Jaq peeled off his own shirt and offered it to Nick. Kate stared at Jaq's wound and bit her lip, but said nothing. As the cool wet cloth touched Jaq's side, he drew a breath. He could feel the flesh knitting. "So the stories are true."

Nick laughed. "That bit of advice happens to have been. Some of the stories are true. Some not. Remember, I didn't write them. I didn't even get to proofread them. And that, my dear Kate, was one of my most significant dilemmas. What I was, what I *am*, is not what people have come to expect. That's why I couldn't simply reveal myself. They would have been disappointed. They wouldn't have understood. Certainly, they would never have believed. No. I had to be recognized."

Nick paused. "I didn't feel I could, nor should, interfere. Now, I don't know."

"You've choices and you've time," Kate said.

"Yes! What a brilliant prospect." Nick rubbed his hands together.

"Prospect," Jaq said. A short distance away the grassland rose to form a high knoll. "I'll have a look!" he cried as he ran toward it.

◨ ◉ ◨

"Are we back on Earth?" Kate asked. She took a deep breath. "It doesn't smell like Idaho. The air's too heavy and humid."

"No, Kate, we're not in Idaho," Nick said.

Kate inhaled again and dropped to the ground, drinking deeply of the sweet, supple atmosphere. "Wherever we are, I don't want to move from this spot."

"We're in New Spall," Nick said.

"Which is where, precisely?" Kate asked.

"As our mutual friend the Indian would say—'elsewhere, where else?'" Nick said with a chuckle.

Kate rolled her eyes and flopped back onto the tall, fragrant grass, which released a pungent, green odor as its stalks snapped beneath the weight of her fall. Kate pulled Ur down gently beside her. She gave her a squeeze and Ur squeezed back. "I never thought I'd feel you do that," Kate said thickly.

"I'm so sorry. Everything was *very* confusing."

"I know. I used to try to put myself in your place. I'd try not to swallow, for even a minute. I don't know how you bore it."

"Kate! Ur! Come on!" Jaq was shouting from the top of the grassy hillock.

"I think we should join your father," Nick said to Ur. "And your husband," he added, addressing Kate. Nick stood quietly for a moment and rubbed the smooth scars on his hands.

They found Jaq pointing at a house set in a shallow valley that was bordered in the distance by a long line of trees that stretched as far as the eye could see.

The house was of a simple design. Victorian, with a high gabled roof, but lacking excessive ornamentation. It had been painted light gray and trimmed in bone white.

A porch, protected by a low overhang, surrounded its perimeter. Many of the windows were open, allowing a light wind to pass through and causing the curtains to billow in and out at its touch.

"We're going home," Jaq said, hoisting his daughter up onto his shoulders and setting off.

"He doesn't know, does he?" Nick said. Kate shook her head. "And how do you feel about it?"

"All I ever wanted for Ur was a chance for her to enjoy life and fulfill her potential. I mourned her loss, not mine."

"Perhaps, then, you ought to start."

Jaq set Ur down in the deep green grass and bounded up the steps of the porch and into the shade, waving to the Kate and Nick to follow.

When Jaq walked through the front door, he was surprised by the amount of detail he hadn't noticed when he had taken that 'trip' on the porch of Coogan & Co. The entry hall was more spacious than he remembered. Walls were painted a delicate cream color, while moldings and baseboards were covered with gleaming white enamel. Floors of fine walnut were streaked with black and blond tones and polished to a satiny luster.

On either side of the hall, double pocket doors faced one another. They were shut. Directly ahead, a narrow staircase to the upper floor hugged the right side wall, then turned back on itself in a gentle curve. Just at the top of those stairs, he thought. Then shuddered. *No, She won't stop us. Not this time.* He returned to the porch where Ur was waiting and motioned excitedly to Nick and Kate to hurry.

"Boy!" a voice barked. "What's your rush?"

Jaq's jaw went slack. Seated on a porch swing were Grannie Jen and Grandma Kattie. Print dresses, steel-frame glasses, gray-blue perms and all.

"We just want to make sure you get home safe," Grannie Jen said.

Jaq could feel a large smile split his face. "And that morning—"

"We wanted you to know we were thinking about you and were here if you decided to come. And who is this?" Grandma Kattie asked in a soothing voice.

"This is my daughter." Jaq heard the clatter of footsteps as Nick and Kate stepped onto the porch. "*Our* daughter. That's my wife, Kate. And that's …."

"We know him," Grannie Jen said perfunctorily. "How'd you do, Kate. I'm Jen. This is Kattie. We're Jaq's grandmas."

"Yes, I guessed that," Kate said. "I've heard a lot about the both of you."

The two grandmothers looked at each other and nodded.

"Kate's very sweet, Jaq," Grandma Kattie said.

Grannie Jen stared hard at Ur. Ur stared right back. A thin smile split Grannie Jen's lips, like the merest crack on a sheet of ice. "What's *your* name? Speak up, girl."

"Ur," she answered quietly. "And you both should be my great-grandmothers," Ur said. "I hope I've got that right. I'm learning, and there are so many things to know."

"You've got it right," Grannie Jen said. Ur might have appeared pleased. It was always so hard to tell.

"Jaq?" Grandma Kattie said. "You looked frightened when you came out of the house."

"I've been here before and the last time something horrible chased me." Jaq shuddered again.

Grannie Jen cackled. "Across the field, through the trees, down the ice road to the cabin?"

"That's right. How did you—?"

"Sometimes she's not very imaginative. You won't have no truck with her again," Grannie Jen said.

"Did you get what you came for, then?" Grandma Kattie asked.

"Yes! I came for Ur, you know. *We* came. And we've gotten her, too," Jaq said brightly. Everyone was silent. Jaq cleared his throat and his rib muscles contracted, making him wince.

"What's wrong?" Grandma Kattie asked.

"I was wounded when I fought Tiamat. She's—"

"I thought we just told you. We know who she is," Grannie Jen said. "Let's see how it looks, boy."

Jaq lifted the shirt Nick had given him. There were no open lesions and the skin was shiny and smooth, though it was pink and slightly inflamed.

"How did it heal so quick?" Grannie Jen asked.

"Just with some water," Jaq said.

"It was very special water," Ur said.

Grannie Jen harumphed. "I'd have washed it down with a good dose of iodine. Don't you remember what I always told you? 'Old Indian says, no smart no cure.'"

"Which Old Indian?" a voice interrupted. "Not this one. I'm a big baby when I'm hurt." Joe was leaning nonchalantly against the frame of the front door.

"Joe!" everyone cried. The time must be very close, Jaq thought.

"Hello, Joe," Ur said.

"Hello, Ur."

"How—" Kate began.

From inside the house came a sound of music. "Hark!" Grannie Jen said. Sweet notes, evocative chromaticisms and lush harmonies poured through the door and out the windows. A piano was playing. Ur drew a deep, whistling breath. "Excuse me, please," they heard her call back after she had disappeared through the doorway.

"Shall we all go?" Kate asked.

"I think we'll listen from right here, if you don't mind," Grandma Kattie said. "Won't we, Jen?" Grannie Jen nodded.

Kate walked over to the two grandmothers and kissed them both on the cheek. Grandma Kattie chuckled hoarsely. Grannie Jen squeezed Kate's hand.

Kate turned, and without a word followed Ur inside. "Such a nice girl, Jaq," Grandma Kattie said.

"Solid, too. Unless I miss my guess," Grannie Jen added.

"You don't miss it," Jaq said.

"Never did," Grannie Jen said.

Jaq rose and leaned over to kiss them both. "I'm very lucky," he said. "All my best girls have always been very nice. Thanks for thinking of me."

"We always will, boy."

"I love you," Jaq said, smiling at Grandma Kattie.

"I love you, too," he said to Grannie Jen. She lifted her chin and gave him a rather stern look. Jaq looked down at his feet, then back at Grannie Jen. "I guess we never said that to one another."

"Didn't have to."

"Run along, Jaq," Grandma Kattie said. "They're waiting for you."

Joe thrust his hands into his pockets and stared at Nick. "So," the Indian said, "back to your old habits? Giving people the shirt off your back."

Beele laughed and shrugged. "It's who I am, after all. For so long I was an instrument of Mother. And others."

"I think what you need is some time for yourself," the Indian said.

The two men were silent. At last Joe spoke. "Let's go. I think it's time."

"Indeed?"

"Yeah, indeed."

When they had gone inside the house, Grannie Jen spoke to Grandma Kattie. The sky had become overcast with dark gray clouds. "Looks like a storm," she said laconically.

"Yes. It's just what we need. It'll clear the air," Grandma Kattie said. Grannie Jen nodded and the two of them sat in their swing, holding hands, staring out over the field of grass, now thick and dark and tossed about by a cool, steady wind. Neither one said another word.

◎ ◉ ◎

Inside the house, strains of music, shaded with nuances never heard before, floated through the semi-dark of the parlor. The walnut floors were now more black than blond. All of the brilliance of the white enamel moldings had faded to flatness. The creamy white walls were now a dark shade of ocher. The room seemed to settle itself, becoming quiet, although there was no absence of sound.

Outside, light was being lost to the thickening gray storm clouds. The adumbration of the porch roof, which extended along the front of the house and both sides, deepened the texture of the atmosphere.

"It has the feel of dusk in here, doesn't it, Jaq?" Kate said. "The French have such a perfect word for it. 'Crepuscule.'"

"Yes, perfect."

"The sound of the word reminds me that there's beauty even in the loss of something as precious as the daylight." Kate stared at Ur and picked at her finger.

Standing next to a brilliant black grand piano, Ur was studying the musician's hands intently. Atop the instrument sat a silver candelabrum set with tapered white candles. Their luminescence waxed with the gathering storm.

At last Mozart lifted his hands off of the keys and set them in his lap. Ur sighed. "Oh, that was lovely. It reflected the light and the sky perfectly. Do you expect the music affected them as well?"

"Isn't that the nature of reflections, after all?" Mozart replied. He noticed Kate and Jaq and his face brightened. Mozart rose and, clicking his heels, inclined his head. "I am so glad to see that you met with success!"

"Thanks as much to you as anyone," Jaq said.

"Ur told me. But the credit for my contribution must really go to Herr Kak Zhal."

Ur's eyes filled with tears. "We all miss him," Kate said.

Ur wiped her eyes with her arm, gathering herself, it seemed. "Herr Mozart claims that he hasn't seen Kak Zhal and that I may not either," Ur said. She looked from her mother to her father, and then to Nick Beele and the Indian, who stood by the open pocket doors.

"That is essentially correct," Nick said.

"But even if I will become—"

"No. Especially not then," Nick said. "Once you involve yourself, consequences are unpredictable."

"It just doesn't work like that," Joe said.

Ur bit her lower lip and nodded. "Herr Mozart," Ur asked, "would you mind playing something else?"

"I would be delighted," Mozart said and sat back down at the piano.

Ur went to her parents and leaned against their legs, while the three of them listened for a time as the piano filled the room with sound and sense.

"It's time to go," Ur said at last to her parents. Joe had left the room.

When they stepped out of the parlor and into the main entry, the air was thick and dark, nearly opaque. Mozart's music, delicate and muted, trailed like a light mist.

Jaq parted another pair of pocket doors. Rumbling along their guides, the doors' passage was echoed by a deep cough of thunder.

The room, though considerably smaller, had a high ceiling. Facing the entrance was a tall pier glass. A spare, gold trail of Acanthus encircled a bevel around the mirror's entire perimeter. Recessed into the wall, the central glass was flanked by two identical mirrors that faced one another.

Outside, the sky was wet and leaden. Jaq was able to see his grandmothers gazing out over the field of grass that surrounded the house.

"Where is Joe?" Jaq asked.

"Look into the glass," Ur cried as she ran toward the mirror with her finger raised. "He's gone ahead."

Through the medium of the reflections in the mirror, Jaq swept his gaze about the room. He began to notice objects at a different level of detail. He heard Kate draw a sharp breath. *She sees it too.* He could discern evidence of minute brush strokes in the enamel of the baseboard and moldings. Bubbles, minute imperfections, could be seen in the panes of glass set in the frames of the windows, panes that had appeared perfect on a gross scale. The glass squares collapsed and he was able to make out the structure of a beautiful crystal lattice. He could see the follicles of hair on the heads of his grandmothers and the molecules of the skin on Kate's cheeks. Everyone, every*thing* perceived, presented itself in both gross and exquisitely fine detail.

"Lovely," Jaq said softly. He shook himself. "But I still can't find Joe. All I see are reflections of myself."

"And everything reflects everything else. Uncle Nick said that, and you believe it as well, Dad. Uncle Joe said you did. So, you see, Joe is right there in those images of your own self, even though he may be a bit hard to pick out at first."

Jaq shrugged and held out his hands to Kate and Ur. "I guess this isn't any screwier than everything else that's happened to us, so let's go. Through the looking glass!"

But neither Kate nor Ur accepted Jaq's outstretched hands. "I'm sorry, Dad. I'm staying."

Jaq hadn't suspected. Not ever. He screamed silently for help from his friend and his wife. All he received was the reflection of profound and gentle pity in their faces.

"I'm not staying *here*, that is. I'm going back to the Lady Tiamat," Ur said.

"Tiamat? Why?"

"Because she needs me."

"What do you mean, she needs you? So do we!"

"I know. And I need you, too. But she needs me more. She doesn't know anything about love, Dad. Or at least, not very much. That's the worst ignorance of all. But you do. And so does Mommy and so do I, because we taught one another. The Lady Tiamat has to know, Dad. She has to learn about it, and I'm the only one who can teach her."

"You have to do this?" Jaq whispered.

"Yes, Dad."

"You want to do this as well?"

"That, too."

Jaq stood up. He took a deep breath, but still, bright moisture filled his eyes. "I thought I came here for a lot of reasons. Now, I realize I came here for only one. For your sake." Kneeling down and squeezing Ur as hard as he dared, Jaq kissed her on the cheek. It was salty, but he wasn't at all sure whether the tears were his or his daughter's.

"Thank you so much for understanding, Dad," Ur said.

Kate bit her lip, but tears did not come. "You are an unpretentious child, Ur," she said. "I do love you so."

Ur spread her arms wide, then ran across the length of the room and did a tight cartwheel.

"I didn't realize you'd be so thrilled to see us go," Jaq said sourly, wiping his face with his sleeve.

"Oh, no, Dad. That's not it at all. I'm just practicing."

"Practicing what?" Jaq asked, a small smile slipping between his cheeks.

"Why, practicing being myself."

"Ah," Jaq said. "That is a wonderful thing to practice."

"I believe she's discovering her own blithe spirit. And perhaps we have Kak Zhal and Herr Mozart to thank for that," Kate said.

Ur smiled her odd, toothy smile as best as she was able, then ran to her parents and hugged them both around their necks as they stooped to embrace her. Then she turned and ran at great speed toward a small door to the side of the pier glass that Jaq had not noticed. She turned another cartwheel and spun right through the closed door.

"Impossible," Kate whispered.

"No," Jaq said. "Just highly improbable. Beyond highly improbable, actually. But not impossible."

"I think Ur has shown you the way home," Nick said.

"You mean she's shown *us*, don't you?" Jaq asked.

Nick shook his head. Kate took Jaq's hand and kissed it.

"Unfinished business?" Jaq asked.

"Some. But mostly I'm going to begin …." he smiled. "Begin practicing being myself."

As they approached the door, Nick stopped them. "I think you'll need these," he said to Jaq, pulling a pair of green surgical slippers out of his rucksack. Jaq accepted them, but he gave Nick a quizzical look.

"An artifact," Nick said. "We needed one to get here and you'll need one to return. I'm sorry. I took this when I, um, 'lifted' Kate's monitor."

"May I have it back?" Kate asked.

"Certainly, but I don't see—"

"Neither do I, but I *feel* it," Kate said.

Nick laughed. "And how can I, who has been so wrong about so many things, question you?"

"Because you may surprise yourself and actually get it right one of these days," Kate said.

Nick smiled broadly. "I certainly hope so."

"I know I'm right," Kate said as she accepted the baby monitor with great care. "Goodbye," she said, leaning forward and giving him a kiss on the cheek.

"Oh!" Nick said. "I believe, Jaq, that you'll find almost a full bottle of Lagavulin remaining," he said, handing him the tiny gold key to the cabinet in his study that held his precious scotch.

"I'll have a sip every Christmas," Jaq said rather hoarsely, surprising himself.

Nick opened the small door in the wall and Kate and Jaq walked through it. Jaq heard it click shut behind them.

They both turned toward the sound. "Jesus," Jaq said in what struck him as an overly loud voice.

"I'm glad neither of us is claustrophobic," Kate said. Facing them was a blank white wall.

"Oh, fuck!" Jaq exclaimed, grabbing Kate's forearm. Off to one side, two metal doors, inset at their tops with large panes of opaque glass, like blank eyes, stared at them. "It's the surgery room where Ur was born." He stared down at his feet, covered by the green slippers. "And this is the prep room. I'm sure of it."

She took a loud, very deep breath. "Do you suppose we get do-overs?"

"I doubt it." Jaq stroked Kate's hair with his hand. "You were asleep, of course, and your hair had fallen across your forehead and lay in a soft pile on your shoulder. And I could see a gold earring resting against your neck."

"The pig with wings. And in a way, it flew," Kate said, turning her head back toward the surgery room. "Look!" Slipped beneath the doors was the gray, black and white quantum carpet.

For a moment they hesitated, then Kate tucked the baby monitor tightly under her arm, grabbed Jaq and pulled him through the doors. Whether she was dragging him into their past or their future he did not know.

◙ ◉ ◙

CHAPTER 17

A fierce white sun shone off rough, buff peaks. It had sucked all of the moisture, as well as the color, from a sky stretched silent and cloudless above them. But the brilliance seemed a trick, for a chilly wind rose from the surface of the Lost River. Vinnie put his arm around Clara and pulled her close.

"That feels better," she said. "I'm sure glad Father Nick left this rug, or my butt would have flash frozen."

"I'd have thawed it out for you," Vinnie said.

"I'll bet you would have!" Clara gave him a snappy slap, as he tried to slip his hand behind her belt.

Vinnie grinned at her. "If you think this is cold, wait until that northwest wind hits you, coming off the Hudson."

Clara slid herself around to face Vinnie. "Can you believe it? We're *both* going to New York."

"Correction. All three of us. Boy, I can't wait to tell Mr. and Mrs. q about it."

"Yeah. I was so excited to tell Jaq when we got to their house yesterday."

"Well, you'll get your chance. Unless I miss my guess, Father Beele's got something cooking."

"I'll say. Like that burning tree?" Clara shivered and Vinnie pulled her a little closer. "Anyway, mostly I'm happy for Levine."

"You know what? When Levine called to tell me about everything yesterday, he just cried for a few minutes. Not blubbering or anything but just, you know, happy fucking tears." Vinnie shook his head. "Head of retail. How do you suppose Mr. q pulled it off?"

"He's good. And Rock loves him."

"And I love you," Vinnie said and kissed her. "And you're good, too. Still scared of screwing up?"

"You bet. But I don't think it would be normal if I wasn't." Clara took Vinnie's hands in hers. "I still don't understand something. You told me that you were afraid to succeed. You're so damned smart. Blabla's going to love you. So what was that all about?"

"Here's how it was. By the end of first grade I was reading above level, so my teacher put me into fourth grade, where I turned out to be the best in the class. Trouble was, the nine-year-olds weren't happy about that. So they beat me up. Suddenly, I encountered problems and was sent back to first grade. Let me tell you, I worked my ass off to read average.

"In junior high, I found that I could look at non-linear equations and visualize them as curves and spaces. I solved problems so quickly that the teacher thought I was cheating. She told my father, and he beat the shit out of me, so I turned stupid.

"Anyway, I took care of my mind at home in the privacy of my room. I matriculated at Baruch over the objections of my old man. He wanted me to go into the 'carting' business."

"Carting?"

"Brooklynese for garbage man. But the prick had lost control of me. Had lost control of me ever since the day he had broken my balls over I don't even remember what. He charged me and I rammed my elbow right into his coconut. He dropped like, well, like a sack of garbage."

"My God, that must have been frightening."

Vinnie chuckled. "It was quite a shit-show. 'You've killed him. You've killed your father!' my mother was screaming. 'Hope so,' my sister had said. That was kind of funny.

"Actually, I thought I *had* killed him. He was laid out for twenty minutes. When he came to, we just stared at each another."

"Then what?"

"I walked out of the room. He never touched me again. But I guess stuff like that has a way of sticking."

"So do things like this." Clara wrapped her arms around Vinnie and hugged him hard. "My God!" she yelled.

Jaq thought he heard a shrill voice. But there was no mistaking a loud "Fangool!" as he hit a surface that was as hard and dusty as his moon had been.

He rolled and sat up as quickly as he could. Standing there were Vinnie and Clara, eyes wide, jaws slack and speechless. Kate was sitting right next to him. "You okay?" Jaq asked, touching her lightly on the thigh. She nodded.

"Well," he said, "looks like the present."

"I'm sorry—" Kate began.

"Later. Just a brain fart I had on the way over." He jumped up, then helped her to her feet.

The high desert sun was blinding off of the white blanket of new snow that surrounded them. Alongside the massive cottonwood where they had left for Luna with Beele, the Lost burbled by, undisturbed.

"Are you two, uh, all right?" Clara asked, shaking slightly.

Jaq and Kate regarded one another for a very long moment. "Yes," Jaq said at last.

"Yes," Kate echoed. Then she shivered and rubbed her arms. "But it's a bit chilly."

"Take this," Vinnie said, handing Kate his black leather jacket, which she accepted with a thank you. "So …." Vinnie paused, closed his eyes and shook his head, as if he were trying to rattle things back into their proper places. "So, where you been?"

"That will take some time to explain," Kate said.

"We've got time. Ay, we've been waiting all day for you," Vinnie said.

Jaq smiled. "Thank you, kids." He rolled up the quantum carpet and threw it over his shoulder. "And what day *is* it?" he asked, tentatively.

"Why, Christmas Day," Clara answered.

All the way back to Ketchum, Vinnie assaulted Jaq with questions about the strange world that he and Kate had visited. Calmly, Jaq answered them all as best he could, appreciating Vinnie's curiosity and simply drained of any emotional reserves that might have caused him to feel irritation or anger. Occasionally, Clara would punctuate the conversation by addressing Kate cautiously concerning Ur and her feelings at critical points in the unfolding narrative. Kate usually politely demurred.

By the time they arrived home, the westering sun was splashing the bottoms of black clouds deep pink. Climbing the steps to the front door, Clara laid her hand on Kate's arm. Jaq and Vinnie were fumbling with the keys. "How can you bear it?" Clara asked, her eyes moist.

"I can't," Kate said. "But I must." She put her arm through Clara's and they followed the men into the house.

"So, I'll bet the Russian expressions mean that, at some point, people from Mir landed on the moon, established colonies, then abandoned them for some reason. And—"

Kate let out a small squeal. "Oh, it's lovely!" she said. Before them stood the crooked Christmas tree, fully decorated. Vinnie popped on the lights. "Why, when did you—"

"We had some time to kill," Vinnie said. "Say, would you guys like—"

"Yes, we would," Jaq and Kate said in unison.

"I'm guessing champagne wouldn't—" Clara began.

"No, it wouldn't," Kate said. "But some red wine—"

"Two," Jaq said. They all toasted a simple 'Merry Christmas' in front of the glowing tree.

"Vinnie has some interesting theories about Mir and my moon, Luna" Jaq said.

"I heard," Kate said.

"And why do you think we could breathe and function normally? Just my imagination?" Jaq asked.

"No, I bet the moon was actually closer to Earth size and Mir was bigger. I mean, you'd have to work out the physics," Vinnie said.

"That might explain why some people were more, you know, robust," Clara said, trying at last to engage in the dialogue between Jaq and Vinnie. "The gravity was stronger on Mir."

"Somehow, I don't really think it needs to be analyzed," Kate said rather abruptly. Everyone fell silent.

"Um, I made some dinner," Vinnie offered. "Last night being Christmas

Eve and all, I threw together kind of a 'Feast of the Seven Fishes.' Like from the old neighborhood."

"We remember," Jaq said.

"I hope you like fish," Clara said.

"Actually," Kate said, "fish would be perfect."

Vinnie and Clara did not leave until after midnight. Climbing the stairs, Kate glanced briefly at the door to Ur's room. "Life goes on, doesn't it," she said. Jaq nodded and put his arm around her shoulder, as they walked through the darkness.

Kate switched the lights on low, while Jaq turned on the tap in the shower. Warm water poured down on them by the gallon. Kate began to laugh—and laugh and laugh. Then she put her arms around Jaq's neck and the laughter changed to tears. Kate cried and cried.

"Fuck," Jaq said at last.

"Fuck is right," Kate said. She grabbed Jaq by the ears, just as she had done that day on the Lost, pulled his face close to hers and kissed him hard. He kissed her back and the two of them dropped to the tile.

Just in case, before they climbed into bed, Kate snapped on Ur's monitor.

◎ ⊙ ◎

CHAPTER 18

————

"Jaq! Wake up!" was all he heard, followed by some violent shaking. Jaq pushed himself up against the head board, eyes still glued together, and began to churn his legs as if he were trying to climb the wall.

"Jaq." He felt a gentle hand on his arm and pried his eyes open. It was Kate. Of course it was Kate. "Jaq, we have to go up to the Lost."

"The Lost? Right now?"

"Yes. No. I mean, not precisely right now, this minute. But yes. Now. Today," Kate said, in a tone that lacked any room for debate.

"But we're going to John and Dana's tonight," he said through a yawn. "Gonna celebrate our new partnership. The bond and stock kings of Ketchum, Idaho. Remember?"

"We'll go," Kate answered, picking at a finger. "Probably."

Jaq slid back down onto the bed and ran his fingers through his hair. "Okay. So what's happened?"

"Well, I've had Ur's monitor turned on all year."

"I know."

"Don't start—"

"I'm not."

Kate sat down on the bed. "Anyway, I heard some crying sounds. Not like a child would make, but a baby crying. I ran to her room and, just like last year—nothing. I came back in here and I could still hear them, though faintly." Jaq got up and walked over to the monitor and put it up to his ear. Nothing. "I know. It's stopped."

"Yes. I can't hear that."

"Don't-be-smart."

Jaq put his hand on Kate's cheek and gave her a kiss. "Let's get dressed," he said.

The Lost was running lower than the previous year and was nearly ice-free, except in a few quiet, back eddies where, clinging to the river's edge, the ice looked like clear Christmas ribbon candy. But the willows had not changed, red branches and yellow providing relief to the eye against the beige backdrop of the high plains in winter.

Meandering through a large stand of cottonwood, hand in hand, they emerged at last into the great open field where cows grazed year-round. But there were none to be seen. Over and across the river, remnants of November's snows had found refuge in hollow and shaded spots and places that faced north and east. Snow was tucked, as well, among the stems of the prairie grass that proliferated in great clumps.

"Feeling better?" Jaq asked.

"Yes. Much." She squeezed his hand. "I just—"

"You don't need to explain. It's been quite a year. Sounds like Levine and the kids are kickin' ass in the Apple." Jaq studied the pasture. "Say, what do you suppose *really* happened to Frankie?"

"Why she fell in love, of course." Kate pulled Jaq close and kissed him. "Maybe we should see if this thing works up here," Kate said, pulling her new cell phone out of her jacket pocket. "We might be late, after all."

A noisy, splashing sound drew their attention back toward the river. "What was that?" Jaq asked.

"I don't ... Look!" Kate said. Pointing to a bend in the Lost where the cottonwood stand ended, Kate cried out again. A spray of water and a flash of pink and purple and silver followed another splash.

"Did you—" Kate began.

"Yes." Jaq grabbed Kate's hand tightly. "Do you—"

"Yes." Amidst the bare black trunks of the cottonwoods stood a young girl.

The hood of her long, gray-blue cloak of Lamikin had been tossed back, revealing a head of auburn hair that shone red-gold in the afternoon light.

"Ur!" Kate cried, running to her child. Jaq sprinted after her.

Throwing her arms around Ur, Kate hugged her daughter close around the shoulders. Ur did not hug back. Kate studied Ur with concern. "Is something wrong?"

"Oh, no, Mother." Ur lowered her eyes. "I'm sorry. You see, my arms are full." Concern on Kate's face faded to a question.

Turning from his daughter to his wife and back to his daughter, Jaq began to fumble and fidget. "You've grown," he said. Although only a year had passed, Ur now appeared to be eleven or twelve.

"Yes, Father. You see, this world and Mir accelerate differentially."

"Right," Jaq said. "Say, what's that—?"

"Ur?" Kate said, paying Jaq no attention. "You said your arms were full." Ur simply stared at her mother. "Ur?" Kate said once again, in that mildly scolding tone that a mother uses with a stubborn child. Jaq grinned.

With a free hand, Ur opened the folds of her cloak. Cradled in the crook of her left arm, fast asleep, lay an infant.

"I don't understand," Kate said.

"I do!" Jaq cried, the smile on his face vanishing. "Ur, that's not, not …." he spluttered. Random thoughts and images raced through Jaq's now rigidly paternal brain.

Blushing and lowering her eyes, Ur replied softly, "No, Father. It's very sweet of you to worry, but the child isn't mine. It's yours, if you'll have her."

"Ours? What do you mean?" Kate asked in a low voice.

"Her? Who is she?" Jaq asked. He wasn't sure he wanted to know.

"Mother, would you mind holding her? My arm is getting very tired."

"Um, sure," Kate said laconically. From the expression on her face, it didn't look as if she meant it.

"You've grown so," Jaq said. "Um …."

"I've explained that and, as you know, Father, neither space nor time is invariant."

Jaq closed his eyes for a moment and rubbed the bridge of his nose. Questions raced through his mind, all competing for immediate expression.

None, however, was able to overcome his desire to walk up to Ur and hold her as tightly and for as long as he could.

He jumped as Kate let out a cry. "Oh, my God!" she said. Kate looked as if she didn't know whether to hand the baby back to Ur right then and there, or simply to drop it and run like hell. The baby began to cry softly. Whether from shock or deeply-seated instinct, Kate simply froze.

"What is it?" Jaq asked.

"Come and see for yourself."

Sidling up to Kate, Jaq peeped over her left shoulder. The child had quieted down and drifted back to sleep. "Looks kind of cute to me," Jaq said brightly. Stretching his hand toward the infant, Jaq stroked its head. It had very thick, very black hair.

Jaq's touch woke the child up and the baby's eyes snapped open. "Aw, Jeez!" was all he could say. Staring at him were two orbs, entirely black.

The baby began to fuss a little more. Reflexively, Kate slipped her hand inside the Lamikin swaddling and felt the creature's bottom. Kate cleared her throat. "Ur?" was all she said.

"I'll explain."

"This had better be good," Kate said. But there was no malice in her voice. Jaq just stood there, struck dumb.

"You see, when Father drove that sword into Tiamat, the wound turned out to be mortal, though not in the usual sense of the word."

With great emotional effort, Jaq's brain coughed up a question. "What do you mean, not in the *usual* sense?"

"The blow was mortal. She *will* die. But it was not immediately fatal. Do you see?" Both of her parents shook their heads, no.

"Tiamat was a creature without lifespan. She was immortal, although that's an imprecise word since time is so elastic. You changed all of that, Father. I don't know how exactly and neither did she. But what she *did* know was that her integrity as an individual being would eventually collapse." Ur took a deep breath and a step toward her parents. "She learned love and found the feeling addictive. She has always found humans interesting; she found you both intriguing. So Tiamat decided that if her time was to be finite, she wished to live it out as a human being. From beginning to end, and with the two of you."

"I really don't think—" Kate began.

"Hey, look," Jaq said, pointing at the baby's torso. Apparently Kate had loosened the swaddling when she had checked for leaks. Directly below the sternum and alongside the ribs sat a tiny scar. "That must be where I wounded her."

"Yes," Kate whispered. "And that's exactly where Ur had her g-tube." Kate shut her eyes tightly. "Ur, I'm sorry. Really, I don't—"

"Mother, please." Ur touched Kate lightly on the arm. "Hold her for a little while. We've time. Let's talk. Then—"

"Time? What do you mean, Ur?" Jaq asked. "How much time? Look at you. You're practically a young lady. What have we seen you for? Three days? Less? In, in … the last ten years it looks like, for cryin' out loud."

Ur grabbed her father and squeezed him hard. *It feels so good.* Jaq wished that he might die right then and there.

"For cryin' out loud," Ur said softly. Then, gently pushing her father away, her expression turned more serious.

"Well, your mother and I have always given you the right to make your own choices." Jaq scuffed at the ground, pawing up a small cloud of dust. "Pretty normal for parents to do just that, I guess. At least it's the right thing to do. But you've grown up so damned fast."

Kate shifted Tiamat. The baby made a single, high pitched creaky sound. "If we've only a little time, what gift could we give *you*? It is Christmas, after all."

"That's right. It's celebrated as Uncle Nick's birthday. He told me all about it." Ur lowered her eyes and fidgeted. At that moment, she looked exactly as a child ought to look before revealing her heart's desire. When she spoke, there was a glow on her face. Although, of course, she wasn't smiling. "Well, I'd love to go for a sleigh ride."

"A sleigh ride," Jaq said. "Sure." He looked around. There wasn't much snow. Besides … "How about a spin around town in our truck? Just like old times. It's not the Chevy, but—"

"Oh, that would be lovely. But Grandma Jen said—"

"Grandma Jen?" Kate said.

"Yes. She was a little girl when everybody used to ride in sleighs in the wintertime. She told me all about it and it sounded *wonderful!*"

"Okay," Jaq said slowly. "We've got a little bit of snow, but where do we get the sleigh?"

"Why, Father, it ought to be so simple for you. You created an entire world, didn't you? Shaped it, anyway."

There was a cajoling tone to Ur's pleas that Jaq found irresistible. He melted. "Fine," he said, not knowing quite what to do next.

"Good, good!" Ur cried, flashing two rows of perfect teeth, though her obvious delight was not reflected in her features. "Shut your eyes if it will help, Father."

"Yeah. Go ahead, Jaq. After all, she's not asking for a pink unicorn. Horse and sleigh ought to be a snap," Kate said.

Glaring at his wife, he fired back, "Okay, wise guy." When he had closed his eyes, Jaq tried very hard to think of a wintry scene but found, instead, that all he was able to do was imagine what Ur might look like with a smile on her face. Opening his eyes at last, he found himself standing shin deep in fresh powder. All about him, large thick flakes were swirling and sparkling in the sunlight. Before them sat an old-fashioned sleigh with large curved runners and a seat wide enough for three.

"So, Mother, what do you think of that?" Jaq said.

"Great! Do you intend to pull it or should we hook it to the back of the Jeep?"

"Guess I forgot the horse."

"Oh, Father, that should be easy enough," Ur said. Jaq shrugged self-confidently. "Could you make it a dapple gray? Grandma Jen would sing a song about going over rivers and through woods and in it she sang about a dapple gray horse."

"Yes." Jaq nodded gently. "I used to sing that song when I was your age."

"We remember," Kate said.

"Splendid. I'd love to see what a dapple gray really *looks* like."

As Jaq was starting to reply, but before he could utter a word, all hitched up stood a gray and white dappled horse. "Could there be anything more improbable than this?" he asked in a hushed voice.

"A pink unicorn. But of course Nick said that wasn't—" Kate began, but stopped abruptly as a bright whirling cloud of snow began to coalesce and pulse pink, like a large wad of cotton candy. Then in an instant, a unicorn stood next to the dapple-gray, chewing on its bridle and pawing and snorting large clouds of steam that swirled around its platinum horn and brilliant white mane. "My God, Jaq, it looks as if Nick was wrong again," Kate said. "How did you—"

"Did *I*?" Jaq interrupted.

Holding Tiamat closer to her and adjusting the Lamikin to protect the child's face from the flying snow, Kate climbed in.

"I think she's getting used to the idea," Ur whispered.

Sneaking a peak at Kate, Jaq whispered back, "I think she *is* used to it."

Nodding in agreement, Ur looked at her father and said, "You don't *have* to take her, you know."

"We'll see."

"Anyway, thank you, Father. This is a wonderful present."

"Hey, guys!" Kate said. "It's starting to get a little cold up here. Not to mention lonely."

On the floor of the sleigh was a throw. Picking it up, Ur did just that, covering their laps.

"Now what?" Jaq asked.

"You drive. What else? You're the man," Kate said.

"Right," Jaq said. Lifting the reins and clicking his tongue as he'd always seen done in the movies, he found to his surprise that the animals responded. The ad-lib worked.

Flying across the frozen field, their spirits were elevated by the speed of the sleigh and by the intoxicatingly cold air. Wheee! They soared over a small hummock. Whoompf! They landed on the other side, careering faster and faster.

"Pffff!" Ur sucked in a breath of air. Both Kate and Jaq stared at their daughter seated between them, her eyes wide with wonder. Could it be, thought Jaq, that a child of her capacities could still find a thrill in such a mundane pleasure?

Pffff! Ur drew in another gulp of air. This time, however, her facial muscles failed to return to their formerly implacable position. Instead, her cheeks, now reddened by the bite of cold and snowflakes, lifted, her lips stretched wide, and her eyes, deep pulsing cobalt, narrowed. It wasn't a perfect smile, for the lips were quite rigid. Still terribly toothy, but a smile after all, Jaq thought.

The lovely, dark dapple-gray and the bright pink unicorn were prancing in their traces, clouds of steam huffing from their flared nostrils and swirling about the unicorn's dazzling silver horn. *I guess if pink unicorns are possible ….* He looked at Kate and saw her eyes brimming with tears as she hugged the infant Tiamat more closely.

Tears were streaming down Jaq's cheeks. He had not cried like this over Ur since the first few hours after her birth. He began to speak.

"Ille me par esse deo videtur

"Ille, si fas est, superare divos

"Qui sedens adversus identidem te

"Spectat et audit

"Dulce ridentem …. *

Ur turned toward the sound of her father's voice. When she saw his tears, her 'smile' vanished, replaced by a look of alarm. "Father," she said, "is something wrong?"

"No. Everything is quite all right."

"Father, what were you saying? I didn't understand."

Jaq collected himself. "You mean the Reverend Father Nicholas Beele of the Society of Jesus has not yet taught you your Latin?" he said in a tone of mock horror. Ur shook her head.

"Shame on him!" Jaq shouted over the noise of the sleigh shaking and creaking and the sound of the runners plowing through the powder. "As soon as you return, tell him to begin your studies. It's my express command. I'll have no daughter of mine wallowing about without the tools of a proper education." Jaq sniffed.

"Oh, Father." Ur giggled. "Mother, what was he saying?"

"Your father's right," Kate said. "Discover the meaning for yourself. It'll have more value."

Smiling in her own way, Ur moved closer to her mother, placing her head against Kate's shoulder. For a while, the three rode through the silence and blindness of a winter whiteout.

Thumping over a particularly large clump of grass, the sleigh yawed, then shuddered as it smashed back on top of the hard ground that lay beneath the fresh snow. Tiamat started, though she did not cry. Of their own accord, the horses began to slow, changing gaits, despite Jaq's urgings. Gradually, they began to dissolve as well. As they shifted gait to a walk, they vanished completely and the sleigh glided to a stop.

Without a word, Jaq hopped down to the ground and offered his hand to Ur. The magical ride was over. Accepting his help, she stepped onto the running board.

When she leapt into the snow, her feet sent up a large plume of powder. "Thank you, Father," she said. "For everything." Sunlight bounced off of her auburn hair and reflected itself off the snow crystals.

"You'll forget about us," Jaq said. "Running the universe and all." He was pouting and he knew it. But he meant it.

"No, Daddy, I will not either." Ur laughed and the sound of bright copper bells poured from her mouth. "Now," Ur said, "I'll have to be going soon." Jaq could feel his guts tie themselves into knots of steel. "So I must ask you both, shall I take Tiamat back with me? Perhaps I shouldn't have …."

"Ur," Kate said. "I'd like to talk with you. Jaq? Here. Take Tiamat, please."

"I, uh, really don't—"

"Don't tell me you've forgotten how to hold one of them."

"No. No. It's not that. It's just that she and I have never quite had the best working relationship."

"Then try and sort it out. Ur said she doesn't have much time and we must give her an answer." Unceremoniously, but with great care, Kate handed Tiamat to Jaq. "Get acquainted. She's actually kind of cute. You said so yourself."

In silence, the two women walked arm in arm toward the Lost, scuffing snow that was now only ankle deep. The sun's light skipped atop the river's surface, illuminating the last vestiges of the local blizzard that had blown itself out.

When they reached the bank, they began, it seemed to Jaq, to engage in deep conversation. But he became so occupied with Tiamat that when they returned, he forgot to ask what they had spoken about. They found him bouncing the baby and chortling and cooing.

"Have you decided?" Ur asked her father.

"I think we can manage her," Jaq said. Kate remained stone-faced. "Um, well, actually, the truth is, I want to take her with us."

"So do I," said Kate.

"She'll be a handful," Ur said.

"We've figured that," Jaq said. Jaq stood quite apart from the women, worry tickling the corners of his mouth. "Um, what were you guys talking about for so long? Secrets?"

Kate walked over to him and took Tiamat. "No secrets. I'll tell you later. I just wanted Ur to myself for a little while. I was feeling—selfish."

Jaq grinned. "That's good," he said. "Say, I was thinking. Tiamat's a little formal, don't you think? How does Mattie strike you?"

"Mattie," Kate said approvingly.

"Look at these eyes," Jaq said.

Kate bent over and they stared at two bright, black beads. "We'll have to figure something out."

"Ur?" Jaq said. But Ur had vanished. He thought that for an instant, he had seen a flash of deep molten copper among the black trunks of the cottonwoods.

As they sailed out of Mackay, Mattie slept. For a time, the only sounds to be heard in the cab were her contented breathing and the whoosh! of the heater.

◙ ◉ ◙

Somewhere, well upstream on the Lost, a fish cut its wake through the water, leaving sets of smooth ripples that spread diagonally and behind it, their surface tension disturbed only by snowflakes, remnants of a recent squall, that vanished almost as soon as they touched the water. At last, she reached the horizon, for the horizon did not recede for her, and, if such a thing can be imagined, made one, magnificent leap, flashing rose and violet and silver, illuminating the snow crystals that swirled about, and hurtled herself toward infinity.

* NOTES

'Behold, even the moon is not bright and the stars are not clean in his sight; how much less man who is maggot; and the son of man, who is a worm.'

—Job 25:5

'Ille me par esse deo videtur
Ille, si fas est, superare divos
Qui sedens adversus identidem te
Spectat et audit
Dulce ridentem ....'—Catullus 51, 84-54 BCE

'He seems to me to be a god,
He, if it can be said, surpasses the gods
Who, sitting opposite you,
Looks at you and hears you
Sweetly laughing, again and again'

ACKNOWLEDGEMENTS

I would like to say thanks to a few people, without whose support and guidance, *Sun Valley Moon Mountains* would never have crept out from between the covers of my composition books. First, to my editors and 'book doctors', Jeanne Cavelos and John Barnes, both of whom are not only great instructors in the craft of creating readable literature, but artful writers.

Jeanne was my first mentor and taught me the rudiments of contemporary stylistic conventions, as well as the need to excise a writer's self-indulgent digressions from the demands of the narrative. John picked up where Jeanne left off and has taught me the elements of driving a storyline forward. I hope I have succeeded with the reader in this effort. John has continued to work with me on the next two novels in the 'Ur Legend' series.

Without the almost magical manuscript typing skills of Kelly Lombardi, the text would never have made it onto a word processor. I am a ten finger typist, only seven of which work at any one time. Special thanks also to Joyce Krieg for doing a clean edit of the book, and Gene Harris for his imaginative realization of my inchoate ideas for cover design. Thanks also to Lynn Pigott for the great photo of Linda and me above my bio.

And *SVMM* would never have made it from Word to Kindle without the continued support and guidance of Patricia Hamilton, my publisher, who proved invaluable in steering me through this new world, in which self-publishing is no longer an exercise in vanity but a true enterprise.

Finally, there are no words to thank my wife, Linda, Katherine's mom, who has supplied me with continual support, as well as hard-nosed critique over the course of the entire project.

◙ ◉ ◙

ABOUT THE AUTHOR

PAUL SINSAR was born in Danbury, Connecticut, on September 11, 1950. He 'prepped' at Danbury High School and received an A.B. from Princeton in 1972. After graduation he moved to New York City and began a career as a bond trader. He and his wife Linda lived in Manhattan and Brooklyn for twenty years, and spent another twenty in Denver, Colorado, where their daughter Katherine was born, and died. Presently they reside in Monterey, California. As for Ajax Minor, you'll have to read about him in the Foreword.

Mr. Sinsar began writing after the death of Katherine. Her passing, and her life, served as the inspiration for the 'Ur Legend' series of fantasies, of which *Sun Valley Moon Mountains* is the first of three books. Though the novel is his preferred medium of expression, he has also written a few short stories and some poetry, available on his website, ajaxminor.com.

Made in the USA
San Bernardino, CA
13 March 2016